A GRAVES TEMPTATION

A GRAVES TEMPTATION

By J.A. Lesser

Published by Sandia Press
Copyright © 2018 Jonathan A. Lesser
Revised 2024

Cover illustration by Nancy Twinem
Design by Cindy Monroe

ISBN: 978-0-9859749-2-3
e-ESBN: 978-9859749-3-0

Printed in the U.S.A.

For Donna

Chapter 1

The vicissitudes of the evening—there were always vicissitudes when dealing with Esperanza and Maria, especially of the slings-and-arrows variety—had depleted body and soul. After downing a bracing glass of Dusty Trail—the whisky real cowboys asked for by name, at least according to the label—I retired to the quiet confines of my bed and drifted into what I hoped would be peaceful slumber.

"Señor Graves," a distant, dreamy voice, sounding like an asthmatic Siren, whispered into my ear.

"Sod off, Tiny. The *sopapillas* were quite hot when I brought them to you," I mumbled, as I slowly emerged from a nightmare about the evening's exertions and yet another unpleasant encounter with Tiny Roybal, the rotund county sheriff of high appetite who, with his equally rotund wife and spawn, frequented the Dos Abuelas cafe.

Through a series of events and my Uncle Bill's desire to ensure the cafe where his late wife Celestina had once worked continued to function, he had asked me—well, manipulated me, really—to "manage" the cafe and save it from Esperanza and Maria, the eponymous *abuelas*, as if my background in London banking somehow qualified me to oversee a small, tumbledown cafe in the equally tumbledown village of Vaca Seca, deep within the Valle de los Lobos in far northern New Mexico.

A chain-smoking, foul-tempered, and vituperative pair, sisters Esperanza and Maria were as far removed from roly-poly grandmotherly types as could be envisaged. After Ernesto Amador, their father, passed away, they had renamed the cafe, which had been called Ernesto's. With Celestina involved, the cafe continued to serve the specialities it was famous for—green chile *enchiladas*, *carne adovada*, *tamales*, and a breakfast dish called *huevos de Ernesto*. Maria, who had inherited Ernesto's gift for cooking but not his easy rapport with customers, would cook, whilst Esperanza took care of the customers and Celestina held everything together. But after Celestina's death, Esperanza and Maria began treating the clientele with the warmth of crocodiles, until at last the cafe closed. Eventually, with Uncle Bill's financial backing, Maria and Esperanza began selling Maria's *tamales* every Saturday. The townspeople would line up with military precision and wait for Esperanza to call their names and dispense a ration of the heavenly mixture of pork and *masa*, wrapped in a corn husk.

Eventually, however, the sisters' refusal to pay what they owed to Joe Garcia, the avaricious proprietor of the town's only store, ended *tamale* day. And it was then that I, Benjamin Charles Reginald Graves, son of Sir Gerald Charles Franklin Graves, MP, and descendant of Sir Charles Reginald Franklin Graves, First Lord of the Admiralty, became involved. I had been summarily sacked from my job as banker to make way for the chairman's mannequin-fondling nephew, and sacked as well from the job of husband by my former better half, Cynthia, who had fallen for her co-worker, Rodrigo Lopreso de Vargas, a swarthy and silken-tongued Spaniard. According to Cynthia, Rodrigo's whisperings made her feel as though she were in a garden of geraniums. Well, one cannot fight a legacy of mannequin-fondling nephews and whispering geraniums, can one? And so, despite my father's considering me a nincompoop and my mother's pleadings that I travel to Cannes, I struck out for the other side of the world, where my Uncle Bill had purchased a ranch many years before. He had been cast out by the Graves family long ago as the blackest of black sheep, for his worship of the cowboy lifestyle of Zane Grey novels in general and, in particular, an ill-timed "Howdy, pard'ner!" slap on the back to Lord Admiral Sir Henry Throckmorton. His victim was an over-aged, over-whiskied, and self-important boor of the highest order, but one whose connections to the Admiralty demanded fawning respect from all persons Graves.

But not even the most fevered imagination could have prepared myself for encounters with the local inhabitants, including the current bedside intruder.

"Señor Graves, it's me," Coronado whispered again. "I know the *sopapillas* were hot. They were real good, too. I ate four of them. But you gotta wake up now."

I perceived a hand shaking my shoulder. A large silhouette stood before me in the darkness, framed by the moonlight streaming in through the window.

"Gah!" I fumbled for the small light by the bed and switched it on. Coronado's rodentary eyes were staring at me, his rounded head, atop his rounded body, nodding slowly.

"C'mon, Señor Graves, wake up."

Coronado claimed to be a descendant of Álvar Núñez Cabeza de Vaca, the Spanish conquistador who had travelled through New Mexico centuries earlier, and who Coronado claimed had founded Vaca Seca. The other residents adhered to a more compelling story of the town's origin: that it had been named for a pile of desiccated cattle bones found near a small creek in the late 1700s by Juan Oñate, a horse thief who had escaped from gaol and imminent hanging in Santa Fe.

Regaining a vaguely conscious state, I rubbed the oculars and goggled him. "Coronado?"

"You okay, Señor Graves?"

"What? Are you mad?"

"No, Señor Graves. I'm not mad. I'm glad you're awake."

"Why? I mean, why are you here in my bedroom? In the middle of the night? And how did you get past Daisy?"

Daisy was Uncle Bill's sombrero-wearing, twenty-five-stone sow who, in addition to her duties hoovering leftovers, acted as porcine sentry. Upon my arrival at the ranch, she had arisen from apparent slumber on the porch of the small house Uncle Bill lived in and, heeding Admiral Nelson's advice to forgo manoeuvres, bore down upon me at dreadnought speed. It was only by diving over the gate that I escaped. She then summarily rubbished my valises, tossing them like a gold medallist Olympian, causing them to explode on impact, and destroying the coddled bottle of eighteen-year-old Scotch malt I had lovingly packed.

"I dunno. I had a couple apples in my pocket, so when Daisy ran up to the gate, I gave her one. She took it and went back to sleep. She's a real friendly pig." He smiled and nodded his head slowly once again, as he reached into his pocket. "I still got the other apple. You want it?" He thrust the grease-covered and much dented fruit towards my face.

"No, I don't want your bloody apple. Why are you here? I mean, it's—" I glanced at the small wind-up clock on the table—"Gah! Does that say three o'clock?"

"I guess so, Señor Graves. Somebody's asking about you."

"Who? Loretta?" I quickly sat up. "Is she hurt?" I had first met Loretta Alvarez, Esperanza and Maria's niece, whilst lying sprawled on my back in the cafe. She was a shapely young lass, possessed of large brown eyes and reddish-black hair that curled about her shoulders. Not only had Loretta become indispensable to the cafe, she and I had set course towards a rather more intimate relationship, despite Esperanza's diligent efforts to cleave us apart as one cleaves a ripe coconut. That she had failed was perhaps a testament to Loretta's patience, not to mention Maria's warnings to her younger sister to cease and desist.

Had it not been for Loretta, I should have returned to London when Cynthia had arrived in Vaca Seca one afternoon, after *l'affaire Rodrigo* collapsed; a Lothario rarely mends his ways, after all. She had travelled to Vaca Seca determined to retrieve me and return us to our previous life. But the shock of encountering both Coronado and Daisy when she arrived proved too much for her English upbringing, and she returned to London. Not that one could fault her; only the Graves legendary fortitude, plus generous quantities of Dusty Trail, Uncle Bill's favoured tipple being the whisky cowboys asked for by name, enabled the soul to endure the labours and tribulations Vaca Seca had forced upon it.

After Cynthia's departure, Loretta and I had embarked on one of those steady-as-she-goes sorts of romances, each possessed of trepidation towards a second marriage, based on our previous experiences. The locals were aghast, torn between a concern for my "doing right by Loretta" and abject horror at the idea of her possibly marrying a *gringo*.

"Loretta? I dunno, Señor Graves. Is something wrong with her?"

"That's what I'm asking you! If you're not here about Loretta, then what? Why have you awakened me at this god-forsaken hour?"

"A bus came into town tonight. It stopped in front of Rudy's Bar."

"Eh? That Greyhound bus stops there every day. God only knows why."

"*Sí.* But this is a different bus. It's all big and shiny and white."

"And?"

"I was coming out of Rudy's and it stopped right by me. Then this *gringo* got out. He was dressed real fancy. He looked around and then pointed at me. Then he shouted 'You!' and asked me where the cafe was.

"I told him it was down the street, but it was closed. Then I told him if he was hungry, he could have some of my *burrito*." Coronado paused momentarily. "I didn't eat it 'cause I had lunch at the cafe. I think I ordered the *enchiladas*, but I forget."

Discussions with Coronado frequently caused a thick fog to envelop the grey matter, and an especially dense one had now assumed its rightful place.

"Never mind the specifics of your luncheon. Why are you here now? Rudy closes the bar at ten o'clock."

"I meant to come over before, but I kinda fell asleep in my truck."

I sighed. "Well?"

"Huh?"

"Why does this chap want to know about the cafe?"

"I dunno. He said he needed to talk to the *abuelas*."

"What?"

"You know, Señor Graves—Maria and Esperanza."

"Yes, I know who they are. *Why* does he want to speak with them?"

Coronado was about to respond to my inquiry when Uncle Bill entered the room, clad in pyjamas and cowboy hat, and cradling a shotgun. "What's goin' on?" Espying Coronado, he stopped suddenly and lowered the gun. "How the hell did you get in?" he said, tossing the hat onto my bed.

"*Buenos días*, El Vaquero," Coronado replied, shrugging his largish shoulders. "The front door. It wasn't locked or nothing."

"What about Daisy?" said Uncle Bill.

"Oh, she's okay, El Vaquero. I gave her an apple. But I think she knocked her *sombrero* off. It wasn't on her head."

Uncle Bill had been nicknamed "El Vaquero" long ago by the townsfolk because of his penchant for all things Zane Greyish. He leaned the shotgun against the wall, shook his head, and sighed. "You know why he's here, Bennie?" he asked, rubbing the grey stubble on his chin.

"From what I can ascertain, a chap motored into town earlier this evening in a fancy white bus. According to Coronado, he wishes to meet Maria and Esperanza."

"What the hell for? And what does it have to do with you in the middle of the goddamned night?"

A hippopotamus-like yawn escaped my jaws.

"Ah. The investigation has not progressed to that stage, Uncle Bill." I turned to Coronado. "Did this chap tell you why he wished to see Maria and Esperanza?"

"*Sí*, Señor Graves. He says he's gonna make a movie about them."

The Graves's collective jaws plummeted. "A movie?" we replied in unison.

"*Sí.*"

"Perhaps a horror film?" I mused. "*Doctor Jekyll Meets Esperanza.*"

"Does Esperanza need a doctor?" asked Coronado.

"Other than a psychiatrist or an African witch doctor? Doubtful."

The thought of someone—well, anyone— seeking out Vaca Seca in the first place, to say nothing of someone wishing to transform Maria and Esperanza into celluloid stars, boggled the neurons.

"So if this chap, Coronado, wishes to meet Maria and Esperanza—may God have mercy on his tormented soul— then why are you *here?*"

"I dunno. He said he needed to talk to you."

The neurons began to throb. "At three o'clock in the morning? Surely—"

"Save your breath, Bennie," Uncle Bill interrupted. "Coronado, what's this fella's name?"

Coronado paused to rub his multiple chins. "I dunno, El Vaquero. Robert, or maybe Roger. He yelled at me real loud."

"Why?" I asked perfunctorily, as attempts at sane conversation with Coronado usually ended with the aggrieved speaker launching a fusillade of expletives at him.

"I dunno, Señor Graves. When I told him the cafe was closed, he shouted, 'Don't you know who I am?' And I said, 'No, señor, who are you?' Then he got real mad, and told me his name. You think he's somebody important, Señor Graves?"

"Why would anyone important wish to visit Vaca Seca?" I asked.

"The governor once stopped here 'cause he had a flat tire. Luis had to come fix it and whilst the governor waited in his car, his girlfriend went into Rudy's. But then she ran out 'cause José Gonzales walked into the bathroom and—"

I held up an unsteady hand. "Please, Coronado, not now."

"Maybe you'd better see what the hell this is all about, Bennie," said Uncle Bill.

By now, several of the more insomniac birds were chirping in the nearby cottonwoods.

"Gah," I moaned softly.

Having herded Coronado out the back door so as to avoid Daisy and promising him that I would rendezvous with him at Garcia's store later that morning, I attempted, unsuccessfully, to return to my interrupted slumber. The grey matter whirred, vainly seeking to comprehend how this Robert or Roger chap knew about the cafe, much less why he wished to make a movie about Maria and Esperanza.

By five o'clock, with dawn emerging and the avian chirping now a cacophony, I arose, dressed, and staggered into the kitchen.

Uncle Bill was already awake. He handed me a cup of his cowboy coffee, a boiled concoction that resembled tar, but which I had come to rely on for its invigorating effects.

"What is it about this place?" I asked him, after several large swallows. "It is a magnet for loonies."

"You live here, too."

I grimaced. "Er, yes."

Uncle Bill shrugged. "Coronado probably has the whole damn story wrong anyway. Or maybe he was drunk and dreamed it up."

"One can only hope."

After draining our mugs, we fed and watered Daisy and Marjorie, Uncle Bill's obstreperous horse. I mucked out Marjorie's stall—I had become convinced she produced copious quantities of dung to spite me—whilst Uncle Bill checked the pasture to make sure the cattle had water and hay.

After breakfast, I put on my overcoat and walked out the back door to the small garage. Although Uncle Bill had purchased a second lorry from Luis Chavez for my use, it was currently awaiting repairs by the same. As I keyed the ignition of Uncle Bill's lorry, the engine coughed, sputtered, and finally started.

By seven o'clock, I was motoring along the pockmarked macadam that served as Vaca Seca's main street. As I passed by Rudy's Bar and Package Liquors, I heard the small neon sign above the entrance humming loudly.

Paco, Nestor Martinez's urine-filled and barkative canine, lay near the bar's front door, as he did every morning. Espying me, the dog growled. It was no doubt planning the day's campaign of stealthy urination on unsuspecting shoes, trouser legs, and doorways. I recalled the day I stepped off the bus that had brought me to Vaca Seca. Paco had calmly approached, urinated on my valises, and then casually walked away.

I drove past the cafe, which was dark and shuttered. Our resident skunk, whom Loretta had named Señor Apestoso (Mr. Stinky), was no doubt sleeping off last night's *ofrenda*, a large plate of Maria's green chile *enchiladas* and a leftover *sopapilla*. He—well, we assumed it was a he, as no one wished to undertake the necessary enquiries—had become noticeably more rotund since these nightly feedings had begun.

Nowhere did I see a bus, shiny white or otherwise, parked on the road. Yawning, I continued my slow progress along the road. When I reached Luis Chavez's Texaco station, which served as the unofficial eastern end of town, I came about and began another slow reconnaissance. Perhaps Uncle Bill had been correct after all and Coronado had imagined the entire thing whilst in a drunken stupor.

After driving past the town square, I glanced down Vallejos Road, which would take the errant traveller north into Colorado. I stopped suddenly, espying not the shiny white bus of Coronado's jabberings, but a dilapidated school bus. The bus was parked in front of an abandoned old adobe building that had once been the town's official bar, before Rudy's.

I reversed the lorry, turned onto the road and drove alongside the bus. Its bonnet was bent open, as if grinning. The windows were curtained in some sort of reddish-purple fabric, and the word "Siddhartha" was painted on the side in largish, wavy orange letters.

"Bloody hell," I muttered, shuddering at the ill tidings which Fate would soon dispatch.

Chapter 2

There was a pronounced hesitancy on my part, if not outright fear, to enquire of the bus's occupants. I mean, one never knew where an enraged and inebriated boyfriend of Esperanza might lurk, and my previous experiences with Hector Castillo—a large and oafish ape who periodically visited from Santa Fe to bivouac with Esperanza—counselled discretion.

I returned to the ranch. Walking into the kitchen, I found Coronado sitting at the table with Uncle Bill, pawing a mug of coffee.

"You're here?" I grimaced, poured myself a cup of thickish coffee, and sat down heavily at the kitchen table.

Coronado smiled. "*Sí*. My truck wouldn't start. El Vaquero says he's got some jumper cables. Did you see it, Señor Graves?"

"See what?"

"The bus. And the *gringo*."

"The white bus? No. Nor did I encounter anyone by the name of Roger or Robert, or whomever you spoke with."

"By the way, Coronado, does the primary school own a bus?"

"Primary school?"

"The elementary school. The one with that old bat of a principal who has outlasted time itself."

Coronado laughed. "I don't think Señora Flores likes you."

"Quite. She made a point of telling Loretta not to trust *gringos*."

"I trust you, Señor Graves."

"Er, yes, well, about the school bus?"

"Oh, yeah. Luis Chavez sometimes fixes the bus that takes kids to the high school in Alta Luna."

"Odd thing is, I espied a school bus parked on Vallejos Road. Definitely not the shiny white variety. Had a most odd paint scheme, too."

"How did you know it's a school bus?"

"Simple deduction of the kind that would warm Sherlock Holmes's heart. The words 'School Bus' were above the windscreen. What colour is the bus that Luis has repaired?"

"It's kinda yellow. Except one corner in the back is painted green where Enrique Montoya backed it into a rock. He was kinda mad at David Sanchez for stealing one of his chickens, and—"

"Yes, yes," I interrupted. Having absorbed painful lessons as to why further enquiries regarding incidents recalled by Coronado were ill-advised, I ignored David Sanchez's thievery of poultry and Enrique Montoya's resulting bus-reversing. "Well, nothing suggested this bus hailed from Alta Luna, nor did I see any greenish corners."

"Maybe the *gringo* drives two buses."

"Eh? Why would he—never mind." I turned to Uncle Bill. "Bloody thing had the word 'Siddhartha' on its side. Do you know what that means?"

"Damned if I know, Bennie," he replied. Uncle Bill raised himself from the table. "Anybody in it?"

"I'm not sure, really. The curtains were tightly drawn."

"Curtains?"

"Quite. All of the windows were draped with a purplish fabric, including the windscreen. Someone may have been inside, but I was reluctant to enquire, especially so early in the morning. Discretion and all that. One never knows where one of Esperanza's paramours lurks."

"Maybe it's a ghost," said Coronado.

The left eyebrow rose. "A ghost? Driving a school bus?"

"*Sí*, Señor Graves. Before he died, Enrique Mora's dad, Alejandro, drove a school bus. Maybe he came over here from Alta Luna for a beer. They got a bar, but it's closed."

I sighed. "Er, yes." I cleared the vocal cords and stood up. "Right, then. I'll be off to the cafe."

"You gonna check this other bus out, Bennie?" Uncle Bill asked.

I glanced at my watch. "I think not. One presumes the locals are already crawling around it like ants. But I may stop at the Texaco station and enquire if Luis Chavez has any ideas."

"A school bus?" Luis Chavez said, his head retreating from its position under the bonnet of my moribund lorry. "I dunno. I fixed one of the Alta Luna buses that broke down here, but that was last year. Did it have a corner painted green? A few years ago, Enrique Montoya was driving and—"

"Yes, yes, Luis," I said. "Coronado informed me about the theft of *gallus domesticus* and ensuing bus-reversing. I rather doubt this is the same bus."

"Whad'ya say was painted on the side?"

"The word 'Siddhartha.' Is that some sort of Spanish name?"

Luis laughed. "If it is, I ain't ever heard it before. Maybe Hector drove the bus up from Santa Fe for Esperanza. ¿*Que no?*"

The stomach lurched, as Luis brought back painful memories of the too-short and too-loosely tied pink robe Esperanza wore whilst cavorting with Hector. "But why Vallejos Road?"

"I dunno, and I don't want to know, neither. Not if it's got something to do with Esperanza."

I grimaced. "Er, yes. Wise counsel, Luis. Thanks anyway."

"Sure, Bennie." He grinned widely. "Hey, I hear you and Loretta went to Santa Fe last week. Big night? When you gonna make an honest woman of her?"

I felt my face beginning to roast itself into a crimsonish colour. "Er, I suppose we are both rather gun-shy regarding a marital union, as it were."

"I dunno, Bennie. Loretta's a real nice girl. Folks want her treated good."

"Say no more, Luis," I said as I raised the right hand. "A Graves is always a gentleman. Speaking of which, I promised Loretta I would retrieve her this morning, and I'm rather late."

"Okay, Bennie, but don't wait too long. Somebody might steal her from you." He shook my hand vigorously. "If I see Hector driving that bus of yours, I'll let you know."

"One hopes even Fate is incapable of such cruelty. Oh, by the way, do you know what's wrong with the lorry?"

"Yeah. I think it's a bad fuel pump. I gotta go to Española to get a new one. Should be fixed in a couple days."

"Thanks, Luis."

After departing the Texaco station, I motored to Loretta's mother's home, where Loretta stayed. It was a small, neatly trimmed abode, possessed of a large garden and a far larger, copiously drooling canine named Chata.

Rather than disembark and face Chata's salivary secretions, I pressed on the horn. Presently, Loretta emerged, wearing blue jeans and a rather translucent white shirt.

"You're late," she said. She climbed into the lorry and kissed me. I yawned.

"So is kissing me boring, now?" She then stared at my sleep-deprived oculars. "Are you okay? You look terrible."

"M-hem, Coronado," I mumbled. "He came to the house at three this morning. Walked inside and woke me up. Some nonsense about a chap in a white bus demanding to speak with me."

"What? I don't understand. Why would Coronado—did you say a bus?"

I groaned. "Indeed. And, like everything else here, it defies logic, at least in any normal sense. According to Coronado, a chap named Roger or Robert—he does not know which—first demanded to see Esperanza and Maria. I gather he is under the mistaken impression they are the cafe's owners.

"Coronado told the chap I was the owner. Hence, the chap's new demand to confront yours truly. Coronado drove out to the ranch—well, first he slept off the evening at Rudy's—mollified Daisy with a greasy apple, and then I was awoken by his silhouette sitting on the bed, whispering for me to wake up. One cannot imagine a more scabrous alarm clock."

"Did you see this Robert or Roger?"

"No. I drove into town after breakfast and espied neither white bus nor its alleged driver. What I did espy was a school bus—those are the words above its windscreen—parked on Vallejos Road, possessing a rather emetic paint scheme. The word 'Siddhartha' is painted in orangish letters on the driver's side. Perhaps you are familiar with the term? Luis Chavez was not. Or perhaps one of the local farmers ingested a bit too much Farm Calm prior to an artistic undertaking."

Farm Calm, I had discovered previously, was a sweet, alcoholic mixture sold at Garcia's store. Although its putative purpose was to treat "the distressed farm animal," the local two-legged varieties were disposed towards its eponymous effects and dosed themselves generously.

"A school bus? But the school doesn't have one. What does *Siddhartha* mean? Is it a town?"

I shrugged. "Coronado believes the bus was driven here from Alta Luna by the ghost of Enrique Mora's father to enjoy a beer. I gather Alta Luna lacks pubs that cater to apparitions."

"Old Alejandro? I remember him. He drove the bus to the high school."

"Perhaps he remains blissfully alive, just like Dora Esquivel, despite Coronado's belief that a mountain lion had consumed her on our opening night."

Loretta laughed. "He means well, Bennie. He admires you."

"Yes, well, in any event, his nocturnal visit was beyond the pale," I said, as I yawned again. "God knows what would happen to a chap like Coronado on a long sailing voyage."

"Well, maybe this Robert, or Roger, will show up at the cafe this morning and solve the mystery. Why don't you drop me off and then go back home to get some sleep? I can handle the prep with Maria." Loretta took my right hand and squeezed it gently.

"Thanks, but a Graves must not abandon his post, as it were. Besides, if this chap shows up, I want to be there. Can you imagine if he encounters Esperanza or Maria unbridled?"

"Suit yourself. But you're as stubborn as Marjorie."

"Perhaps. I do have other, offsetting qualities, though."

"You do," she replied with a rather lascivious smile. "By the way, you promised we would take another trip to Santa Fe."

"Yes, I know. But with Esperanza's enfeebled back, I don't know how we can trust her to keep things shipshape."

"I think *Tia* Esperanza is fine. She's just pretending to make you mad."

"Esperanza? Malingering? Pshaw. Still, I would prefer to avoid her erupting with epithets. Perhaps you would speak with her?"

"She's mad because she expects you to marry me. And she's mad because she hates the idea of my marrying a *gringo*."

"Trapped between her own Scylla and Charybdis, your aunt is. Most gratifying."

"Bennie, she's still my aunt."

"One cannot imagine a more cruel irony." I glanced at Loretta and winked, only to be met with a sharp jab to the right shoulder. I parked the lorry in front of the cafe. "Right, here we are. No buses about, either. Perhaps we shall survive the day, after all."

"You're such a pessimist."

"Rather the coin of the realm in Vaca Seca. Speaking of which, I need to dash over to your uncle's store. Time for the weekly mollifying purchases."

"I know he appreciates it."

"A small price to pay for a disarmed and un-pyromaniacal Joe. I rather doubt Maria or myself would survive another rattlesnake tossed into her kitchen. Nor do we wish your uncle to attempt to set fire to the cafe again."

Before we reopened the cafe, Joe Garcia had placed the snake in the kitchen as punishment for my decision to purchase lower-cost supplies elsewhere. It was Coronado who, in an amazing feat of knife-throwing dexterity, despatched the snake, to our astonishment. Subsequently, on opening night, an inebriated Joe attempted to set fire to the cafe.

"You don't need to remind me, Bennie. He was desperate. He likes you now. You're going to be part of the family, after all."

"Er, yes," I said with a cough, reminded of Tennyson's *Charge of the Light Brigade*, what with the poor chaps facing cannons to their left, right, and front. Only in my case, it was Loretta's barmy aunts and uncles, who could inflict damage that would shame the largest cannon.

Chapter 3

L oretta stepped through the cafe's front door, whilst I hoofed towards Joe's store. Joe, as usual, was not in attendance, as he preferred the alcoholic comfort provided by Rudy's Bar. Instead, Coronado manned the mercantile tiller, ready to confuse and exasperate the few customers who ventured inside.

"*Buenos días*, Señor Graves," Coronado said. He was grasping what appeared to be a well-gnawed *burrito*. "You want some of my *burrito*? *Frijoles y carne.*"

"Er, most kind, Coronado, but I have already breakfasted, thank you. You were sitting at table with Uncle Bill and me, as you may recall."

"Oh, yeah, I forgot." He inserted the remainder of the *burrito* into his agape mouth, which looked like the maw of a steam shovel.

Having observed Coronado's table manners in the cafe on numerous occasions, I raised an eyebrow halfheartedly.

"We are in need of our weekly supplies, Coronado. Has Joe set them out?"

"I dunno. You want me to look in the back?"

I sighed. "Only if he wishes to sell his over-priced wares to us."

"Uh, I guess he does. He didn't say nothing about you owing him money."

"What? Why would he?" The grey matter began to spin. Had something taken place that I was not told? Had Esperanza mucked about with the cafe's finances? My experience in Vaca Seca had demonstrated that what one would dismiss as raging paranoia elsewhere was best contemplated here.

"Look, Coronado, please just retrieve the supplies from the back of the store or wherever Joe has hidden them. I need to return to the cafe presently, unless of course you wish to inform Maria that she will be unable to prepare *enchiladas* today."

"I sure like Maria's *enchiladas*," he said. His countenance took on a trance-like appearance, neurons scuppered away by visions of steaming plates.

"Er, Coronado?"

"Oh, sorry, Señor Graves. I was thinking about *enchiladas* for lunch today." His hand patted his ample stomach.

"The supplies, if you please."

"Uh, okay. If anybody comes in the store, can you tell them I'm in back?"

"I always do, Coronado."

"Thanks." He waddled slowly down the middle aisle and through a swinging door at the back. I sighed again, amazed by the dim-witted and unchanging nature of this weekly routine.

I leaned against the front counter, waiting impatiently for Coronado to return with the supplies. Presently, he returned, wheeling a hand lorry with several boxes. These were the supplies I had agreed to purchase as a *modus vivendi*, despite the punitive prices Joe charged, when we first opened the cafe.

As Coronado wheeled the boxes towards me, I heard the front door open and the small bell mounted on top of it chime. Turning around, I espied a barefoot, unshaven, fortyish chap, with dishevelled hair—well, what remained of it—and bloodshot eyes. He wore blue coveralls over a protruding stomach, and sandals sans stockings. A red bandana was tied about his forehead. In his right hand, he held a small, stubby cigarette, whose acrid odour quickly filled the store.

"*Híjole*," Coronado muttered under his breath, goggling at the chap. "*Hola*, señor. Joe's not here, but if you need something, I can get it for you."

"Peace, man," he replied, raising his right hand and displaying Churchill's "V-for-victory" symbol. He inhaled deeply of the cigarette, held his breath, and then exhaled a large cloud of smoke far different from that produced by the unfiltered

Camels on which Esperanza and Maria chimneyed. "You got any coffee, man? We could use some, at least until we get set up."

I coughed as the remnants of the smoke cleared.

The chap looked out the store window, which was streaked with dirt. "So, this is Vaca Seca," he said, patting his stomach. "I can dig it."

"Eh?"

"This town, I can definitely see our centre here."

"Your centre?"

"Spiritual centre, man. We're gonna open one here. You can feel the energy."

"Energy?" I said, as I raised an eyebrow. I was familiar with the basic laws of thermodynamics, of course, and I suppose if one were struck by lightning, one would indeed feel the energy, if only momentarily, before one was crisped.

"Yeah, man, energy. You can feel it all around you." He rotated himself around slowly, reminding me of a barbecue at Ernesto Morales's farm at which Ernesto had rotated several sides of beef slowly over a large fire. Ernesto was a friendly-giant sort of chap who owned a large ranch north of town, and from whom Uncle Bill frequently purchased hay for his own cattle.

"Er, did you say *spiritual* centre?" One wondered whether a white rabbit would soon come through the door, followed by a young girl and Cheshire cat.

"Yeah, man. A place where people can boost their *chi*." He stared out the front window again, gazing at the hills in the distance. "Wow. I can really dig it."

"You want to dig something, señor?" Coronado asked. "Like a gold mine? We got some shovels on aisle four."

"Huh, man?" The chap inhaled deeply again.

"*Sí*, señor." Coronado pointed to the same hills. "There's supposed to be gold in the mountains. That's why my ancestor Cabeza de Vaca came here. The town's named after him."

"Cool. *Chi* and gold."

When a chap answers one's questions by spewing gibberish, one usually concludes he is barmy, inebriated, or both. And, whilst I was accustomed to the locals' mental gibberish, this chap seemed possessed of a wholly different form.

I extended a trepidatious hand. "Er, I'm Benjamin Graves. And you are?"

"Sky Blue," he replied, continuing to stare out the window.

I glanced upwards. In an otherwise azure sky, several puffy, grey-white cumulus floated over the nearby hills. "Well, yes, the sky is rather blue here. What did you say your name is?"

"Like I said, man, Sky Blue."

"What? You mean your name is ... I say, Mister, er, Blue, this spiritual centre, do you intend—"

My question was interrupted by Coronado, who emitted a loud yelp and pointed towards the front door.

"*Híjole!*" he shouted.

I glanced at Coronado and then turned my gaze towards the front door. A rather tall, long-legged young woman, perhaps the same age as Loretta, had walked in. She was dressed—perhaps undressed would be more accurate—in the same sort of blue coveralls Sky Blue wore, and apparently little else. The view from the perpendicular afforded the oculars a rather stunning profile, as her ample bosom strained against the coveralls, which seemed sorely inadequate for their eponymous task. A mane of curly blond hair draped over her shoulders, and she seemed to possess an aura of anodyne fecundity.

Coronado stood transfixed, jaw trespassing on his dirty shirt collar.

She glanced at Coronado innocently, smiled, then walked over and embraced him. "Hi," she warbled, "I'm Sunflower."

Next, she shimmied towards me, revealing large blue eyes, a perfectly proportioned nose, and soft lips that were curled into a luminous smile. Quite simply, she was perhaps the most beautiful member of the fairer sex I had ever seen.

As she approached, the luminosity of her smile increased. She enveloped me in an embrace, which quickly fogged the brain. "Hi," she repeated.

I coughed, feeling quite febrile. "Er, did you say your name is Sunflower?"

"Uh-huh. Well, my real name is Jane Myers, but I became Sunflower in Sky's renaming ceremony. You're English, aren't you? I love your accent. It's so sexy."

The neurons had begun to overload. "M-hem, yes, I suppose it is. I mean, yes, I am. Did you say *renaming* ceremony?"

"Yeah. It was so powerful. Would you like to have one?"

Glancing down at her coveralls, I could see her bosom undulating rhythmically as she breathed. "Both, actually," I muttered under my breath. "What? That is, no, I, er, am rather used to my given name, Benjamin. Thank you just the same."

"Benjamin. That's my brother's name."

"Indeed? Well, lucky chap, eh?" I forced a smile, anxious to retreat before my behaviour devolved into something rather more simian. "Yes, well, Miss Sunflower, a pleasure to make your acquaintance." I glanced artificially at my watch. "Sorry, but I manage the cafe down the street and really must be going."

I was about to doff a nonexistent cap when Sky Blue interrupted loudly. "You manage that cafe down the street? Dos Abuelas, right?"

"You know the name?"

"Yeah, man. We're gonna be neighbours."

"Neighbours?"

"Yeah, man. I can show you. It's gonna be cool."

He walked out the door, followed by Sunflower, and then down the road towards the cafe. Coronado whimpered softly and followed Sunflower like a forlorn puppy, whilst I brought up the rear. Sunflower's coveralls could not conceal the other attributes of her stunning figure.

Sky Blue stopped in front of the cafe and pointed to a dilapidated and vacant structure down the street from the cafe, which, in prehistoric times, had been the town's only bar.

"You see that building? That's gonna be our spiritual centre. And we're gonna have a restaurant and art gallery, too."

"Art gallery?" I mumbled, as the neurons waved a white flag of surrender. "Restaurant, you say?"

"Yeah, man. People are craving spiritual healing, too. Siddhartha will nourish their souls, not just fill their stomachs."

What the well-nourished soul wished to dine upon was not something I had previously contemplated, although the baron of beef the Graveses traditionally devoured for Sunday dinner after the local vicar's droning sermon always seemed a respectable choice. It was not soul-nourishing sustenance I now craved, but a cavernous glass of Dusty Trail.

"Well, Maria's *tamales* are heavenly."

"That's cool, man."

"Did you say 'Siddhartha'? Do you own a rather dilapidated bus?"

"Yeah, man." Sky Blue laughed. "Sunflower and I have travelled all over the country in that old bus. It's been our spiritual centre." He wrapped a large, hairy arm around her midriff, fingers disappearing into what one could only imagine was a rapturous netherworld lurking beneath her coveralls.

I coughed. "Er, quite."

"*Madre de Dios*," Coronado whimpered. I could see beads of sweat clotting his brow. "I don't feel so good, Señor Graves. Maybe I better go back to the store."

"*Adios*, Señor Blue. You too, Señorita Flower. Sorry, but Joe gets real mad at me if I leave the store."

Coronado waddled away, not towards the store, but towards Rudy's Bar. Admiral Nelson himself surely would have approved, what with his "never mind manoeuvres, always go straight at 'em" approach.

"Is that poor man all right?" asked Sunflower. "He looked like he was turning pale."

"Ah, yes. A bit of an odd duck, Coronado. Worry not, though. A beer or two will restore him to health." I coughed again. "Er, what were you saying about a restaurant?"

"Oh, yeah, man. It's gonna be all-natural. Vegetarian food is good karma."

"I've always been a rather cheerful carnivore myself," I replied, as the brain served up an image of Daisy providing copious *tamales* and mounds of *carne adovada*.

"That's cool, man. The guy who sold us the building told us you could use some competition, anyway. He told us all about your cafe. Sounds like you got some real uptight *abuelas*."

"Uptight?"

He shrugged. "Yeah, man. You know . . . uptight." I espied Sky Blue's fingers burrowing themselves more deeply into Sunflower's coveralls, as she giggled softly.

I turned my gaze towards the cafe. "Well, Esperanza and Maria are rather high-strung, if that's what you mean. By the way, from whom did you purchase the building?"

"Guy named Joe Garcia."

Upon hearing that Joe had sold Sky Blue the building, the jaw weighed anchor.

"Sorry? Did you say Joe Garcia sold you that building?"

"Yeah, man. He gave us a real good price, too. When I told him we were gonna open a restaurant, he was real enthusiastic. Said he could sell us whatever supplies we needed for the restaurant. You know him?"

"One could say that, yes."

"Said if it wasn't for him, your cafe wouldn't be in business. That guy's got good *chi*."

"Well, Joe possesses copious quantities of something, although one might not call it *chi*."

"You know where he is, man?"

"Alas, with Joe, there are several alternatives. I might suggest reconnoitring Rudy's Bar first." I pointed towards the bullet-riddled sign hanging over Rudy's front door. "If he's not there, then he has likely gone to Santa Fe for the day."

"That's cool, man. If you see him, can you tell him I gotta speak to him?"

"Don't we all," I muttered to myself. "What? Yes, of course. Happy to do so."

Sky Blue paused. He stared off at nothing in particular. Then, he looked at Sunflower and removed his fingers from under her coveralls. "C'mon baby, let's drive over to Taos and check it out."

"Okay, Sky. It was nice to meet you, Benjamin." Sunflower enveloped me in a second embrace. "Won't it be fun to be neighbours?"

"You have no idea," said I, as beads of sweat began erupting on my forehead. Fate, it seemed, had delivered a Siren.

Chapter 4

I wandered back towards the cafe, mind reeling from the effects of Sunflower's incomparable figure, as well as the disintegrating modus vivendi with Joe Garcia. As I opened the front door, Loretta came out of the kitchen.

"Hi, Bennie. What took you so long?"

I massaged my chin slowly. "Ah, well, it seems we are to have competition in the near future."

"Competition? What do you mean?"

"A restaurant. Well, spiritual centre, art gallery, and soul-nourishing restaurant, to be exact."

Loretta cocked her head. "What are you talking about? What's a spiritual centre?"

"It seems your uncle has struck once again."

"Uncle Joe? A spiritual centre and art gallery? Uncle Joe may be a lay priest, but he's not spiritual. As for art, the only pictures he's got in his entire house are portraits of President Kennedy and Elvis Presley."

"Yes, well, apparently, he sold that rundown building down the road, the bar that predated Rudy's. The new owner intends to open a spiritual centre on the premises—whatever that may be—as well as art gallery and cafe. The latter, if I am to understand, will serve soul-nourishing cuisine to patrons. When he heard about the cafe, I gather your uncle reduced the selling price in hopes of supplying the new owners with overpriced supplies."

Loretta burst out laughing. "Uncle Joe sold them the old bar? How?"

"I assume property is exchanged here in the States via contracts, as we have in England."

"No, Bennie, I mean how did he sell a building he doesn't own?"

The already knitted Graves brow knotted itself tightly. "Joe doesn't own the building?"

"Nobody does. In fact, nobody will go inside it."

"Why not? Well, other than the fact it appears to be crumbling into dust."

Loretta offered one of those embarrassed looks. "It's been like that for decades. The building is supposed to be haunted."

"Haunted?"

"I know. It's a silly superstition. Uncle Joe told me the story. He said it's haunted by the ghost of Alejandro Mora. His wife, Rosanete, shot him dead one night in there."

"I shall no doubt regret asking, but what were the circumstances that caused her to shoot him?"

"He was cheating on her," said Loretta. Her eyes narrowed, inducing me to offer her one of those guilt-ridden, innocent-on-all-charges looks. "Like I said, the place used to be a bar—a wild one, according to Uncle Joe. Anyway, Alejandro had been flirting with Adoncia Aguilar, who was the daughter of Prudencio Aguilar, the owner. I guess Adoncia didn't live up her to father's name—Prudencio means "prudence"—because she had been telling everyone in town how much she loved Alejandro.

"The whole town knew. For a while, Rosanete ignored them, but everybody kept telling her about Alejandro dancing with Adoncia. Finally, Rosanete couldn't take it anymore. So, one night she grabbed Alejandro's shotgun and walked into the bar. It was pretty dark inside, but she saw Alejandro dancing with Adoncia. She was going to shoot Adoncia, but her aim wasn't real good and she hit Alejandro instead.

"Rosanete screamed, 'Alejandro, Alejandro, *mi amor*,' but it was too late. He was lying on the floor, still breathing. She bent down to him. 'Alejandro,' she whispered, 'I'm sorry. But why did you have to dance with her?'

"Alejandro tried to speak, but she couldn't hear him. She bent down and put her ear next to his mouth. With his dying breath, he whispered, 'Rosanete, I was dancing with her mother. ¡Vete a la chingada!' Then he died. Since then everybody has been afraid to go in there because of Alejandro's ghost."

I smiled. "Yes, well, not the last words one envisions hearing from the about-to-be departed. Although one imagines an errant shotgun blast could induce discontent within one's ghostly spirit. As we shall have an art gallery in a supposedly haunted bar, one wonders what sort of art the discriminating ghost favours. Hieronymus Bosch? The mind boggles, really."

Loretta laughed. "All I know is you'd better behave, Benjamin Graves," she said. "I know where Maria keeps her shotgun."

An image of Sunflower's ample bosom, bursting from her coveralls, detoured through the cranium, causing me to shudder. "Truth, honour, and fidelity are a Graves's highest callings," I said, raising the right hand in full scout fashion.

"What about that relative of yours, the sea captain you told me about who deserted in Jamaica during the War of 1812?"

"Ah."

One evening, as a bit of leavening to amuse ourselves whilst washing dishes, I had told Loretta the story of Captain Archibald Graves, who scuttled his ship so he could stay with a Jamaican woman with whom he had fallen in love.

"Well, whilst all Graveses have been called, a few have failed to answer, one might say." I glanced at my watch furtively. "Right, I should assist Maria."

The front door opened again and Coronado walked in quickly, if somewhat unsteadily.

"Señor Graves. Are you gonna tell Loretta about that girl, Señorita Flower?"

Loretta's brow narrowed. "Girl? What girl, Bennie?"

Coronado's eyes widened. "The one from the bus, Loretta. *Híjole*, she sure is pretty. She even hugged Señor Graves and me."

Loretta's eyes narrowed. "Bennie?" she hissed.

"Fear not, Loretta," I replied, raising my hands in mock surrender. "Sunflower is bespoken to the bus's other passenger, a Mister Sky Blue."

"Her name is Sunflower? His name is Sky Blue? Who are these people?"

"I gather from the licence on the bus they are from California."

"And this Sunflower is pretty?" Loretta asked.

"*Sí*, Loretta. *Muy, muy bonita*," Coronado replied, unhelpfully. "I sure liked her."

"Is she prettier than me, Bennie?" Loretta asked, hands set menacingly upon her hips.

When a woman of one's romantic acquaintance enquires as to how her beauty compares to another's, one's answer must be artfully constructed, lest broken crockery or the deafening retort of a shotgun ensue. I mean, Loretta was most attractive, as I have previously described her. But there is beauty, and then there is Helen-of-Troy-face-that-launches-a-thousand-ships beauty. Sunflower was definitely of the dreadnought-launching category.

I took Loretta's hand in mine. "Jealousy does not become you. I'm quite sure you and, er, Sunflower will get along famously, assuming they really do open this spiritual centre and such. Well, I suppose I should get to work."

"I still don't understand how Uncle Joe managed to sell that building."

As far as I could tell, the creativity of Joe Garcia's avarice was unlimited, not that I would express such a thought so bluntly to Loretta, for whom her uncle was the kindly, doting type.

"Perhaps you should ask him."

"I will."

Sufficiently placated for the moment—I had no illusions as to the explosion of jealousy that would erupt once she encountered Sunflower in the flesh, as it were—Loretta planted a kiss on my cheek and returned to the kitchen. I followed, wondering what sort of gastronomic competition we would soon face.

Inside the kitchen, I found Maria stirring a large pot of *posole*, whilst Esperanza slowly chopped onions for the evening's *enchiladas*. Both were smoking furiously, large ash plumes dangling ominously from their cigarettes. A blue haze hung in the air, despite a blowing fan and the open back door.

"About time, *Pendejito*," Esperanza grumbled. "Where the hell have you been? My back's real bad."

Although Esperanza had promised, reluctantly, not to address me as *Pendejito* as a condition of my staying in Vaca Seca to oversee the cafe, her promise had been shed like a snake's skin in short order.

"And a most pleasant good morning to you, too, Esperanza. In fact, I was taking stock of our competition."

"Huh? What competition?"

"A new restaurant will soon be opening nearby. Well, actually a restaurant, art gallery and spiritual centre."

"What the fuck is a spiritual centre?" Esperanza asked, as she blew a large cloud of smoke towards me.

"I haven't the vaguest notion. We shall find out soon enough, however."

Maria looked up at us and growled. "¡*Cállate*! We got lots to do. Bennie, start grating cheese."

"Of course, Maria." I retrieved the large block of cheddar and began to scrape it against the grater.

"Where is this new cafe gonna open?" Maria asked, as she stirred the *posole* violently.

"Apparently, Joe sold the old bar to the new buyers. How he managed to so, as I gather he does not own the building, is rather a mystery."

Esperanza shrugged. "If somebody's stupid enough to buy a haunted bar, then Joe can sell it."

"He can't sell a building he doesn't own."

"Why not? If I could sell that shit pile to somebody, I would. Nobody here wants it. Only a *gringo* would be stupid enough to buy it."

"Well, in fact, a couple has purchased it."

"*Gringos*?"

"Yes. From California."

Esperanza laughed. "I told you, *Pendejito*. You watch, Alejandro will frighten them off. Then Joe can sell it to somebody else."

"You don't really believe in ghosts and such, do you Esperanza?"

"*Sí*, I believe in ghosts. You go in there. You'll see. That bar's haunted by Alejandro."

I sighed and resumed my cheese-grating efforts.

The evening had proceeded uneventfully. There had been a steady but manageable flow of customers. Maria remained civil as orders were brought in and plates of *enchiladas, carne adovada,* and *tamales* were whisked out, along with baskets of *sopapillas*. With the exception of an inebriated Pedro Aragón, who had staggered into the cafe from Rudy's and staggered out towards same after consuming a large bowl of green chile stew, all of our customers had paid for their meals.

Around seven o'clock, a dozen or so of the locals were grazing away, including Coronado and his equally dull-witted sister Maria, who oversaw the local bank branch. Maria was nattering loudly whilst Coronado would periodically interject, "*Sí*, Maria," as he devoured a large plate of *enchiladas*. Rudy and his grandson Antonio, a lad of eleven whom Rudy had already trained to tend bar, were also eating, albeit quietly.

I was clearing off a table when the front door opened, admitting a tall, tan, crisply attired fiftyish chap. He strode in, turned around, and regally surveyed the dining room. He wore crisp white trousers, brown cowboy boots polished to the extreme, a light blue shirt, dark blue jacket, and sunglasses. His hair was greyish-blonde, with a slight curl at the sides. But what I most noticed was his teeth, which were large, perfectly straight, and luminously white.

Forks were set down on tables and silence enveloped the dining room, as everyone present simply goggled at the chap.

"I say, may I help you?" I stammered. "Please sit where you like."

"Is this the Dos Abuelas cafe?" he barked.

"Y-yes, it is," I replied, with measured trepidation.

He glanced at his watch. "Good. Then I need to meet them right now. I'm a busy man."

"Meet whom?"

"The ah-boolas, son." He surveyed the room until his eyes encountered Coronado, who blinked back timidly from over his plate. "You! I saw you last night. You're the one who said he didn't know me."

"Sorry, señor," Coronado said, a wisp of cheese hanging from his chin. "I still dunno who you are. But if you're hungry, Maria's *enchiladas* are real good."

"That's why I'm here. I want to see Maria. And her sister, the other ah-boola. What's her name?"

"I take it you mean Esperanza?"

"Yeah, that's right. British, aren't you?"

"You Americans are especially perceptive," I replied.

"Well, cheerio and all that, old chap," he replied, in a grating imitation of a British accent. "I need to see your father."

"What?" The mind reeled, wondering how he could possibly know my father.

"That's right, old chap," he replied with the same grating accent. "Right after I speak with the ah-boolas. My time is far too valuable to waste. Got that? Now, where is he?"

"Who?"

"Your father. He owns this—" the chap paused, glanced around the room again and frowned—"place, doesn't he?"

"The cafe?" I laughed and shook my head. "My father owns the cafe?"

"That's why I'm here, old chap. I need to speak with him and the ah-boolas." He raised the cuff of his shirt and glanced at the large golden watch that enveloped his wrist. "Now!"

By now, the Graves patience had thinned. "My father is a member of Parliament," I replied. "He does not own this establishment. In fact, I'm quite sure he is unaware of its existence.

If you still wish to dine, there is a table in the corner. Now, if you'll excuse me."

I turned and was about to return to the kitchen, when I perceived a hand around my forearm.

"Now hold on, son," he said. "I'm Roger Victory." He paused and glanced around the room, only to be met with blank stares, shrugs, and the odd muttering about the crazy *gringo*.

I goggled him blankly.

"Roger Victory," he repeated. "Jesus, doesn't anyone here ever go to the movies?" he asked, as he shook his head in disgust.

"There's a drive-in in Española," Coronado said. "I saw a movie there last summer with my sister. It was about a giant spider. Do you like to go to movies, too, Señor Victor?"

"I'm an actor and a director, you idiot. *Everyone* knows me. I won an Oscar for *Devil in Blue*."

"How come the Devil was wearing blue, señor?" Coronado asked. "Isn't he kinda red 'cause it's so hot?"

"What? I played a parish priest in a small village in Italy on the Mediterranean and— "

"I say, Mister, er, Victory," I interrupted, desirous of preventing an extended descent into Coronado's illogic. "Why exactly are you here?"

"I told that fat idiot why," he said, pointing to Coronado. "I'm here to make a movie. About this cafe. Now, where's your father and where are the ah-boolas?"

"First, Mister Victory, there is no call for invective. Second, Maria and Esperanza are in the kitchen at present. And the correct pronunciation is 'ab-way-las.' Third, my father does not own the café. My uncle is the owner and I am the manager."

"The ah-boolas are in the kitchen? Good. I'll speak to them first." He began to rocket towards the kitchen door. I caught his arm and pulled. "What are you doing?" he snapped, pulling his arm from the hand's grip.

The grey matter was unable to fathom how this rude, over-toothed sod even knew of the cafe, much less why he, or anyone, would wish to make a film about it. Granted, our existence was perhaps miraculous, especially given Esperanza's continued and mercurial involvement.

"Neither Maria nor Esperanza appreciates customers in their kitchen, and you would be wise not to enter their lair." I led him to the table in the corner. "Now, kindly sit down and I shall ask them to come out and see you. As for my uncle, he is at home. You may see him tomorrow, if you like."

Roger sat down. "Fine," he growled, as he glanced at his watch. "Bring me a glass of your best cabernet."

"We do not serve alcohol. Would you care for iced tea?"

"What? Iced tea?" He shook his head in disgust. "Fine. Bring me a goddamn glass of iced tea."

I strode into the kitchen to assess Maria and Esperanza's mental status. Despite wishing to inflict both of their most vituperative selves upon the over-ivoried Roger—vituperation that would have withered Admiral Nelson himself—the Graves code frowned upon mayhem.

Chimneying on their ubiquitous cigarettes and jabbering in Spanish, they glowered at me with the usual disapprobation.

"What do you want, *Pendejito*," growled Esperanza. "You got any new orders?"

"No, I don't." I looked about. "Where's Loretta?"

"She's in the storeroom," Esperanza replied acidly. "You miss her already, *Pendejito*?"

"Sod off, Esperanza." I had long ago decided to meet Esperanza's insults with heavy return fire. "In any case, there is an out-of-town visitor in the dining room who is anxious to speak with you both."

Maria and Esperanza looked at each other quizzically. "Who?" Esperanza asked. "We don't know nobody."

"The chap's name is Roger Victory. He assures me that everyone in the States knows him."

"Roger Victory? Sounds like a *gringo*. Who the fuck is he? The only *gringos* we know are you and El Vaquero. "What does he want?"

"He says he is a famous actor. He wishes to speak with both of you about making a film about the cafe."

"Huh? You mean he's a movie star?"

"Apparently. And, he wishes to make a film about the two of you."

Maria shook her head, unable to contemplate even the idea. She grasped her largest chef's knife for comfort and began to savage an onion.

"How come some *gringo* wants to make a movie about Maria and me?"

I paused, not wishing to reply that he was mad as a March hare. "I haven't the foggiest notion," I said. "Nevertheless, he is here and, as there are no new orders at present, would you both kindly step into the dining room and speak with him."

Maria shook her head and continued to chop away. "*Hermana*, you talk to this *gringo*. I'm gonna stay here. And don't let him come into my kitchen."

"Okay." Esperanza dropped the remains of her cigarette onto the floor, grinding it mercilessly into the linoleum with her shoe. For months, I had reminded Esperanza not to fly about the dining room whilst smoking, as ash-laden plates were not favoured by the customers. Despite her uncivil responses to such reminders, I had apparently won a small battle.

"Let's go, *Pendejito*. Where's this fucking *gringo*?"

I poured a glass of iced tea and walked back into the dining room, with Esperanza following behind. We strode to the table where Roger sat, impatiently drumming his fingers on the table.

I placed the glass in front of him. "Mister Victory, allow me to introduce Esperanza Fuentes, one of the *abuelas* you asked to speak with."

Roger stood up forcefully. "Glad to meet you, Esperanza." He grabbed her arm and began pumping it heavily. "I've heard a lot about you."

She eyed his well-tanned finery and glowing teeth. "You sure look like a rich *gringo*." Then, waving her thumb towards me, she added, "*Pendejito* says you want to make a movie about Maria and me. How come?"

Roger smiled. It was one of those Cheshire cat smiles one instinctively reacts to by grabbing one's wallet and searching for the nearest exit. "Because I think your story is fascinating," he replied. "Resurrecting this cafe against all odds to save the town and preserve your heritage against the encroaching march of progress."

Esperanza cocked her head slightly. "What the fuck you talking about?" I pondered the same question, although I might have phrased it in a rather more civil tone. The other customers in the cafe had all turned towards Roger and were listening intently. I espied Loretta, who was peering through the kitchen door.

"It means I see a great story here. Your entire town is struggling to save itself from oblivion. The cafe is a metaphor for that struggle, rising up out of the ashes."

"Huh? The cafe didn't burn down or nothing. Fucking Coronado tried to shoot it to pieces and that *pendejo* Joe Garcia tried to set it on fire with some matches, but he was too drunk."

"Well, I'm just speaking metaphorically. The cafe is a metaphor for the triumph over adversity."

"Me-ta-phor?" Esperanza repeated. "What's that?"

Roger exhaled deeply. "A metaphor? Um, well, it doesn't matter. It means a story."

"You talk worse than *Pendejito*. Maria and me, we ain't interested in no movie or nothing. ¡*Vete a la chingada!*"

"I'm sorry, I don't speak Spanish. What does that mean?"

Esperanza stared at him but remained silent as she slowly extended the middle finger on her right hand.

"Esperanza," I said sharply. The finger retracted reluctantly.

Roger appeared taken aback by Esperanza's tone. "You know," he said softly, "making a movie can mean a lot of money for you. Of course, I will purchase the rights to your story." He reached into his right trouser pocket and removed a large sheaf of bills. "How about five hundred dollars for you and your sister Maria? Think of it as a token of good faith, even if you decide not to proceed?"

He counted off five hundred-dollar bills slowly. Esperanza's eyes widened. She snatched the bills away from his hand with a speed that would have shamed the fastest iguana.

"Okay *gringo*, Maria and me will listen. How much for this movie?"

"Well, that's hard to say. Now, I understand you and your sister do not actually own the cafe, but that it's named after you."

Esperanza glared at me. "*Sí*, El Vaquero, he lent us the money to pay off Joe Garcia, so he kinda owns it. But Maria and me, we're gonna pay him back real soon. Maybe if you give us some more money, we can buy it now. *¿Que no?*" Her eyes brightened at the thought of further lucre.

At this point, Roger turned to the assembled customers. "A movie like this means a great opportunity for all of you," he shouted. "The crew will need supplies, catering, and lodging. We'll also need extras. That means all of you can be movie stars."

He looked around, displaying his fluorescent teeth in a large grin. There was a low hum of discussion and much head-nodding to the affirmative.

"Señor Victor," Coronado shouted, waving his hand about as if he were in school hoping to be called upon by a hapless instructor. "I got an extra room in my house. It's got some chickens in there now, but I can move them out if you want to stay there."

"Chickens? Uh, no. Thanks for the, er, offer, but I have my bus. I wouldn't want to impose. Well, I am glad you are all on board." He turned to me. "Now, son—what is your name by the way?"

"Graves," I replied slowly. "Benjamin Graves."

He reverted to the grating British accent. "Right ho. Ben, old chap. You said your uncle owns the cafe? When can I see him, old chap?"

Having observed the toothy fungus before me ensnare Esperanza, the internal alarm bells now tolled loudly. I did not relish the thought of his visiting Uncle Bill's ranch.

"We live outside of town. Perhaps you can visit the ranch tomorrow. Or I can ask Uncle Bill to come into town."

"Excellent, old chap," he replied, patting me on the shoulder. He glanced at his gold watch. "We will meet here, then. Nine o'clock. By the way, can I meet Maria? I understand she's a hell of a cook."

"Maria, she don't like people much," Esperanza said. "But she's gonna like your money a whole lot."

"Well, I'll need to meet her soon so I can cast an actress to portray her."

"You mean, you're gonna get somebody else to be Maria and me?"

"Well, yes, of course. There are some very fine actors who would be delighted to portray either of you. But, as I said, you and Maria can certainly be extras."

Esperanza's eyes narrowed again. "Extra what?"

"Extras. Ordinary people who appear in movies, in the background. For example, when we film scenes in the cafe, we'll need to hire extras as customers."

"You mean, like these *lobos*?"

"What?"

I coughed. "Er, Roger, let me inform Uncle Bill you wish to meet him. Nine o'clock may be a bit early, what with chores at the ranch and such. How about ten o'clock?"

Roger glanced at his watch and scowled. "Nine-fifteen, old chap. I've got far too much work to do whilst I'm here."

"Señor Graves," Coronado shouted. "I could bring Señor Victor to the ranch if you want."

Roger looked away, drumming his well-manicured fingers.

"Thanks, Coronado, but no need. Uncle Bill needs to come into town tomorrow anyway."

"Excellent, old chap," Roger said, using the same grating accent. "I look forward to meeting him."

"By the way, would you like something to eat? You've already heard about Maria's cooking. Perhaps you should try it yourself."

"Of course, old chap. What do you recommend?"

"Coronado, how are the *enchiladas*?"

"Real good, Señor Graves." Coronado patted his ample stomach. "You should get them with green chile, Señor Victor. And some *sopapillas*, too."

Roger nodded. "Uh, okay, *enchiladas* it is."

As I turned around and walked towards the kitchen, the front door opened, admitting Sunflower and Sky Blue. Although Sky Blue was dressed in the same coveralls, Sunflower had changed into blue jeans and a light yellow, tight-fitting shirt that revealed an erupting décolletage. The room descended into silence again as every pair of eyes focused on her.

"*Híjole*," Coronado yelped.

"¡*Que chichona!*" Esperanza gargled, as she sprinted towards the kitchen.

"Jesus," Rudy muttered, as a large forkful of *enchiladas* fell into his lap.

Roger remained silent. He simply smiled, staring at Sunflower like a vulture anticipating its next meal. No doubt, he and Rodrigo could compare notes on techniques for ensnaring the fairer sex.

"Hi, Benjamin," Sunflower said, waving her hand. She strode over and embraced me yet again. "So this is your cafe?"

I retreated from her embrace before the heart could explode. "Er, yes, I suppose it is."

I espied Loretta, whose eyes were wide with fury. She turned around and retreated hastily into the kitchen. Fate, I feared, was about to enliven the evening.

Chapter 5

Sunflower seemed oblivious to the attention she had engendered. "I say, perhaps you and Sky Blue would like to sit down?" I glanced about, espying a table in the corner farthest from the kitchen—and Loretta. "How about there?" I said, pointing to the table.

"Thanks, man," Sky Blue replied, snaking his arm around Sunflower's waist and guiding her towards the table.

I followed them, guiltily admiring the outline of Sunflower's encased derriere until it was comfortably seated in a chair. "Would you care for something to drink?"

"Sure man. You got any *lassi*?"

"Eh, what?"

"*Lassi*, man. It's made with yoghurt."

"Er, afraid not. Sounds rather too exotic for the local clientele. Something else, perhaps? Iced tea?"

"How about a bottle of wine, baby?" he asked, turning to Sunflower, who nodded her assent.

I pointed a thumb towards Roger. "Sorry. As I just told that other chap, we don't serve alcohol. No liquor licence and such. You're quite welcome to purchase something from Rudy's and bring it back here, if you wish, although I rather doubt Rudy has much of a wine selection. The locals seem to prefer beer."

Sky Blue grunted. "No wine?"

"Sorry."

"Just water then, man. But we're gonna have wine and *lassi* at our restaurant."

"Right. Two glasses of water."

I noticed Sunflower staring intently at Roger. She stood up and walked towards his table. "Oh my God! You're Roger Victory, the actor. I've seen all your movies. I loved *Devil in Blue.*" She covered her hand with her mouth and emitted one of those schoolgirl giggles.

"Why, yes, yes I am," Roger replied, as he fluffed himself like a peacock. His eyes swivelled, targeting Sunflower's chest. "I'm glad somebody knows who I am." He took her hand in his. "And you are, miss?"

"I'm Sunflower." She giggled again. "I can't believe this. Roger Victory!" She turned back to Sky Blue. "Sky, isn't this cool? Roger Victory!"

Aware that Roger's eyes were aimed squarely at Sunflower's décolletage, Sky Blue squirmed in his chair. "Yeah, that's real cool, baby."

"Sunflower," Roger said smoothly. "What a beautiful and charming name. How would you like to be in my new movie? It's going to be about this cafe."

"Me? In your movie? That would be so cool!" She embraced him tightly.

"Well, Sunflower," Roger said, taking her hands in his perfectly manicured ones, "I'll be her for a few days scouting locations. We can discuss a suitable role for you."

Sunflower nodded silently and returned to her table. She sat down and continued to stare at Roger, who, I observed, offered her a wink of the eye. No doubt, Rodrigo would be proud.

Having watched Roger scout his prey, I retreated to the kitchen. The door had not even swung behind me when the first verbal fusillade struck.

"So that's Sunflower," Loretta growled. "Care to explain why you were hugging her?"

"Er, to be fair, she embraced me. Seems to possess rather a fondness for the tactile. I mean, she embraced Coronado."

"No she didn't. He was sitting at a table."

"I don't mean just now. When we first met. She waltzed right up to him and, well, embraced him the way you saw her embrace me. Really, Loretta, there is nothing to be jealous about." I moved towards her, but she receded from me step for step.

"Don't touch me, Bennie."

"You better watch out, *Pendejito*," Esperanza added. "I see how you looked at that *chichona*. You're just like Hector."

"What?" I spluttered, appalled at the comparison to Esperanza's ape-like paramour.

"You heard me, *Pendejito*." Esperanza placed her arm around Loretta's shoulders. "You better not do nothing to upset my Loretta."

"Your Loretta?"

"*Sí*, and she deserves better than some *lobo* who's gonna sniff around that *chichona*, especially a *gringo*."

Maria, who had been listening silently, picked up a large knife and plunged the point into a cutting board. "¡*Cállate todos!*"

Everyone froze.

"*Hermana*," Maria said in a measured tone, "Don't you get involved no more. You remember what I said? *No más*." Maria strode over to the kitchen door, opened it slightly, and looked towards the corner table where Sky Blue and Sunflower now sat. "*Madre de Dios*," she whispered.

Esperanza waved her hand in disgust, tracing arcs of cigarette smoke. It was she who had spread rumours about Loretta and me when we first opened the cafe, hoping to drive me away, and had almost succeeded.

Maria turned to me. "Bennie, that one, she's a *bruja*."

"A what?"

"It means a witch, *Pendejito*," said Esperanza. "The kind who cast spells over stupid *gringos*."

"You gotta be real careful," Maria said, patting my forearm gently with her chef's knife.

I sighed and offered a scout's salute. "Not to worry, Maria. I am pledged to Loretta."

Loretta seemed unconvinced. "Okay, Bennie, but I don't like her here."

"Well, she does appear to be, er, rather involved, with Sky Blue, although the allure is rather mysterious. And, Mister Victory appears to be—how might one put it?—sniffing about."

Esperanza rudely cupped her hands in front of her apron. "It's real obvious, *Pendejito*."

"Never mind, Esperanza. Now, if you will excuse me, I promised them two glasses of water."

"You stay in the kitchen and help Maria," commanded Loretta. "I'll wait on them."

"Yes, er, okay," I said.

Loretta filled two glasses and disappeared through the kitchen door. She returned several minutes later with their order.

"Two orders of cheese *enchiladas*, Maria. And they don't want any green chile sauce because it's got meat in it."

"*Enchiladas sin chile*? Maria said, shaking her head. "I think maybe Alejandro's ghost, he's gonna be working real hard."

Maria prepared the two plates of cheese *enchiladas*, whilst I fried several *sopapillas*. The comestibles readied, Loretta picked up the plates and the basket of *sopapillas*. She marched into the dining room as Esperanza and I peered discreetly from the kitchen door.

Loretta walked over to Sunflower. "Two cheese *enchilada* plates, no chile." She began to lower the plate, which suddenly tipped forward. A river of steaming *enchiladas* and *refritos* poured over the side and into Sunflower's lap. Sunflower screamed and stood up, frantically wiping off the cheesy mess from her jeans.

"Oh, I'm so sorry," Loretta said dryly. "How could I be so clumsy?"

"My jeans," Sunflower cried. "They're ruined."

I rushed over towards their table. "Are you all right?" I asked, as I resisted the urge to secure a serviette to clean her lap. "I am terribly sorry. Of course, we shall pay for your jeans."

I turned to Loretta, meeting her dagger-like stare with my own. "Loretta, please ask Maria to prepare another plate of *enchiladas* for our guest." Then, turning back to Sky Blue, I added, "of course, there shall be no charge."

"No thanks, man," Sky Blue replied. He stood up and glowered at Loretta. "This place has bad *chi*." He placed his arm around Sunflower, who was sobbing lightly, and escorted her towards the front door. "Come on, baby, let's get you cleaned up." Then, before shutting the front door behind them, he turned around and said to no one in particular, "Real bad *chi*."

Everyone watched as they exited the front door. Loretta and I returned to the kitchen, where I confronted her. "How could you be so childish? That poor girl didn't do anything."

"It was an accident. Besides, you shouldn't have let her press herself against you like that. Sorry I don't have that kind of equipment, Bennie."

"Loretta, please. I mean, she's obviously quite smitten with Sky Blue."

"Then why did you have your arms around her like that?"

"What was I supposed to do, shoot her when she approached? Run away? For God's sake, I told you, she embraced Coronado."

"I don't want to talk about it." Loretta grabbed a tray and returned to the dining room.

Esperanza laughed. "*Híjole, Pendejito*, you got her real mad now. Better apologise."

"Apologise? For what? Loretta deliberately spilt that plate of *enchiladas*."

Esperanza shrugged. "Okay, don't apologise. What the fuck do I care? Maybe she's gonna cut off your *cojones* while you sleep." Esperanza grinned like a hyaena.

Before I could respond, Roger glided through the kitchen door.

"Excuse me—" he began.

"Get the fuck out of my kitchen," Maria yelled, brandishing her chef's knife, reddish-hued from the tomatoes she had just decapitated.

Roger stopped suddenly and his eyes widened.

"*Hermana*," Esperanza said calmly, "it's okay. This is Señor Roger. He's the *gringo* with all the money ... for the movie." She retrieved the five hundred dollars from her pocket and waved them in front of Maria. "And you and me, we're gonna get paid more for some 'rights' or something. And we get to be in the movie, too, like Hollywood stars."

Maria lowered her knife and stared, first at the money and then at Roger. "*No entiendo.*"

"Allow me to explain, Maria," said Roger, who oozed well-oiled charm. His eyes glinted. "The five hundred dollars I gave your sister are just an initial payment—to show my good faith. When I told your lovely sister I wished to buy the rights to your story, I meant that I would pay for the right to do so. It's very common in my business. We pay authors for the rights to their stories, too."

"How much you gonna pay for these rights?" Esperanza asked.

"Well, I hadn't settled on a final number. How about, oh, a thousand dollars. That's five hundred for each of you."

"*Hermana*, five hundred dollars each," whispered Esperanza. Her eyes brightened with avarice, reminding me of Joe Garcia.

"M-hem," I said. "Not that I particularly care, Esperanza, but as you mentioned to Roger, you and Maria do not actually own the cafe at present. As for the cafe's phoenix-like resurrection, as I recall you were distinctly opposed."

"Huh? I'm real glad Maria and me got the cafe, *Pendejito*. I just don't want you here. Maybe Roger can pay you money so you can go home."

I sighed. Before I could respond, Loretta burst through the kitchen door and slammed into Roger, sending the large stack of dishes she was carrying crashing to the floor.

"I'm terribly sorry, miss," he said. "Are you all right?" He looked into Loretta's eyes and flashed the fluorescent grin.

"Yes, I, I'm fine," Loretta replied slowly. "I'm sorry I ran into you like that."

"Entirely my fault, miss . . ."

"Loretta Alvarez." She wiped her hand on her apron and extended it towards him.

He took her hand gently, raised it to his lips, and kissed it. Observing what I took to be Rodrigo-like behaviour, the grey matter began beating to quarters.

Loretta's face reddened. "I thought they only do that in the movies."

"They do, and I have," Roger replied. "It's not often I encounter as charming and beautiful a woman as yourself. How would you like to be in my movie?"

Roger appeared to be corralling members of the fairer sex like the cowboys in Uncle Bill's Zane Grey novels corralled horses.

"Me? I don't know anything about acting."

"Don't worry," he said, kissing her hand again. "I can teach you everything you need to know."

"Tosser," I muttered under the breath.

Roger turned to Maria. He extended his hand towards her but, noticing her hand was still wrapped around the large knife, withdrew it quickly. "Well, Maria, very nice to have met you and your lovely sister. Tomorrow, after I sign a contract with Benjamin's uncle, we can begin." Roger paused and smiled yet again. "Big changes are in store for your little town."

Between Sunflower's rapturous beauty, Roger's lupine tendencies, and the prospect of a competing restaurant, the grey matter cried out for a large whisky, even one with the battery-acid-like qualities of Dusty Trail.

"Right, then, er, Roger," I said. "My uncle and I shall see you tomorrow at ten. Now, we really must—"

"Say no more, old chap. What do I owe you for dinner?"

"You already pay us, Señor Roger," Esperanza replied, reaching into her pocket where she had stuffed the five hundred dollars.

"Thank you, Esperanza. That's very generous of you."

"*Sí*, Maria and me, we're real generous."

As soon as Roger walked out, Esperanza smiled. "*Hermana*," she said, "I think we got us a real rich *gringo*."

Maria shook her head. "You never gonna learn, *Hermana*."

Later that evening, after Señor Apestoso had received his nightly *ofrenda* and the cafe had been spiffed, Loretta bid me a distinctively cool goodnight.

"Aren't you overreacting, Loretta? There's no reason for you to be jealous."

"Oh, really? I saw two very good reasons," she replied as she scowled deeply. Loretta then walked to the back door. "I'll see you tomorrow morning, *Tia* Maria. You too, *Tia* Esperanza."

"*Buenas noches*, Loretta," they replied in unison.

Esperanza smirked and cupped her hands in the same rude manner. "I think maybe you're gonna need a new girlfriend, *Pendejito*. You sure got Loretta real mad."

"What am I supposed to do, tell them to leave town, like those yobs in Uncle Bill's Zane Grey novels?"

"Don't worry, Bennie," Maria said. "Loretta, she won't stay mad real long. Maybe you can bring her some flowers tomorrow. She'd like that."

"Capital idea, Maria. Although I'm not sure where one obtains flowers at this time of year. Perhaps Uncle Bill has an idea." I exhaled deeply. "Well, cheer-o."

Returning to the ranch, the feet set course for the sitting room, where several bottles of Dusty Trail were anchored. Pouring out a bracing dose, I sat down heavily on the sofa.

Uncle Bill stared up at me from his chair. "Bad night?"

"Nightmarish."

"What'd Esperanza do this time?"

"Not Esperanza, Uncle Bill. She was merely her usual vituperative self. It's rather our visitors. We are to have competition soon."

"Competition? For what?"

"Apparently, our new visitors will be opening up a spiritual centre, art gallery, and vegetarian restaurant."

"What the hell's a spiritual centre? Art gallery? In Vaca Seca? What's it gonna have—pictures of Elvis and the Virgin

Mary? And who's gonna eat at a vegetarian restaurant? Besides, I thought this Roger or Robert fellow Coronado was jabbering about was making a movie or something."

"Er, yes, Roger is the movie chap. Perhaps you know him. Roger Victory? Apparently, he is a famous American actor. Well, he insists he is famous."

"Roger Victory? Nope. But then I ain't much of a movie fan. Now, if it was Bogart, that'd be different. Celestina loved Bogart. She always wanted to see his movies." Uncle Bill stared wistfully at the picture of Celestina that hung above the mantelpiece.

He turned back towards me. "Why does he want to make a movie about Maria and Esperanza?"

I drained my glass. "Something about their heritage and the encroaching march of civilisation. You can ask him yourself tomorrow."

"Me? What for?"

"Well, as you are the legal owner of the cafe, he wishes to purchase the rights to the story from you."

"What story?"

"The phoenix-like rise of the cafe from the ashes, or, in this instance, Coronado's shotgun. He gave Esperanza five hundred dollars, which she hoovered up like a famished iguana."

"Five hundred bucks?" Uncle Bill's eyes widened.

"Indeed. And with a promise of more lucre. I gather, however, he requires your assent, something about buying the rights to the story. I told him we would meet him tomorrow morning at ten o'clock to discuss it."

Uncle Bill refilled his glass and laughed. "Well, if he wants to pay me so he can make a goddamn movie about Maria and Esperanza, why the hell not?"

"Rather the oily sort, this Roger," I said. "An American Rodrigo."

"What about those other folks, the ones who plan to open this spiritual centre and art gallery or whatever?"

"That would be Sky Blue and Sunflower."

Uncle Bill rolled his head to starboard. "What the hell kind of names are those?"

"Well, Sunflower informed me her Christian name is Jane, but Sky Blue changed it to Sunflower during her renaming ceremony."

"Renaming ceremony? What in goddamn—"

I held up my right hand. "Merely the messenger of madness, Uncle Bill. I must say, however, this Sunflower, er, Jane, is quite—well, I mean she is simply stunning."

"What about this Sky Blue fellow?"

"Older chap. Perhaps fortyish. Has a most odd way of speaking."

"So do you, Bennie, at least to folks here."

"Yes, but this chap speaks of *chi*, whatever that is. Muttered something about bad *chi* in the cafe this evening. I haven't the foggiest notion what he means."

Uncle Bill took a large swallow of whisky. "Jesus, what the hell's going on in this town?"

"Perhaps God has decided to freshen the biblical plagues." I paused. "Er, there is one other matter. It's, well, Loretta."

"Trouble in paradise, pard'ner?"

"Eh? No, I mean, Loretta espied Sunflower embracing me and, well, a spot of jealousy has arisen, if you know what I mean."

Having read several Zane Grey novels, I had discovered that fidelity to one's betrothed and, especially, to one's horse, was a centrepiece of the cowboy creed, which Uncle Bill adhered to with rigour. A chap was expected to rebuff all immodest advances, even those of grateful members of the fairer sex whom he had saved from debauchery by ruffians, thieves, or savage Indians.

"Goddamn it, Bennie, I thought you and Loretta were engaged."

Had Uncle Bill seen Sunflower, he need not have asked. Although the Graves coat-of-arms proclaimed *Vires – Fidelitas – Honoris*, few had been immune to the Sirens' calls.

"We are, well, informally. Besides, you have it entirely wrong. I'm truly innocent. It took place inside the cafe. She—Sunflower, that is—simply walked up and wrapped herself around me. Loretta then retaliated by emptying a plate of *enchiladas* into the poor girl's lap. Hence Sky Blue's remarking about bad *chi*, by the way. In any event, I admonished Loretta about the incident. Said admonishment was not well received, if you take my meaning."

"Sorry, Bennie, I shouldn't laugh. She's a pistol."

"Are you comparing Loretta to a firearm?"

"What? No, it means she's got spunk. Stands up for herself."

"What do you suggest I do? I mean, with Sky Blue and Sunflower prowling about, resurrecting the allegedly haunted bar—"

Uncle Bill's eyebrows rocketed upwards. "Where Rosanete Aguilar shot Alejandro? *That* old dump's gonna be their spiritual centre and whatever the hell else?"

"So I gather. Apparently, Joe Garcia sold the, er, 'old dump,' as you call it, to them, despite not having title to the property."

"Sounds like Joe. Well, I guess they're gettin' a true Vaca Seca howdy."

"Quite. However, you still haven't addressed my, er, problem. What should I do?"

Uncle Bill rubbed his chin slowly. "Well, pard'ner, whenever Celestina went on the warpath—and talk about a pistol, well, I've told you some stories—I'd eat crow and come back, hat in one hand and flowers in the other."

"I understand the flowers. Maria suggested the same, although there are no floral shops in Vaca Seca. But how would consuming a local avian prove one's faithfulness?"

"I forget you still don't understand English here. It means apologise."

"But I have nothing to apologise for."

"When the hell does that matter with a woman? You must have done the same goddamn thing with Cynthia. From what I saw, she must have required a hell of a lot more maintenance than Loretta."

"Well, there were several occasions, usually after tardy returns from the Jolly Rooster. This, however, is different. I simply can't avoid Sunflower, not in Vaca Seca. Nor do I wish to see plates dumped into paying customers' laps. Bad for business, that."

"Yep, I suppose that's gonna be a problem. Look, why don't you apologise to Loretta tomorrow. Smooth things over. Maybe take her to Santa Fe for a night on the town. Since I got to meet this Roger fellow tomorrow anyhow, I'll have a word with Josefa." Josefa was Loretta's mother, whom Uncle Bill had dated briefly a few years after Celestina's untimely death.

"Besides, if this Sky Blue fella is gonna fix up the old bar, odds are he won't get real far. I don't know anybody around here who'll even set foot in the place." He glanced at his watch. "Jesus, I got to get me some shut-eye. You'd better, too, Bennie."

I grunted. "I suppose you're right. I shall consume crow, as you call it, tomorrow."

Chapter 6

The following morning, I staggered towards the barn, bleary-eyed and insufficiently braced with cowboy coffee, to mix the witches' brew of 'slops', as Uncle Bill called the previous day's leavings, and various other ingredients that formed Daisy's breakfast. The sow followed me about, carefully supervising the preparations. As I poured the mixture into her trough, she pushed me aside—a trivial task for a twenty-five–stone rasher—and rapidly devoured the contents.

The morning's equine care was of a similar nature. Except, whereas Daisy was motivated by hunger, Marjorie was motivated by spite; at least, the condition of her stall suggested such.

"Many cultures consider horsemeat a delicacy, Marjorie," I said. She eyed me balefully and aimed a well-placed kick in my direction. Fortunately, through painful experience, I had become rather adept at remaining outside of firing range.

After the four-leggeds were properly serviced, Uncle Bill and I sat in the kitchen, breakfasting. "I still don't understand why I need to meet Roger," said Uncle Bill, as he finished the last bite of his *tortilla*. "If he wants to make a movie about Esperanza and Maria, what the hell do I care?"

"A noble sentiment," I replied. "But you might as well earn a bit of brass, especially if Roger disrupts operations at the cafe. Besides, there is your legacy to consider. And what about Celestina and Ernesto? A phoenix rising from the ashes is all well and good, but without them, the phoenix would have never hatched, if you will forgive the metaphor."

It had been Ernesto, father to Esperanza and Maria, for whom the cafe was originally named. Celestina had worked tirelessly with Ernesto until the afternoon of her untimely death. Uncle Bill's efforts to resurrect the cafe, including large loans to Esperanza and Maria, were his way of ensuring Celestina's legacy.

"I dunno, Bennie. I got a bad feeling about this."

"A less noble but doubtless more apt sentiment, Uncle Bill. All the more reason to pocket a bit of brass. Insurance, one might say."

"What time did you say we got to meet this fella?"

I glanced at my watch. "Ten o'clock. By the way, do you know where I might secure something of a suitably floral nature for Loretta?"

"How about giving her some wild daisies? I used to pick those for Celestina. Maria's got a few rosebushes, but they aren't in bloom now. Or you could drive to Santa Fe."

"Rather a long trip for a single bouquet. Besides, I had hoped to present them to Loretta this morning."

Uncle Bill contemplated briefly. "Look, you go on out to the pasture. There's bunches of daisies there. In the meantime, I got to hitch up the trailer. I'm gonna head on up to Morales's ranch for some more hay. What's this Roger like, anyway?"

"Er, rather an oily sort of chap. Possesses a disturbingly large and fluorescent set of ivories, which he flashes rather like a well-brushed baboon. Definitely not British."

Uncle Bill grunted but said nothing further. I stood up from the table, stretched, and walked outside. The air was brisk, but the sun shone bright and warm. The cattle were huddled together, some standing, others lying down leisurely as they chewed. A few eyed me as I climbed over the gate and walked into the pasture. Although there was ample bovine fertilizer, I espied little of a floral nature.

Continuing the walkabout, I came upon a rock, next to which was a small cluster of fatigued-looking daisies. "Flowers, ho," I muttered, as I bent down. After harvesting them carefully and arranging them in the right hand, I stood up and turned around.

A bovine crowd was gathered behind me, curious as to my intentions. I doffed an imaginary hat. "Cheer-o, chaps."

I detoured around the group of onlookers and began to walk back towards the house. The group retreated cautiously, except for a bull named Malcolm, who possessed a formidable set of horns. Rather than retreating, he began to move towards me in a most Admiral Nelson-ish manner.

"Avast!" I shouted. "Off with you."

The bull stopped and snorted loudly. Then he lowered his head and stamped his hoof.

"Avast! Sod off!"

Having been almost skewered by Daisy on the day of my arrival, I did not wish to repeat the experience, especially by an even larger beast possessed of actual horns. I moved away, cautiously, eyeing the gate in the distance.

The bovine enemy advanced and, judging by the noticeable odour, maintained the weather gauge.

I continued to retreat towards the house, hoping a devil-may-care pretence might discourage it. Malcolm again snorted loudly. I espied Uncle Bill, who was trotting towards the gate.

"Stay calm, Bennie."

"Er, thanks, Uncle Bill. Would you suggest I run?"

"Nope. He'll catch you. Just keep walking towards the gate. Don't look back." Uncle Bill removed the large white cowboy hat that graced his head whenever he was outdoors. "Yee-hah!" he shouted as he ran towards the gate.

I glanced over my shoulder. The bovine *Victory* was now anchored and staring at Uncle Bill.

"Yee-hah!" Uncle Bill shouted again. He climbed onto the gate and continued to wave his hat wildly. "Yee-hah. Git along!"

The gate was now perhaps ten yards in front of me.

"You're okay now, pard'ner," he shouted. "Just keep walking real nice and smooth."

I reached the gate unskewered and climbed over it to safety. "Thanks, Uncle Bill. I don't recall Malcolm being ill-tempered."

"I dunno, Bennie. Maybe he didn't like you picking his flowers."

"Ah," said I, whilst I stared at the crumbled mass in my right hand. "Perhaps a pine bough or an exhausted hollyhock would suffice?"

Uncle Bill adjusted his hat and jerked his thumb towards the pasture. "Yep, you could try that, but I think I'd rather take my chances with the bull."

"M-hem, yes."

We arrived at the cafe slightly before ten o'clock. Paco had left his morning calling card by the front door. No doubt Lucifer, after stepping into one of Paco's puddles by his doorstep, had rung up Saint Peter, muttered something about a clerical mistake, and returned the dog to Heaven. Saint Peter, golden shoes soon soiled, then presumably despatched the dog back to its earthly reward.

We stepped over the shimmering pool and went inside. Maria had not yet arrived, and the kitchen was deserted. "I'll start some coffee, Uncle Bill, and then mop up. Gah! I detest that cur."

"Yep. But somehow he manages to survive. Gotta give him credit for that."

I grunted and walked into the kitchen. Having set the coffee to brewing, I retrieved the mop and pail, filled the latter with water, and walked back into the dining room.

"Right, coffee's on. I shan't be a moment."

I stepped outside, set the mop down, poured water out of the pail, and began to swab the now diluted mixture.

"Top o' the morning, old chap," a voice shouted.

The grating British accent was now an equally grating Irish one, except no Irishman ever said "old chap." I looked up and espied Roger approaching me at dreadnought speed. He was dressed much the same as yesterday, with the exception of a bright pink shirt. Its two top buttons were undone, revealing a mane of hair and a thickish gold chain about his neck.

Roger smiled. He bounded up the stairs and extended his right arm towards me. Just then, his well-polished left boot dropped onto the pool of liquid and rocketed forwards, spiralling his upper torso back and downwards onto the *portal*, with an audible thud.

"My back," he cried, as the mixture oozed under his trousers and jacket.

"Here, let me help you up."

Uncle Bill came out the door. "Jesus, what happened, Bennie?"

"Paco," I replied. "Roger stepped into the pool, slipped, and fell backwards. Apparently, he has injured his back."

"Let's see if we can get him inside." We reached behind Roger's shoulders and began to hoist him up.

"Ow!" he cried. "My ankle. I think it's broken."

"Right, let's try to get you inside," I said. With Roger's arms about Uncle Bill's and my shoulders, and jacket dripping, we moved him slowly towards the front door.

"C'mon, pard'ner, almost there," said Uncle Bill. We manoeuvred Roger over the threshold and lowered him gently onto a nearby chair.

He gripped the seat of the chair tightly and grimaced.

"How is your back?" I asked.

"I think it's okay," Roger said. He leaned forward slowly. "Ow," he groaned, leaning back in the chair. "No, goddammit, it's not okay." Roger next attempted to rest his left foot on the floor. "My God that hurts. I think my ankle's broken. I need a doctor."

"Let's get his boot off, Bennie." Uncle Bill looked at Roger. "Probably just a sprain," he said, as he began to pull Roger's boot off.

"Ow! Careful, goddammit."

"Sorry, pard'ner, but we need to get that boot off before your ankle swells too much."

"I say, Uncle Bill, perhaps the chap's correct. Where is the nearest doctor?"

"Nearest one's in Española."

"How far is that?" Roger groaned.

"A couple of hours' drive," Uncle Bill replied, as he manipulated the boot off Roger's foot. Roger began to whimper and his head lolled to port.

"I say, Uncle Bill, he appears to be perspiring rather profusely. Looks rather poorly, as well." Roger's tanned facial visage had taken on a distinctly greyish pallor.

"Yep, I know, Bennie. I got the boot off, though."

"Should we call an ambulance?"

"Take too long. Bennie, you go find Nestor. I'll stay here with Roger."

"Nestor?" I replied. "What on earth for? I mean, a large dose of Dusty Trail might provide a bit of relief. But surely it would be quicker if I retrieved a bottle from Rudy's."

"Not booze. Nestor was a medic during the war. He can help."

The mind boggled at the thought of Nestor as anything but an inebriate.

"Bennie, you remember where he lives?"

"Difficult to forget, really. One can almost smell the angels' share in the nearby air, not that any self-respecting angel would care to imbibe Nestor's brand of tipple. Besides, God only knows what state he will be in."

"He won't be too bad this time of morning," Uncle Bill said. "Unhitch the trailer real quick and take the truck. Nestor's got some sort of black medical bag somewhere in his place. Make sure he brings it."

"Black medical bag. Right, then." I dashed out to the lorry, disconnected the trailer, and motored to Nestor's ramshackle house, incredulous that a chap one rarely observed sober could have dashed about the front, Florence Nightingaling the troops.

I stopped sharply in front of Nestor's house, raising a large cloud of dust, which enveloped the lorry. The front of the house had a screened porch, access to which was gained by an open door hanging limply by a single hinge. Several chickens milled about, pecking at the ground. Another emerged through the open door, cluck-clucking its way into the front yard and disappearing under a rusty, abandoned lorry that sat on concrete blocks. I stepped out and dashed to the front door.

"Hullo?" I shouted. "I say, Nestor? Are you there?" I pounded on the door frame and peered into what appeared to be a sitting room. "Hullo? Nestor?"

The intense stench of alcohol and cigarette smoke began to have an emetic effect on the stomach. Covering the nostrils, I walked into the house. I passed a small kitchen, which was overrun with dirty dishes stacked in the sink, on countertops, on a small table, both chairs, and the Frigidaire. I glanced into the nearby loo and turned away quickly.

"Hullo?" I called again, approaching the remaining two rooms near the back of the house. In the farthest room, I espied Nestor, asleep on his bed and snoring loudly. Curled up next to him was Paco, who began to growl.

"Shut up, you bloody cur." I shook my fist at the dog and walked over to Nestor. "I say, Nestor, wake up. We have rather a medical emergency for you."

He grunted and rolled onto his side.

"Nestor! You need to wake up now. Please!" I pushed his shoulder and rolled him onto his back. "Nestor!"

He opened his eyes slowly and blinked. "Who the fuck are you?"

"You know who I am. Benjamin Graves, El Vaquero's nephew. You've eaten in the bloody cafe enough times." Nestor's manner at table was rather Neanderthal-like, and his habit of allowing Paco to hoover up the detritus that spilled onto the dining room floor was off-putting, to say the least.

"El Vaquero? You don't look like El Vaquero."

"I'm his nephew, Bennie. Look, we have an emergency." I pulled Nestor into a sitting position. In addition to the unpleasant aroma of alcohol and cigarettes, the olfactory detected a pressing need for a rigorous wash and brush-up.

"Come on, Nestor, we've a patient for you. Just like the war."

"Huh? How come you woke me up?" He fell back onto the bed.

"Damn and blast." I pulled him up again. "We have a patient, Nestor, and need your help."

He stared at me blankly. Presently, an idea formed in the grey matter. "Medic!" I screamed. "Man down! Medic!"

Nestor jumped up. "Medic? I'm the medic."

"Man down, Nestor. Where's your bag?"

"My bag? My bag. Uh, it's in the closet." He pointed to a small closet in the corner. "How bad is he?"

"He, er, was hit in the ankle. Seems to be sweating a lot." I navigated around the debris strewn about the floor to the closet. There was a black satchel in the back of the closet, half buried in dirty laundry. I pushed away the laundry and retrieved the bag. The smell reminded me of Daisy. "Got it."

"It sounds like shock. Okay, let's go. You got the jeep?"

"Eh, what? Oh, the jeep? I mean, yes, it's outside."

Nestor snatched the bag from my hand and dashed towards the front door. "You see any Krauts?"

"Krauts?" I repeated, slowly realising that Nestor had transported himself mentally to the war. "Er, no. Our boys beat them back. One soldier injured. We need to hurry."

I pointed to Uncle Bill's lorry. "There's the jeep."

Nestor trotted over to the lorry and opened the passenger door. As he raised himself into the seat, Paco leaped inside and sat down on the seat next to him.

"Get out, you damn cur," I shouted. Paco growled and refused to move. "Bloody hell," I mumbled.

We motored quickly back to the cafe. Before the lorry had fully stopped, Nestor had hopped out with the black bag, displaying astonishing agility for someone who was at least several sheets to the wind.

"Where's that soldier?" Nestor asked.

"Inside," I said. "Hurry."

Nestor ran up the stairs, followed by Paco, and through the front door. Roger was lying on the floor. Uncle Bill had found a dish towel and placed it under his head.

"We've got a man who needs your help, Nestor. It's his ankle and his back. I think he's in shock, too."

Nestor nodded. "Okay, let's have a look." He lowered himself to the floor and brought his face near Roger's. "Can you hear me, soldier?" he shouted.

"Soldier?" Roger moaned. "Who are you? "My God, your breath. Are you drunk? Ow!"

"Don't worry, soldier, I've got something for the pain." Nestor opened up the black bag and removed a small phial.

"What's that?" I asked.

"Morphine." He slammed the phial into Roger's leg.

"Ow! Jesus, what did you do?" Roger cried.

"Gave you some morphine, soldier. It's gonna help the pain."

I glanced at Uncle Bill. "Is that really morphine from the war? I mean, does it not go bad?"

"I dunno, Bennie. Let's hope not."

Nestor rooted through the bag again, removing various bandages and a wood splint. He began to entomb Roger's ankle. "It's just a sprain, soldier. We'll have you back to your unit in no time."

Despite its age, the morphine appeared to have taken effect; Roger's eyes closed and he began to drool.

"What about his back, Nestor?" I asked.

"Bruised ribs." Nestor rifled through his black bag and retrieved a small bottle of pills, which he gave to me. "Aspirin. Not much else to do for bruised ribs."

I glanced at the bottle and placed it inside my trouser pocket. Uncle Bill's medicine cabinet contained what I believed were less aged pills. "Er, thanks, Nestor," I replied. I eyed Roger and turned to Uncle Bill. "I believe he's asleep. What should we do with him?"

"He'll sleep for a few hours," Nestor said. "Get him back to his bunk." Nestor stood up and stretched. "Guess you can take it from here."

"Yep. Thanks, Nestor," Uncle Bill said. "Always knew I could count on you."

"Any time, Sarge." Nestor marched out the front door, followed by Paco, who paused to urinate in precisely the same spot that had caused the mayhem. I watched through the front window as he marched to Rudy's Bar and disappeared inside.

I raised an eyebrow. "Sarge?"

Uncle Bill glared at me. "Don't even ask. What are we gonna do with him now?"

"Well, we can't let Roger lie here on the floor. We could find his bus."

"Hell, let's get him back to the ranch. He can sleep there, at least until we figure out something else. He's gonna need some new clothes, too."

I glanced at Roger's soiled and sodden jacket and trousers. "Er, yes. Shall we hoist him up and load him into the lorry?"

We carried Roger to the lorry and gently placed him in the cab. He was slightly conscious and moaned softly.

After a slow and kidney-jarring ride to the ranch, we carried him into the house—observed by Daisy, whose porcine brain presumably hoped the new chap had brought a set of valises to be tossed—and placed him on the small bed in the back room. Then, removing Roger's jacket and trousers, Uncle Bill draped several blankets over him.

"Now what?" I asked.

Uncle Bill removed his cowboy hat and scratched his head. "I guess one of us better stay here, just in case. You mind, Bennie? I gotta go back to town and get the trailer so I can get my hay from Ernesto Morales."

"What about the cafe?"

"What about it?"

"I'm expected, not that Esperanza will mind my absence." I glanced at the watch. It was now almost eleven o'clock.

"I'll tell 'em what happened. Besides, this gives you a chance to pick some more daisies for Loretta. Course, maybe you ought to stay outside the fence." He laughed.

"Yes, well, perhaps you can tell Loretta that I risked life and limb to prove my honourable intentions."

Uncle Bill grinned. "Sure, I'll let her know. I'll be back mid-afternoon or so. Why don't you grab us a few steaks from the freezer for dinner, and an extra one for Roger. I got a feeling he's not going anywhere for a few days."

Chapter 7

A round one o'clock, I heard an anguished cry from the back room. I walked in and espied Roger sitting on the bed, trouserless. His countenance reminded the self of one of those times at university when I had imbibed to excess at the Jolly Rooster and awoken in the flat of one of the school chums.

"How are we feeling?"

"Where am I?" Roger asked. He stared at me blankly. His countenance was less ashen, but still pallid. "Where are my pants?"

"You're at Uncle Bill's ranch. As for your trousers and jacket, I've laundered them. They're hanging outside and should be dry shortly."

"What happened?" He pointed to his bandaged ankle. "I remember falling on the porch of the cafe and being carried inside. And I remember dreaming I was in the army."

I coughed. "Indeed? Were you? In the army, that is?"

"I was assigned to entertain the troops. Worked with Bob Hope, made some training films, that sort of thing." He attempted to stand, unsuccessfully. Groaning, he fell back onto the bed. "Is the ankle broken?"

"Nestor diagnosed a sprain and wrapped your ankle. A few days' rest and you should be right as rain. As for your back, you probably bruised a few ribs."

"Nestor? Is he the doctor?"

"Er, not exactly. He was a medic in the army."

"Medic?"

"That's right. Nestor gave you a shot of morphine for the pain. Uncle Bill and I didn't want to leave you alone in your bus, so we brought you here. You've been asleep for several hours."

"I have to get back to Hollywood. What am I going to do?"

"Afraid you're in no condition for any sort of voyage at the moment. You can stay here for a few days whilst your ankle and ribs mend."

Daisy, who had been asleep in her usual place on the front porch, grunted loudly. "What was that?" cried Roger.

"That would be Daisy, Uncle Bill's pet sow. She usually sleeps on the front porch. I would be happy to make a formal introduction, should you wish. Marjorie, too."

"Marjorie? Is she your uncle's wife? I'd like to meet her."

"Eh? No, Marjorie is a rather cantankerous mare. Afraid Uncle Bill is a widower. He should tell you about Celestina— that's his late wife. The cafe would not exist if not for her."

"Sorry. I didn't know about that. Will your uncle let me buy the rights to the story, and let us film in the cafe?"

"I'm confident he will. Of course, you will need to reimburse us for the lost revenues whilst you are filming, no customers and all that."

"Sure, that's no problem." He attempted to raise himself again. "Uh, Ben, I need take a leak. Can you help me up?"

"What? Oh, right, the loo." Roger placed an arm about my shoulder, and together we hobbled down the hallway to the loo. "I say, can you, er, manage?"

"Yeah, I think so." He shut the door.

"Right, give a shout when you're ready." I strode into Uncle Bill's bedroom. Having recalled the story he told me about being gored by a bull, I assumed he would still possess the cane he had used afterwards. I peered into the small closet. The cane was leaning against the back corner.

"I'm ready, Ben."

I retrieved the cane and gave it to Roger as he exited the loo. The colour slowly returned to his face. I eased him down the hall and into the sitting room. With the cane, he was able to walk, albeit at a tortoise-like pace, which seemed to please him greatly.

"Would you care for some lunch?"

"Uh, yeah, sure."

"You can try Maria's *tamales*. They're quite good."

Presently, there was a loud knock at the front door. I strode over and opened it. Standing before me was Coronado, breathing heavily and scratching under Daisy's *sombrero*-covered ear. Daisy grunted. I groaned softly.

"Señor Graves, I just heard. Nobody's been shot here for a real long time. Is Señor Victor gonna live?"

"Shooting? What are you talking about?"

"Nestor told me in the bar. He said the *gringo* movie star got shot in the leg. Maybe we better call Sheriff Tiny, especially if there's a murderer on the loose." He looked over his shoulder, apparently fearing that the murderer was lurking behind a rock, ready to shoot.

"Sorry to disappoint you, Coronado, but there was no shooting. No need to call Tiny."

"Tiny" Roybal—I had never heard anyone use his Christian name—was the obese, ill-tempered, and wholly ineffectual county sheriff. On the night of the cafe's grand reopening, I had crisped my forearm with fry oil whilst cooking *sopapillas*. This had caused a delay in providing the same to Tiny's brood of oafish children. Tiny had grabbed the burnt and bandaged wing, which was rather painful, and told his spawn that the *gringo* would bring their *sopapillas* presently. I suggested he cease and desist, albeit in a rather severe tone, which caused Tiny to erupt and march his entire rotund family out the door.

"But Nestor said the *gringo* was shot by a German," Coronado said. He looked at me uncomprehendingly.

"Ah. Yes, well, Nestor may have misunderstood. He splinted and bandaged Roger's ankle, but there was no shooting. Paco left his liquid calling card in its usual spot by the front door of the cafe. Alas, when Roger came up the steps, he slipped and sprained his ankle."

"He sprained his ankle and then he got shot?" Hope glinted in Coronado's eyes.

I was about to reply when Roger hobbled up behind me and stared at Coronado. "Oh, it's you. Sorry, Ben, I heard voices and thought I would try to walk a bit."

"*Hola*, Señor Robert. I'm real glad you're not dead. I told Señor Graves that nobody in Vaca Seca has been shot since when Esteban Romero accidentally shot Billy Mondragón. He was gonna shoot Billy's dog, 'cause it killed two chickens, but the dog bit him on the leg and he shot Billy in the arm by mistake."

"Shot?"

I rolled my eyes, desperate to avoid descending into one of Coronado's many circles of Hell, this one populated by Billy Mondragón's chickens and dog. "Coronado, no one was shot. As I explained, Robert—I mean, Roger—slipped and fell."

Coronado stared at Roger. "Does that mean you're still gonna make your movie, señor? Can I be in it? I could be a *vaquero*, like El Vaquero."

I glanced at Roger, whose countenance registered the grim confusion often felt by those who engaged in conversation with Coronado. "Roger, perhaps you should sit down in the kitchen. Rest the ankle and all that."

Roger hobbled away towards the kitchen, muttering something about inmates and an asylum. I turned to Coronado. "Can you do me a favour? Well, several, actually."

"Sure. I like to help."

"Yes, I know. Most kind of you. First, can you stop by the cafe and tell Maria and Esperanza I will attempt to be there before we open for dinner? Second, do you know where I may purchase flowers?"

"Flowers? What for?"

"Er, for Loretta, actually."

"Is she still mad at you?"

"What? No, I mean, who said she was mad? I, er, simply thought she would enjoy some flowers."

Coronado paused, perhaps lost in what for him constituted thought. "You could ask Sunflower. Maybe she's got flowers, 'cause her name's one. Or, I could ask my sister. She planted some flowers last year, but the deer ate them. Maybe she's got some more by now."

"Thanks all the same."

Coronado shrugged. "Sorry, Señor Graves. Maybe you should get Loretta something else, like a pickup. Everybody likes pickups."

"A rose by any other name would smell as sweet, eh?"

"I dunno. Antifreeze kinda smells sweet. Maybe El Vaquero's truck's got a leak. You better get Luis to fix it for you."

I sighed. "Never mind. But do please tell Maria and Esperanza about my coming in before the dinner crowd."

"Okay, but I don't think anybody's gonna show up tonight."

"Why not?"

"Nobody wants to get shot, even if it means no *tamales*. I better get back to the store. *Adios*, Señor Graves."

Coronado exited out the front door, scratched Daisy's *sombrero*-covered ear, and waddled away to his lorry. I watched the lorry disappear down the road, then returned to the kitchen.

After making short work of three *tamales* and drinking a cup of Uncle Bill's "cowboy" coffee, Roger's neurons appeared to recover from the day's ordeal.

"Do you have a phone? I should call the studio and tell them what's happened."

"Er, afraid not," I said. "Although I have convinced Uncle Bill of the efficacy of such a modern device, the telephone company has yet to run the assorted wires to the house. We hope it will be installed in the next month or so."

"No phone? How do you live?"

"There is a certain inconvenience. However, the locals generally share their connections—I believe they refer to it as a party line. I rather doubt Uncle Bill would care to listen to the conservations."

"But I must call the studio."

"Garcia's store has a telephone. So does Rudy's Bar. Also, Luis Gonzalez—he owns the Texaco station on the west end of town—has one as well."

"Can you drive me there, the Texaco station?"

"Ah. That would be rather difficult at present."

"Why?"

"The lorry Uncle Bill purchased for my use—it is currently at the same petrol station undergoing repairs. Something about a fuel pump."

"What am I going to do? I have to let them know what's happened to me."

"After Uncle Bill returns, I will be going to the cafe. I can initiate a trunk call from Garcia's store and speak with whomever you wish."

Roger looked at his wrapped ankle and grimaced. "You can call my secretary at the studio. Her name's Sharon. Tell her, I'll—tell her my bus broke down and is being repaired and I asked you to call for me. I don't want anyone to know I'm laid up."

"Why not? I mean, it was an accident and all that."

"My image. I'm the rugged outdoors type, the one who always gets the girl. If word gets out that I fell on the café's porch, I'll be a laughingstock. They're like hyaenas there, ready to rip apart anyone who's down."

"Hyaenas, eh? Sounds rather like my prior career in banking. One would never imagine the movie business to be so vicious."

"There's nothing worse. Years ago, I was supposed to try out for a part one afternoon. I don't even remember the name of the movie now. All I remember is that I got into my car to drive to the studio and it wouldn't start. Another actor had cut the distributor wires."

"Outright sabotage, eh? How did you find out?"

"One of my neighbours said he saw the car with its hood up and a man hunched over the engine. He thought it was a mechanic working on it."

I grunted. "Well, I shall be happy to tell your secretary your bus is undergoing repairs. Should I tell Sharon you are here? Or will that similarly unleash the hyaenas?"

He rubbed his leg. "Tell her I'm walking around town scouting locations and that I'll call her soon."

"Right. Er, I shall need the telephone number."

"Oh, yeah. I can write it down for you. Do you have a pencil and paper?"

I brought Roger the requested writing supplies and he scribbled the number down.

"Uncle Bill should return soon. He can assume your Florence Nightingaling, whilst I return to the cafe and call your secretary."

"Thanks. I think I better lie down again. My ankle's throbbing. I don't suppose you have any more of that morphine?"

"Afraid not. There's a bottle of aspirin in the cupboard."

"Okay. By the way, those *tamales* were great. Did you say Maria makes those?"

"By the hand of God, some believe. Of course, if true, then He does work in truly mysterious ways."

Uncle Bill returned around four o'clock, ferrying a large trailer's worth of hay. I quickly explained to him the current state of affairs, then motored into town, wondering what sort of insults Esperanza would hurl at me when I arrived.

I parked the lorry, then walked to Garcia's store to make Roger's call. Fate must have been napping, because Coronado was not about. Rather, Joe Garcia himself was at the front counter.

"I say, Joe, may I use your telephone? I need to make a trunk call."

"What kind of call?" he growled.

"A trunk call. Long distance."

"Long distance? That costs a lot of money."

"Yes, well, after you receive your bill, I shall pay you."

"How do I know that? Maybe you're gonna stiff me, *gringo*."

"What? How can I pay you if I don't know how much the call has cost?"

"Ten bucks. You want to use the phone now, you gotta pay me ten bucks."

As I perceived little choice in the matter, I retrieved my wallet and removed a ten-dollar bill. Joe snatched it from my hand, almost as quickly as Esperanza had taken Roger's five hundred dollars from his.

"Thanks. Who you gonna call? Your old girlfriend in England?"

"She is my ex-wife, and no, I am not calling her. I need to call California."

"California? You got a girlfriend there? You cheating on my Loretta, *gringo*?"

"What? No, and it's none of your bloody business. I'm calling Mr. Victory's secretary."

"Who?"

"The chap who hurt his ankle this morning. Coronado must have told you."

"The rich *gringo* who got shot? *Sí*, he told me. Said you and El Vaquero took him to the ranch. Is he okay? Who shot him?"

I groaned. "Not you, too. He was not shot. He slipped and fell."

Joe looked crestfallen, perhaps because he had started ludicrous rumours of his own—including the rumour that a mountain lion had somehow attacked and consumed Dora Esquivel in the cafe the night it first opened. "Not shot, huh?"

"No. Nor was he bitten by a rattlesnake, devoured by a mountain lion, or whisked away by space aliens."

"Huh? Is the *gringo* hurt real bad?"

"A sprained ankle and bruised ribs. He is recuperating at the ranch for a few days until the swelling decreases."

"If he ain't hurt bad, how come you didn't bring him here to make his own call?"

"Because Luis Chavez is repairing my lorry," I yelled. "I told Roger I would call his secretary on his behalf when I returned to work this afternoon, not that it is any of your bloody business. Now, may I please use your phone?"

"Okay. You don't gotta get mad." Joe pulled the phone out from under the counter. "El Vaquero needs to get his own phone. Five minutes, no *más*." He eyed his wristwatch intently.

"Fine." I made the call to Roger's secretary, introducing myself as the owner of the cafe on which his movie was to be based, and then lying about Roger's situation, per instructions. She seemed satisfied—well, at least one did not hear the baying of hyaenas in the background—and asked that Roger call as soon as he could. Something about executives rather upset over expenses, from what I could gather.

I hung up the phone. "Satisfied?"

"Four minutes and forty seconds. You coulda talked twenty seconds more if you wanted."

"Indeed? Then I am owed a refund of sixty-seven cents, if my arithmetic is accurate."

"No refunds, store policy." He pointed to the small piece of paper taped to the countertop. "Is that *gringo* still gonna make a movie about Esperanza and Maria?"

"I haven't heard him say otherwise. Why?"

"All those rich *gringos* are gonna come here and spend lots of money. Then I'm gonna get rich. Maybe I'll raise my prices."

"Why? Are they insufficiently stratospheric?" I replied.

"Huh?"

"Just idle chatter. Now, if you will excuse me, I must get back to the cafe."

Although I had survived one Herculean labour, another awaited. Fearing Loretta would still be brassed off about yesterday's encounter with Sunflower, I entered the cafe laden with trepidation. The dining room was deserted. I gingerly opened the door to the kitchen. Maria and Loretta were both chopping away, cheerfully nattering on in Spanish. Esperanza was nowhere to be seen, which, given the circumstances, meant that I would face incoming fire from only one direction.

I coughed. "Er, good afternoon. Sorry to be so late. I hope Coronado explained the situation with Roger and all that."

Loretta looked at me and smiled. She placed the knife down, walked over, and embraced me heartily. "Oh, Bennie," she cooed, "they're beautiful. That was so sweet of you. I'm sorry about yesterday." She glanced to the left and I espied a floral bouquet resting in one of the glass pitchers we used for iced tea.

I raised an eyebrow as a wave of confusion washed over the grey matter. "How did he—" I muttered. "I mean, I'm glad you like them."

"You don't need to explain, Bennie. Coronado told me."

"Oh God," I whispered. "I mean, yes, he was over at the house earlier today. I, er, well, I did not expect him to deliver them to you so quickly."

"I love them, Bennie. It's been a long time since anyone gave me flowers. I guess that's why I love you, because you're such a gentleman. I'm going to put them next to the cash register, so everyone in town can see how wonderful you are."

I glanced at Maria. She pointed her chef's knife at me and smiled.

"Er, yes, well, part of the Graves code, Loretta." Sweat began washing over the brow. "I say, would you know where I could find Coronado? I mean, I really should thank him for the delivery and all that."

Maria shrugged. "If he ain't here eating, he's at Joe's store or Rudy's."

"Right, well, I've just come from Joe's store. Perhaps I shall just dash over to Rudy's. Won't be a minute."

I bounded over to Rudy's Bar and walked inside, assuming Coronado would be hunched over in his usual chair. Although several of the regulars were sitting in the dimly lit, smoke-filled room, Coronado was not one of them.

Thinking Rudy might be aware of Coronado's current location, I walked down the hallway to his office and knocked on the door.

"C'mon in," he shouted.

"Hullo, Rudy."

"Hey, Bennie. How's everything going? You see your *chichona* friend today? ¡*Madre de Dios*! If she's gonna be at the cafe tonight, I want to reserve a table."

"I sincerely hope she and Sky Blue do not dine with us this evening. Besides, she's rather young for you, is she not?"

"Hey, a guy can dream. ¿*Que no*? Wonder what that boyfriend of hers has got that I don't?"

"I would prefer not to speculate. Doubtless, you have heard they intend to open a spiritual centre and vegetarian restaurant."

"Yeah. I guess Pedro's gonna have his work cut out for him, fixing up that dump. That is, if he's even willing to work on it."

Pedro was Nestor Martinez's nephew. Whilst he was a skilled carpenter, his work habits were irregular, to say the least. "Why wouldn't he?"

"Pedro's afraid of ghosts. He's convinced Alejandro Mora haunts that old bar."

"I suppose he will have to decide between fear of ghosts and love of money."

"Yeah, I guess so. Loretta still mad at you? That was some scene last night."

"Actually, her demeanour at present is most exuberant. I had asked Coronado if he knew where I might purchase flowers for her. He didn't know. Yet, somehow, he delivered a bouquet to Loretta earlier this afternoon. I'm flummoxed. I thought he might be occupying his usual bar stool."

"Nope, he ain't here. Flowers, huh? Only flower store I know is in Santa Fe. Maybe he's working at Joe's."

"No, I was just there."

Rudy paused, no doubt salivating over a mental image of Sunflower *au naturel*. "Hey, how's that movie director? El Vaquero said he's staying at the ranch for a couple of days. Funny how everybody thinks he got shot."

"Indeed. Coronado visited the ranch around noon, enquiring if Roger had survived the shooting. The mind truly boggles." I glanced at my watch. "Right, I must return to the cafe."

"Hey, Bennie. One more thing. Don't let that Sunflower girl hug you anymore, if you value your *cojones*. And find out where Coronado bought those flowers. You're gonna need to buy some for her every day, as long as that *chichona's* around."

I grimaced. "Rather a mystery, that. Then again, I've always thought Coronado is one of those 'riddle wrapped in an enigma' sorts Churchill spoke of. Well, cheer-o."

I left Rudy's office. As I opened the door to leave the bar, I nearly collided with Coronado. "*Hola*, Señor Graves. You getting a beer before the cafe opens? You can sit with me, if you want."

"Er, no, Coronado. I was just speaking with Rudy. By the way, thank you."

"Sure. What for?"

"The flowers, of course. Loretta is ecstatic. Where did you get them? Rudy said the nearest floral shop is in Santa Fe."

"Um, I guess so. I didn't buy them in a flower shop."

"One of the locals a secret gardener, is that it?"

"I guess," he shrugged. "I got the flowers from Luis Obrador."

"Luis Obrador? Does he come into the cafe?"

"He used to, Señor Graves, but he doesn't no more."

"Why not? I can't recall anyone not liking Maria's cooking."

"Oh, he always liked Maria's food real good, Señor Graves, especially her *tamales*. He liked Ernesto's *carne adovada*, too."

"Well, if he is housebound, like Dora Esquivel, I would be delighted to deliver some *tamales* and *carne adovada* to him. What do I owe you for the flowers?"

"Huh? The flowers didn't cost nothing, Señor Graves."

"He gave them to you? That was most magnanimous. I shall deliver a dozen *tamales* to Luis as thanks, forthwith. Where does he live?"

"Uh, he ain't eating *tamales* now, Señor Graves."

"Why not?"

"He's dead."

"Good God, you mean he died just this afternoon? After you saw him?"

"Oh, no, Señor Graves," Coronado said, as he shook his head. "Luis died two years ago. I think it was a heart attack or something."

"What?" I spluttered, as the grey matter began to take on water. "Two years? Then—that is, how exactly did you obtain these flowers from him?"

I shuddered. Was Coronado some sort of dim-witted Frankenstein? Had he reanimated Luis Obrador with one of those lower-quality brains—a Scotsman's perhaps—to wreak havoc throughout the valley?

"Oh, they were on Luis's grave. He's buried at the cemetery just outside of town."

Coronado paused whilst the few mental gears he possessed revolved slowly. "You know, Señor Graves, your name is the same as where dead people get buried."

"What? I mean, yes, I suppose it is." The full weight of Coronado's floral theft now scored a direct hit. The jaw, having already grounded itself, now began to excavate the macadam. "Gah! You pinched the flowers off Luis's grave?"

"Pinched? I didn't pinch them, Señor Graves. I held them real careful."

"No. I mean, you stole them? From his grave?"

Coronado nodded. "Oh, sí. I didn't think he would mind. Luis never liked flowers much 'cause he was afraid of bees."

"Yes, but—I mean, what about Luis's family? They put the flowers there for him."

"Oh, I guess so," Coronado said, apparently not having considered that particular aspect of his floral theft. "You want me to take them back to Luis, Señor Graves? I can ask Loretta for them."

"No!" I screamed. "I mean, no need to upset Loretta." I shuddered, conjuring up an image of Luis's family wandering into the cafe and espying the departed's gravesite flowers sitting next to the cash register. "Er, Coronado, whilst I do appreciate your efforts in obtaining flowers for Loretta, let's not disturb the dead any more, shall we? I will call the flower shop in Santa Fe and ask if they will deliver flowers here next time."

"Do you think I should apologise to Luis? I don't want his ghost getting mad at me."

"Eh?"

"What if Luis's ghost comes after me tonight 'cause I took his flowers?"

"Yes, well, if Luis was as afraid of bees as you said, one imagines his ghost will be delighted that you removed them. Surely his ghost will be happy that Luis won't be stung by bees."

Coronado emitted a sigh of relief. "I didn't think of that. Thanks."

Instead of entering the bar, he turned around and walked back to Garcia's store, behind which he had parked his lorry. I watched him disappear. Then, realising Fate would insist the Obrador family dine at the cafe this evening, the grey matter began a frantic search for ways to hide the flowers without incurring Loretta's wrath.

Chapter 8

I walked into the cafe and groaned softly. Loretta's flowers were displayed prominently in a large green vase next to the cash register. I retrieved the vase and walked into the kitchen. As I entered, Maria, Esperanza, and Loretta all goggled me.

"Bennie, what are you doing with my flowers?" Loretta asked.

"I, er, I thought they would be safer back here, what with all the customers and such. We shan't want someone to knock the vase over."

"What are you talking about, *Pendejito?*" said Esperanza suspiciously. "Nobody's gonna knock it over. Anybody pays, they stand to the left of the cash register." Esperanza motioned with her left hand. "Loretta, she put your flowers on the other side." Here she motioned with her right hand, looking like a bird flapping its wings singularly.

"Yes, well, even if that's true, a customer could, ah, mistakenly come to the wrong side, accidently biff the vase, and, well, why tempt Fate, eh?"

Maria glared at me, but said nothing. Loretta placed her hands firmly on her hips. "You're acting very strange, Bennie. I want my flowers in the dining room."

"Of course you do, Loretta," I stammered. "But we must also consider, er, possible allergic reactions. I mean, you wouldn't want a customer to begin sneezing uncontrollably and such."

Loretta's face began to redden from rage. "Allergies?"

"Or, er, bee stings. I mean, what if a bee hides in the flowers, pops out, and stings a customer?"

"Nobody's allergic to no fucking flowers and there ain't no fucking bees," Esperanza snarled. "Maybe a bee stung your fucking *gringo* brain."

"It's her, isn't it, Bennie?" Loretta said, tears welling up. "You don't want her to know about us, do you?"

"What? No, I mean, of course not, Loretta." I moved towards her, arms extended.

"Don't touch me," she snarled. Tears began to cascade down her cheeks. "How can you be so cruel?" Loretta untied her apron and threw it to the floor. "I quit," she screamed. "I don't want to see you ever again, Bennie." She rocketed out the back door and slammed it shut behind her.

I stared at the door blankly. "Gah," I moaned.

Esperanza shook her head and pointed her burning cigarette at me. "I told you, *Pendejito*, don't you never hurt Loretta. I never wanted her to get involved with no *gringo*, but she did. You want to get in that *chichona's* pants, go ahead. But don't embarrass my Loretta. She's been hurt enough. Now get the fuck out of here."

I stood there, seemingly frozen to the floor. In the space of a few minutes, I had been transformed from a gentleman to an inconsiderate yob. Fate had performed her job quite well.

"I, I didn't mean to hurt Loretta's feelings," I stammered. "I don't understand."

"Bennie," began Maria softly, emerging from her long silence, "you gotta decide: Loretta or that *chichona*. It ain't right what you done."

"Yes, but, I haven't done anything." The cranium lowered itself.

"Maybe you better go, Bennie," Maria said. "Esperanza, she can waitress tonight." Maria turned to Esperanza and spoke firmly. "*Hermana*, go see if Antonio can clean tables for us and wash dishes. Maybe even Rudy can help some."

"Maria, I'm sorry, but you don't understand."

Maria looked at me, struggling not to explode. "Maybe I don't. All I know is my *sobrina* is real upset. I don't want to be mad at you, Bennie. You done a lot for us, but if you work here tonight, I'm gonna. Like I said, you gotta decide about Loretta."

She turned away and focused on a large pot of green chile, which she commenced to stir angrily. The ash from her cigarette dangled dangerously over the pot.

"Very well, I shall leave." I retreated out the kitchen door, swooped through the dining room and out the front door, whereupon I stepped into a fresh pool deposited by Paco.

"Gah!" Needing a large whisky to calm the embattled neurons, I returned to Rudy's Bar. In the smoke-filled darkness, I espied Coronado, occupying his usual spot. Two empty beer bottles stood on his table. Rudy's grandson Antonio was standing behind the bar, almost hidden from view.

"Hullo, Antonio," I said, sitting down heavily. "A large whisky, if you please."

"You okay, Señor Graves?" he said as he wiped down a glass expertly and set it down before me. "You look like you saw a ghost." He poured a large dose of Dusty Trail into the glass.

"Ghost? If only." I raised the glass to the waiting lips. "Cheers," I said, as I vanquished the contents.

"*Hola*, Señor Graves," Coronado slurred. "Did Loretta like her flowers?"

"She did. Regrettably, however, she is not overly endeared to me at the moment."

"Huh?"

"I've made a grave mistake."

"If she likes her flowers, isn't she supposed to like you, too?"

"Not in Vaca Seca. Another round, if you please, Antonio."

Suitably whiskied, I wandered down the hall, banged on Rudy's door, and walked in.

"Bennie," Rudy chirped. "What's up? You look like the walking dead."

"An apt description, perhaps. Although the non-walking dead are rather more problematic, specifically Luis Obrador."

"Luis? I don't get it. He died before you even got here. It was a heart attack or something. Right around this time of year, come to think of it."

"Well, it's not so much Luis, may he rest in peace, but his family."

"Huh? Teresa moved to Santa Fe after he died. I don't remember where the kids are. Texas, maybe? But I still don't get it."

I sat down heavily. "You said earlier you had no idea where Coronado would purchase flowers. Well, he did not purchase them."

Rudy sighed and rubbed his eyes. "What are you talking about? You were just in here, saying Loretta loved them. Besides, what does Luis Obrador's family have to do with this?"

"Coronado pinched them, actually. Right off Luis's grave, as it were."

"*¡Madre de Dios!*" exclaimed Rudy as he straightened up in his chair. "Coronado took flowers off Luis's grave? That Teresa and the kids put there? Why the fuck would he do that?" Rudy retrieved a glass and bottle of whisky from the lower right drawer of his desk. He poured out a dose and downed it quickly. "I don't get it, Bennie. Coronado's weird, but he's not a ghoul."

"Coronado's explanation to me had a certain un-ghoulish logic, if one wishes to use that word. I gather Luis disliked flowers, owing to the bees which hovered about them. According to Coronado, the poor chap was most frightened by them."

"So, Teresa came up here on the anniversary of Luis's death and put flowers on his grave. And then Coronado took them and gave them to Loretta on your behalf. Do I have that right?"

"Quite."

"He didn't tell Loretta where he got them, did he?"

"No, actually, he did not. A surprising measure of tact in that regard, one must admit."

Rudy eyed me with trepidation. "If Coronado didn't tell Loretta where the flowers came from, what's the problem?"

"Ah, yes. Prideful of the floral delivery, Loretta displayed them in the dining room for all to see. One can only imagine the grieving Obradors walking into the cafe and espying the flowers they had placed on their dear departed's grave cheering up the dining room."

Rudy ran his hand over his face slowly. "This doesn't sound real good. What did you do?"

"I muttered something idiotic about customers, allergies, and stinging insects. Then I suggested the flowers remain hidden in the kitchen. Loretta naturally assumed my trepidation over the public display of her flowers was caused by Sunflower. Hence, Loretta burst into tears, announced she was quitting, and ran out the back door. As you might further imagine, Loretta's actions did not endear me to Maria and Esperanza, who, er, suggested I depart the cafe environs immediately. And here I am. I mean, had I informed Loretta her flowers were stolen from Luis Obrador's grave—"

Rudy leaned back in his chair and exhaled loudly. "*Híjole.* What are you gonna do?"

"I was always under the impression one's bartender could provide answers to such conundrums."

"Answers? Fuck no, we just listen to the customers complain, then grunt, and nod. Most folks are so drunk, they think that's an answer."

"M-hem, yes. I could use rather more than a grunt and a nod at present. Should I go see Loretta? Explain the entire bloody mess?"

"I dunno, Bennie. I've been divorced four times. Number two took a shot at me with my rifle. No, that was number three. Number two went after me with a baseball bat. Anyway, maybe I'm not the best guy to ask for advice."

"Well, Loretta has not reached the rifle-shooting or bat-wielding stage yet, but point taken."

"Somehow, you gotta get Loretta to believe she's got nothing to fear because Sunflower's crazy about—what's that guy's name she's with?"

"You mean, Sky Blue?"

"Yeah, that's it. Jesus, I never thought the really crazy *gringos* would find Vaca Seca. Not you and El Vaquero, of course."

I coughed, as glimpses of various Vaca Secans and their, well, eccentricities, streamed through the grey matter. "Well, thanks all the same, Rudy. I suppose I shall have to sort it out myself."

I drained the last remnants of Dusty Trail from my glass, stood up, albeit rather wobbly, and departed. Outside, I espied a few of the early customers standing on the patio waiting for the cafe to open. Throughout history, the Graveses had always been inspired by Admiral Nelson's "straight at 'em" approach. Deciding it must still be so, I staggered to the lorry.

I rolled to a stop in front of Loretta's mother's home. Chata bounded over to the lorry, wagging her tail and, as always, drooling copiously. I exited, thumped her enormous head heavily, walked to the front door, and rang the bell.

After what seemed an interminable wait, the door opened slightly. Loretta stood before me, her eyes red and swollen. "What do you want, Bennie?"

"May I at least attempt to explain?" Chata pushed her head under my right hand.

"There's nothing to explain. I'm not a fool."

"Of course you're not. But you must believe me when I tell you it has nothing to do with Sunflower. Luis Obrador, actually."

"Luis Obrador? He's dead."

"Yes, I know. His widow, Teresa, places flowers on his grave around the anniversary of his death, and—"

Loretta gasped. "My God, you stole flowers from a grave and gave them to me? What kind of monster are you?"

"Coronado took them. He was at the ranch earlier today, asking about Roger. I asked him where I might purchase flowers for you. He said he did not know, although Rudy told me the nearest flower shop is in Santa Fe. I had attempted to retrieve wild daisies from the pasture, however, there was rather a cantankerous bull, and—well, I arrived at the cafe and discovered Coronado had brought you flowers. That's why I dashed out to find him and enquire. He espied the flowers on Luis's grave. Coronado reasoned that, because Luis was never especially fond of flowers—something about a fear of bees lurking within—pinched the lot and brought them to you."

Loretta placed her left hand over her mouth and goggled me silently.

"A reaction similar to my own. I mean, how would we explain to the grieving widow who, upon entering the cafe, confronts the bouquet she placed at her husband's grave displayed in a vase next to the cash register? 'Right ho, your late husband wasn't especially keen on flowers, so Coronado pinched them and gave them to Loretta.' The mind boggles."

Loretta maintained her silence and slowly shook her head.

"What would you have me do, Loretta?"

"You could have told me the truth."

I sighed. "Yes, I know. But you were so happy to have them. Besides, had I rushed in, grabbed the flowers, and said, 'Right, back to the grave for you,' I suspect you would have been rather displeased."

"Haven't you ever asked for flowers to be delivered? You must have sent flowers to your ex."

"Er, yes, but London is replete with florists. I gather the nearest shop is in Santa Fe. One might as well ask the shop to deliver to the moon."

Loretta's countenance relaxed. She took hold of my arm and kissed me softly. "Bennie, for someone who complains about how crazy the locals are, you fit right in."

I coughed. "M-hem. Well, regarding the local loons, would you please not quit the cafe? I cannot possibly cope with Maria and Esperanza alone."

"Can I have a raise?" she asked, as a sly grin appeared on her face.

"Raise, eh? What did you have in mind?"

"Come in and I'll tell you."

When I returned to the ranch that evening, I found Roger and Uncle Bill in the sitting room, a half-empty bottle of Dusty Trail on the table between them.

"'Bout time you showed up, pard'ner. Grab yourself a glass. Big night?"

I paused to consider what, if any, of the evening's floral debacle to relate, and decided the less, the better. "Er, one could say that. How's the patient?"

"Top o' the morning, old chap," he replied in the grating British accent. "Your uncle has told me some interesting stories. I may make a movie about his life, too."

I suppressed a grimace, not wishing to explain the expression was Irish. "Indeed? Well, I'm glad you are improved. What shall you do next?"

"As soon as I'm a bit more mobile, old chap, I plan to scout out some more locations for filming, because I want to make it authentic. Plus, I want to interview the locals for bit parts. I've already got a scriptwriter working away back in Hollywood. Once he's finished with the draft, I can start casting the leads. I may even work in a story about the new couple, too."

"Eh?"

"What was her name, Sunflower?" Roger asked, with feigned nonchalance. "The cafe struggles, first to reopen and then, against the competition from the outsiders, Sunflower and—what was his name? She seduces the men, while he, a traveling preacher, promises them a new religion of free love. Maria and Esperanza fight valiantly to keep the town's pure spirit. The way Charlton Heston delivered the Jews from bondage in Egypt."

I goggled at Roger, speechless. He had moved far beyond the amateurish efforts of the likes of Rodrigo to ensnare the fairer sex. Uncle Bill slowly reached for the bottle of Dusty Trail and refilled our glasses.

"Sunflower and bondage," Roger muttered under his breath.

An image of Esperanza and Maria leading the Israelites out of Egypt formed in a scrum of neurons, but was thankfully erased. One doubted that Charlton Heston would have been as effective declaiming to Pharaoh, "Let my *pendejitos* go." Then again, a plague of Esperanzas dressed in too-short pink sateen robes would surely have dampened the appetite of the hungriest locusts and induced a coronary in the most steadfast Angel of Death.

Roger smiled. "Sunflower will sell more tickets than Jayne Mansfield ever did."

"I gotta get a look at this gal," said Uncle Bill.

"I say, Uncle Bill, not you, too?"

"Oh hell, Bennie," he replied. "I may be gettin' old, but I ain't dead yet."

"Lest you forget, you are still dying of cancer, at least as far as Esperanza and Maria are concerned."

"Yeah, but I've been telling 'em it's in remission now." As part of a rather elaborate ruse to convince Maria and Esperanza I was needed to manage the cafe, Uncle Bill—with a bit of assistance from Rudy—had informed them of his impending demise. As Maria and Esperanza were in arrears to him rather heavily, owing to their previous failed attempts to reopen the cafe, they asked me to stay, rather than see the cafe sold.

Apparently enamoured with this grotesque new cinematic plot, Roger finished his whisky. Bracing himself with the cane, he rose up slowly, groaning softly as he did so. Then, he flashed the fluorescent ivories. "Well, goodnight. Bill, thank you for your hospitality." He leaned on the cane and hobbled down the hall.

When Roger shut his bedroom door, I turned to Uncle Bill. "How much has he offered to pay you, if I may enquire?"

"Ten thousand," he whispered. "Can you believe that? Just so he can film in the cafe. I can get me another bull and some good breeders, too. We'll be able to improve the stock."

"No doubt, although one fears that Roger's interest in casting Sunflower is similarly aimed at 'improving the stock,' so to speak."

"Is she really that good lookin'?"

"Joan of Arc would be your old aunt, by comparison."

"Damn. I guess that Hollywood grin of his reels 'em in like hooked fish. Just don't you try, Bennie. Loretta's too good a gal."

"Eh? I mean, no, of course not." The brain quickly hid an image of Sunflower beneath the mental sofa. "This entire film idea is barmy."

"Yeah, but if it gets me a better herd, then I'm all for it."

"Rather a mercenary-like perspective, don't you think?"

"Yep. All those damn naval officers my father—your grandfather—told me stories about. I guess he hoped it would inspire me. Bunch of goddamn drunken pirates, if you ask me."

I laughed. "Perhaps. Then again, they were not bankers. One could not find a more rapacious, piratical lot, excepting Joe Garcia and Esperanza, of course."

"You miss the old life, pard'ner?"

I paused, contemplating both Rodrigo and the bank chair's mannequin-fondling, fire-starting nephew, for whom I was made redundant. "I suppose, now and again. At least, I understood most of its aspects. One despairs of ever understanding life in Vaca Seca."

Uncle Bill raised his glass. "Nobody does. That's the most important thing to remember."

Chapter 9

The next day dawned crisp, like burnt toast. Roger hobbled to breakfast with greater ease, announcing he felt well enough to return to his bus, for which I was grateful, as his oily nature was disquieting.

"Glad the ankle is feeling better, Roger," said Uncle Bill, slurping the last remnants of his coffee. "How are the ribs?"

"Still sore, but I can breathe more easily. I'm anxious to get things rolling. I need to return to Hollywood, get more sign-offs on the budget, that sort of thing. It's going to be a hell of a movie, and the temporary disruption will be worth it. Whenever we film on location, the locals always benefit. It's not everybody who can say they were in a big movie." Roger now smiled, reminding me of an over-tanned Cheshire cat.

"How long do you plan to film in the cafe?" I asked.

He waved his hand dismissively. "A few days, a week, tops." Then, reverting to his discordant accent, he added, "Don't worry, old chap, we'll be finished filming before you can say Rob's your uncle. By the way, can you talk to Maria?"

"The correct expression is 'Bob's your uncle,'" I replied. "As for speaking with Maria, about what exactly?"

"I want Maria to play herself. She has a presence about her. I want that onscreen."

I eyed Uncle Bill, who shrugged. "Er, Maria is rather a force to be reckoned with, Roger. The topic must be approached with caution."

"No caution when money's involved, Ben. She'll be eating out of my hand."

I raised an eyebrow as I contemplated how little Roger understood of Maria.

"Well, any time you're ready, old chap. Time is money, you know."

"So I have heard."

I brought the lorry around to the front of the house. Uncle Bill relocated Daisy to her feeding trough so Roger could hobble out the front door and down the steps undisturbed. As we drove into town, he was uncharacteristically silent. We passed by the cafe. He nodded slightly and whispered "*Adieu, Dos Abuelas.*"

I parked the lorry next to Roger's bus. During his recovery, the bus appeared to have become a target for the local avian population.

"God, what a mess," Roger said as he eyed the windscreen, which was the apparent avian aiming point. "Is there a car wash in town?"

"You can probably clean the windscreen at the Texaco station. There is a garden hose on the side of the building."

"How do you live in this dump, old chap?"

Although Vaca Seca could be described as rundown, even decrepit, I was taken aback by Roger's description. "I grant there is an aura of deferred maintenance about it, but Vaca Seca does possess its peculiar charms. Besides, one must accept the oddities of the local domicile, wherever it may be. No doubt Hollywood has its own peculiarities."

"Sure it does, but getting bombarded with bird shit isn't one of them. And there are lots of car washes."

"A hazard of the more pastoral existence, I should think."

Roger mounted the steps into the bus slowly, pulling himself up with his arms. He then gazed back at me and waved. "Cheerio, old chap. As MacArthur said, I shall return."

"God help us all," I thought as I waved back silently.

After watching Roger's bus exit stage left, so to speak, I returned to the cafe. By some miracle, or perhaps because Señor Apestoso was hidden nearby, Paco had not yet soiled the entrance. Granted, he would probably attempt an especially large urinary bombardment later in the day, but I was nevertheless momentarily pleased.

Entering the kitchen, I found Maria and Esperanza chimneying away. Maria was stirring a large pot of beans whilst Esperanza jabbered away in Spanish, gesticulating wildly, as if she were drawing on a large, invisible canvas.

"*Pendejito*," she said, pointing her cigarette-grasping hand at the self, "how's that rich *gringo*? He gonna be okay? We heard he's staying with you and El Vaquero. You ought to charge him a lot of money, like a fancy hotel."

"What? Anyway, he just left."

"You let him leave? What about our money?"

"He was a guest, Esperanza, not a prisoner. What money? He gave you five hundred dollars."

"Yeah, but what about this movie. He said he's gonna pay us a lot more money."

"He shall return. He said so himself."

"But we need our money now."

"So you can repurchase the cafe from Uncle Bill? Nothing would please me more. Although one doubts that Uncle Bill would wish to see you run the cafe aground yet again."

"So what if me and Maria want to own the cafe again?"

"*Hermana*," Maria interrupted, "you know what will happen if Señor Bennie leaves. ¿*Que no*? Things are okay now."

Esperanza waved her cigarette-grasping hand dismissively. "We don't need *Pendejito* no more."

Maria stared at Esperanza silently, shook her head, and moved towards the counter, where she commenced ruthlessly chopping several tomatoes.

"You will have to be patient, Esperanza. Once Roger returns, you can negotiate with him directly. I certainly want no part of it."

"Negotiate? I just want that *gringo's* money."

I shook the cranium resignedly. Esperanza, I had concluded, was the human equivalent of Marjorie—vain, moody, recalcitrant, and thoroughly disagreeable. Although tempted to reply with an acidic remark of the "a fool and her money are soon parted" sort, I decided, as with my regular morning encounters with the equine Marjorie, that the preferred strategy was to remain well outside of hoof range.

"As you wish, Esperanza," I said. "Now, I need to prepare the dining room. Maria, are we in need of additional supplies? I had planned to motor to Sabrosa Foods once my lorry was repaired."

"*Sí*, Bennie, I got a list in my pocket." She removed a small piece of paper and handed it to me.

"You still waiting for that *pendejo* Luis to fix your truck?" Esperanza asked. "He can't fix nothing."

Esperanza had an especially strident dislike of Luis Chavez. After the cafe was rebuilt, he had publicly mocked her tendency to break wind. Although the townsfolk were wildly amused by Esperanza's embarrassment, they were rather less mirthful when Esperanza was in the dining room. Not only did customers fear receiving cascades of steaming enchiladas or iced tea on their laps, depending on what Esperanza was carrying at the time, but her emissions could be off-putting to the dining experience.

Rather than enter into yet another pointless discussion, I retreated to the dining room to undertake preparations for the dinner crowd. I then set course for the bank to deposit the previous night's earnings, which also meant a painful dialogue with Coronado's sister, who favoured me with repeated complaints about her lumbago, arthritic knees, and the countless failings of her brother.

The morning banking always created a strong desire for a glass of whisky to help erase the memory of the just-finished encounter. And, whilst no Graves would allow himself to descend into a state of perpetual inebriation, despite the strength of the Graves liver, I felt unprepared for further assaults by Esperanza.

I detoured into Rudy's and asked Antonio for a cup of strong coffee. Although Rudy did not prepare his coffee "cowboy style" like Uncle Bill, the liquid Antonio dispensed into the cup was similarly tar-like.

"Here you go, Señor Graves," Antonio said. "You want anything in that? I think we got some milk in the refrigerator."

"Thank you, no, Antonio. Bitter and unadulterated is called for this morning."

Presently, Coronado walked into the bar. "*Hola*, Señor Graves. Is that coffee? Smells real good. I had some this morning before I left the house. Joe won't let me drink none when I'm working."

"Why not?" I asked automatically, before the vocal cords could be detoured. One was often torn between immediate curiosity over Coronado's statements and subsequent regret at the answers he provided.

"I dunno. I guess 'cause I broke two of his coffee pots. They get real hot."

"Yes, but the handles—"

"You broke some pots, too, Señor Graves? Did Maria get real mad?"

"What? No, no broken coffee pots as yet, Coronado."

I motioned to Antonio. "Could you add a small tot?"

"Sure, Señor Graves," the lad responded. He retrieved the bottle and filled the cup to the top with whisky. "My grandfather calls this stuff rotgut."

"A wise man, your grandfather. But one must be braced for action, as Admiral Nelson would say."

"Who's Admiral Nelson?"

I sat at attention, as no Graves would ever countenance discussing the great man whilst slouched on a barstool. "Admiral Lord Viscount Nelson was the bravest British naval warrior of all time. Commanding the *Victory*, he died in the Battle of Trafalgar in 1805, struck down by a Frenchman's bullet. Before he died he said, 'Thank God I have done my duty.'"

"Are you fighting a war, Señor Graves?"

The question gave the grey matter pause, during which time I ingested a large swallow of the whisky-infused coffee. "Er, yes, I suppose I am, Antonio."

"Can I fight, too? I can borrow my grandfather's twenty-two."

"Er, no, but most kind of you to volunteer." I thought of Esperanza's earlier assault. "Rather a more private battle, I'm afraid."

I finished the coffee and returned to the cafe. During my short absence, and as I had feared, Paco had struck, and heavily. I sighed, opened the front door, and stepped over the shimmering pool.

"Hi, Benjamin," a sweet voice called out.

I glanced up. Sunflower was standing before me, dressed again in her ill-named coveralls, holding a hammer.

"Gah! I mean, er, hello, Sunflower," I said as the Graves eyes were drawn inexorably to the Siren-like visage. "I, er, I'm afraid the cafe is closed at the moment. Something else I can, er, help you with?"

She offered a golden smile. "Sky and I are starting to remodel the old bar. But I think we're in over our heads. Do you know anyone in town who can help us? I'm not very good at this sort of thing."

"I'm sure you're very good," I replied softly, before the grey matter biffed itself back to reality. "That is, you probably want Pedro Martinez. He is the local carpenter. Helped rebuild the cafe after we had a slight mishap."

"What happened? Your cafe looks wonderful."

"Oh, nothing serious," I lied with a dismissive wave of the hand, whilst the image of the cafe lying in ruins thanks to Coronado's demented fusillade appeared. "We were attempting to rid ourselves of a skunk and, well, an errant shot caused a spot of damage. Nothing serious. Spiffed up the cafe whilst we were at it, what?" Large beads of perspiration were now forming on the forehead. I swallowed heavily.

"Are you all right, Benjamin?"

"Eh, what? I mean, yes, quite well. A bit warm, that's all. Must be the sun." The sun, as it happened, had disappeared behind a cloud bank a half-hour earlier.

"The sun?" Sunflower eyed the now overcast sky and placed her left hand gently on my right forearm. "I don't bite, Benjamin."

How unfortunate, I thought, as I gazed at the delicate hand. "I mean, no, of course not. It's just that, well, the townsfolk do tend to gossip rather heavily. Small town and all that." I swallowed again as drops of perspiration fell to the floor.

"I'm not trying to seduce you, Benjamin," cooed Sunflower. "But you are cute." Her right hand now moved slowly up my back, somehow draining the lungs of oxygen.

"Gah."

"Is everyone from England so uptight?"

"Uptight? I mean, no, of course not," I stammered, as an image of Sunflower seducing me *sans habillement* knocked on the mental door, whilst shouting like a drunkard to be let inside. The kitchen door opened suddenly and Esperanza steamed through, chimneying heavily. She glanced at Sunflower, who now had both arms wrapped around my torso, and shook her head, as she mouthed the word *chichona* in my direction.

"M-hem, Sunflower, you remember Esperanza, don't you?"

"Sure. She told me to wait here for you."

"What?"

"Uh-huh. I asked her who could help Sky and me. She told me to ask you."

"*Sí*. Looks like you got a lot to tell her, *Pendejito*."

I glowered at Esperanza. "Well, as I said, Pedro Martinez is your man."

"Where can I find him?"

I pondered Pedro's likely mid-morning whereabouts. "Best to try him at home. He lives with his uncle, Nestor Martinez."

"Okay. Where's that?"

Finding Nestor's ramshackle home was not especially easy for the uninitiated. "You'll want to drive south about, oh, half a mile or so, and turn right onto a narrow dirt road. There is a large lilac bush at the corner that obscures a small road sign for Ramirez Road. After a mile or so, you will pass an old adobe shack with a collapsed wall. There will be two roads to your immediate right, one before the bridge over the *acequia* and one past it. Make sure to turn onto the one past the bridge. The other road will take you into the mountains, as I discovered some months ago. Then, one—"

"Benjamin, I'm sorry, but I don't have a car and I don't know how to drive Sky's bus. Could you take me there?"

"Gah! Me? I mean, well, I'm rather busy. Er, perhaps Esperanza would do so." I delivered a hopeful glance towards her, but she shook her head in the negative.

"Sorry, *Pendejito*," Esperanza said, "I gotta help Maria cook." She smiled artificially at Sunflower. "Bennie, he'll be real glad to drive you to Nestor's."

"That would be great. I promise to return him to you soon." Sunflower hooked onto my arm. "Thanks for doing this, Benjamin."

"Sure, take your time. We don't need no *Pendejito*." She pointed her burning cigarette at me and waved me off.

A thick fog descended over the brain as Sunflower pulled me out the front door and towards Uncle Bill's lorry. She slid into the front passenger seat. I had just opened the driver's side door when Fate intervened.

"Hi, Bennie," Loretta said, stopping beside me. "Where are you going?" Presently, espying Sunflower, Loretta's eyes narrowed into volcanic slits. "Taking your friend somewhere special?"

"No, L-Loretta," I stuttered. "It's not what you think. I mean, she merely wants Pedro Martinez to help repair the old bar and, well, as you know Nestor doesn't have a telephone. So, she enquired whether—"

"I don't want to know." Loretta marched up the steps and through the front door, which she slammed shut behind her.

"Is that Loretta, Benjamin? She seems real uptight, too."

"Eh? I mean, no. All's well. Er, would you mind waiting here for a moment?"

"Do you want me to talk to her?"

"God no. That is, I rather doubt your speaking to Loretta would be useful at the moment."

"Sky taught me jealousy leads to bad *karma*. We have a very open relationship, you know." She seemed like a hungry lioness eyeing the slow and dim-witted Graves gazelle.

"Indeed? How, er, cosmopolitan, that. Er, just wait here." I dove out of the lorry and hurried into the cafe.

"Loretta," I called, walking towards the kitchen door and crashing through it, startling Esperanza and Maria. "Where is Loretta? I must speak with her."

"She walked out the back door, *Pendejito*," Esperanza crowed. "I guess you can't help yourself with that *chichona*. Like a *gringo* fly on horseshit. *¿Que no?*"

"Bugger off, Esperanza. And as to flies on horseshit—" I paused, and eyed her with the most dagger-like Graves stare. "And what about you, Maria? After what you told me yesterday, why didn't you volunteer to motor Sunflower to Ernesto's house? Or are you now of the same opinion as your sister?"

Maria shrugged. "Esperanza said you need to pass a test."

"What test?"

"She says as long as that *chichona* is here, you're gonna be tempted. You gotta pass a test, so Loretta don't get hurt."

I moaned. "God help us all. What do you suggest I do? Shoot Sunflower? For good or ill, Sky Blue and Sunflower are here. Let me emphasise—the two of them, *dos*—as in 'together'. *¿Comprende?*"

"You're the one who's upsetting Loretta," yelled Esperanza.

"I am trying to avoid upsetting Loretta," I shouted, "despite your puerile attempts to make me do just that. Now, would one of you please take Sunflower to Nestor's house?"

Maria turned to Esperanza. "*Hermana*, maybe you better drive the *chichona* to Nestor's. I gotta finish my green chile."

"No way. That *chichona* is scary."

"What?" I said, sputtering.

"I ain't scared, *Pendejito*. But that *chichona*, I think she's been possessed. I don' want to go nowhere with El Diablo."

"Possessed? Surely, even you don't believe such rubbish, Esperanza?"

"*Sí*, I believe in El Diablo. I see him. When Maria and me were real little, Antonio Martinez, he got possessed. Antonio was always real nice. Sometimes, when we saw him in town, he would give Maria and me candy. One night, he was in the bar and he started screaming real funny, saying words nobody understood. He went home and killed all his chickens and goats. Then he shot himself. Everybody in town knew he got possessed by El Diablo."

"A lurid story, whose veracity I quite doubt. Nevertheless, someone may go stark staring bonkers for reasons having nothing whatsoever to do with possession by the Devil, or anyone else. My ancestor, Captain Archibald Graves of the Royal Navy, scuttled his ship and ran off with a Jamaican woman during the War of 1812."

"Nobody cares about your fucking *gringo* ancestors, *Pendejito*. But Maria and me, we know what happened to Antonio Martinez."

I sighed, wondering if Fate, having created a circle of Hell for my dealings with Coronado, had created another for those involving Esperanza.

"Esperanza, unless the Devil is himself stark staring bonkers, he would never wish to possess you."

"I dunno. How come he wanted to possess Antonio Martinez? He didn't do nothing to nobody. And he gave us candy."

I had reached the limit of my patience. "Shut the fuck up with your bloody nonsense and drive Sunflower to Nestor's home. Now!"

Esperanza's eyes widened. Her mouth gaped, apparently to respond, then closed again silently.

I exhaled deeply. "Please forgive the language, Esperanza. A Graves never employs such vulgarities under normal circumstances, but I have lost all patience with these ridiculous games of yours."

Esperanza remained silent. Her brow furrowed as the anger welled up within her.

"And if it is any comfort, should the Devil decide to pop out from Sunflower and possess you, I promise to organise the exorcism myself. After all, even the Devil himself should not suffer so."

Maria laughed.

"¡*Vete a la chingada, Pendejito*! screamed Esperanza. "If I get possessed, I'm gonna come after you first.

"I would expect nothing less." I tossed Esperanza the keys to the lorry. "Oh, and Esperanza?"

She returned fire with ocular daggers. "What?"

"*Muchas gracias*," I said.

Esperanza raised her middle finger. Then she turned around and stormed out the front door.

I exhaled deeply. "Well, Maria, do I pass the test?"

Maria drew deeply on her cigarette. "*Sí*, I guess. But as long as that *chichona's* here, there's gonna be trouble. I can feel it."

"There's always trouble in Vaca Seca. The town is a veritable boiling cauldron of trouble."

"*Sí*, but trouble with pretty girls, that's always the worst kind."

I could not disagree with Maria's philosophical observation, as my own experience had proven. What with the ex-wife's dalliance with the flower-whispering Rodrigo and now Sunflower, trouble orbited the fairer sex. One could even include the bank chairman's nephew's fondness for mannequins, which had resulted in my redundancy. After all, the mannequins were used to display women's raiment.

Back in the kitchen, I stirred a large pot of *frijoles* and contemplated a defensive strategy. I would inform Loretta that Esperanza had chauffeured Sunflower. This, I hoped, would ease Loretta's mind that my intentions were noble.

I tasted a spoonful of the *frijoles*. "Mmm, quite satisfactory. I believe these are ready, Maria."

"*Bueno*. Maybe you better go find Loretta now. She probably went back home. If you want, you can use my truck. I'm gonna need her help tonight."

"Thanks, Maria. One doubts Esperanza's chauffeuring of Sunflower will set tongues wagging."

As soon as I uttered those words, Fate tapped the shoulder to remind me of Esperanza's acid tongue, which could inflict untold damage.

"Gah," I whimpered as a cavernous feeling grew in the stomach.

Chapter 10

I sat down in Maria's lorry, which was parked in the alley behind the cafe. Waves of trepidation swamped the grey matter as it contemplated the nonsense Esperanza was surely spewing to Sunflower. No doubt, heavy weather lay ahead. Even the most redoubtable Graves might breach when pitted against Typhoon Esperanza.

I manoeuvred the lorry through the alley, which was strewn with garbage cans and fallen adobe bricks from crumbling walls, and turned onto the main road. Presently, I espied Sky Blue standing outside the allegedly haunted bar. He appeared to be in a sweaty trance as he stared at the front door—well, the opening where the front door ought to have been. A handle dangled from his right hand.

Curious, I stopped beside him. "I say, are you all right?"

He turned around slowly and goggled at me. "Huh? Oh, it's you, man. Did you see Sunflower? I thought she went over to the cafe to talk to you."

"Er, yes, she did, actually. She and Esperanza have set off to find Pedro Martinez."

"Who?"

"Pedro Martinez. He's a carpenter. As I explained to Sunflower, he provided repairs to the cafe." I scanned the crumbling façade and wondered what horrors lay inside. "Pedro should have no trouble sorting things out for you."

"Thanks, man." Sky Blue turned back towards the building. "I guess we should have looked the place over more. Joe said it would be easy to fix, but I don't know. Maybe we shouldn't have trusted him. He's got bad *chi*."

"M-hem," I replied, not wishing to reinforce Sky Blue's doubts regarding Joe Garcia's lack of trustworthiness. Having sold a building not his own, it was not surprising Joe had not accurately represented its condition, which could best be described as a mix of ancient ruin and victim of modern artillery barrage.

A brick fell from the edge of the roof and landed with a distinct thud. "I'm sure it's not as bad as it looks," I chirped. "You may wish to consult the Ortiz brothers, Ray and Manuel, who are masons. They repaired the cafe's foundation. Doubtless they can repair your parapet."

Sky Blue directed his stare to the fallen brick. "Yeah, man. I hope Sunflower and me have enough bread for this."

"Bread?" I asked. Though I was well-versed in the biblical 'loaves and fishes', and the repairs required on the falling-down bar were of the 'miracles needed' sort, I could not fathom how loaves of bread—traditional cottage loaf? baguette?—would be useful for construction.

"You know, man, money."

"Ah. I suppose a not insignificant sum may be required. Yet, surely it will be worth the expense, what with creating your spiritual centre and such."

"I guess so, man." Sky Blue returned his gaze to the missing front door. "Lot of bad *chi* in this town."

"Well, best of luck with the repairs," I said. "One hopes Pedro and the Ortiz brothers can improve the overall *chi* of your endeavour."

"Yeah, man," Sky Blue muttered, his eyes reconnoitring the crumbling facade.

I resumed the short voyage to Loretta's mother's house, carefully rehearsing the forthcoming apologies and explanations. When I arrived, I espied Loretta's mother carrying an armload of wood towards the front door, followed by Chata.

The dog bounded over and leapt on the door, per her usual greeting. I rolled down the window and offered a half-hearted "good dog," which appeared to increase her production of drool.

"Oh, it's you," Mrs. Alvarez said in a distinctly unfriendly tone.

"Hullo, Mrs. Alvarez," I replied, with false cheer.

"Why are you driving Maria's truck?"

"Er, Esperanza has Uncle Bill's lorry at the moment. She went to find Pedro Martinez."

"Pedro? Did something happen to the cafe?"

"No. Thankfully, the cafe needs no repairs at present. The, er, new couple in town, the ones who intend to convert the old bar into a spiritual centre, need a bit of assistance. Sunflower, I believe that is the young lady's name, enquired whether were any carpenters in town and I suggested Pedro."

"She's the one driving all of the men in this town crazy, isn't she?"

I coughed. "Oh? I had not noticed."

"Don't bullshit me, Bennie. Loretta has told me all about her. And you."

"M-hem. I have assured Loretta she has no cause for concern. The Graves heart is pure."

"Your heart isn't the problem," said Mrs. Alvarez, pointing an accusatory finger towards the lower Graves extremities. You've upset Loretta. As her mother, that upsets me. ¿*Comprende?*"

"Er, yes, which is why I am here, actually. As I attempted to explain to Loretta before she ran off, Sunflower, that is, Sky Blue's girlfriend, asked about Pedro and, well, finding Nestor's home is rather involved. I mean, I was simply attempting to be courteous. Sky Blue and Sunflower are here. And their intended spiritual centre is the old bar, which is rather near the cafe. I mean, one could not very well tell Sunflower to sod off merely for making inquiries about the availability of carpentry services."

"Fine," she said. "I guess I can't argue with that. I don't even know if I understood what you said." She paused, then raised the accusatory finger towards my countenance. "But that better be all. You ever lie to her, Bennie—"

Chata barked loudly and jumped on the lorry's door again.

"Gah! That is, I shan't. Now, may I speak with Loretta? She is here, isn't she?"

"No, she's not. She borrowed the car and left. She told me she had to meet someone in Santa Fe."

An air of trepidation arose from within. "Santa Fe? Who?"

"I didn't ask," she replied.

"I, er, that is, when Loretta does return, please tell her I—I mean, well, we rather need her help at the cafe."

"I'll tell her that. Is there anything else I should tell her?"

I inferred that Loretta's mother wished me to utter an emotive expression of the Lord Byron or *Cyrano de Bergerac* undying-love sort. However, the male Graveses have always been instructed to avoid poetic declamations, other than to one's mistress, for whom such utterances are considered *de rigueur*. Besides, when one utters poetic declamations, one expects *l'amour* to be listening, not her mother.

"Er, well, you can tell her I am anxious to see her." I smiled artificially.

Mrs. Alvarez rolled her eyes in a manner indicating disgust, disappointment, or both.

I glanced at the watch. "Well, I must return to the cafe. Cheer-o."

"Goodbye, Bennie. And please behave, for your sake and Loretta's."

I nodded hurriedly, started the lorry's engine, and returned to the cafe. Walking into the kitchen, I found Maria constructing *tamales*.

"Where's Loretta?"

"According to her mother, Loretta went to Santa Fe to meet someone. Her mother does not know who, although she assumes it has something to do with the cafe."

Maria exhaled a large cloud of cigarette smoke. "We don't need nothing from Sabrosa Foods. Who's she gonna meet?"

"I don't know," I shouted. "Gah! Hector lives in Santa Fe. What if she is meeting him?"

"Hector?" Maria laughed as she waved her chef's knife at me. "You think Loretta went to Santa Fe to see Hector?"

I began to shake with anger. "Why not? Your bloody sister has never ceased her attempts to poison our relationship. What better way than to use Hector?"

"Hector? *Madre de Dios.* That's crazy. Loretta don't like Hector. Nobody likes Hector."

"But why else would Loretta run out of the cafe and motor to Santa Fe?"

"Señor Bennie," Maria said quietly, "you want Loretta to trust you. *¿Que no?* You gotta trust her."

One could almost hear Fate sniggering. Presently, I heard the front door open, followed by laughter. Stepping through the kitchen door, I espied Esperanza and Sunflower. "I say, did you find Pedro?

"*Sí, Pendejito.* Sunflower, she talked to Pedro. He drove back with us. I dropped him off at the old bar."

"Indeed? Unusually punctual of him."

Sunflower offered a polite laugh. "He told me about all the work he did on the cafe, Benjamin. You're very lucky, after all of the damage you caused."

"What? It was Coronado who reduced the cafe to rubble."

"Don't get mad, *Pendejito.* Pedro, he was just showing off some for Sunflower."

Sunflower's bare arms glistened as the sunlight from the front window reflected off them.

"Esperanza told me all about the cafe, Benjamin. And you, too." She smiled radiantly.

I eyed Esperanza coldly. "No doubt, Esperanza has embellished the truth."

"Don't be shy, Benjamin. You obviously have great *chi.*"

"What?"

"*Chi?* Don't you know what that is?"

"I have heard Sky Blue use the term, but I confess to not knowing its meaning."

"It's what the Chinese call the life force. Your life force is very strong."

"Life force?" I said.

"You know, what's inside." Sunflower pressed her finger on her coveralls at the precise location where her bosom was attempting to escape. "Some people have a great life force inside. Sky Blue says I have great *chi.*"

The throat constricted as I attempted to swallow. "Pearls of great price," I muttered absently.

"What about pearls, Benjamin?"

"Eh? Oh, sorry. I was merely thinking about *chi*, life force, and all that. Has rather a religious connotation, one imagines."

"That's why our bus is named Siddhartha. That's the Buddha's real name. Are you a Buddhist?"

"I rather doubt it. The Graveses have always been Church of England types. Why?"

"What you said, it's very Zen."

"How kind of you to think so," I replied, having no idea what she meant.

Esperanza, who had been silent during the discussion of *chi* and pearls, waved her arms. "Look, *Pendejito*, you and Sunflower talk, I gotta help Maria some more." She started towards the kitchen door.

I pried my eyes from Sunflower and turned to Esperanza. "Did you tell Loretta to go to Santa Fe to meet someone?" I asked severely.

"Huh?"

"Her mother said Loretta left for Santa Fe as soon as she arrived home. Told her she was meeting someone there. Is it Hector?"

Esperanza's eyes narrowed. "Hector? What the fuck are you talking about?"

"That's what I am attempting to find out," I shouted.

"What sort of sabotage have you attempted now?"

Esperanza retrieved a cigarette and placed it between her lips. "You're crazy, *Pendejito*. If Loretta ain't here tonight, who's gonna help us? My back hurts real bad."

"I can help you, Esperanza," Sunflower chirped. "It's the least I can do."

I whimpered softly.

"You been a waitress?" Esperanza asked.

"Well, sort of. I worked at a drive-in. I had to wear roller skates."

Esperanza's eyes widened. "Roller skates?"

"What is a 'drive-in'?" I asked, as an image appeared of Sunflower's décolletage roller skating about.

"It's just what it sounds like, Benjamin. You drive your car to the restaurant and park outside. A waitress, like me, comes out, takes your order, and you eat in your car."

"One dines in one's vehicle? Barbaric. Why would anyone wish to do such a thing?"

"It's fun. Mostly a teenager thing. Don't you have drive-ins in England?"

"Well, perhaps there are such things in the less civilised regions—Scotland comes to mind. As lads, we would sneak into the local pub."

Sunflower laughed. "Well, you missed some fun. So, what do you want me to do?"

"Why don't you show her, *Pendejito*. I'm gonna go help Maria." Esperanza smiled at me rather lasciviously, which provided a painful reminder of several previous encounters when she wore a too-short, pink sateen robe whilst "entertaining" the oafish Hector. She turned around and disappeared into the kitchen.

"Er, it's, most kind of you to offer to assist, but there really is no need. I am sure we can manage without you. Besides, one would not want to keep you from Sky Blue and all that."

Sunflower approached until her coveralls pressed against my shirt. "I want to help you, Benjamin," she cooed, oozing fecundity. She passed her right hand smoothly across the left side of my face and took hold of my hand.

The sustained sensory bombardment was weakening the Graves resolve. "Sunflower, please," I croaked, reluctantly removing my hand from hers and stepping away. "I mean, you're most attractive and I'm flattered but, I mean, circumstances being what they are, this isn't an especially good idea."

"Sky won't mind, Benjamin." She kissed me softly. "I love your accent. It's so sexy."

The Graves resolve was ready to strike its colours. "Sunflower, you don't understand, Loretta and I—"

"But I do understand. Esperanza said you and Loretta broke up. She has real bad *chi*, Benjamin. And Esperanza told me you wanted to get to know me better."

"Gah! Esperanza told you that?"

"Yes. She just wants you to be happy. By the way, what does *pendejito* mean?"

Sunflower stroked my face again. "I'd like to get to know you better, too." Dull-witted as I could be in matters of the heart, I gathered Sunflower was referring to knowledge of the biblical sort.

Caught between Esperanza's duplicity and Sunflower's ardour, the cranium felt as if a large axe had been driven through it. I fumbled for a nearby chair and sat down heavily.

"Is something wrong?" said Sunflower as she caressed my shoulder.

"What?" I moaned, feeling like a fly entangled in Fate's web. "Esperanza, well, what she told you wasn't true. About Loretta and me, that is. What I mean is, well, we're to be—"

"You don't have to explain, Benjamin." She knelt down by the chair, revealing the coveralls to be even less aptly named, and kissed me again. "There are no rules, you know."

I had reached the point of unconditional surrender when the front door opened. Coronado and Mrs. Alvarez stood before us, goggling as Sunflower ended her kiss.

"*Híjole!*" Coronado exclaimed, staring at Sunflower.

"Your word, is that what you said, Bennie?" Mrs. Alvarez growled. "I don't like being lied to. You should be ashamed of yourself."

I rocketed upwards, knocking the chair over. "Wait, you don't understand, Mrs. Alvarez."

She glared at Sunflower, who had stood up beside me. "I understand perfectly, Bennie. If I ever see you around my daughter, I'll shoot you myself." She turned around and stormed out, slamming the front door behind her.

"*Híjole,*" Coronado repeated.

"What do you want, Coronado?" I mumbled.

"Uh, I forgot, Señor Graves." He stared at Sunflower hungrily, as if she were a large *tamale* ready to be unwrapped. "Sorry, Señor Graves." He continued to stare at Sunflower, looking as if he might begin drooling as copiously as Chata.

"The cafe is closed at present, Coronado. You need to leave."

"Uh, okay, Señor Graves." Coronado walked through the front door. He turned around, eyed Sunflower and muttered *híjole* yet again, then shut the door and waddled down the stairs.

I turned towards the kitchen, contemplating the disaster that had just swept over.

Sunflower slipped her arm about my waist. "Don't worry, Benjamin."

A state of mere worry would have been welcome. I was far beyond worry, having catapulted into full terror, only to discover Fate considered terror to be small beer.

The front door opened again, revealing Sky Blue's large form, hammer in hand.

"Hey, baby, there you are." He stared at her arm, which was wrapped around my waist. "Not cool," said Sky Blue. "Not cool."

Chapter 11

It's okay, Sky," cooed Sunflower, as she oozed towards his side. "I was just thanking Benjamin for helping us find a carpenter. She snaked herself around Sky Blue, taming the beast with a soft kiss.

"You know how much I dig you, baby," Sky Blue said. He eyed me suspiciously.

"I know, Sky. I dig you, too."

"Yes, please," I mumbled to myself, still under Sunflower's spell.

Esperanza burst through the kitchen door. She stopped and glanced about the dining room. "Too many fucking *gringos*," she said, then retreated back towards the kitchen.

Although I normally dreaded Esperanza's appearances, the present one vanquished Sunflower's carnal spell. "Esperanza, wait!" I shouted. I turned to Sky Blue and Sunflower, who were cooing like doves to each other. "Right, I really must speak with Esperanza."

I marched into the kitchen to confront her about this new depth in her efforts to sabotage my relationship with Loretta. Esperanza stood outside the open back door, chimneying away and howling with laughter. Maria, who was still in the kitchen, glanced at me, shook her head, and proceeded to behead a carrot.

"Your bloody sister has struck yet again," said I.

"*Mi hermana*? She told me about you and that *chichona*. I guess you made your choice, Señor Bennie. ¿*Que no*?"

"What? No, I mean, nothing has changed between Loretta and me. Your sister is again resorting to sabotage."

"Huh? That *chichona's* got a boyfriend already. You gonna make him real mad, too."

"Er, well, Sunflower's views regarding monogamy appear to be rather more elastic than what most might consider traditional. But your sister is encouraging her. This is a nightmare."

"*No entiendo nada,*" said Maria, eying me as if I were a Martian. She walked to the back door and stepped outside into the alley.

"*Hermana,*" I heard her growl, "*venga aca.*"

Esperanza turned around. Maria exploded with a fusillade of Spanish, none of which I understood. Esperanza's face turned a dark crimson. She returned verbal fire, waving her arms wildly. Maria remained motionless. Esperanza threw down the remains of her cigarette, crushed it mercilessly with her shoe, and crossed her arms over her chest.

Maria stepped back inside and looked at me. "*No más,*" she said, and walked into the storeroom. I remained motionless, unsure as to what I should do next. Presently, Esperanza stormed inside and launched a dagger-like stare at me.

"Don't say nothing to me, *Pendejito,*" she snarled. "Maria said to tell you I'm sorry. *Bueno,* I'm sorry, but I didn't tell your *chichona* nothing that wasn't true. I see how you look at her; real hungry, just like Hector looks at me. Loretta, she's got no chance."

I strained to dissolve the emetic image of Hector hungering after Esperanza. "You do realise Loretta and I are engaged to be married. Therefore, I would appreciate your ceasing these puerile efforts to sabotage our pending nuptials."

"What the fuck are you talking about, *Pendejito?*"

"I said, Loretta and I are engaged to be married. Are you deaf?"

In truth, even though Loretta and I had broached the matrimonial subject rather tentatively, we were not engaged. And with Loretta's most recent encounter with Sunflower, the prospects of a forthcoming engagement seemed grim indeed. Yet the words had erupted from the vocal cords.

"Engaged?" Esperanza shouted. "When? Loretta didn't say nothing to me."

"Er, quite recently, actually. Loretta and I, I mean, we thought a formal announcement seemed premature."

"How come Josefa didn't say nothing? You tell her, too?"

"No, I mean, we were waiting until I, er, had purchased a ring and all that."

Maria, who had heard Esperanza, walked back into the kitchen. "You and Loretta are engaged? *¡Felicitaciones!*"

"*Hermana*, he don't deserve our Loretta," said Esperanza.

"Why not?" I shouted. "Because I'm a *gringo*? Because I've prevented you from bankrupting the cafe yet again? Or do you have some other ridiculous reason you wish to enlighten me with?"

Esperanza pointed an accusatory finger at my countenance. She appeared ready to unleash a verbal fusillade, but shouted only "*¡Pendejito!*"

Maria shook her head. "I'm real glad. I know you're gonna treat Loretta real good. Maybe you better tell that *chichona*."

"I shall, Maria. Only, as I have told Loretta, Sunflower appears to have rather, er, tactile tendencies, which are difficult to discourage."

Maria inhaled deeply on her cigarette and blew a huge cloud of smoke towards the kitchen ceiling. "Huh? Don't let her put her hands on you no more, Bennie. *¿Comprende?*"

"Er, yes. Rather the nub of the problem, that. How does one discourage Sunflower?"

"You need an *acompañanta*," said Maria.

Esperanza burst out laughing.

I raised an eyebrow. "An *acomp*—what?"

"She makes sure a girl don't get in no trouble," Maria replied.

"Do you mean a chaperone?"

"*Sí*, a chaperone, *Pendejito*," said Esperanza. "But this time, for a *gringo* so he don't get into the *chichona's* pants."

"For God's sake," I spluttered.

Maria shrugged. "*Sí*, especially if the *chichona* is possessed by the Devil."

"Possessed?" I replied. "What are you suggesting? Some sort of exorcism?"

Maria pondered the suggestion momentarily. "*Sí*," she said, "exorcism would be real good, but we don't got no priest here. So, we got to get you an *acompañanta*. No more *tentación*. *¿Que no?*"

"You mean temptation? A chaperone to ensure I do not succumb to Sunflower's, er, charms? But this is madness."

"*Sí*," the sisters responded in unison.

I stiffened. "I say, I'm quite capable of taking care of myself. The Graves spine is made of stern stuff. It can and shall resist the advances of even the most determined Siren."

Maria shook her head. "Siren? *¿Quien es ella?*" she asked.

"The Sirens are from Greek mythology," I said. "They lured sailors with their—"

"I don't care about nobody luring no sailors," Maria said. "I mean the *chichona*."

"Er, yes."

Maria continued. "Luis, Pedro, Joe Garcia, Rudy, I seen them look at that *chichona* just like you, Bennie. Only they ain't engaged to Loretta."

Despite my protestations about the stiffness of the Graves spine, it was noodle-like in Sunflower's presence. "Well, if I must have a chaperone, I can think of no one better suited than you, Maria."

"I don't got no time to babysit. Too much work."

"Then who—gah! No! Not your sister, Maria. Simply beyond the pale."

"Yeah, I ain't gonna chaperone *Pendejito*," Esperanza shouted.

I breathed a large sigh of relief. Given a choice between Esperanza serving as a chaperone or being ripped apart by famished hyaenas, one would be hard-pressed not to prefer the latter. "Well, whom do you have in mind, Maria?"

An hour later, I motored back to the ranch, accompanied by an unwelcome passenger in case Sunflower should suddenly appear in the road like a fecund ghost.

"Shouldn't you be at work?" I sighed.

"It's okay, Señor Graves," Coronado replied. "Joe told me I should watch you real close, 'cause he wants Loretta to be happy. And Maria said if I let Señorita Flower come near you, I won't get no more *enchiladas* or *tamales*."

I grimaced.

"Señor Graves?"

"Yes, Coronado?"

"I ain't been a chaperone before. What should I do if Señorita Flower comes after you?"

"I'm quite sure your presence will be off-putting enough, Coronado."

We arrived at the ranch. My rotund chaperone lowered himself slowly out of the lorry and glanced around furtively, as if checking for well-endowed enemy soldiers.

"I don't think Señorita Flower is here, Señor Graves."

Daisy had come around to the lorry to investigate. She grunted loudly and sniffed Coronado's trouser pockets. He raised his hands. "Sorry, Daisy, I don't got nothing for you. I'm guarding Señor Graves now." As if she could understand, Daisy eyed me, grunted dismissively, and walked away.

Uncle Bill emerged from the barn and walked towards us.

"Hullo, Uncle Bill," I said.

"Howdy, Bennie," he replied. Uncle Bill then looked askance at Coronado.

"*Hola*, El Vaquero," Coronado chirped, extending a pudgy hand. "Did Señor Graves tell you the news? He and Loretta are gonna get married."

Uncle Bill's eyebrows shot up. "Bennie, you asked Loretta to marry you? Well, I'll be goddamned." He shook my hand vigorously. "Congratulations, pard'ner! She's a mighty fine filly."

"*Sí*, El Vaquero," Coronado interrupted. "And Maria told me I got to be a chaperone so he don't kiss Señorita Flower no more."

Uncle Bill turned to Coronado. "Did you say *chaperone*?" he asked. "Kiss? Bennie, what the hell is going on?"

I disgorged a large sigh, which sounded like a deflating tyre, and attempted to explain, including Coronado's current presence. After Uncle Bill listened to the sordid details, his eyes narrowed.

"Fooling around with some other gal when you're engaged to Loretta? That ain't the cowboy way, pard'ner."

"Uncle Bill, I am not 'fooling around' with Sunflower, as you put it," I replied in protest. "That is a calumny of the worst order, promoted by Esperanza."

Uncle Bill removed his cowboy hat, dusted it off against his trouser leg, and replaced it onto his head. "Jesus, Bennie, how'd you get yourself into this mess?"

"Me? It is entirely the result of Esperanza's meddling. She remains committed to my abandoning Loretta and the cafe."

"Yeah, but you just told me you kissed that gal in front of Josefa."

"I did not. She kissed me."

Uncle Bill again removed his hat and then scratched his head. "You think that makes a difference?" he asked.

I turned to Coronado. "Would you be kind enough to wait in the lorry? I must speak with Uncle Bill privately."

"But Maria told me I gotta stay with you, Señor Graves, so you don't kiss Señorita Flower."

"She is not here!" I cried. "She is miles away." Feeling the blood pressure rising to volcanic levels and not wishing to explode, I paused and inhaled deeply. "Look, Coronado, you can watch for Sunflower from the lorry. If you see her approach, then, er—"

"What, Señor Graves?"

"Head her off at the pass. You know, the way Zane Grey would do."

Coronado's rodentary eyes blinked in non-comprehension.

"Now what?" I asked.

"Is Zane Grey gonna chaperone you, too, Señor Graves? I don't know him."

Presently, Uncle Bill intervened. "Go wait in the pickup, Coronado. Bennie and me gotta talk over a few things privately. I'll get you a beer. You can take it back to the lorry and wait for us."

Coronado smiled. "Sure, El Vaquero."

Uncle Bill trotted onto the front porch, interrupting Daisy's siesta. She raised her head, which was still sombreroed, eyed him as he disappeared into the house, and resumed her slumber.

He re-emerged momentarily, two bottles of beer in hand. "There you go, Coronado," he said, extending the bottles to Coronado, who quickly enveloped them in his own pudgy appendage.

"*Gracias*, El Vaquero," Coronado said. He turned around and heaved his bulk towards the lorry. When he was seated inside, Uncle Bill turned to me and jerked his thumb towards the lorry. "You want to tell me what the hell's really goin' on, Bennie?"

"Er, yes. Well, Loretta and I are not actually engaged."

"Huh? You just told me you were."

"To be accurate, Coronado told you. There is, ah, no engagement at present. I told Esperanza and Maria we were engaged, hoping to, well, stave off Esperanza's continued sabotage."

Uncle Bill grabbed his hat and slammed in onto his knee. "Goddamn it, Bennie!" he shouted. "It's that Sunflower gal, ain't it. Well, no nephew of mine is gonna behave like a goddamned bull, breaking down fences to get into some other pasture. You lose Loretta and I'll whup you myself."

I stepped back, alarmed by his fury. "I, that is, I am attempting to remain on the straight and narrow path, Uncle Bill. But I confess Sunflower has a rather intoxicating effect. More to the point, what do I tell Loretta?"

"First thing you're gonna do is ask her to marry you. Then, you're gonna talk to that Blue Sky fella. Tell him he's got to corral his filly."

"Eh, what?"

"He's got to make sure that gal of his don't stray."

"Ah. Easier said than done, I'm afraid. Perhaps her amorousness could be directed elsewhere."

Uncle Bill growled. "What a goddamn mess. Let's go."

"Go?" I asked. "Where?"

"The Texaco station, to get your truck. I gotta run some errands and I need mine."

With myself squeezed between Uncle Bill and Coronado, we drove to Luis's garage. After paying Luis an exorbitant charge for installing a new fuel pump, Uncle Bill departed for parts unknown. Coronado and I then motored to the cafe in the now operational lorry.

I walked into the kitchen, followed closely by Coronado. Inside, Maria and Esperanza were again chimneying and jabbering away.

"Where's Sunflower?" I asked. "Did she change her mind about this evening?"

"You miss her already, *Pendejito*? I told her be here at five."

"Merely enquiring. Oh, by the way Esperanza, where's Hector? Doubtless he would enjoy meeting Sunflower."

"¡*Vete a la chingada, Pendejito*! If Hector goes near that *chichona*, he ain't gonna have no *cojones* left."

"Are you and Hector are engaged, too, Esperanza?" Coronado asked. "I can chaperone Hector if you want."

"¡*Cállate, gordo*! Only *Pendejito* needs a chaperone."

I shook my head in disgust and began walking towards the kitchen door.

"Where you going, *Pendejito*?" Esperanza shouted. "You know I can't work much 'cause of my back."

"Sod off. You and your malingering back."

Coronado trailed me out the front door and down the road towards the old bar. As Uncle Bill might say, the time had come to grab the proverbial bull by the horns.

Chapter 12

I walked briskly, followed by a huffing and puffing Coronado. As we approached, we heard Sunflower screaming. Presently, she shouted, "Kill it, kill it, Sky!"

I ran inside. Given past experience, I assumed Sunflower and Sky Blue were face to face with a rattlesnake. "Is it a rattlesnake?" I shouted.

Coronado arrived shortly thereafter. "Don't be scared, Señorita Flower," he said, whilst attempting to breathe. "I like snakes."

She screamed again at an especially painful frequency.

"Stay centred, baby," Sky Blue said calmly. "I'll get it."

"I hate mice! Kill it." She screamed again at a frequency that caused me to expect any nearby glassware to shatter.

"Stay centred, baby," Sky Blue said again, this time in a noticeably less calm tone.

"Maybe it's a rat, Señorita Flower," Coronado said. "I see a lot of those."

Upon hearing the word *rat*, Sunflower's screams reached a decibel level one thought humans incapable of producing.

"Easy, baby," Sky Blue shouted. He enveloped Sunflower and squeezed her tightly. "You're okay. Deep breaths, baby. Find your centre."

Sunflower stopped screaming and began to sob.

"Capital job, Coronado," I muttered. "Telling Sunflower it could be a rat was most comforting."

"Sorry, Señor Graves."

"Can you find the offending rodent?"

"Sure. It's probably in a corner or something." Coronado bent down and peered along the walls of the bar. "I don't see it. Maybe it ran out the door."

I was about to reply when Sunflower emitted the loudest, most piercing scream the ears had ever experienced. She exploded out of Sky Blue's embrace and raced outside. The three of us followed. Sunflower was running straight towards the cafe at dreadnought speed. Maria and Esperanza, apparently hearing Sunflower's screams, had walked up the alley to the road. They goggled as Sunflower approached.

"Stop, baby, stop," Sky Blue shouted, as he ran after her. "Please, stop her."

Esperanza stepped into Sunflower's oncoming path and motioned for to stop.

As Sunflower fast approached Esperanza, the screams continued, unabated, as did her velocity. She rammed Esperanza forcefully—Admiral Nelson would have approved—knocking Esperanza onto the macadam and falling upon her. Presently, a small field mouse emerged from Sunflower's cleavage. It walked slowly for several feet, then stopped.

Sky Blue reached the scene of the collision first and scooped Sunflower into his arms. She was again sobbing. "It's okay, baby, you're safe now."

Coronado picked up the mouse, which appeared rather dazed and doubtless unaware it had successfully plumbed a region of Sunflower's geography of which others only dreamt. He held the rodent in the palm of his hand and smiled. "See Señorita Flower? It's just a little mouse."

Sky Blue helped Sunflower to her feet. The sobbing had quieted to soft moans. "Don't show it to her, man. She's got this thing about mice."

Esperanza groaned as Maria knelt down on the macadam next to her. "*Hermana*, you okay?" Maria asked.

"I think my arm's broke," Esperanza said. Maria and I assisted Esperanza to a sitting position. She groaned again, clutching her right arm. "Why the fuck was that *chichona* screaming? She see Alejandro's ghost?"

"She was frightened by a mouse," I said.

"She saw a mouse? A fucking mouse!" shouted Esperanza. "Is that how come she ran into me?"

"Er, I gather the offending rodent had burrowed, if you will, into her coveralls and was crawling about her—well, Sunflower experienced rather a high degree of mental anguish."

Esperanza eyed me suspiciously. "Help me the fuck up."

Maria and I slowly uprighted Esperanza. She cradled her right arm and staggered over to where Sky Blue and Sunflower stood.

Sunflower, eyes reddish and swollen, glanced at Esperanza. "I'm sorry, Esperanza," she whimpered. "I've always been terrified of mice. Are you all right?"

"You broke my arm, *pendeja*, 'cause of a fucking little mouse. You ain't gonna work at the cafe. We got mice in the kitchen and a fucking skunk outside."

Sunflower shrank back into Sky Blue's arms. "It's okay, baby," he whispered again. He turned to Esperanza. He pointed a large finger at Esperanza's face. "Don't yell at her, man. She's got a phobia. This town has some real bad *chi*."

"¡*Vete a la chingada* and your fucking *gringo chi*! My arm's broke. How am I gonna work?"

Although Esperanza appeared to have forgotten her spinal malingering, I thought it best to defuse the approaching explosion. "Esperanza, please. Let's get your arm examined. Nestor gave Roger some pain medication that was most effective."

"That fucking *borracho*? I don't care if he was a medic. He ain't coming near me." She turned to Maria. "*Hermana*, take me home. And get me some whisky. That's the best medicine I know." She turned around and began walking up the alley where Maria's lorry was parked, all the while emitting a torrent of Spanish invective.

Maria looked at me and shook her head. "Señor Bennie, maybe we better stay closed tonight. I gotta help her."

"Of course, Maria. I will take care of it. And I believe you should convince Esperanza to see a doctor, or at least Nestor. He seemed surprisingly competent ministering to Roger's ankle."

"I dunno," Maria said. "She always hated doctors. And she hates Nestor. But, maybe I can convince her. ¡Ay, cabrón! You gotta get Loretta back, Señor Bennie. You and me, we can't run the cafe alone."

Maria escorted her sister with a damaged wing down the alley towards the cafe, as Esperanza continued to spew invective. Fate, it seemed, had just provided an odd mix of credits and debits. On the credit side of the ledger, Sunflower's phobia of rodents and unsuitability for work at the cafe eliminated the carnal temptations I would experience if she waitressed. On the debit side, Esperanza's efforts in the cafe, though not extensive, were nevertheless useful. This made Loretta's return more imperative. Then again, she would be inundated with congratulations about her still unbeknownst engagement.

"Gah!"

Coronado came up to my side. "Are you really gonna close the cafe tonight, Señor Graves?" he asked. "Can I still get some enchiladas?"

"What? No, you may not have enchiladas this evening. The cafe will be closed. Furthermore, your chaperoning duties will not be necessary."

"But Maria told me I got to stay with you."

"Yes, yes, however, Sunflower will not be working at the cafe. And after I prepare Señor Apestoso's ofrenda, I shall return to the ranch forthwith."

Presently, Sunflower and Sky Blue approached. "I'm sorry, Benjamin. I didn't mean to hurt Esperanza. Will she be okay? I can still help you at the cafe."

"No! That is, a most generous offer. However, we shall manage. Besides, the cafe has, er, its own rodentary issues. I should not wish to expose you to—to mice, that is. Besides, Esperanza is rather a tough old bird, as they say. I am quite certain she will return to her duties shortly."

"Sky has tried to help me with my mouse phobia," Sunflower whimpered. "I guess I'm not over it." She offered Sky Blue one of those helpless, doe-eyed looks for which the fairer sex is well known.

"That's okay, baby," said Sky Blue, as he caressed the nape of her neck and then kissed it softly.

"M-hem. Well, Garcia's store sells various compounds designed to eliminate infestations. Perhaps you and Sky Blue should distribute them liberally throughout the old bar."

"Yeah, man," Sky Blue said. "The *chi* around here is real bad."

"Er, yes," I replied.

Sky Blue snaked his arm around Sunflower's waist. "Let's go to that store, baby. I'm gonna get rid of all of the mice. You won't have to be afraid anymore."

Sunflower nodded silently and then leaned her head onto his shoulder.

"Er, I say, Sky Blue, might I have a brief word with you in private? Coronado, perhaps you could stay with Sunflower, whilst I speak with Sky Blue."

"Sure. I can guard Señorita Flower."

"Guard, man?"

"Afraid the explanation is rather involved," I said, directing Sky Blue towards the old bar.

"I hope you will not be offended by what I am about to say. It concerns, er, Sunflower's behaviour."

"Huh? I'm real sorry about her knocking down the old lady, man."

"What? Oh, no, accident and all that. I mean, she appears to care a great deal for you."

"Yeah, we've been together almost two years. It's real cool."

"Quite. However, she seems to have a rather, er, tactile nature, if you know what I mean. And her views on monogamy are unconventional, to say the least."

"Tactile, man?"

"I mean, she seems quite fond of touching people, does she not, what with various embraces and such."

"Yeah, Sunflower is real physical. That's how we got together."

I swallowed with difficulty, as a particularly tactile image entered the grey matter. "Let me assure you, there's no cause for jealousy. It's just that, well, Loretta—my, er, fiancée—has been rather distressed recently, having seen Sunflower, er, embracing me and such."

"Yeah, man." He scowled at me. "Not cool."

I coughed. "Yes, I mean, no, of course not. She does have rather an effect on the local male populace, given her physical, er, gifts."

"Yeah, she's got a great pair."

"God, yes," I muttered under the breath, a vision of Sunflower's erupting bosom sweeping into mental view. "I mean, no, not that I have noticed. I, er, merely an observation on my part concerning the local populace and such."

"Guys dig looking at her, man."

"Well, she seems to have formed an attachment of sorts to me."

"Huh?"

"Fear not. A Graves always behaves honourably, especially when pledged to another."

"You mean Sunflower's come on to you, man?" Sky Blue scowled again.

"Eh? If you mean has she directed what I perceived as a, how shall we say, carnal interest, towards me—of course I have discouraged it, in light of my relationship with Loretta."

"Sunflower's a real free spirit, man. Most times it's real good, but not always."

"One supposes such a certain *freedom of spirit*, as you call it, can lead to poor, er, *chi*."

"Yeah, man."

I was about to suggest he direct Sunflower's free spirits elsewhere, when Sunflower approached, seemingly recovered from her trauma. Her arm was snaked around Coronado's large girth. Coronado was grinning wildly.

"Thanks again for understanding, Benjamin. Coronado just told me he's your chaperone. That's so cute."

"*Sí*, Señor Graves. I told Senorita Flower about your engagement to Loretta and why I gotta chaperone you 'cause you were kissing her."

Sky Blue turned to me. "Hey, man, I thought you said you tried to discourage it."

"Well, I, er, I have—"

Sunflower glided over to Sky Blue. "Don't be jealous, Sky. You know I love you."

Sky Blue wrapped his arm around Sunflower's waist, reeling her in like a large fish. "Sorry, baby, but you mean so much to me."

She kissed him and laughed. "Maybe we should go back to the bus." Sunflower escaped from his embrace, then pulled on his arm.

"Cool, baby." They walked down the road, presumably for a tête-à-tête within the confines of the wheeled Siddhartha.

Coronado and I watched until they disappeared behind the old bar.

"How come Señorita Flower wants to go back to the bus? Are they gonna leave town?"

I sighed. "If only."

With Esperanza escorted home to nurse her damaged wing and Sunflower occupied with Sky Blue, a momentary calm settled over the grey matter like a comforting fog.

"I sure am hungry," said Coronado, which returned reality with a jolt. "Are you gonna make some *enchiladas* for Señor Apestoso? I think he likes those best."

I glanced at the watch and grumbled. "I have not found Señor Apestoso to be especially discriminating in his tastes. Very well, come inside and I shall prepare your enchiladas. You shan't forget to feed Señor Apestoso his meal?"

He licked his lips. "*Sí*, Señor Graves. I won't forget."

With Coronado fed and watered, and Señor Apestoso's *ofrenda* readied, I bid Coronado good evening.

"Wait, Señor Graves, you can't leave."

"Why not? We are closed this evening."

"Don't I still got to chaperone you?"

The eyes rolled heavily. "I am returning to the ranch. Uncle Bill can assume the chaperoning duties. He may not possess your indomitable skills, but I shall instruct him to remain vigilant by thinking of you."

Coronado puffed his chest outwards and smiled. "Thanks, Señor Graves. I guess I'll go to Rudy's for now. I'll come back later and feed Señor Apestoso."

I watched Coronado disappear into Rudy's bar, then returned to the ranch. After informing Uncle Bill of my battle plans, I set course for Mrs. Alvarez's house, hoping to add my own mewling apology to Uncle Bill's presumed discussions with her earlier in the day.

Before the lorry had stopped, Chata was running madly towards it. She leaned her massive front paws on the door, barking and drooling. It was a frightening sight, eased only by her wagging tail. I heaved the door open, presuming the canine battleship had not been informed of my transgressions, at least not all of them.

"There's a good dog," I said, patting her massive head.

Chata turned around and walked back towards the house, tail wagging. As a wave of trepidation swept over me, I envied her innocent happiness. I knocked on the front door and stepped back to await Fate's judgement.

The door opened slowly. Before me stood Loretta, grim-faced and arms folded across her chest. "Hello, Bennie. I understand congratulations are in order. I didn't know I was the lucky girl. Am I?"

The heart, or what was left of it, was now becalmed. "Er, hullo Loretta. I have made a complete hash of things. The last thing I wished to do was hurt you, although I surely have done just that."

Loretta remained silent.

I sighed. "I cannot excuse my behaviour and shall return to London. I do have one favour to ask. Some months ago, you offered to manage the cafe. Uncle Bill would be most pleased if you do so. I know how much the cafe means to him. Of course, Esperanza will be delighted to learn of my departure.

Well, cheer-o, Loretta. I hope someday you find it in your heart to forgive me."

I began walking back towards the lorry, head lowered to half-mast. Chata followed me, tail wagging as if it to dissipate the melancholy surrounding the self.

"You don't get off that easy, Benjamin Graves," shouted Loretta.

I turned around. "What more do you want from me? Flogging around the fleet? *Auto-de-fé*? I grant Esperanza would delight in both, but have I not already humiliated myself sufficiently?"

She pointed towards the sitting room like a stern schoolmistress. "Inside. Now."

Chata ran ahead of me, tail down, and rushed inside the house, apparently convinced Loretta was expressing severe canine disapprobation. I followed, stepped inside, and stood at attention in the sitting room.

Loretta walked towards me, arms still folded and countenance still grim. "Sit down."

I sat as commanded. "Right, er, I mean—"

"Shut up. Do you know what you've put me through?"

"Well, one can imagine. Hence my announced departure."

"No, you can't. Earlier today, I stopped at the Texaco to get gas. Do you know what happened?"

"Er, no. Problem with your vehicle?"

"No. Luis Chavez runs out and yells '¡*Felicitaciones,* Loretta! I'm real happy for you. It's about time that *gringo* did the right thing. ¿*Que no?*' Then he hugged me.

"I just stared at him because I had no idea what he was talking about. I must have looked funny, because he asked me, 'You okay, Loretta?'

"'I'm fine, Luis, I guess.' I smiled and asked him to fill up the tank. I pulled out five dollars to pay, but he told me, 'Forget it, Loretta. It's on me.'

"As I drove away, Luis was smiling, whistling, and waving a dirty rag. Next, I get to the cafe. It was dark inside. Nobody was there. I got out of the car to see what was going on, and do you know who I saw?"

Fate would insist on only one possibility. "Coronado, no doubt."

"That's right." Loretta's tone had become more acidic. "So Coronado rushes over to me. He says '¡*Felicitaciones*, Loretta! I'm real glad for you. That's why I'm chaperoning Señor Graves.'

"I stared at him. 'Chaperone?' I asked him. 'You mean, Bennie?'

"'*Sí*, Loretta. Maria told me I got to make sure he don't kiss Señorita Flower no more, 'cause of your wedding.'"

Hearing the word *wedding*, I groaned, which caused Chata to sit up and growl in my direction. "Loretta, please let me explain."

I sat silently, words unable to form. I mean, admitting one succumbed to a Siren's song might be all well and good over a few pints with one's mates; doing so whilst pleading for mercy with one's girlfriend, with whom one has broached the marriage bond, is quite another. Besides, even as the fairer sex were allowed to fall under the spell of flower-whispering Lotharios, they were singularly unmoved by claims of insanity brought on by heaving bosoms and soft lips.

"Loretta, please," I stammered, "I'm sorry. I'm not a cad. You must believe me. After the, er, incident, I was confronted by Esperanza and, well, telling her we were engaged seemed the best way to squelch her meddlesome efforts."

"Well, are we?"

"Sorry?"

"Engaged. The whole town thinks we are. Only you haven't asked me."

"I, er, I mean, would you like to be?"

"What the fuck kind of marriage proposal is that?" she shouted. This caused Chata to glare at me and emit a cavernous and cringe-inducing bark.

I swallowed heavily and perceived the forehead dampening with perspiration. "Yes, well," I began, attempting to clear the vocal cords. "Will you, er, marry me?"

Loretta eyed me silently. "Aren't you supposed to get down on your knee?"

"What? I mean, right, bent knee it is."

I knelt down, feeling rather unsteady. Immediately, Chata stood up and ran straight into me, capsizing the Graves matrimonial ship. I stared up towards the ceiling whilst Chata proceeded to debride the side of my face with her tongue. "Gah," I cried.

Loretta walked over and stood next to me. "Isn't this how I first met you?" she asked, a broad smile slowly emerging.

"I do recall a similar geography, absent the canine. Shall I propose from here?"

Loretta tapped her foot. "I'm waiting."

I reached into my trouser pocket and extracted a small ring, which I handed to her. "M-hem, Loretta Alvarez, will you marry me?"

She held up the ring. It was a simple gold band with a small diamond.

"Uncle Bill gave it to me some weeks past," I said nervously. "It belonged to Celestina. I was waiting for an opportune moment."

"It's beautiful, Bennie. I accept, but only on one condition."

"Of course," I replied as I raised myself to a standing position.

"Do you promise to behave?"

"A Graves always does his duty," I replied stiffly, "and a betrothed Graves is always a gentleman."

"Even around *chichonas*?"

I swallowed. "Er, yes. I will even maintain Coronado as my chaperone. That should put even the most determined Sunflower off her feed, so to speak."

"No excuses, Bennie," growled Loretta.

"Word of honour, my dear," I replied, raising my hand and offering a three-fingered salute. "If we are making promises, I do have one request of you."

Loretta scowled. "Like what?"

"Do you promise not to run off with any chap who whispers to geraniums?"

"Even if he has rippling muscles, thick hair, and is from Spain?"

"Especially one of those."

Chapter 13

The next day, having reached a matrimonial *modus vivendi* with Loretta, I hoped for a brief respite of normalcy, even by the rather dim standards of Vaca Seca. Thus, when I arrived at the cafe the next morning, I was unperturbed by Paco's galloping over to the front door, copiously urinating, and then disappearing around the side of the building. God might not be in his Heaven and all was certainly not right with the world, but one could at least take comfort in such daily annoyances.

I exited the lorry, walked up the steps, and detoured around the fresh pool. As I entered the cafe, the aroma of green chile enveloped the olfactory, overwhelming even the stale odour of Maria's ever-present cigarettes. I entered the kitchen and espied Maria savaging a scrum of onions and tomatoes. Hearing the door swing open, Maria looked up at me briefly before returning to her chopping.

"Well?" she asked. She pointed her chef's knife towards my chest.

"Sorry?" I replied.

"You just asked Loretta to marry you. About fucking time."

I glanced at the watch. "How can you possibly know already? It was less than an hour ago." I took a deep breath, having temporarily forgotten the rapidity of the town's gossip telegraph. "I mean, yes, we are officially engaged."

"*Bueno*. You better behave. *¿Comprende?*" She pointed the knife menacingly.

"Yes, Maria."

"Now we got work to do. You get the dining room ready. And get me two bags of corn tortillas. Then you gotta cook chicken and some hamburger."

I began to laugh.

Maria looked up at me and exhaled a large cloud of smoke. "What's so fucking funny?"

"Nothing, Maria. Nothing whatsoever. Merely the modicum of normalcy, that's all."

"Huh?"

"Not important," I replied.

"You want something important? Get to work." Maria wiped her arm against her forehead, removing several beads of sweat.

"Please do not worry, Maria. We'll manage for a few days without your sainted sister. How is she? Did she see a doctor about her arm?"

"*Sí*, I guess. Hector's here. He said he was gonna drive her to Española. I ain't seen her today. I hope she didn't get hurt real bad."

"Probably just a sprain. I'm sure your sister will be—what's that expression Uncle Bill uses?— 'back in the saddle' quite soon."

Maria shrugged and returned to her chopping.

I exited the kitchen and began preparing the dining room. Shortly thereafter, Loretta arrived. "Hi, Bennie," she said. She walked over and kissed me as she waved her ring-anointed left hand in the air. "There's a puddle outside the door."

"Yes, I know. I was just speaking with Maria. Afraid we will be rather short-staffed for a few days until Esperanza recovers.

"How is *Tia* Esperanza?" Loretta asked.

"According to Maria, Hector has taken Esperanza to Española to see a doctor. I rather doubt it's serious, although doubtless Esperanza will use her injury as an excuse to do as little work as possible for as long as possible."

"She's not that bad, Bennie," Loretta replied, as she strode proudly into the kitchen to tell Maria the news and show off her ring.

I nodded, not wishing to argue with the newly betrothed, having long ago learned discretion to be far superior to valour, at least in dealings with the fairer sex.

We survived the lunch crowd with relative ease. Mid-afternoon found the three of us in the kitchen. Loretta and Maria were making preparations for the evening, whilst I washed dishes. Presently, we heard the front door open, followed by a stream of Spanish invective. Esperanza had returned.

She burst into the kitchen, followed by the oafish Hector. Her right wing was encased in plaster and held aloft by a sling about her neck. Her demeanour, unpleasant at the best of times, was especially vituperative.

"Six weeks I gotta wear this fucking cast, *Pendejito!*" shouted Esperanza, shaking her left fist at me whilst spewing a cloud of cigarette smoke. "All 'cause of that fucking *chichona.*"

"How long you got to wear that?" Maria asked.

"That *pendejo* doctor says six fucking weeks," Esperanza hissed. She then turned to me. "Six fucking weeks, *Pendejito,*" she shouted again.

I was about to return fire, when I espied Loretta shaking her head. "Er, yes. Sorry about the arm. We shall have to manage, difficult as it shall be."

Esperanza, no doubt having expected a more acidic response, grunted.

"*Tia* Esperanza," Loretta chirped, walking up to Esperanza. "What do you think of my engagement ring?"

Esperanza grabbed Loretta's hand and inspected the ring closely. "Uh, *sí*, Loretta, it's real nice." Then she eyed me. "Where'd you get the ring, *Pendejito*? You steal it from somebody?"

"Actually, it belonged to Celestina. Uncle Bill wished Loretta to wear it, now that she and I are engaged."

"Uh, oh, okay," Esperanza said, apparently unwilling to sully the memory of Celestina.

"Hey, Esperanza," Hector grumbled, "I gotta get back to Santa Fe. I'm gonna go to Rudy's and get some beer before I go. You want some before I take you home?"

"I don't want no beer, Hector."

He shrugged his shoulders. "Okay." He leered at Loretta. "You sure you want to marry a *gringo*? They don't got much where it counts. *¿Que no?*" He jerked his thumb towards me and gestured rudely.

"Always the gentleman, eh, Hector?"

He laughed. "I'm just telling Loretta the truth, *gringo*. She should marry a real man."

With the Graves honour at stake, a challenge was called for. Of course, given Hector's simian bulk, the Graves honour would be pummelled mercilessly. Thus, rather than an outright challenge, I decided upon a verbal assault.

"Perhaps Esperanza needs a real man as well, Hector."

"What did you say, *gringo*?"

"*¡Cállate, todos!*" Maria roared. "Get the fuck out, Hector. You talk about Loretta again and you ain't gonna have no *cojones*. Maria brandished her knife. *¿Comprende?*"

Hector raised his hands in mock surrender. "Okay, okay, Maria. It was just a joke." He jerked his thumb towards me and shook his head. "You want Loretta to marry *that gringo*?"

Loretta eyed me but Maria remained silent.

The silence appeared to unnerve the brute. He turned to Esperanza. "Let's get the fuck out of here," he said, "before your sister does something crazy."

"*Hermana*," Maria said softly, "I'll bring you some *enchiladas* tonight."

"Okay, *gracias*." Esperanza replied. She walked out the front door, followed by a subdued Hector.

"Er, thanks for defusing the situation, Maria," I said.

Maria grunted. She turned to Loretta. "It's real nice of El Vaquero to let you wear Celestina's ring, Loretta. I remember it."

"Thanks, *Tia* Maria. I like it a lot."

"Señor Bennie, you want some advice?"

"Er, I suppose, Maria."

"When Hector starts talking, just don't say nothing. Okay?"

"Er, yes, Maria," I replied meekly.

"I know Esperanza don't do much, but we're gonna need more help."

"Any suggestions?" I asked.

"I dunno," Maria said. "One of you gotta help me in the kitchen. The other's gotta work in the dining room. How about somebody to wash dishes?"

"Yes, quite."

"You go ask Antonio, Bennie. Rudy won't mind."

"But Maria, the lad is only eleven. Or is it twelve now? Regardless, he is rather young for late-night dishwashing, especially as he has school in the mornings. I could enquire of Pedro."

Maria shook her head. "No. We need somebody who is gonna be here every night."

I recalled Pedro's penchant for extended absences and nodded in agreement.

Whilst Maria and Loretta remained in the kitchen, I returned to the dining room to finish preparing the tables. The grey matter continued to ponder suitable personnel. One could not very well ask Uncle Bill or Rudy, although both had assisted bravely when the cafe first opened. Presently, the front door opened, admitting Coronado.

"*Hola*, Señor Graves. Kinda cold outside, huh?"

"Indeed. The temperature in the dining room seems to be dropping as well. Would you mind closing the front door?"

"Oh, sorry." Coronado shut the door and sniffed the air. "Sure smells real good."

"I shall pass along your olfactory approval. Anything else?"

Coronado shuffled his feet. "I gotta ask Maria something. Can I?"

"Can you ask Maria a question? You don't need my permission."

Coronado continued to shuffle his feet.

"Are you all right, Coronado?"

"Uh, I guess so, Señor Graves. But I don't want Maria to get mad at me."

"Well, entering Maria's kitchen always carries a risk, even at the best of times. Would you like me to see if she can spare a moment?"

Coronado shrugged his round shoulders. "Maybe you can ask her for me, Señor Graves."

I felt the sudden presence of an intense headache and sighed. "Ask her what? A bit early for dinner, is it not?"

"Oh, I ain't hungry, Señor Graves. I just ate a *burrito*."

"Then what?" I asked impatiently.

"Can you ask Maria if I still gotta chaperone you tonight? I'm supposed to see my sister."

"Er, yes, Coronado. Kind of you to report in." An idea rose from the depths. "Coronado, how would you like a free dinner every night at the cafe?"

"Every night?"

"Well, every night we are open, that is."

"Sure, Señor Graves." He licked his lips.

"We need someone to wash dishes, Coronado. With Esperanza's arm broken, we are rather short-handed, or short-armed if you prefer."

"I can wash dishes real good, but Maria wants me to chaperone you."

"Precisely my point, Coronado. Because I will be working at the cafe whilst you wash dishes, you will be chaperoning as well."

Coronado stared at me whilst he attempted to comprehend the ability to accomplish both tasks simultaneously. "Uh, I guess. What time do you want me here?"

"Shall we say, five o'clock, Coronado?"

"Okay. But I don't gotta watch."

"Yes, well, I suppose I can retrieve you. Will you be at Joe's store?

"*Sí*, we close at five. I can ask Joe what time it is then."

As there was nothing to be gained attempting to disentangle Coronado's unique logic, I simply ignored it. "Er, yes, an excellent idea," I said.

"Thanks, Señor Graves." He shook my hand vigorously, then turned around and exited the cafe.

I walked into the kitchen. "We have our dishwasher," I announced.

Maria and Loretta looked at me. "Who, Bennie?" Loretta asked.

"Coronado."

Maria's gaze took on a distinctly unforgiving hue. "You hired El Gordo? In my kitchen?"

"Hear me out, Maria. You asked Coronado to act as my chaperone. Well, he can now wash dishes whilst he chaperones. If he is going to sit in the cafe every night and enjoy a free meal, we might as well employ him to perform a useful task."

"Keeping you away from Sunflower is real useful," Loretta growled.

"Of course, Loretta," I stammered. "As I've told you, 'truth, fidelity and honour always' is the Graves motto. It's on the family coat-of-arms."

"And my motto is, I'll cut your *cojones* off if I see you near that *chichona*. ¿*Claro*?"

I grimaced. "Er, quite. For a gentle soul, Loretta, you do seem to share your aunts' warlike tendencies."

"What the fuck is a coat-of-arms?" Maria asked. "How come you write stuff on your coat?"

"What? No, I, well, perhaps I shall show you a picture someday. Besides, Maria, who else is there?"

Maria shrugged, then wiped a wisp of grey hair from her forehead. "*Sí*, okay. I'm too old for this."

By half-four Friday afternoon, Maria, Loretta, and I were in the kitchen, ensuring all was shipshape for the anticipated crowd that evening. Presently, we heard an odd rumbling noise, rather like a train approaching. I had read stories of approaching storms, but the sky was clear. The volume steadily increased as the rumbling began to sound more like a crowd shouting.

Curious, and rather frightened, we dashed out into the dining room. A huge crowd stood in the road in front of the cafe. They all seemed to be fixated on something approaching. Loretta and I rushed out the front door. There we espied, slowly rolling towards the cafe, Roger's massive white bus.

"He's come back!" Loretta shouted, jumping into the air, rather like a schoolgirl. "Roger's back."

"Gah!"

The bus stopped in front of the cafe, whilst the crowd continued to shout and cheer. The windows were heavily tinted, making it impossible to see inside. Suddenly, the *1812 Overture* filled the air. The crowd roared its approval. After a minute, the door opened. Roger emerged. He wore white trousers, white shoes, a bright pink shirt, a dark blue blazer with gold buttons, and sunglasses. He stepped down and onto the macadam as the crowd clapped. Next, three rather ordinary-looking chaps, all of whom carried clipboards, disembarked. They stood behind Roger like midshipmen awaiting inspection.

The music stopped and the crowd began to quiet. "Thank you, all," he shouted, flashing his luminous smile. "I have returned."

"I say, your General MacArthur promised something along those lines in the war, did he not?" I said. Loretta did not hear the question.

Espying us on the *portal*, Roger pointed his forefingers into pistol-like shapes, and quickly lowered and raised them, like a gunfighter shooting an outlaw. He walked towards us, taking extra care on the steps.

"I say, old chap," he said in his atrocious British accent. He extended the well-manicured hand towards me. "I've been a bit of a bounder. But here I am, as promised."

Roger looked hungrily at Loretta and extended his hand to her. "Hello, my dear. You're even more beautiful than I recall. Have you changed your hair?"

Loretta blushed and laughed softly. I cringed. "Bounder, indeed," I thought.

Roger turned around and addressed the crowd from the *portal*. "Thank you all. I've brought a few of my crew with me." He pointed at the leftmost chap. "Jim Peters. He's my cameraman and location scout. And that's Sam Epstein," he said, pointing to the middle chap. "He's my head scriptwriter." He then pointed to the third chap. "Last, but certainly not least, this is Alex Reynolds, my assistant director." The three chaps nodded slightly, but otherwise remained frozen in place.

Presently, like a shark drawn to the odour of blood, Esperanza arrived, the brakes on her lorry screaming to a stop. She jumped out of the lorry, using the plaster cast on her damaged wing like a bulldozer to push her way through the crowd, and rushed up the steps to the *portal*.

"You ready to make the movie?" she said, shaking his hand wildly. "Remember, you said you were gonna pay my sister and me. How much you got? I promised Hector some money to fix his truck."

Roger grimaced. "Uh, that's right." He paused. "You're Maria, right?"

"Fuck no. I'm Esperanza. Don't you remember? You gave me five hundred dollars."

"Uh, yes, of course. My apologies, Esperanza. What happened to your arm?"

"That stupid *chichona* knocked me over, 'cause some fucking mouse was crawling inside her shirt."

"Who?"

"The *chichona*, you know, Sunflower." Esperanza made a rude gesture in front of her chest.

"Oh, yes, of course," Roger replied, a carnal grin spreading across his face. "I must see Miss Sunflower. Where is she?" He glanced amongst the crowd.

Esperanza pointed up the road. "See the old bar? She and her *gringo* boyfriend, they been fixing it up. That's how come I got my arm broke."

Roger placed his hand over his sunglassed eyes and stared down the road towards the old bar. As he did, Sky Blue and Sunflower walked out the front door, which they had demanded

Pedro install immediately following the rodentary incident. Sunflower's curvaceous form was easily discernible.

Noticing the gathered crowd, she and Sky Blue walked towards the cafe, arm-in-arm. Roger followed her movements closely with a vulture-like stare.

The crowd parted for Sunflower. "Hi," she shouted, waving her arm wildly. "You came back!"

Roger raised his sunglasses and rested them on the crown of his grey-golden mane. "How could I not," he said, "when such rapturous beauty awaited? Yours is the face that launched a thousand ships."

Sky Blue tightened his arm around Sunflower's waist.

Roger eyed Sky Blue. "You're a lucky man, sir. Such beauty rarely walks the Earth." He recast his gaze to Sunflower. "I've got my scriptwriter working on a part for you."

Roger turned to Sam Epstein, who nodded and began scribbling on his notepad.

"That's so cool." She slipped from Sky Blue's grip, ran up the steps, and embraced Roger, who allowed his hands to linger casually on her waist.

I arched a sceptical eyebrow and saw Sky Blue grimace. One sympathised; after all, he seemed no match against the well-coiffed, well-ivoried, and oily charm of a Hollywood star in a battle for the attention of the fairer sex, especially one with the attributes and demeanour of Sunflower.

"What a splendid welcome," he shouted to the crowd. "Well, there's much work to be done—locations to be checked, several key roles to be cast—" He paused to study Sunflower. "And script modifications to capture the local flavour. By the way, everyone who wants to be an extra in the film, just give Alex your name. You'll each be paid fifty dollars once we finish filming. And we'll be sprucing up the town. By the time we're done, I promise you Vaca Seca will be transformed!"

The crowd erupted with applause and shouts of "¡Viva Roger!"

Roger flashed his fluorescent, Cheshire cat-like smile to the crowd. "Thank you, thank you all. I'll announce a town meeting soon to go over the details. This is indeed a great day for Vaca Seca!"

I espied Paco, who had surreptitiously climbed up to the *portal*, presumably to provide his particularly liquid opinion of Roger's speech.

The crowd cheered yet again. Roger now raised his hands to quiet them. "You are all so kind. Thank you, *amigos*. Now, I need to speak with Benjamin about some of the details, but I promise to speak with all of you shortly. We're going to make a great movie!"

As the cheers erupted yet again, Paco struck, lifting his leg and depositing a copious volume of urine onto Roger's trouser leg.

"Jesus," he shouted, as he unsuccessfully attempted to place an expensively leathered shoe onto the dog's backside. "Somebody shoot that fucking—" Roger glanced at the crowd, who appeared suddenly displeased with the attempted dog-biffing. Regaining his composure, Roger swallowed and shook the excess liquid off his trouser leg.

"Uh, well, maybe the dog can be in the movie, too," he said as he grimaced. "He can be the town's version of Lassie."

I was vaguely familiar with Lassie, who as I recall was a friendly and well-behaved collie, adjectives that no sane individual would use to describe Paco. But the crowd appeared mollified. Roger waved again, as if he had just been awarded an Olympic gold medal. He then grasped my arm and led me inside, followed by his assistants, and then Esperanza and Loretta.

"Details?" I asked.

He waved his hand dismissively. "Sorry," he said, as droplets of urine fell onto the floor I had mopped an hour before, "but I needed an excuse to get away from that damned crowd. You know what they say about the tired, unwashed masses, eh, old chap?"

"They don't seem to be fatigued, if that's what you mean."

Esperanza, arms crossed, glared at Roger, no doubt waiting for him to open his billfold and disgorge its contents like a cash register. Loretta stood back quietly. She appeared to be entranced by Roger, an ominous sign, especially for one who had been previously cuckolded. Only Maria seemed thoroughly unaffected. She shrugged and returned to the kitchen.

I cleared the throat loudly. "M-hem, Roger, you mentioned transforming the town. What, exactly, do you intend to transform it into?"

He grinned. "Well, old chap, it's like this. First, Jim and I will scout locations—the cafe, the old bar where that lovely Sunflower is, your father's ranch, that sort of thing. We're going to need to build a few sets. And I want to clean up the town square. The locals can earn a lot of money doing that."

Roger then began to inspect the cafe, carefully eying the walls, tables, and floor. "Good God," he muttered, "this won't work. It needs to look much more rundown." He turned to the assistants. "Alex, let's get a few location shots inside. Maybe some dirt for the tables and floor. We could break that front window, too. Then we can build a more realistic-looking set at the studio."

I goggled Roger. "You want to spread dirt inside? And break the front window? Then you intend to construct a movie set cafe because the cafe doesn't look realistic? This is madness."

Roger tut-tutted. "Sorry, old chap. When you're in my business, looking real and being real are completely different. Fake always looks more realistic than real."

"What?" I grimaced, unable to comprehend Roger's gibberish any more than I could Sky Blue's rantings about the local *chi*.

Roger waved his hand dismissively and returned his predatory gaze to Loretta. "Well, my dear, what do you think? Are you ready to star in my movie? You may well end up being famous. And men *love* beautiful movie stars."

Loretta glanced rapturously at Roger. "Famous? But I'm just a waitress. It's *Tia* Esperanza and *Tia* Maria that should be famous. Isn't your movie about them?"

"Yeah, *gringo*," Esperanza said, growling. "Me and Maria, this is our cafe. We done all the work to bring it back and fought those progress roaches you talked about. So when we gonna get our money?"

I shook my head, but remained silent.

"Soon, Esperanza, very soon, of course," said Roger as he flashed the glowing ivories. "But there are a few details we must take care of first."

"Like what? You got Maria and me. You got the cafe. You even got fucking *Pendejito*." She pointed her cigarette dismissively towards me.

"A backstory, for one. And a subplot or two to keep the audience interested."

"Huh?"

"You've seen movies, haven't you? We're telling a story. Well, we need to fill in the details for the audience. Tell them what's happening first, so they'll know. Adding a subplot or two provides some relief. Breaks up the action and lets the audience catch its breath."

"Huh?" replied Esperanza, who now looked uncharacteristically like the proverbial deer illuminated by headlamps.

Roger turned to his scriptwriter. "Sam, I want a love interest as part of the backstory." He then returned his gaze to Esperanza. "Are you in love with anyone, Esperanza?" he asked with a hint of sarcasm.

A vision of Esperanza, clad only in the too-short and loosely tied pink sateen robe, crashed over the neurons. "Gah! Er, sorry," I muttered.

"Are you fucking crazy?" she replied.

Roger laughed. "No love interest, then." He turned back to Sam, who was scribbling away madly. "Sam, make a note. I may have to reserve that role for myself and one of our stars."

Whilst the brow attempted to knot itself, Maria burst through the kitchen door, trailing cigarette smoke. "How come all of you still talking? We got to get ready for tonight. ¡*Vamanos*!" She waved the large butcher's knife in our direction, whilst tossing the onion she held in her left hand into the air.

"Entirely my fault, Maria," Roger said with a wink. "I need to speak with my assistant director anyway. Perhaps I shall return for dinner this evening."

Maria stared at him. "We ain't gonna have no dinner unless everybody gets to work," she said angrily, then turned around and rocketed back towards the kitchen.

"She's got spunk, that one," said Roger. "I like that."

He looked around the room until his gaze settled upon Loretta. "Yes, I see big things for you, my dear. *Very* big things."

Loretta giggled softly and returned to the kitchen.

"Cad," I muttered under my breath.

Roger patted me on the shoulder. "Well, cheerio and all that, old chap," he said. "Jim and I will need to look around your uncle's ranch, too. That's going to be part of our back-story, too."

"Of course," I replied, feeling as if I was listening to an inebriated Martian.

Roger waved his hand nonchalantly and then walked to the front door. He opened it and reconnoitred for Paco and any puddles. Then, satisfied he could escape unscathed, he walked down the steps and disappeared into the white bus, which motored away quickly, leaving a large cloud of dust in its wake.

Chapter 14

He's barking mad, Uncle Bill," I said as we breakfasted the next morning. "Bloody, barking mad."

"What exactly did he say?" Uncle Bill asked rather matter-of-factly, before swallowing a large bite of his *tortilla*.

"Rather a lot of twaddle about backstories and romantic interests, which brings me to Loretta. He leered at her like some lecherous hyaena. Rodrigo is a choirboy by comparison."

Uncle Bill drained his coffee cup, then refilled it with more of the sludge-like brew. "Well, pard'ner, I don't know much about Sunflower, but I know Loretta's a good gal. She's not gonna wander off the pasture. Besides, aren't you two engaged now?"

"Well, yes, we are, of course. But I was married to Cynthia. Look where that got me."

"From what I saw, Loretta's a lot more down to earth than Cynthia. That gal was one high-strung filly."

"Er, yes," I replied. "But what should I do about Roger? I mean, isn't that every girl's dream, to be swept off her feet by some Hollywood star, whisked away to, well, wherever it is Hollywood stars whisk girls off to?"

"I wouldn't know, Bennie. Kinda ironic, if you ask me."

"Eh?"

"You and Loretta. You start sniffing after Sunflower. Now you got Roger sniffing after Loretta. Course, I don't think he's really doing that. Hell, he's almost as old as me."

"M-hem. I was not 'sniffing after Sunflower', as you put it, Uncle Bill."

"Yeah, okay, pard'ner," Uncle Bill replied. He grinned at me, shook his head, and took another swallow of coffee. "By the way, where's your chaperone?"

"On his way to Santa Fe with his dim-witted sister. Something to do with her employment at the bank, I gather. One tends to benefit by not enquiring. We've engaged him to be our dishwasher whilst Esperanza recovers. In that way, he can continue his duties as protector of my virtue, at least the tattered remains. Coronado promised to return this evening to undertake his dishwashing duties. However, one doubts he will report on time, if at all."

Uncle Bill finished his coffee, stretched, and stood up. "I dunno, Bennie. Things sure have gotten mighty complicated since you've been around here."

"Me?" I spluttered. "How is any of this my fault?"

Uncle Bill rubbed his stubble-encrusted chin. "I'm not saying it's your fault, except sniffing around that Sunflower gal like a dog in heat. *That's* your fault. I'm just saying—oh, hell, we've got work to do. Daisy's dug a hole under the porch. I want you to fill it in whilst I get some wire to string beneath it. That ought to keep her out."

Hearing her name, the sow emitted a loud grunt, evidently expressing displeasure.

"Perhaps an extra heavy dose of Farm Calm would suppress the subterranean porcine urges," I said.

"Yep. A good dose might do her some good. We got any more?"

"I believe so. If not, Garcia's store always seems to be well-stocked. One of the few items one can rely on his having in inventory."

I walked outside, into the cool morning air. What with the yet-to-be-scheduled nuptials with Loretta, the looming competition from the under-construction art gallery, spiritual centre, and vegetarian restaurant, and the frenzy over Roger's movie, the Graves life had steered into heavy weather.

I found the shovel and a half-full bottle of Farm Calm. As I left the barn, I heard Marjorie, ever baleful, deliver a loud kick to her stable door. I then returned to the house to effect repairs. Daisy, *sombrero* askew, eyed me warily from her usual position on the porch. Then, espying the bottle of Farm Calm, she became noticeably friendlier. I emptied the remains of the bottle into her trough, which she hoovered up. Then, presumably convinced my activities would not adversely affect access to her trough, she returned to the *portal* and fell asleep.

As I filled in the porcine excavation, I heard a lorry speeding down the road towards the ranch, and turned around. It swerved to avoid a large pine tree on the side of the road, then careened around the garage, and sped towards the pasture beyond. Daisy rose up instantly and descended the steps of the *portal*. I opened the front gate. She pushed me out of the way, and trotted around the house ahead of me.

I followed her, walking around to the back of the house. There I espied Joe Garcia, who was scratching Daisy's ears and speaking with Uncle Bill.

"Hey *gringo*—I mean, Señor Bennie," Joe said as he observed my approach. "Uh, how's it going?" he said, with a noticeably strained amicability.

"Eh? That is, I suppose steady-as-she-goes," I replied. "Er, what brings you here?"

"Seems as though Joe wants some of your business advice, Bennie," Uncle Bill said. He paused to straighten his cowboy hat.

"Advice?" I replied warily. Other than avoiding dodgy practices such as selling buildings he did not own, dropping enraged rattlesnakes through windows, and attempted arson, the mind boggled at what sort of business advice to provide him.

"Uh, yeah," Joe mumbled. "I was telling El Vaquero, I was wondering if you could make one of them business strategies for me."

"What? A business strategy? For you? What on earth for?"

Joe removed his hand from underneath Daisy's *sombrero*. "You know, like you did for the cafe. I figure, with the new *gringos* and this movie thing, I could make a lot more money if I had one of them strategies of yours. *¿Que no?*"

I thought back to the business strategy I had put into force for the cafe, which consisted almost entirely of Herculean labours to prevent Esperanza from sabotaging our efforts. "Well, I'm not exactly sure how I could help. After all, yours is the sole mercantile establishment in town, and monopolists tend to do quite well."

"Huh? You think I sell some of those monopo-things? What are they? Do they got them in Santa Fe? What are they for?"

"No, you don't understand. I mean, you own the only store in Vaca Seca. 'Mono' means one."

"But none of the movie *gringos* are buying nothing," Joe said, crossing his arms across his chest.

"Yes, well, they have only just arrived," I replied. "Besides, I'm not sure what sorts of items one purchases when making a movie. Perhaps you should ask Roger. Then you can stock the items he requests."

"I tried, but he just looked at me real funny. You're a *gringo*. Maybe you could ask him."

I glanced at Uncle Bill, who smiled and then surreptitiously drew an index finger across his throat, a most inauspicious sign. "Er, I don't know, Joe. Roger, well, he's rather an odd chap."

Joe grinned and grabbed my hand, then pumped it vigorously, "*Gracias*, Señor Bennie."

"But, I—"

"*Bueno*. I gotta get back to the store. That fat *gringo* said he was gonna come in to buy some more construction supplies for the old bar. I hope his *chichona* comes with him. ¡*Hijole*! Coronado told me she likes you real good." Joe paused and made the same rude gesture Esperanza had made. "You better make sure that fat *gringo* don't got a shotgun. ¿*Que no*?"

I groaned. "If you wish me to help you, I suggest you avoid that rude gesture. ¿*Comprende*?"

"Yeah, okay. I didn't mean nothing."

"M-hem. By the way, how did you manage to sell Sky Blue the old bar? You don't actually own it, do you?"

Joe shrugged. "Nobody does. So, he coulda bought it from anybody in town, even you. I just done it first."

Deciding a response would be futile, I remained silent.

"Okay, I guess I better go," Joe said. "Let me know what that movie *gringo* wants to buy so I can make some money."

He placed his hands in his trouser pockets and sauntered back to his lorry. I watched him drive off in a cloud of dust and then turned to Uncle Bill. "Did I just agree to act as Joe's intermediary regarding his desire to sell obscenely priced supplies to Roger?"

"Yep."

I shook my head and groaned. "Why?"

Uncle Bill grinned. "Why? 'Cause you're living in Vaca Seca, that's why."

"I should have told Joe to put several rattlesnakes in Roger's bus and then hire himself out to retrieve the bloody things."

"He's probably thought of that already," Uncle Bill said.

I raised an eyebrow. "Quite. Well, I must be off to the cafe."

"Don't forget to buy me some more Farm Calm."

On hearing the name of the elixir, Daisy grunted. "Er, yes."

Later that afternoon, after we had survived the luncheon crowd, I decamped to Rudy's bar for a restorative and any accompanying advice he might have about our decision to engage Coronado as a temporary dishwasher.

"You sure about this, Bennie?" asked Rudy, taking a large draw on a Montecristo.

I emptied the last drops of Dusty Trail from my glass. "Only that we're desperate for help, Rudy. With Esperanza having run herself aground, as it were, for, well, knowing Esperanza, time immemorial, we must have some additional help."

Rudy shrugged. "You want Antonio to wash dishes for you? He could probably do it a couple nights a week instead of the bar."

"I shouldn't want him working on school nights. He is only eleven, is he not?"

"Twelve, actually. His birthday was last month. Kid wants me to buy him a pickup. He's always borrowing one of mine so he can drive to Española. He says he's going to the library, but I think he's got a girlfriend there."

"Antonio? You allow him to drive your lorry?"

"Why not? I was driving my dad's old Model T when I was nine."

"Yes, but surely such youthful motoring cannot be legal."

Rudy eyed me quizzically. "Tiny doesn't care. Hell, he wrecked his dad's DeSoto when he was thirteen. Besides, Antonio gives Tiny free rounds at the bar." Rudy smiled to himself, then muttered, "Boy's a natural businessman."

Although thoughts of young children tending bar and motoring about were rather disconcerting, I banished them to the far recesses of the grey matter. "Well, as your grandson's, er, entrepreneurial and romantic activities would appear to preclude him from providing regular assistance, there seems no other alternative than Coronado."

"Hey, you're the boss, Bennie."

"Besides, he will be a vigilant chaperone. If anyone can cool the ardour and keep Sunflower at bay, Coronado can. More importantly, Loretta approves."

Rudy laughed softly. "Yeah, I guess that's right. What's my *querida* think of it?"

"If you mean did Maria threaten violence to Coronado's person, then no. Not yet, at least. She seems rather resigned to the concept. I believe she is rather fatigued by the machinations."

"You make sure she's okay. *¿Que no?*"

"You really are quite fond of her, aren't you, Rudy?" I said.

"Of Maria? Yeah, I guess. I dunno why, but I am." Rudy leaned his desk chair back. "Bill ever tell you the story how we convinced Maria to reopen the cafe and cook?"

I laughed. "He did, actually. I gather you took heavy fire."

Rudy rubbed his right shoulder. "Maria could have pitched in the majors with that arm. Hurt like hell. But we convinced her. Maria can act real crazy, but when the chips are down, she always comes through."

"Indeed. Admiral Nelson would have approved. Not only is Maria fearless, but her aim is true. She would have put the master gunners in the Royal Navy to shame."

"I hear Loretta is wearing Celestina's ring. That was real nice of Bill. You set a date yet?"

My heart skipped several beats. "Er, no, we haven't yet established a precise date. One assumes next summer."

"You having second thoughts, Bennie?" Rudy asked.

"What? I mean, no. That is, I lost a previous marital battle."

"Hey, I've been married and divorced four times," Rudy said, his eyes revealing a slight sadness. "She's a real good gal, Loretta."

"Yes, of course she is. It's just that, we're from two different worlds, aren't we?"

"So? You both tried your own worlds once. That didn't work out real good for either of you. Besides, Vaca Seca's its own world."

"More a world apart." I glanced at the watch, which showed half-four. "Well, thanks for the tipple, Rudy. I must be getting back."

"Bennie?"

"Yes?"

"Make sure Coronado stays out of Maria's way. We don't need any more bloodshed around here. And for God's sake, behave yourself around that *chichona*."

"M-hem," I said, clearing the throat. "Scout's honour." I raised my right hand and made the three-fingered Boy Scout salute—despite having never been one.

Upon returning to the cafe, I found Coronado beavering away in the kitchen, scrubbing detritus off Maria's pots.

"You're early, Coronado," I said. "I thought the store does not close until five o'clock."

"*Sí*, Senor Graves, but Joe told me to leave early. I spilled a bag of sugar on the floor and he got kinda mad."

"Ah," I replied coolly, wondering when Coronado would begin dropping Maria's pots and pans onto the kitchen floor.

"Señor Graves, am I washing dishes okay?"

I peered into the vat of soapy water. "Er, appears to be shipshape."

"Stay out of my way, *gordo*," Maria growled as she passed by us carrying a bag of *masa*.

"Sorry, Maria," whimpered Coronado.

"He's not in your way, *Tia* Maria," Loretta said.

"Good," she replied. "He gets in my way and he's gonna lose his *cojones*."

Coronado nodded as he swallowed heavily. "Sorry, Maria," he repeated. "I won't get in your way."

I glanced at my watch. "Maria, we open in a half hour. Is everything ready?"

"*Sí*. Can you wait tables? I need Loretta to help me in the kitchen."

"Er, any objections, Loretta?"

"That depends on who shows up tonight."

"If you mean Sunflower," I said, as I pointed to Coronado, "my chaperone is sworn to vigilance. Besides, Sunflower's rather pronounced rodentary fear would counsel avoidance of the café, what with the ever-present local population."

"*Sí*, Loretta," Coronado said. "I'm gonna make sure Señorita Flower don't come near Señor Graves." He paused. "I sure am hungry now."

"You get to eat later, *gordo*," said Maria. "You gotta get everything washed first."

The early regulars were gathered at the front door when we opened. The first hour proceeded apace with a steady, but manageable, trade. Around half-six, I stepped out of the kitchen carrying a tray of enchiladas for a waiting Luis Chavez and his brother, Sammy.

"Thanks, Bennie," Luis said, eyeing the steaming mass and golden-coloured basket of *sopapillas*. "Smells real good."

I nodded to Luis. Before I could retreat to the kitchen, the front door opened, admitting Sunflower and Sky Blue. Fate was apparently less indisposed towards mice than Sunflower.

"Hi, Benjamin," cooed Sunflower, whilst she nervously eyed the floor in search of any scurrying rodents. "I told Sky I would try to stay centred."

"You got real good *chi* tonight, baby," Sky said, eyeing her straining shirt.

"Ravishing *chi*," I thought, attempting to resist the Sirens' call. "Er, mice? I shouldn't think so. They generally prefer the kitchen."

Sunflower glanced about, breathed deeply, and secured Sky Blue's hand in hers. "Thanks, Benjamin. It's embarrassing to be so afraid of stupid mice."

"Say no more," I replied as I raised my hand. "We all have our, er, idiosyncrasies, do we not?" Having always sought to avoid Coronado, I now found myself willing him to appear. "Would you like to see the menu?"

"No thanks, man," Sky Blue said. "I think we know what we want."

"I'll have the cheese *enchiladas*," Sunflower said, offering me a luscious smile.

"Same for me, man."

"Two orders of cheese *enchiladas*. I shan't be long."

I retreated into the kitchen. The heart pounded. Droplets of perspiration were erupting on the forehead. "Two orders of cheese *enchiladas*, if you please, Maria."

Maria and Loretta turned to me. "What's wrong, Bennie?" Loretta asked. "Are you sick?"

"Sick? No, merely—gah!" I leaned over and braced myself on a nearby countertop.

"Maybe you better sit down," said Loretta. "There's a chair outside the back door in the alley. Some fresh air will help."

"You see a ghost, Señor Graves?" said Coronado, as the sponge he held dripped soapy water onto the floor. "I don't think it's Alejandro. He always liked *carne adovada*."

I dismissed thoughts of ghostly dining preferences. "Perhaps I should wash dishes. Coronado, you can wait upon the customers."

"Okay. What do I do?" Coronado dried his hands on a nearby towel.

"You keep washing dishes, *gordo*," Maria growled. "Loretta, you help Bennie outside. He don't look good."

"I, uh—"

Loretta removed her apron. She took hold of my elbow and guided me out the back door. "Here," she said as she helped lower me onto the chair. "You just rest for now. I'll wait tables."

"No, Loretta," I groaned. I gripped her right arm tightly. "You should stay in the kitchen."

"Why?" Loretta removed her arm from my grip as her face darkened. "It's her, isn't it?" Loretta pulled off her apron and threw it upon the ground. "I knew it. I'll handle this."

"Please, no, Loretta." I stood up and walked back into the kitchen. "We cannot have another incident like the previous one. Whatever you may think of Sunflower, you cannot continue to spill plates of *enchiladas* in her lap. They are paying customers, after all. You remember what happened when Esperanza frightened all of the customers away? Uncle Bill would not want that." I paused. "Neither would Celestina."

Loretta rested her hands on her hips defiantly. "Fine," she growled, "you take the *enchiladas* to them." She turned to Coronado. "Sunflower is in the dining room. If she tries to come near Bennie, shoot her."

"What?" I said.

"*Tia* Maria, where's your shotgun?" Loretta's countenance had turned red with fury.

"I don't think I should shoot Señorita Flower," Coronado said. "She's real nice."

Maria turned to Loretta. "It's okay. Señor Bennie, he's gonna behave good." Maria then eyed me. "Real good," she repeated.

Maria prepared the two plates of cheese enchiladas, whilst Loretta fried the *sopapillas*. I lifted the plates onto the tray and retrieved the basket of *sopapillas*.

"You watch him real good, Coronado," commanded Loretta.

"Okay, Loretta." Coronado crouched down, as if he were ready to spring out of a trench. "You want me to go first, Señor Graves? I can protect you."

I lifted the tray to my shoulder and groaned. "No."

I walked into the dining room, followed closely by Coronado, and set the tray down on an empty nearby table. "Two cheese *enchilada* plates," I announced, as I set the plates before Sunflower and Sky Blue. Coronado looked on hungrily. It seemed he would begin to drool momentarily.

"*Hola*, Señorita Flower. *Hola* Señor Blue," Coronado said. "I wash dishes now. But I still gotta chaperone Señor Graves."

I placed the basket of *sopapillas* on the table and cringed.

"Chaperone?" asked Sky Blue. He looked at me and scowled.

"Chaperone?" asked Sunflower. "What for?"

"Maria says I got to make sure Señor Graves don't kiss you no more, Señorita Flower, 'cause he's engaged to Loretta."

Sky Blue continued to scowl. "Not cool, man," he said.

Sunflower offered a strained smile. "Congratulations, Benjamin. She's a lucky girl."

"Er, yes, thank you. Of course, you and Sky Blue shall be invited to the wedding. Afraid we have not set a date as yet."

"Sunflower and me talked about getting married," Sky Blue said, "but we decided it's too constricting."

The cranium formed an image of Sunflower wrapped about myself like a python. "Constricting?" I asked.

"Yeah, man. That 'until death do us part' stuff is too heavy. It could really mess up your *chi*."

Although I could not judge the effect of the previous marriage on the tidiness of my *chi*, my own experience had been of the "until a geranium-whispering Spanish Lothario do us part" variety. And, disinclined toward all things Sisyphean, I did not wish to repeat the experience. "Yes, I suppose one should endeavour to not disturb one's *chi*," I muttered. "Well, I trust you will enjoy your *enchiladas*."

With the image of Sunflower as the bewitching *P. reticulatus* still floating in the cranium, I slithered back towards the kitchen, followed closely by Coronado.

Upon entering, Loretta eyed me severely. "Did he behave, Coronado?" she asked.

"*Sí*, Loretta. He told Señorita Flower and Señor Blue about your engagement. Then Señor Graves invited them to your wedding."

I emitted an audible groan.

"What?" shouted Loretta. "You invited them to our wedding? Why would you do that?"

"Er, merely exchanging meaningless pleasantries. I mean, in England one might tell an acquaintance, 'We must have tea one of these afternoons.' And the acquaintance will reply, 'Yes, we must.' Of course, both know there shall never be an invitation to afternoon tea. Merely the obligatory social pleasantry."

"I don't care how fucking unpleasant you have to be. She better not be at *my* wedding." Loretta eyed me in rather a Maria-like manner, *sans* the cutlery.

"Might we postpone this argument until we set an actual date for *our* wedding?" I replied coolly.

Loretta's demeanour devolved into one bearing closer resemblance to Esperanza. She lifted her hand and pointed towards me. Before she could speak, Maria reached out, took Loretta's hand, and pulled it down. "I'm only gonna say this once," she said slowly, "so you both better listen real good."

"Yes, Maria," we replied in unison. Coronado nodded his head with trepidation.

"Loretta, Bennie wants to do what's right. That's how come he wanted Coronado here to chaperone him. You start yelling at him, and he's gonna leave. Once you get married, you gonna have lots of time to yell at each other."

I raised an eyebrow, but remained silent. "Yes, *Tia* Maria," Loretta replied softly.

"And you, Bennie, you remember Loretta's been hurt real bad before. I ain't gonna let nobody do that again. *¿Comprende?*"

"Never in life, Maria," I replied.

"*Bueno*. Now I got two orders of *tamales* ready."

"You want me to remember something, too, Maria?" Coronado asked meekly.

"You? *Sí*. Wash the fucking dishes real good."

Chapter 15

Over the next fortnight, a disquieting appearance of normality enveloped the town. The fauna at Uncle Bill's ranch remained uncharacteristically docile. The cattle refrained from pushing down the fences and invading Felipe Aragón's pasture. Daisy allowed me to straighten her *sombrero* and scratch under her ears. Even Marjorie appeared to have accepted a temporary ceasefire from planting her back hooves into my torso.

Business at the cafe hummed. Paco was content to urinate on vehicles parked in front of Rudy's Bar and any nearby boots. Señor Apestoso continued to arrive precisely at nine o'clock each evening for his *ofrenda*, whilst extending patrons the courtesy of not doing so through the front entrance. No rattlesnakes were nocturnally bunged into the kitchen, nor did any new rumours of ravenous mountain lions devouring hapless patrons circulate.

During this period of preternatural calm, Pedro sawed and hammered—with a punctuality and dedication never before observed by any Vaca Secan—to transform the decrepit old bar into the spiritual centre, art gallery, and vegetarian restaurant.

An overnight voyage to Santa Fe, including dinner and dancing at La Posada, noticeably calmed Loretta's demeanour. Coronado had sought to accompany us, but Loretta had convinced him that she would maintain a weather eye on any errant behaviour on the part of myself.

At the cafe and in town, Coronado maintained his hovering, rodentary presence. He would sleuth about, ensuring Sunflower was not lurking under any of the tables or within the dark surroundings of Rudy's Bar. One afternoon, he burst into the loo in Rudy's Bar, enraging Joe Gonzalez, known by all as Old Joe, who threatened to shoot Coronado if he ever did so again. All in all, the bluebird of happiness, whilst perhaps not singing gaily, was no longer cursing like a sailor.

The calm respite was broken on a Thursday afternoon when Esperanza unexpectedly appeared at the cafe. Although her arm was still encased in plaster, it was no longer in the sling. She burst through the kitchen door whilst venting a large cloud of smoke. "Anybody seen that *gringo*?"

"*Tia* Esperanza," said Loretta, brushing a wisp of hair off her forehead, "You said you weren't going to call Bennie that anymore."

Esperanza pointed her cigarette menacingly at me. "I don't mean fucking *Pendejito*. I mean the movie *gringo*, the one with all the money." She threw the remains of her cigarette onto the floor and crushed it mercilessly.

"Most delightful to see you again, as well, Esperanza," I said icily. "If you mean Roger, we've heard nothing. Perhaps he reclaimed his sanity and rubbished the entire movie idea."

"Huh? But I got to get some more money. I already spent the movie *gringo's* money and Hector needs to fix his truck."

"Then perhaps you should consider returning to work to earn sufficient brass, rather than malingering."

"That doctor says I got to wear this fucking cast on my arm for two more weeks. After that, maybe I come back to help—if the cafe's still in business." She spun the plastered wing and pointed towards Coronado. "With *El Gordo* eating everything, you ain't gonna make no money."

"*Tia* Esperanza," Loretta interjected, "that's not nice. Coronado's doing a very good job. He works hard. Besides, he's Bennie's chaperone."

Coronado, resembling an aproned hippopotamus, nodded whilst scrubbing a large pan.

"Actually, cash flow has been quite acceptable," I said. "We may even remain what we bankers call a 'going concern'.

Perhaps you wish to earn a bit of brass with your labours? Your arm seems rather functional."

"I don't care about your fucking flowing cash or where you're going, *Pendejito*," snarled Esperanza. "I need two hundred dollars now. That rich *gringo* promised me some."

"*Hermana*," said Maria, "Why you want to give more money to that *borracho*?"

"Don't you say nothing about Hector," replied Esperanza. She retrieved another cigarette, ignited it, and tossed the match onto the kitchen floor. After exhaling another cloud into my already watery oculars, she aimed the cigarette at her sister. "You're just jealous 'cause I got a boyfriend. Besides, we both got to get enough money to pay El Vaquero. Then we can get rid of *Pendejito*."

Maria shook her head, then proceeded to stir a cauldron of green chile sauce violently.

"No doubt, we have seen the last of Roger," I chortled. "Your choice is quite simple, Esperanza: either languish in penury or return to work. The manner in which you are waving about that injured wing makes me believe you are quite capable of rendering assistance."

"¡*Vete a la chingada!*" Esperanza blew another large cloud of smoke into my face, then stormed out the back door and disappeared down the alley.

I watched her disappear, then turned around and retreated into the dining room. Loretta followed.

"Bennie, do you really think Roger won't come back?" asked Loretta. "After everything he said? Wouldn't it be fun to be in a movie?"

I had learned one must always exercise extreme caution when replying to rhetorical questions posed by the fairer sex. And so, whilst the Freudian id urged the vocal cords to scream "Are you bloody insane?" the calmer neurons managed a preventative binding and gagging.

"Eh? That is, Roger must consider the profitability of such an endeavour. I mean, a film focused on your barmy aunts? Not exactly one of those Charlton Heston epics."

"I guess you're right," said Loretta, her countenance sagging. *Tia* Esperanza is going to have to come back to work after all. She won't like that."

"Yes, well, neither shall I. Then again, every silver lining must have its cloud."

Chapter 16

The next morning, I arrived at the cafe and discovered that during this fortnight's respite, Fate had been beavering away. She had collected a veritable typhoon's worth of clouds and dutifully pinched any linings that remotely resembled silver.

I stopped the lorry in front of the cafe and espied a large crowd gathered in the town square, which enveloped Roger's large white bus.

"God help us," I muttered, as I exited the lorry and began walking towards the crowd. Luis Chavez's wrecker was parked on the other side of the bus. And next to that was Coronado, who was hopping about like an overweight rabbit.

"*Hola*, Señor Graves," he said. "Did you hear the news?"

"Eh? What news would that be, Coronado?"

"Señor Victor's come back to make the movie! But his bus has got a flat tyre, so Luis is trying to fix it. Otherwise, Luis is gonna have to tow it back to the Texaco station or even Santa Fe."

I was about to comment, when Roger stepped out of the bus. He scowled and eyed Luis Chavez, who was manoeuvring a jack behind the deflated front tyre. "Well?" he growled. "Can you fix it?"

"I dunno," Luis replied, leaning against the bus. "It's pretty bad. You got a spare?"

"A spare? How the hell should I know? I'm not a grease monkey."

Luis stared malevolently at Roger. "Maybe I'm a grease monkey who don't like *gringos*. You want my help or you want to sit here until a tow truck arrives from Santa Fe?"

"Look, I'm sorry, Mister, er—" Roger read the name stitched onto the pocket of Luis's coveralls—"Luis. We have much work to do. I've spent a whirlwind two weeks in Hollywood with scriptwriters and studio bigwigs. I have a very tight schedule to meet. I don't care what it costs, I just need that tyre fixed."

Luis squatted down and inspected the tyre again. "I don't think I can patch it. Looks like it was sliced open, like somebody gutting a trout. I don't know if I got a spare that big at the shop." He stood up, transferred the dirt and grease on his hands onto his coveralls, and then hid his now marginally cleaner hands in the coverall pockets.

"Can you tow it to your shop?" Roger asked.

Luis eyed his wrecker, which was dwarfed by the bus. "I dunno. I better see if I got a spare first." He drove off, then stopped suddenly in front of Rudy's and disappeared inside.

I walked over to the bus and inspected the tyre. A large piece of rubber appeared to have been surgically removed from its side. I glanced at Roger. "Er, damaged rather severely, it would appear," I said.

"Ben, old chap, you understand these people," replied Roger, reverting reflexively to the scabrous British accent. "Can't you get them to speed things up? Time is money, you know."

"So I have been told. However, *mañana* is not something one trifles with in Vaca Seca." Out of the corner of my eye, I espied Luis emerging from Rudy's Bar, cradling a large paper bag. The search for a spare tyre no doubt would be an extended one.

"*Mañana*? asked Roger, as he tapped the face of his golden watch. "What does that mean?"

"Tomorrow," I replied.

"Tomorrow? What the hell happens tomorrow? I need this fixed *now*."

I rubbed my chin. "Nothing, so far as I know. Rather an, er, cultural sort of thing. Nothing so important it cannot wait. Rather reminds me of my banking days. No decision was so important it could not be delayed with an interminable meeting."

Roger kicked the knackered tyre with a well-polished shoe and muttered to himself. Then Joe Garcia approached, whistling some sort of Spanish tune.

"Looks like you got a flat, señor," said Joe gaily.

"Of course I have a flat, you idiot," Roger shouted, "That grease monkey Lewis, or whatever his name is, may not have a spare, either. What am I going to do?"

"Yeah, sometimes Luis don't got stuff you need," replied Joe, whilst he attempted to suppress a Cheshire cat-like grin. "You know, I think I got one. Might even fit your bus."

The eyebrows raced upwards. Joe stocked a variety of goods in his store, but one would not espy bus tyres rubbing shoulders with the *masa* or motor oil.

Roger's eyes lit up. "A spare? That's great! Where's your gas station?"

"Oh, I don't got a gas station, señor. I own the General Store." Joe pointed down the road.

"The store," Roger said. "Yes, yes, I remember now, Mister, er—"

"Joe Garcia, señor," he said, as he extended his arm.

Roger shook Joe's hand vigorously. "You stock bus tyres? That's a miracle. Thank you!"

Indeed, a most convenient miracle, I thought. Although one might accept miracles of the Red Sea-parting or loaves-and-fishes sort, a Joe Garcia miracle was akin to an elephant biffing a snail. Yet, I was unable to fathom how Joe left the ranch, arrived in town, nobbled Roger's tyre, and located a spare in so short a time. Even for someone possessing Joe's avariciousness, this seemed above and beyond.

"Well, I don't really stock 'em, but I got one at the house. I can sell it to you, if you want. Got a rim and everything for it."

Roger smiled and reached for the billfold in his jacket. "Perfect. How much do I owe you?"

"Five hundred dollars," said Joe. One almost expected his eyes to reveal pound signs like a cartoon character.

An errant laugh escaped the Graves vocal cords. Roger turned towards me, then scowled at Joe like an infuriated baboon.

"For one damn tyre?" he spluttered, as his tanned face turned a deep crimson.

"Tyre like that's real hard to come by," said Joe, with feigned innocence. "They don't always got 'em in Santa Fe. You might have to go to Albuquerque to get one otherwise."

Roger stared angrily at Joe, who maintained the artificial innocence. "All right, dammit. Five hundred dollars. I assume you will take a check. I don't have that much cash."

"I don't let nobody except locals pay with checks, and then only if it's less than twenty bucks."

"What? But you know who I am. What about everything I'm doing for this town?"

Joe looked around the square. Two of the *viejos* were asleep under Rudy's *portal* and Paco was quietly urinating on one of the *viejo's* boots. Weeds grew along the sides of the road.

"Sorry, señor."

Roger snorted. "Look, I've got two hundred dollars cash. I'll ask the crew for the rest of it." He handed Joe the money. "Well?"

Joe looked at the money in his hand and smiled. "I don't usually give people no credit. But seeing as you're a Hollywood *gringo*, I guess it's okay."

"Good. When can you have the tyre fixed?"

"Maybe a couple hours. I got to get the tyre, then Luis and me can put it on for you." Joe turned around and walked jauntily to the store; a jaunting Joe presaged further events, none of which would likely be pleasant. But the grey matter could not piece the puzzle together and so instructed me to return to more mundane tasks. I turned around and began walking towards the cafe.

"Just a minute, old chap," shouted Roger, before I could escape. He pulled at my arm. "I must speak with you."

"Damn and blast," I muttered, before coming about.

I sighed. "Yes?"

"Little bastard," said Roger. "Overcharging me like that."

"I'm afraid Joe has you over the proverbial barrel. Unless, of course, you promise him greater riches in the future. We employed such a strategy with success regarding supplies for the cafe. More of a payoff, what? He no longer attempts to set the cafe on fire and the kitchen has remained blissfully free of rattlesnakes."

Roger's eyes widened. He glanced at the bus. "A rattlesnake? In your cafe? You don't think he would—"

I offered a diffident shrug of the shoulders, but remained silent.

"Doesn't he realise what I'm going to do for this town? I mean, look at it." Roger pointed to several buildings in more advanced stages of decay along the road.

"Er, I am quite sure he does, actually. Now, I really must return to the cafe." I gave him a languid salute and walked back to the cafe. As I opened the front door, I turned around and espied Roger driving off in a small car piloted by his cameraman.

For the next several hours, the many-wheeled leviathan remained beached at the side of the road. The crowd had dispersed, other than Paco, who must have thought himself to be in a canine Heaven that offered tyre-urinating opportunities exceeding even his capacious bladder. Maria's radio blared from the kitchen whilst she and Loretta beavered away with the evening's preparations.

Around two o'clock, there was a loud knocking at the front door. Thinking it was Coronado in search of an early dinner, I ignored the knocking and continued my duties as scullery maid. Presently, the kitchen door swung open, admitting Sky Blue, Sunflower, and a panting Coronado.

We turned around and eyed them in unison, and my trepidation rose, what with Loretta within knife-throwing distance of Sunflower, to say nothing of me.

"We're closed," growled Loretta. "What do you want?"

Although she looked stunning, Sunflower was uncharacteristically subdued and said nothing.

Sky Blue moved his fingers to create his peace symbol. "Yeah, we're sorry to bother you, but I was wondering if you could help us out."

"What kind of help?" Loretta said.

"Uh, yeah, well, it's that Pedro dude."

I laughed. "I shouldn't worry. Pedro's binges tend not to last more than a few days."

"No, man. He's quit, for good."

"Eh? He's never mentioned having any other work." I recalled how Pedro had eyed Sunflower previously and been notably punctual. "I thought he rather enjoyed restoring the old bar."

"Yeah, man. He seemed to dig it. Until yesterday."

"Yesterday?" I asked. "What happened?"

Sky Blue looked hungrily at Sunflower. "Me and Sunflower took off in the afternoon. You know, to, uh, get some stuff. When we got back, the door was wide open and Pedro was gone."

"Did you check Rudy's Bar?"

"No. He had brought a six-pack with him and there were still four cans left."

"Perhaps he had to attend to his uncle? Spring him from gaol, that sort of thing."

"I dunno, man. He just grabbed his tools and left. Told us he wasn't coming back and that he was going to Santa Fe. Said he had to get away from here."

I glanced at Loretta and Maria, both of whom wore quizzical expressions. "Why?" I asked. "Pedro seems the rather unassuming, trouble-free type."

"The ghost, man. He said it shook his ladder and threw a hammer at him."

"Sí, Señor Graves," Coronado interjected. "Alejandro must be real mad 'cause Señor Blue and Señorita Flower are fixing up the old bar."

"Stuff and nonsense, Coronado," I sniffed. I turned to Sky Blue. "You don't seriously believe this ghostly bilge, do you?"

"I dunno, man. How else did the ladder get on top of the roof? It's sticking out over the side of the building. Nobody could get down from that."

I waved a dismissive hand. "A trifle, that. I saw a similar trick performed at Cambridge."

Coronado's eyes radiated fear. "Did they have a ghost there, too, Señor Graves?"

The grey matter replayed the fond memory, which had included placing a commode on one of the taller chimneys. It was then I had realised the usefulness of the chaps studying engineering and physics.

"Eh, what?" I said as I returned to the present. "I mean, no, of course not. College prank and all that."

"There was a knife stuck in the wall, too," Sunflower sobbed, "with a furry tail hung over it."

"Sí, Señor Graves," Coronado said. "I think it was a squirrel."

Maria, who had been listening expressionlessly, spoke. "Señor Bennie, you think maybe it's Joe?"

"I was entertaining the very thought, Maria. But Joe is not wont to frighten off paying customers. Of course, your sister is the other likely suspect, although one doubts whether she could hoist a ladder with her damaged wing."

"Why would Joe want us to leave?" Sunflower asked. "He sold us the building. Besides, he paid us twenty dollars just this morning to borrow one of the tires off our bus. Said it was an emergency, and he would put it back real soon."

"Bloody sod," I muttered, reluctantly admiring Joe's creativity.

"What did you say?" Sunflower asked.

"Eh? Oh, nothing."

"Maybe Alejandro's ghost slashed Señor Victor's tyre, too, Señor Graves," Coronado said.

"¡Cállate, gordo!" shouted Maria.

"One doubts Alejandro's ghost would have had the time, Coronado, what with placing ladders on roofs and tossing knives into walls."

"I guess so." Coronado paused, in what for him constituted thought. "Maybe there's another ghost," he said as his rodentary eyes lit up.

"Never mind, Coronado," I interrupted, wishing to avoid reminding Loretta of the floral incident. "Vaca Seca is surely not experiencing some ghostly epidemic. One suspects someone is having a bit of fun, that's all."

"How do we convince Pedro to return, Benjamin?" Sunflower asked. "Sky and I can't do the work on our own."

I pondered the benefits of Sky Blue's and Sunflower's departure, whether ghost-driven or no. But the Graves code did not allow for misplaced fears, even serendipitous ones, to nobble the opponent; the code insisted on victory with honour.

"Er, no, of course you can't. If you wish, I shall speak with him when he returns from Santa Fe."

"You think he's gonna come back, man?" Sky Blue asked.

I hadn't a clue about Pedro's mental process, other than supposing it would not willingly abandon proximity to Sunflower. Then again, Pedro had no apparent conception of time. Nevertheless, one preferred to speculate on the optimistic side, even though optimism and Vaca Seca were generally estranged.

"Well, Pedro did leave four beers unconsumed, did he not? Surely that is an inducement to return."

"Thanks, Benjamin," Sunflower replied. "It's nice of you to offer to speak with Pedro." She started towards me, but was restrained by Sky Blue, if not the ocular daggers I felt in the back of my neck being launched by Loretta, who stood behind me.

Sunflower and Sky Blue departed, mollified that their project would continue. Coronado followed them out, presumably to return to Garcia's store until five o'clock. As soon as Loretta saw the front door close, she rocketed her fist into my shoulder.

"Gah!" I cried. "What was that for?"

"Why did you say that, Bennie? They were ready to give up. You could have told them Pedro was never coming back and they might as well leave now."

"Hasn't Pedro lived here his entire life? I mean, the chap is not the adventurous, swashbuckling type."

"So?" Loretta crossed her arms across her chest.

"Well, did Pedro tell you he wasn't returning?"

"No. But that's not the point. They could be packing up and leaving right now. Instead, you offered to help them."

Maria eyed both of us, shook her head in exasperation, and walked back into the kitchen.

"You want her to stay, don't you?" Loretta continued, readying her fist to strike another blow against the now throbbing shoulder.

The Graves ponderousness in matters of the heart had re-emerged. "Yes. I mean, no. That is, I didn't realise—"

"Forget it," said Loretta, interrupting my mewling apology. "Something else is bound to work." She exhaled loudly. "I guess we better get back in the kitchen and help Maria."

Loretta's anger soon appeared to have blown over. Instead, she seemed almost entranced as she stirred a large pot of *frijoles,* and I heard her laughing softly to herself several times as I chopped and scullery-maided to Maria's orders.

Several hours later, whilst giving the dining room a final inspection, I espied Luis's lorry driving up to Roger's still becalmed bus, followed by Roger and his crew. A large tyre with an emetic orange rim, presumably the one Joe had borrowed from Sky Blue and Sunflower, sat in the bed. Out of curiosity, I ventured onto the *portal.*

Joe and Luis exited the lorry, retrieved the tyre, and effected repairs, attracting several onlookers, including Paco, who christened it in his inimitable fashion.

Roger eyed the orange rim and the worn tread. "Where did you get this?" he asked.

"From the other *gringos,*" Joe replied, making the now common gesture to describe Sunflower. "They had an extra one."

Roger's mood brightened considerably upon hearing that Sunflower and Sky Blue had supplied the tyre. "I'll thank her—uh, them—in person," he said, flashing a lupine smile.

He paid Joe the balance of the promised five hundred dollars. Joe pocketed the money and set sail for Rudy's, whistling gaily.

Luis turned to Roger. "That's gonna be fifty dollars."

"What? I just paid that Joe Garcia fellow five hundred," Roger cried.

Luis shrugged. "Yeah, you paid Joe for the tyre. You still gotta pay me for putting it on your bus."

Roger removed his wallet from his jacket pocket, extracted fifty dollars, and handed the money to Luis. "Are we done?" he asked.

"We sure are, *gringo*," Luis replied, stuffing the bills into his pocket. He then walked towards Rudy's and disappeared inside.

Espying me on the *portal*, Roger trotted over. "Those two ought to work in Hollywood," he said. "They'd fit right in."

"Well, Joe is by far the more avaricious," I replied. "As for Luis, may I suggest a bit more courtesy?"

Roger shrugged. "By the way, I want to bring the crew out to your uncle's ranch tomorrow morning to scout some scenes. Is that okay?"

"I shall inform Uncle Bill."

"Thanks, old chap."

Roger opened the bus's door and ascended the steps slowly, favouring the previously maimed ankle. Then the bus pulled away, leaving a cloud of exhaust-infused dust behind it. I nodded my head slightly and returned to the cafe, prepared to do battle with the evening's customers.

Chapter 17

The next morning, I sat at the breakfast table Florence Nightingaling the left shin, which had suffered a direct hit from a water bucket launched by Marjorie with a precise kick. No gunner could have aimed more true.

"Don't you say a goddamn thing about my little girl," growled Uncle Bill, "or you're gonna be eating beans, and only beans." He slid a large piece of ham out of the frying pan onto the self's waiting plate.

"Twenty-five stone is hardly diminutive, Uncle Bill," I replied. Wistful musings on Daisy's ultimate fate vanished like the steam rising off the plate. "As for any future porcine trans-mogrification to, er, something more utilitarian, perish the thought."

Uncle Bill grunted. We proceeded to discuss, as we did every morning, the upcoming events of this day—fence mending, wood stove cleaning, and hay stacking, to say nothing of my cafe-related duties for the evening. Presently, the roar of an engine was heard outside.

"Who the hell is that?" asked Uncle Bill. He stood up, then drained the viscous remains of coffee from his mug, before setting course for the sitting room window.

I stood up and followed. The time was half-seven.

From the window, we espied Roger's bus. It was parked in front of the small garage, engine idling loudly and belching sooty black exhaust. Roger stood beside it, carrying a clipboard and a tape measure. Jim Peters, the cameraman Roger had introduced to us on his previous visit, stood beside him. A large, silver-coloured metallic case lay on the ground between them.

Roger was pointing to various objects, including the large steer that had thrust its head over the fence to investigate. Jim held a small instrument, something like a compass, up to his eye with his right hand and rotated to and from it whilst gesticulating wildly with his left.

"I say, I distinctly informed Roger to arrive at ten."

"Hell, we might as well get it over with, Bennie," replied Uncle Bill. "You say he wants to look the place over?"

"Er, yes. I gather he wants to evaluate the scenery. After all, one supposes the ranch is like Genesis—resurrection of the cafe began here."

Uncle Bill walked towards the front door, where on a small coat rack hung his cowboy hat. "I dunno. I just tell myself I'm gonna be able to buy a real fine bull 'cause of this nonsense."

We stepped outside the front door onto the *portal*. Daisy was pushing on the gate, wishing perhaps to enquire of Roger about a larger role.

"Hullo, Roger," I shouted, waving my hand. He raised the clipboard slightly in acknowledgement and continued pointing at various objects—the barn, the ranch house, the staring steer, as well as the mountains to the north.

Presently, Roger walked towards the front gate, where Daisy remained on guard. Her *sombrero* was tilted to the side and had slid over her eyes. As Roger approached, she grunted loudly.

"There's a good pig," he said, extending his arm over the gate and scratching her ear.

Uncle Bill pushed his cowboy hat higher upon his forehead. "Not many city folks would come right up to her. I guess Daisy took a liking to you when you were here."

"Er, yes," I said, recalling my own, rather less cheerful, introduction.

"May I come in?" asked Roger, his hand on the gate latch.

Uncle Bill nodded. "Yep. Daisy's being mighty neighbourly this morning. How's the ankle?"

"Still a bit sore, but not bad." Roger looked at me and reverted to the tawdry accent. "Stiff upper lip, eh Ben?"

I sighed deeply. As difficult as the locals found my speech, at least the accent was authentic, rather than some clownish Hollywood imitation.

Roger opened the gate and continued to scratch Daisy's ears. The sow seemed unusually docile, more so than after a dose of Farm Calm. She trotted beside Roger like a puppy as he approached the *portal*. He scaled the steps slowly and carefully. On deck, as it were, he shook Uncle Bill's hand vigorously, then repeated the exercise with me.

"Good to see you again, Mister Graves. I hope we didn't arrive too early this morning. I wanted our cameraman to test the morning light and shoot some film. Do you mind if we film in your living room, too? After all, the story begins right here."

Uncle Bill adjusted his cowboy hat and pulled up his jeans. "Okay, c'mon in," he said. "You and your cameraman want any coffee? I still got some in the pot."

Roger, likely recalling the strong flavour from his previous, involuntary stay, grimaced. "Uh, no, I, uh, already had several cups and, uh, Jim doesn't drink coffee," he said. "Thanks anyway."

We stepped inside the house. Roger glanced about the sitting room, stopping to focus on the framed picture of Celestina on the mantelpiece.

"Your wife was quite beautiful," Roger said, lowering himself slowly onto the sofa. "I've got a few actresses in mind to portray her."

Uncle Bill looked wistfully at the picture. "Yep, she sure was. Not a day goes by that I don't miss her."

"Of course not," Roger replied. "Now, I know we've had a few discussions about the rights to your story. So, I've got some figures in mind for that, plus filming some scenes right here."

"How much we talking about?"

Roger cleared his throat. He raised his fingers slowly, interlocking them and extending the two index fingers over his chin. "Well, typically we option rights, but in this case, I've been given the green light by the studio. Er, how about two thousand, total? You could do a lot with that much money."

I raised an eyebrow, but remained silent. Uncle Bill removed his hat and ran his fingers through the thinning pate beneath it. "Two thousand, huh?" he said, no doubt calculating the equivalent bovine purchasing power. "Well, I reckon—"

Before Uncle Bill could say anything more, he was interrupted by a loud crash and Jim screaming "No!" There followed the sound of Daisy squealing and then a loud moan. We dashed outside. Jim lay face-down upon the ground outside the fence. The large metallic case that had been beside him earlier was nowhere to be seen. Nor was Daisy. Presently, we heard a second squeal, the sounds of pine tree branches snapping off, and a second, rather more violent thud.

"Goddamn it," shouted Uncle Bill as he raced down the steps and out the open gate. I followed quickly, dreading discovery of the extent of the porcine destruction.

"Jim, what happened?" Roger shouted. He hobbled after me.

We reached the still-prone cameraman. Jim groaned and lifted himself slowly onto his hands and knees. "Ohhh," he groaned.

"Jim, what happened? repeated Roger. "Are you okay?"

The cameraman rose up, holding a hand against his ribcage. "Pig," he moaned. "Knocked me over. Light meter. I think it ate it." Jim glanced around. "Pig," he repeated as he stared at Roger.

Daisy was nowhere to be seen. Presently, we heard her squeal and yet another loud thud. The sound came from down the road towards Felipe Aragón's ranch. Uncle Bill and I ran down the road. Before us, Daisy was standing over the crumpled and open camera case. She bent down and took the handle in her teeth, ready to launch another fusillade.

Uncle Bill waved his arms wildly. "Daisy! Put that goddamn thing down!"

Daisy released the handle. She looked at us, although her *sombrero* had slipped down and was covering her eyes, and grunted contentedly. Uncle Bill ran up to her whilst unleashing a torrent of obscenities. I followed at a discreet distance, not wishing Daisy to mistake me for a two-legged valise.

A large camera lay next to a rock perhaps ten feet from the case. Jim walked over to the camera and began to inspect it. "My Bolex," he whimpered.

Uncle Bill removed his hat and placed it over his heart. We stared at the damage mutely. Daisy grunted again, no doubt proud that her valise-tossing record remained unblemished, and sat down on her haunches.

Roger hobbled up to us. "Sorry," Uncle Bill said.

"Jim!" Roger shouted. "How bad?"

Jim looked at Roger and shook his head. "Bad. The lens is broken and the film holder is bent. I dunno, maybe it will still work. I can check the rest of it out when I get back to the bus." Jim turned to Uncle Bill. "What got into that pig of yours?" he asked.

"She's got a mind of her own," said Uncle Bill. "I'll pay for the damaged camera. You can take it out of what you were gonna pay me."

Roger grimaced. "Christ, this place must be cursed," he muttered. "All right, change of plan Jim. Let's head back to town. Might as well start lining up our town location shots, even if we can't film them." Roger then turned to Uncle Bill. "Maybe we won't bother filming here," he said. "One ranch will look like any other to moviegoers. There's a few north of L.A. we can use. Probably some stock footage, too."

Uncle Bill shrugged. "Suit yourself. Like I said, I'll pay for the damage."

Roger grunted. "Yeah, okay." He turned to Jim. "Let's get back to town."

They walked slowly back to the bus and hoisted themselves inside. The bus's engine roared to life and drove away, leaving a cloud of dense black smoke in its wake.

"Wonder how much that camera's gonna cost me," said Uncle Bill. He took off his hat and slapped his leg with it. "Goddamn that Daisy."

"I shouldn't worry about the camera," I replied. "As for Daisy, perhaps you should post a sign on the front gate: 'Abandon all valises ye who enter here.'"

Uncle Bill laughed. "Yep. I dunno what about 'em gets her so riled up."

"Perhaps a porcine intolerance for sharp corners," I said. "Well, I should motor into town myself before Maria becomes overly enraged."

"You gettin' by without Esperanza?"

"In a manner of speaking, but we are rather strained at present, even with Coronado's help. Her ability to avoid gainful work is rather disconcerting, especially as she seems quite fixated upon the prospect of Hollywood lucre."

ROGER VICTORY
PRESENTS:

TOWN MEETING
1 P.M. SATURDAY
Old Church

Roger will brief the town on movie preparations, schedules, and <u>your</u> duties.

Remember—<u>you</u> want Roger's movie to be a **BIG** hit.

Please be prompt! Refreshments will be served.

"Sounds like Esperanza. Hey, before you go, can you give me a hand hitching up the trailer? I gotta get some more hay."

I assisted Uncle Bill as requested, then motored into town. When I arrived, I espied a large sign posted on Rudy's front door. Several of the local *viejos* were gathered around it.

The sign was also posted on Joe Garcia's front door. Coronado stood before it, staring intently despite his inability to read. I parked the lorry in front of the cafe. The same sign was posted on the front door of the cafe. I exited the lorry, climbed the steps to the front door, and proceeded to read.

"Mad as a hatter," I muttered, before opening the front door and stepping inside. I strode into the kitchen, where I found Maria and Esperanza jabbering and chimneying away. Esperanza held a small paring knife in her hand and gesticulated frenetically. A small scrum of chopped tomatoes lay in front of her upon the cutting board.

"*Buenos días*, Maria," I said cheerily. I then turned to Esperanza. "Should you not be in hospital? After all, your arm may become gangrenous should you use it to perform actual work."

"Fuck you, *Pendejito*," replied Esperanza with a reptilian stare. "My arm's okay. I just gotta get this fucking cast off, that's all."

I glanced at the chopped tomatoes. "Are you quite sure you are not suffering from the vapours, or some other mental depredation which has caused you to act so rashly? Then again, perhaps I am hallucinating."

"What the fuck are you talking about, *Pendejito*?" she snarled.

Maria proceeded to laugh in a most un-Maria-like manner.

Esperanza folded her arms across her chest and scowled. "What's so funny, *hermana*?"

"I don't understand what Señor Bennie says," replied Maria, as she pointed to the tomatoes with her knife, "but I think he's making fun of you chopping tomatoes."

Esperanza eyed me and hissed. "I work plenty, *Pendejito*."

"Far be it for me to disparage productive activity, Esperanza," I replied. "One is merely confused, as you previously appeared to be in no hurry to return. Why the sudden change?"

Esperanza stabbed the cutting board with the paring knife. "I need the money. And, 'cause Hector's staying at my house. He's making me crazy."

"An experience we have all shared. In any event, welcome back. We have been rather disadvantaged without your assistance."

"Uh, okay, *Pende*—Bennie. You gonna fire El Gordo now? I don't want him eating all our profits."

"Actually, I would like to retain his services, if that's all right with Maria. He has proven to be a most diligent dishwasher. Besides, Loretta will insist on his continuing to serve as my chaperone."

"*Sí*, okay," muttered Maria from behind lips that tightly grasped her cigarette. "Long as he don't get in my way."

"Never in life, Maria," I replied. "And Esperanza, you would not wish to disappoint Loretta, not with our impending marriage, now would you?"

Esperanza erupted with a shotgun blast of Spanish, the majority of which, excepting several especially colourful words one would not use in mixed company, escaped my translation. Then she paused. "Uh, *sí*," she added.

"Did you see the sign on the front door?" I asked.

They both stared at me quizzically. "Sign?" asked Esperanza. "We came inside through the kitchen."

"There is a sign on the door announcing a town meeting this Saturday at the old church. Apparently, Roger shall deliver our marching orders Saturday regarding his movie."

"*¿Que?*" Maria asked.

"Sorry, Maria," I replied. "The sign says that Roger will inform us of his schedule and what he expects from all of us."

Maria looked at me blankly and shook her head. She turned away and began to mince the green chiles that lay upon her cutting board.

"What he expects from us?" repeated Esperanza. "I don't understand."

I shrugged. "A riddle, wrapped in a mystery, inside an enigma, as Churchill said."

"This Churchill makes movies, too?"

"Eh, what? You know, Winston Churchill. Prime minister. Led my country during the war. Surely you've heard of him?"

"Another fucking *gringo*," muttered Esperanza. "Now, I gotta see this sign." She rammed through the kitchen door and disappeared.

Esperanza soon reappeared with a quizzical expression. "Duties?" she asked. "What duties we got?"

"One presumes we shall be informed on a need-to-know basis," I replied.

Esperanza shook her head and retrieved the paring knife, then proceeded to chop the remaining tomatoes. "*Gringos*," she hissed.

A half-hour later, we heard the front door open and I stepped into the dining room to investigate. Standing before me, resplendent in navy blazer with gold buttons, crisp white trousers, and light blue shirt, stood Roger.

"I say, old chap," he said, shaking my hand with an odd vigour, "good of you to receive me on such short notice."

"Eh?" I replied, as the grey matter began beating to general quarters.

"About Saturday's meeting."

"Yes? I have read the sign you posted on the front door."

"Good. Then the Dos Ah-boolas will provide the mentioned refreshments?"

"What?"

"Nothing fancy, of course," said Roger. He waved his hand casually. "A light luncheon menu will be acceptable. I find *canapés* and *petits fours* are always appreciated.

"*Canapés* and *petits fours*?"

"Precisely, old chap. Enough to serve several hundred people."

I inhaled deeply. "Anything else?" I replied dryly. "Several cases of Louis Jadot and Dom Perignon, perhaps?"

Roger's eyes sparkled. "That would be splendid, old chap! I do especially love Dom. I would recommend the fifty-five. The fifty-four is a bit disappointing, don't you think?"

"M-hem, yes. Er, about your menu, Maria is in the kitchen at present. I am sure she will wish to discuss it with you directly."

"Of course, old chap. Lead on."

We stepped into the kitchen. Maria and Esperanza looked up and eyed Roger suspiciously.

"My dears," he said gaily. "How very nice to see you again." Roger held out his hand and displayed the fluorescent smile.

Maria and Esperanza exhaled large clouds of smoke simultaneously, but remained silent.

"I was just discussing Saturday's meeting with Bennie," continued Roger, unawares. "I am hoping the cafe will provide refreshments. I suggested to Ben that a light luncheon, including *canapés* and *petits fours*, would be acceptable. I'm not sure how many of your townspeople will attend, but I would plan for several hundred."

Maria raised her chef's knife. "*¿Que?*" she said, eyebrows knitting together.

"You want us to make lunch for two hundred *lobos?*" Esperanza growled. "What the fuck are canopies?"

I retreated to the relative safety of the kitchen door in the event a hasty retreat would be required, and waited for the forthcoming eruption.

"*Canapés*, Esperanza," corrected Roger haughtily, in a French accent as phoney as his English one, "are small appetizers. *Petits fours* are bite-size cakes, hence the word 'petite'."

Esperanza eyed Roger coldly. "We ain't gonna make none of your petite canopies shit."

"But I always find meetings to be more productive when refreshments are served," replied Roger.

"You want *enchiladas* and *tamales*, we can make those." She jerked her thumb towards the self. "Even *Pendejito* knows how to make *tamales*. Five bucks each. You want enough for two hundred *lobos*, that's gonna cost, uh—"

"One thousand dollars," I interjected.

"You expect me to pay?" Roger sniffed. "I'm making a movie that will allow your town to rise up from its decrepit ashes. The townspeople will earn money as extras. You and Maria will have small but consequential roles, for which you shall be paid. And yet you expect *me* to pay for this lunch?"

One detected both grandmotherly fuses smouldering towards detonation. "Look, *gringo*," said Esperanza, "you want lunch, you gonna pay like everybody else. We already got too many *lobos* trying to sneak outta here without paying."

Roger turned around and stared at me. "Ben, old chap, surely you can talk some sense into Esperanza and Maria? This entire effort—my effort—is for your town's benefit."

"Er, afraid not—old chap," I replied, haughtily. "Immovable object, what?"

"What am I supposed to do?" he asked.

"Perhaps you should enquire of Joe Garcia," I replied. "For the right price, he will motor to Santa Fe and return with whatever comestibles you wish to serve. Then again, Santa Fe is not St. Moritz, and I shan't imagine you will find *canapés* and *petits fours* on offer. Perhaps a luncheon of *frijoles* and *tortillas* instead?"

Roger scowled. "To hell with lunch." He turned and limped past me into the dining room and out the door.

"*Pendejo*," Esperanza muttered.

Half-twelve on a cold and grey Saturday found us—Uncle Bill, Loretta, Esperanza, Rudy, Maria, and the self—huddled in the cafe kitchen. Maria was immovable, reminding me of Marjorie at her equine worst, less the well-aimed hooves.

"Maria, surely you are curious to learn more about Roger's movie," I said, watching as she cycloned a large pot of red chile sauce. "The movie is *about* you, after all. None of us would be here if it were not for your cooking."

"Bennie's right, Maria," said Uncle Bill. "Every time I come in here, I think about Celestina. That's all 'cause of you."

"Please, *Tia* Maria," Loretta added.

"You'll be famous, *querida*," said Rudy.

"*Hermana*, we need that *gringo's* money," Esperanza whined.

Maria glared at the assembled group, looking like an aproned and knife-wielding cobra ready to strike. "I got work to do."

She turned around, walked into the storage room off the kitchen, and slammed the door shut.

"Stubborn as a mule," Uncle Bill grumbled, as he shook his head. "Always has been. Guess she's always gonna be."

"*Sí*," said Esperanza.

"She's just shy," added Rudy.

"Perhaps you could speak with her, Rudy," I said. "She listens to you, albeit in her own, rather unique way."

Rudy shrugged. "Okay, I can try." He gave us a mock salute and walked over to the storage room door.

"*Querida*," he said gaily. "Can I come in?" Rudy opened the door slowly and disappeared from view.

Presently, we heard a torrent of abusive Spanish.

"*Querida*, no!" shouted Rudy. There was a loud thud. "Ow!" he cried. "C'mon, Maria, put that down!" We heard a second loud thud. The storage room door opened. Rudy emerged and the door quickly slammed shut behind him. He was rubbing his left shoulder and I espied a large, reddish depression above his right eye.

Uncle Bill raised an eyebrow. "Looks like Maria's aim is still real good."

Rudy groaned.

"Let's get you into the dining room so you can sit down," said Loretta. "Bennie, get some ice and a dish towel." Loretta then put her arm around Rudy's waist and escorted him out of the kitchen.

"Esperanza, you talk to her," Uncle Bill said.

"Are you fucking crazy?" shouted Esperanza. "I ain't going in there."

Possessed of ice wrapped inside a towel, I walked into the dining room, followed by Uncle Bill and Esperanza.

Rudy glanced up at me, then reached for the towel and placed it on his forehead. "Bennie," he moaned, "could you run over to the bar and bring me some whisky? And you got any aspirin? My head hurts like hell."

"Right ho. The first-aid kit contains aspirins, and I shall return with your liquid restorative momentarily."

I rushed out the front door, narrowly averting the small puddle Paco had deposited, and bounded towards Rudy's Bar. Approaching the front door, I encountered Coronado, who was exiting, the pudgy fingers of his right hand grasping two beer bottles.

"*Hola*, Señor Graves," he said. "Are you getting some beer for the meeting, too?"

"Er, no, Coronado. Merely retrieving something for Rudy, who has suffered a slight accident."

"An accident? Is his truck okay?"

"What? No, I mean, in the cafe."

Coronado's eyes widened. "Rudy crashed into the cafe? It looks okay to me."

"What? No, I shall explain later," I said, not wishing to prolong the grey matter's agony further. "Are you attending the meeting?"

"*Sí*, Señor Graves. What time is it?"

"Almost one o'clock. Off you go, then." I went into the bar, asked Anthony for a bottle of whatever whisky his grandfather favoured, and exited, only to encounter Coronado again.

"Maybe I should ask Luis Chavez to drive over to the cafe. He's said he was gonna be at Señor Victor's meeting, too."

"Luis? What on earth for?"

"To tow Rudy's truck. Once, I wrecked my truck and tried to drive it back home. But the front wheel came off in a ditch. Then I gotta ride with Old Joe 'cause he was—"

I sprinted back to the cafe, abandoning Coronado in midsentence. Inside, Rudy was still sitting at the table, holding the ice pack to his forehead. Loretta and Uncle Bill sat next to him. Esperanza was absent, perhaps in the kitchen.

"Bushmills, eh?" I set the bottle down upon the table.

"Huh? Anthony give that to you? That's supposed to be just for real special occasions."

"I asked him for your favourite. Let's get you a glass."

I poured Rudy a bracing dose, which he gulped down.

"Another?" I asked.

"Hell, yes," Rudy replied. He quickly extinguished the second glass.

"Whoa, pard'ner," said Uncle Bill. "We don't want you falling down and hurtin' yourself."

"Yeah, I know," Rudy replied. He removed the towel from his forehead. "How's it look?"

Three sets of eyes surveyed the damage. "The area appears to be swelling and has acquired a purplish hue," I said.

"What'd she hit you with?" Uncle Bill asked.

"She hit my shoulder with one of those big cans of *posole*. And this," said Rudy, pointing to his bruised forehead, "was a goddamn potato."

Loretta stifled a laugh. "I'm sorry, Rudy. I shouldn't laugh."

Rudy smiled. "That's okay, Loretta. I'd laugh, too." Which he did. "Now you know how to keep Bennie in line."

"I would prefer not to be endangered by tuberous artillery," I said.

"You better remember that, Bennie," said Loretta. She wagged her finger.

"Er, yes." I glanced at my watch, which read almost half-one. "I say, should we decamp to the town meeting? Rudy, do you wish to remain here?"

Rudy removed the ice from his forehead. "No, I want to hear what Roger has to say."

We walked over to the old church. On the front of the door a new sign, *sans* mention of refreshments, was posted.

"Rather surprised he did not include a list of *dramatis personae*," I said.

ROGER VICTORY
PRESENTS:

TOWN MEETING
1 P.M. SATURDAY
Old Church

Roger will brief the town on movie preparations, schedules, and <u>your</u> duties.

Remember—<u>you</u> want Roger's movie to be a **BIG** hit.

We walked inside and sat down on one of the well-worn wooden pews. There were perhaps ten people seated inside. Roger paced at the front of the church, resplendent in his Hollywood finery. He glanced at his watch, then at the small audience, and then at his watch again.

"Where is everyone?" he asked.

Coronado raised his hand. "My sister said she was gonna be here, Señor Victor," he said. He slowly removed a wrapped package from a greasy shirt pocket. "If you're hungry, you can have some of my *burrito*. I made it myself."

"No I don't want your *burrito*," replied a scowling Roger. He glanced at his watch and tapped lightly upon its face.

"Folks 'round here have a different sense of time than they probably do in Hollywood," said Uncle Bill. "They call it '*mañana*.'"

"Tomorrow? They think the meeting's tomorrow? My God, don't you people even know what day of the week it is?"

Uncle Bill rubbed his chin. "No. What I was tryin' to say is that folks 'round here aren't real punctual. Not much you can do about it, either."

"Well, time is money in my business."

"I expect they'll show up soon enough," said Uncle Bill.

Presently, Sky Blue and Sunflower entered the church. She wore a light green blouse and jeans, both of which strained to enclose her curves.

"Hi, Roger," Sunflower said, waving excitedly.

"Well, hello, my dear," he replied, as he examined her carriage. "What a delight to see you again. Would you care to sit up front near me?"

"Sure," chirped Sunflower, who detoured towards the frontmost pew. Sky Blue grunted and followed her.

I felt a sudden pain in my right shoulder. "Ow," I muttered. I turned to Loretta and raised an eyebrow.

"You stop ogling her," she hissed.

"But, I—"

"Shut up," said Loretta.

I shrugged, knowing this particular skirmish was lost. I glanced to my left. Coronado was standing next to me, smiling and nodding. His right hand held the now half-consumed burrito; his left a half-drained beer bottle. "*Hola*, Loretta. You want me to chaperone Señor Graves so he don't look at Señorita Flower?"

"Please do, Coronado," said Loretta. "Bennie, scoot over and make room for Coronado."

"Bloody hell," I muttered again as we slid right. Coronado sat down heavily next to me, followed by a strong odour of alcohol and overcooked beans. "You want the rest of my *burrito*, Señor Graves? I'm kinda full."

"No, I do not want the remainder of your bloody *burrito*," I said through clenched ivories.

More individuals dribbled into the church, including Coronado's rodentary sister. By two o'clock the church was nearly full and infused with chatter in Spanish and English.

Roger stood at the pulpit and raised his hands. "Excuse me, everyone," he said. "Everyone, please!" The church quieted. "Shall we start?" He cleared his throat. "Thank you for coming. Today is a glorious day for your little town because—"

"—Hey *gringo*," one of the *viejos* shouted, "that sign on Rudy's door said there was gonna be refreshments. You got any beer? I could sure use one."

"We have no beer," said Roger icily. He glared at the self. "I'm afraid we have no refreshments of any kind."

"Now, if there is nothing else," continued Roger, "let's get started. We're in your church today, which is appropriate. My movie, which I am going to call *The Miracle Cafe*, will be your town's salvation.

"After people see my movie, they're going to want to come here and see for themselves where the miracle of the Dos Ah-boolas took place. Tourists will flock to your town; tourists, who will bring money for all of you.

"And some of those tourists will decide they want to live here. Think of that. New jobs, refurbishing the crumbling hovels you live in and building new houses. Money that can be used to repair buildings and open new businesses. Money to restore this fine church we are in today. A health clinic to take care of the sick and injured. New equipment for schools, to better educate your children." Having witnessed far too many political speeches, the Graves eyes rolled and the ears shuddered.

Roger paused—one of those dramatic pauses intended to allow the audience to applaud—and displayed his luminous ivories. The room remained silent.

Presently, Sunflower began to clap enthusiastically. The locals smiled—well, the male locals smiled as their wives scowled—and began to clap, too. Roger lowered his eyes towards Sunflower's blouse.

"It sounds wonderful, Roger," said Sunflower. She turned to Sky Blue. "Doesn't it sound wonderful, Sky? Just think about those tourists who will come to our Siddhartha."

Sky Blue espied Roger ogling Sunflower. "Yeah, baby, it's real cool."

"Your enthusiasm is contagious, my dear," said Roger. "I may have a special role in the movie in mind for you."

Roger appeared ready to resume his soliloquy when the church door opened, admitting Esperanza and Maria, the latter's left arm within the iron grasp of the former's right hand.

"Ladies and gentleman," Roger shouted like a traveling carnival barker, "please welcome the two, er, ah-boolas, Esperanza and Maria. *The Miracle Cafe* is about them."

More clapping erupted. Maria wrenched her arm free from Esperanza's grip and crossed her arms tightly. She sat down in the last pew and attempted to hide behind Sheriff Tiny's girth.

"What a bloody charlatan," I whispered to Loretta.

"Don't be a killjoy, Bennie," replied Loretta, staring reverently at Roger. "Just think what our little town could become."

The grey matter displayed an image of thundering herds of swivel-eyed tourists crashing through town, led by a blueblazered Roger sitting upon a white stallion.

"Thank you, thank you all," Roger continued, motioning for silence. "Now, there's much work to be done if my vision is to come true. First, if you want to be an extra and earn fifty dollars, you'll need to sign my standard contract." He retrieved a sheaf of papers from behind the pulpit and waved it in front of everyone.

"Second, I would like to begin location filming in town right away. That means I need a really rundown building to serve as the "before" picture for the cafe. Any suggestions?"

There was a momentary silence and then Coronado raised his hand.

"Uh, yes," Roger said. "Do you have a suggestion?"

"*Sí*, Señor Victor. My house is kinda run down. Last week, part of a wall fell over. I put a tarp over it."

"Er, yes. I, uh, I'll keep that in mind. Thank you. Anyone else?"

Sunflower raised her hand.

"Yes, my dear?" Roger said.

"Well, we're still working on building our cafe and spiritual centre. It's kind of a mess inside. Would that work?"

"I'm sure you would," he said. "I mean, yes, excellent. Perhaps I should have a closer look later this afternoon, or this evening."

"Okay," said Sunflower, as she rocked up and down in the pew.

I detected a low groan from Sky Blue.

"Maria and Esperanza, where are you hiding?" Roger said, peering into the crowd. "Ah, there you are. Since you will have larger roles in the movie, I've got a special contract for each of you to sign." He reached behind the pulpit and waved another sheaf of papers.

"You gonna give us some more money when we sign?" shouted Esperanza.

"Uh, well, not right away, but we can discuss the contract terms after the meeting."

"No more money now?"

"Esperanza, I already paid you five hundred dollars as a goodwill gesture."

"Yeah, but I spent that. I need some more."

"You gonna buy a new dress and wear it for Hector?" Luis Chavez shouted from across the room. "Maybe one that covers your face? Or you just gonna buy lots of beer so he don't care no more?"

The room exploded in laughter.

"¡*Veten a la chingada, todos!*" roared Esperanza. She stood up and began to move towards Luis. "You want ro say that to Hector, *pendejo?*"

Luis shrugged. "I could, but he's probably too drunk right now to hear me." The room again exploded in laughter.

Esperanza's hands had contracted into fists. Luis stood up and faced her. Then other locals stood up. I envisioned a riot starting within the holy confines.

"Everyone," shouted Roger. "Everyone, please! If my movie is to be a success, I must have all of your cooperation. Now, Esperanza, why don't you sit down? We can discuss your contract terms afterwards."

Esperanza glowered at Luis. "*Pendejo*," she hissed, before returning to the rearmost pew and sitting down next to Maria.

Fisticuffs averted, the crowd murmured as everyone resumed their seats.

"That's better," said Roger. "Now, just a few more matters. Whilst we are filming, would anyone care to cater meals for my crew? Moviemaking is hard work, and I always ensure my crew eats well. If you would like to provide them with breakfast, lunch, and dinner, please see me afterwards and I'll have you sign a contract."

The audience sat stone-faced.

"Okay. Well, just one more slight matter," Roger continued. "As you know, my bus is parked nearby. However, because we will be filming in many locations, I would like to rent several vehicles for the crew. Pickup trucks would be ideal. If you have a truck that you would be willing to rent, please see me afterwards and we can sign the necessary contracts."

He glanced at his watch. "Well, that's all I have. I would like to thank each and every one of you for coming here today. Now, let's go make a movie!"

Chapter 18

Many of the locals shuffled to the front of the church, waiting to sign contracts to appear as extras in Roger's movie. Esperanza, with Maria reluctantly in tow, manoeuvred her way to the front of the line in true Admiral Nelson form. "Get the fuck away from me," she roared. "Maria and me got to sign first, 'cause this movie is gonna be about us."

Ignoring the various epithets hurled at her, Esperanza demanded the contracts for herself and Maria. Roger obliged, retrieving two copies of a bound document about as large as the London telephone directory.

"Here you go, ladies," said Roger. "Now, you both must sign and date each copy. Keep one for yourselves and return one to me. Then we're all set."

Esperanza grabbed both copies. "We got to read this shit?" she shouted.

Roger coughed. "Well, I would never advise anyone not to read a contract, of course, but it's mainly boilerplate. You know how attorneys are."

"What the fuck is 'boilerplate'?" Esperanza asked.

"Oh, that's just another word for standard contract language," Roger replied as he waved his hand dismissively. "No need to concern yourselves with that."

Loretta and I approached. "Problem, Esperanza?" I asked.

Esperanza turned to me and hoisted the documents. "You know about this contract shit?"

"Er, well, I used to deal with contracts when I was employed at the bank, although not of the movie-appearing variety. Perhaps best to engage a solicitor."

"Huh?" Esperanza said.

"What we Brits call your lawyers. No doubt, there are attorneys in Santa Fe whose services you could engage."

"You mean we got to pay an attorney to read this shit?"

I raised an eyebrow. "Well, they're not an especially charitable lot, so, yes, you and Maria will have to pay."

"How much?"

I considered the size of the contract, which would certainly require hours of reading. "Er, perhaps a few hundred dollars. I shan't think more than five hundred dollars for a comprehensive review."

"Huh? But we're only gonna get five hundred to be in the *gringo's* movie," Esperanza said.

I shrugged. "Horns of the proverbial dilemma."

"Fuck this shit," Esperanza said, turning to Roger. "Where do me and Maria sign?"

Roger opened the contract to the last page. He pointed to several spots on the page. "Here and here," he replied, retrieving a pen from his jacket pocket.

Esperanza grabbed the pen and signed both copies angrily. She gave the pen to Maria. "You gotta sign, too, *hermana*. Then we can get outta here."

"You sure?" Maria asked.

Esperanza waved her hand. "*Sí*. We sign this and then we get our money."

Maria shook her head. She took the pen and signed the contracts, then gave the pen back to Roger.

"Okay, *gringo*," said Esperanza, "*now* do we get our money?"

Roger tut-tutted. He took Esperanza's hand and patted it gently. "I'm delighted you're so excited, my dear. But you must be patient. There's much to do before we begin filming. My scriptwriter has to write the scenes where you and your sister will appear. You and she will have to memorise your lines. Wardrobe will need to prepare your costumes. And we still have to prepare sets and our location shots."

A shroud of incomprehension descended over Esperanza, rendering her blissfully, if only momentarily, speechless. Maria shook her head, turned around, and set course for the church door.

"Now, if you'll excuse me," said Roger, "I must deal with the contracts for all of the extras." He released Esperanza's hand, stood up, and walked towards a beaming Sunflower, who embraced him with fecund fervour.

"C'mon, Bennie," Loretta said. She heaved my arm as if raising anchor. "We've got to get ready for this evening."

"Eh, what?" I replied absently, as the oculars focused on Sunflower. I felt a sudden sharp pain in the right shoulder. "Gah!"

"Now!" Loretta heaved the arm again, then towed me out the church door. A still shell-shocked Esperanza followed, carrying the now signed contract.

Back in the cafe, Esperanza sat down, setting the contract upon a table.

"Are you okay, *Tia* Esperanza?" asked Loretta softly.

"You do look rather poorly," I added.

"I can't memorize nothing," Esperanza said.

"What?" I asked.

"The *gringo* said Maria and me got to memorize our lines. I can't memorize nothing. Maria and me were in a Christmas play at school. When I got up, I couldn't remember what I was supposed to say. Everybody laughed and I ran."

A measure of sympathy arose in the Graves heart. "Surely just a modicum of stage fright, Esperanza. You shall be playing yourself in Roger's movie and will be able to say what comes, er, naturally. Besides, unlike the stage production you and Maria appeared in, when making a movie, if one errs in reciting one's lines, the scene is simply redone."

"So I don't got to memorize nothing?" she asked.

"Worry not, Esperanza. Your *abuela*-ish self will surely shine through."

"Bennie's right, *Tia* Esperanza," said Loretta. "You don't have anything to worry about."

Esperanza sighed. "Okay, thanks, Loretta. You, too, *Pende*—Bennie."

"M-hem. As we have addressed these film production issues, perhaps you would care to help ready the dining room for this evening?"

Esperanza glanced about the dining room. "Uh, I can't," she said. "My arm hurts real bad. I guess I shouldn't have carried that contract thing. Maybe I better go home and get some, uh, ice." She arose, lit a cigarette, and headed out the front door, leaving the contract upon the table.

I sighed. "Back to her old self, I gather."

"Never mind, Bennie," said Loretta, "we can take care of it."

I hoisted the contract off the table. "I suppose someone ought to read this. Esperanza most certainly will not."

"Can you please read it, Bennie," Loretta asked soothingly.

"I suspect my legal counsel would be as useful to Esperanza as advice on how to land on the moon. Still, one wonders." I thumbed through the contract. "What rubbish. Where should we put it?"

"Give it to me," said Loretta. "I'll put it on a shelf in the storeroom for now."

"Right, then." I glanced at the watch, which read half-three. "I say, we've much work to be done before we open for dinner. If you will help Maria, I shall attend to the dining room."

Loretta disappeared quickly into the kitchen and I proceeded to prepare the tables.

A half-hour or so later, the front door opened, and through it waddled Coronado. His pudgy hand held a small bound document, which I presumed was his contract to appear as an extra.

"*Hola*, Señor Graves," he said. "Sure smells good in here."

"Er, yes. Rather early for your dishwashing duties, is it not Coronado?"

"I dunno. What time is it?"

"Not quite four o'clock," I replied. "Though one appreciates your enthusiasm, the normal starting hour is five o'clock."

"Do I got to wash dishes tonight?" he asked.

"We do rather count on your diligent dishwashing, Coronado."

"Sorry, Señor Graves."

"What? No, you're a most accomplished dishwasher. That's why we count on your assistance."

Coronado nodded. "Oh, okay."

I laughed. "Is there a problem? A date with a beautiful señorita perhaps?"

"Kinda. Señorita Flower asked me to help her."

"Eh? Sunflower asked you . . . to help . . . her? Er, what sort of help does she want?"

"I dunno. She asked if I could help her down at the old bar tonight." Coronado paused as his appearance became dreamy. "She asked me real nice." He paused again. "She sure smells good."

I fought back the attacking olfactory thoughts of Sunflower emerging in the grey matter. "Yes, well, one cannot expect you to resist the Siren's call."

Coronado stared at me blankly. "Is someone gonna call me? I don't got a phone. Maybe I should go to Rudy's so I can use his."

"No, I meant—that is, we shall manage without you this evening."

"Thanks, Señor Graves," he said. "Oh, I got my movie contract, too." He waved the document at me. "Señor Victor says I get fifty dollars. Are you gonna be in his movie, too?"

"I certainly hope not."

"Don't you like movies?"

"Whereas I enjoy watching the occasional film, I have no interest in appearing in one, especially one about the cafe. Now, if you'll excuse me, Coronado, I really must finish preparing the dining room."

"Okay, Señor Graves." He stood motionless.

"Something else?" I asked.

"Can Maria make me a burrito? She always makes me one when I wash dishes and I'm real hungry."

I sighed. "Sit down and wait here. I shall enquire."

"Thanks," he said, as he entered a caloric trance.

Five minutes later, after enduring a stream of invective from Maria, I emerged from the kitchen with a large, tinfoil-wrapped burrito. Coronado's eyes lit up as he reached greedily for the package.

"Thanks, Señor Graves," he said, putting it into his coat pocket. "I guess I can't chaperone you tonight. Is Maria gonna be mad at me?"

"She already is," I muttered. "That is, there's no need. As you will be with Sunflower, you shall be chaperoning in absentia."

"Uh, okay, I guess. Maybe Loretta can chaperone you instead."

The blood pressure was fast approaching the volcanic stage. "No doubt," I replied, stepping to the front door and opening it. "Good day, Coronado."

He eased by me and stepped outside onto the *portal*. Then he turned around. "Señor Graves?" he asked.

"Yes, what now?"

"What if Alejandro Mora's ghost is in the old bar tonight?"

I pondered an appropriate response. "Perhaps you could offer to buy him a beer at Rudy's. Any self-respecting ghost is sure to appreciate such a magnanimous gesture."

Coronado dug through his trouser pocket. "But I don't got any money."

I retrieved my wallet and gave him two dollars. "Here," I said, thrusting the bills into his pudgy hand. "You now have money to purchase a beer for Alejandro, should he, or it, appear."

"Thanks, Señor Graves." Coronado pocketed the bills. He stepped off the *portal* and set course for Rudy's. As he disappeared into the bar, I thought any ghost wishing to survive Coronado would need a far stronger tipple.

By half-four, the dining room was prepared and pots were simmering, ready for the evening crowd. Loretta was assisting

Maria with last-minute preparations whilst I scrubbed pots at the sink. Suddenly, the kitchen door burst open, admitting Sunflower.

"Hi, everyone," she gushed.

"Sunflower," I said, "what a, er, pleasant surprise." Then, applying the Graves iron will, I fixed my gaze on the dishwater and whistled, whilst preparing the shoulder for yet another blow from Loretta's fist.

"Don't never come into my kitchen," said Maria, as she continued to stir a large pot.

"What do you want?" growled Loretta. I sensed the ocular daggers aimed at me as I mindlessly scrubbed an already clean pan.

"I'm really sorry," Sunflower said in an excited tone, "but I have to speak to Bennie about Roger's movie."

I rotated the cranium slowly as I readied myself for any upcoming blows. My gaze settled on Sunflower. "M-hem. Ah, Roger's movie?" I croaked. "That is, I mean, I have nothing to do with it."

"Roger insisted I speak with you," said Sunflower.

I grimaced. "He did? Why?"

"Yeah, why?" said Loretta. I espied one of Maria's knives in her hand.

"Roger said I'm going to have a starring role," she said.

"What?" exclaimed Loretta.

"*Que chichona*," Maria muttered.

"Isn't it cool?" gushed Sunflower. "I'm going to play your uncle's—what's his name?—wife, Cele-something. Celery? Anyway, Roger said she started your cafe, so I should talk to you and your uncle about her."

Maria turned to Sunflower. Her eyes darkened and her brow knitted together into a half-hitch. The point of her chef's knife flashed in the light, and I detected what sounded like a guttural growl, rather like an enraged leopard.

"Steady, Maria," said I, raising my hands.

"*Mí padre*, Ernesto," said Maria, as she waved the knife menacingly. "Celestina, she helped." Maria turned around and attacked the head of lettuce on her cutting board.

"I don't understand," Sunflower said.

"Er, Roger may be rather confused," I said. "You see, the cafe was started by Maria's and Esperanza's father, Ernesto. Celestina was Uncle Bill's wife. She worked for Ernesto. After Ernesto fell ill, Celestina worked with Maria and Esperanza. They ran the cafe until Celestina's untimely death."

"*Chichona*," Maria hissed.

"What did she say?" asked Sunflower.

"Er, nothing important," I quickly replied. I glanced at Loretta and visually begged her not to translate. "One tends to talk with oneself when engrossed in one's work, that's all."

"Roger wants *you* to play Celestina," Loretta said. "I wonder why." As she moved her hands to make a rude gesture, I intervened, quickly securing her hands in mine.

"M-hem. Loretta is merely, ah, expressing surprise because you lack previous, er, experience—acting, that is." One of Loretta's fingernails was now gouging into my palm like a steam shovel. "Gah!" I cried, letting go of her hands.

"Are you okay?" Sunflower asked.

I inspected the small, oozing gash in my palm. "No, I mean, yes. That is, a cramp of the hand is all."

"Roger said I'm a natural actress," said Sunflower in a rather trance-like voice. "He wants to be known as the director who discovered me. Isn't that cool?" She approached me, readying an embrace, until Loretta manoeuvred between us and stood athwart as she placed her arms across her chest.

"Bennie and I are engaged, remember?" said Loretta.

"Sky's right," Sunflower said dismissively, "you have bad *chi*. Bennie deserves someone better."

"There's gonna be a lot more than bad *chi* real soon," Loretta said. "*Vete a la—*"

"Ladies, please," I glanced at the watch. "Ah, look at the time. We open presently, Sunflower so, er, much work to be done. And, ah, I gather you have asked Coronado for assistance this evening."

Loretta appeared ready to erupt, when Maria interrupted. "Get the fuck out of my kitchen, *todos*," she yelled. "I ain't gonna listen to this shit no more. We got work to do. Loretta, you get into the dining room and see if we got customers waiting. Bennie, you start mashing beans for the *refritos*. And you," she said, as she pointed her knife at Sunflower, "don't ever come in my kitchen no more. ¡*Vamanos*!" Maria turned around and began stirring a pot of red chile sauce, continuing to mutter to herself in Spanish.

"Wow, bad *chi*," said Sunflower. She backed away towards the kitchen door and opened it. "Oh, I almost forgot, Bennie. Pedro came back. He said he would have our place finished in a few days so we can open. Sky says the *chi* at the spiritual centre will be really positive. You can even come into the kitchen."

Sunflower turned around and disappeared through the kitchen door.

"Damn," said Loretta, "I thought he would stay away."

"Surely not even Pedro believes all of that nonsense about Alejandro's ghost," I said.

"Shut up, Bennie," Loretta said. She pushed the kitchen door open violently and stormed into the dining room.

What next? I wondered, convinced Fate would soon provide an answer.

Chapter 19

By the following week, an eerie, eye-of-the-stormish calm
had descended upon Vaca Seca. Roger and his cameraman, Jim, made brief appearances at various locations throughout the town, including the cafe, the old church,
Rudy's Bar, Joe's store, even the Texaco station. Roger would
bark various orders and Jim would film something of interest
for a few minutes—the cash register in the cafe appeared to
be of interest for an entirely unknown reason—and then they
would depart.

I saw nothing of Sky Blue and Sunflower, although the
changes to the old bar were noticeable when I motored past
along the main road. Pedro, doubtless inspired by Sunflower's
propinquity and strategically deployed raiment, had made significant progress using Joe Garcia's overpriced materiel. And
despite Loretta's hopes for Pedro's permanent exile, she said
nothing about the building's ongoing metamorphosis.

Thursday found me clearing detritus off one of the dining
room tables. The cafe was filled with the luncheon crowd. I
heard the front door open and then a large crash of shatter-
ing glass. There, amongst the glass shards, stood Coronado. He
held a large wooden sign, which he set down against the wall.
Then he closed the defenestrated front door. I surveyed the
damage and shook my head.

Coronado glanced at me and then lowered his head. "Sorry,
Señor Graves. I guess the sign kinda slipped out of my hand.
You want me to get a broom and sweep it up?"

I put the tray of dishes down upon the table and examined
the wreckage. "I will take care of it, Coronado."

Esperanza, who had returned to work, and Loretta emerged from the kitchen and surveyed the damage.

"You gonna pay for that door, *gordo*," shouted Esperanza. "Go get some plywood from Joe. We gotta board the door up."

"Okay, Esperanza," Coronado replied. "Can I get some money?"

"Get your own fucking money, *pendejo*. I don't care if you gotta steal the plywood from Joe."

As Esperanza's voice rose further, customers streamed out of the broken front door, plates abandoned.

"That's quite enough, Esperanza," I said.

Esperanza glared at me. She exhaled a large plume of smoke and returned to the kitchen.

I glanced at Loretta and sighed. "Perhaps we should stock the first-aid kit with a bottle of Farm Calm. In any event, I shall clean up the mess."

Loretta, whose anger last week at the return of Pedro had dissipated several days ago, smiled. "I'll get the broom and dustpan. Don't cut yourself on the glass."

I surveyed the debris. "If I do, you shall be the first to know."

Presently, Loretta returned with the broom and dustpan. "What's the sign for, Coronado?" she asked.

"Señorita Flower asked me to make it," Coronado said proudly. "I told her I made real good signs, like the one I made for the cafe." He picked up the sign and displayed it for us.

"You like it, Loretta?" he asked, beaming.

"Satisfying your hunger and nourishing your soul," she read aloud. "What's that supposed to mean, Bennie?"

"Never mind the nourished souls and whatnot, Loretta," I said. "They intend to serve beer and wine. We shall be ruined."

"Why? We're doing fine, and we don't serve beer or wine."

"Yes, but, we've had no competition until now. Their customers shan't need to purchase beer at Rudy's and bring it with them."

"Don't be such a pessimist, Bennie," chided Loretta. "Everyone loves Maria's cooking. They won't give that up."

OPENING SOON!

Siddhartha Restaurant,
Art Gallery

and

Spiritual Center

Satisfying your hunger and
nourishing your soul

BEER AND WINE SERVED!

"*Sí*, Loretta," said Coronado, patting his stomach. "I like Maria's cooking a lot, especially her *enchiladas*."

"Er, Coronado. About the statement they will serve beer and wine."

"Señor Blue told me to write that."

"Does he have a liquor licence?" I asked.

"I dunno, Señor Graves. What's a liquor licence?"

"A liquor licence allows an establishment to serve alcohol," I said. "We lack one, which is why we cannot serve beer or wine."

"I got my driver's licence in Española when I was thirteen," said Coronado absently. "The sheriff asked me if I knew how to drive. I told him I did, so he gave me my licence."

I shuddered. The day of my arrival in Vaca Seca included a singularly unpleasant journey to Uncle Bill's ranch in Coronado's lorry, driven by its inebriated owner. "Yes, well, the rigour of your driver's licence examination is certainly illuminating, but I am speaking of a liquor licence, not a driver's licence."

"What's the difference, Señor Graves? The Drive 'n' Go in Española has a drive-through window. You can buy a couple of six-packs without getting out of your truck. But there's a real long line on Friday and Saturday nights."

"Indeed? How thoughtful of them." I issued a mental warning to the grey matter to remain as far away as possible from Española on Friday and Saturday evenings.

"Maybe Señor Blue and Señorita Flower will have a drive-through window, too," added Coronado. "Then I wouldn't have to drive to Española no more."

As Coronado attended Rudy's most days so as to besot himself with beer, I could discern no reason for his stated need to drive to Española, other than a desire to extinguish the more careless, or suicidal, local fauna who might dare cross the narrow road that led there. Yet, his tortuous logic had stumbled onto an important issue. If Siddhartha served beer and wine to diners, and sold it to those too lazy to decamp from their lorries, not only would the cafe be ruined economically, but so would Rudy's.

I turned to Loretta. "Perhaps I should go to the old bar and speak with Sky Blue about his liquor licence."

"And see her?" said Loretta. "Not without me, you don't."

"Really, Loretta, this is most childish."

She glared at me, but said nothing.

"What if my chaperone accompanied me?" I asked. I pointed my thumb towards Coronado. "Or would you prefer to speak with Sky Blue and Sunflower yourself?"

"That *chichona*," hissed Loretta. "If I see her, I'm gonna punch her in the face."

"I can chaperone Señor Graves if you want me to, Loretta," said Coronado. "I won't let him kiss Señorita Flower again."

"I have no intention of kissing Sunflower or anyone else, Coronado," I shouted. Loretta responded with an especially reptilian stare. "Right, then. We'll not discuss this with Sky Blue or Sunflower. I shall finish the cleanup and repairs and then speak with Rudy instead."

"Do you want me to chaperone you when you speak to Rudy?" Coronado asked.

"What? No. Shouldn't you be obtaining a sheet of plywood from Joe's store so I may effect repairs on our front door?"

"Oh. Sorry, I forgot." Coronado retrieved the sign and waddled out the door.

I looked at Loretta and shook my head. "He manages to create a new circle of Hell each day."

"Don't talk to Sky Blue," commanded Loretta. "I've got a better idea."

"You do? What?"

"You'll see. Tell Esperanza and Maria I'll be back soon." She rushed out the front door and disappeared.

After cleaning the broken glass off the floor, I awaited Coronado's return with the plywood. I returned the broom and dustpan to the kitchen storeroom and retrieved a small toolbox, under the withering stares of Esperanza and Maria.

"Loretta said to tell you both she will return shortly."

"Where'd she go?" Esperanza asked, as her cigarette ash dripped onto the kitchen floor.

"I have no idea," I replied. "Though I suspect it has to do with our latest competitive challenge."

"What the fuck does that mean?"

"Sky Blue and Sunflower's restaurant intends to serve beer and wine."

"How'd they get a liquor licence?" asked Esperanza. "We ain't gonna have no more customers." I goggled, wide-eyed, at Esperanza, astonished she grasped the nature of the competitive challenge.

"I had intended to enquire of Sky Blue and Sunflower regarding how they acquired a licence. However, Loretta, er, suggested in rather strong terms I not do so."

Esperanza made her now-familiar rude gesture to describe Sunflower. "Yeah, you're like Adam eating that snake's apple in the Garden of Eden, *Pendejito*. Only this time it's the *chichona*."

"Are you suggesting—that is, Eve was the offending *comedenti malum*, not Adam."

"Huh?" Esperanza exhaled a large cloud of smoke into my face. "You gotta get us a liquor licence or nobody's gonna eat here no more."

I coughed. "Such a licence would require rather a large cash outlay, which we cannot afford."

"Where you think Sky Blue and the *chichona* got the money?" she asked.

"Perhaps you should ask them."

Esperanza inhaled deeply on the cigarette. I stepped away quickly to avoid the impending exhalation. "Okay." She turned to Maria. "*Hermana*, I'm gonna talk to that fat *gringo* about his liquor licence."

Maria nodded. "*Bueno.*"

Esperanza opened the outside kitchen door and stepped into the alley, then walked to the main road at dreadnought speed.

Maria turned to me. "When's Loretta coming back? I'm gonna need her help."

"Er, she did not say, actually. The dining room is shipshape, well, other than the front door. May I be of assistance?"

Maria appeared to weigh my request. "Can you make some more *tamales*?"

"Of course. After all, you taught me how to do so."

She laughed. "*Sí*, I remember when we showed you. Your *tamales* looked like horseshit."

"M-hem. Well, with perseverance and a large quantity of masa, I succeeded, did I not?"

"*Madre de Dios*," muttered Maria. "Okay, get the masa and the pork. Don't fuck them up."

"Have no fear, Maria."

A half-hour later, I had constructed two dozen *tamales* that met Maria's standards, and a dozen she deemed to resemble equine effluvium.

Presently, the door to the alley opened and Esperanza entered. "Nobody there. No yellow bus, neither." She ignited another cigarette. "I guess they're busy," she said sarcastically, making another rude gesture with her fingers.

"Did you happen to espy Coronado?" I asked, hoping to change the subject.

"*El Gordo*? How come you want to see him?"

"The front door, remember?"

"Oh, *sí*," she muttered.

By five o'clock, Coronado had still not arrived with the plywood. Nor had Loretta returned from her unstated destination. The dinner crowd had gathered on the *portal* and were now goggling the wreckage.

I stepped into the dining room. "Just a moment, everyone," I shouted. "Yes, as you can see there was a slight incident with the front door. We shall effect repairs presently."

I returned to the kitchen. "The dinner crowd awaits," I said.

"*Hermana, los lobos están aquí*," said Esperanza. "You ready?"

Maria nodded.

"Right, Esperanza," I said. "Would you like to wait tables, or shall I?"

"Maybe you better, *Pendejito*," replied Esperanza. "It's a girl's job."

"Bloody hell," I muttered, as I resisted a strong urge to reply with one of Esperanza's gestures. After tying on an apron, I stepped into the dining room.

The defenestrated door had admitted a large herd of the local flies, which were now buzzing throughout the dining room and crawling over the tables. Several large wasps had also joined the merriment and were investigating one of the small bottles of honey that stood on each table.

Reasoning *Vespula vulgaris* were the more immediate problem, what with a tendency to inflict painful stings, I gently raised the bottle of honey off the table, hoping to escort them outside. However, apparently upset by the rude disturbance of their meal, the wasps proceeded to set course for my head.

"Gah!" I dropped the bottle onto the floor. The bottle top separated and a small wave of honey proceeded to ooze onto the floor.

"Wasp attack," I shouted. "Abandon ship!" I ran out the front door, past the waiting crowd and into the street, where I collided with a plywood-absent Coronado.

"*Hola*, Señor Graves," he said. "Are you okay? I saw you running. Is the cafe on fire or something?"

"Wasps," I said, heart still pounding.

"Wasps set fire to the café? ¡*Hijole*! You think it was Joe? He tried to set fire to the cafe on your opening night, remember?"

"Yes, one recalls Joe's inebriated pyromania. And no, wasps did not set fire to the cafe."

"That's good. How come you're running away? Is Maria mad?"

"Wasps have invaded the dining room, as have flies. Do you know why, Coronado?"

"Maybe they're hungry, Señor Graves," said Coronado, "like me." He patted his ample stomach.

"Where's the bloody plywood?"

"Huh? Oh, Joe said he don't have any. He can get some tomorrow if you want from Pacheco Lumber in Española. Sorry."

"Coronado, there is a gaping hole in the front door because you broke the window with your sign. Now every fly in the county has congregated in the cafe, as have the local wasps. We must have something to cover the door."

"Maybe some newspaper would work."

I paused. "Newspaper? Yes, I suppose that will work until we have a more permanent repair. Do you have any?"

"I can't read."

"Yes, I know, but what about the store? Surely Joe sells the Santa Fe and Albuquerque newspapers."

Coronado shook his head. "I don't think so. Sorry."

"But he must sell some periodicals," I said, exasperated.

"I dunno. What's a periodical?"

"What? They're, well, Uncle Bill subscribes to one—what is it called?—*Life*, I believe."

"Oh, you mean magazines?" Coronado smiled and nodded.

"Yes, yes, that's it, magazines. Does Joe sell any of those?"

Coronado shook his head in the negative.

I grasped my hair and pulled. "Gah!"

Coronado stared at me. "Joe sells paper plates," he said.

"Does he sell insecticide? Anything that kills insects?"

"Sure. We sell flypaper, and we got lots of cans of Raid, too. You want me to get you some?"

"Yes, please."

Coronado thrust his hands into his pockets and remained immobile for several moments.

"What now?" I asked.

"The store's closed 'cause Joe left early today."

Fate was surely enjoying my current visit to this newest circle of Hell. "Coronado," I said slowly, as I resisted the urge to scream, "would you please do me a small favour?"

"Sure, Señor Graves. I like to help."

"Please tell everyone waiting on the *portal* the cafe is closed this evening."

"Okay. How come the cafe is closed?"

"Because giant, man-eating plants from outer space have invaded. Why do you bloody well think?"

Coronado shrugged. "I thought it was 'cause of the flies and wasps inside." He looked timorously up and down the street, presumably in search of large carnivorous plants.

"For the love of God," I shouted, "just . . . please . . . tell . . . the . . . customers . . . the . . . cafe . . . is . . . closed . . . tonight. And then tell Maria and Esperanza I shall return shortly."

"Okay, Señor Graves."

I watched as Coronado waddled towards the cafe, then set course for Rudy's.

"Feeling better?" asked Rudy. He leaned back in his desk chair and propped his boot-shod feet on his desk.

"Thank you, yes," I replied, as I drained the last drops of whisky from my glass.

"How about another? You look like you could use it."

"Thank you, Rudy, but unlike Oscar Wilde, I shall attempt to resist temptation at present."

"You know, most people around here don't mind the flies," Rudy said.

"Yes, well, I am rather more concerned about the wasps, which seem to have a fondness for honey."

"Yeah, they like anything sweet. Put a glass of sugar water outside the front door. That'll attract 'em. "

I drummed my fingers on the desk. "I almost believe Coronado could have defeated Napoleon's army by himself."

Rudy laughed. "Yeah, I suppose he could have. But he means well."

"M-hem. Do you have any cardboard boxes I can use to cover the front door?"

"Sure, I got lots of 'em, out back. You need any help covering the door?"

"Would you possess any tape?"

"Yep." He reached into the centre drawer of the desk, extracted a large roll, and bunged it towards me. "This work?" he asked.

"That should work, yes. By the way, I meant to ask you about Coronado's sign. Apparently, Sky Blue and Sunflower shall be serving beer and wine at their restaurant. As I recall, you told me liquor licences were rather expensive to obtain."

Rudy's eyes widened. "How the hell did they get a liquor licence so fast?"

"I was hoping you would inform me. As I recall, such a licence for the cafe would cost several thousand dollars."

"Yeah, they ain't cheap. Worse for a bar like mine. Plus, it can take a few months to get one issued, at least, without *la mordida*." He rubbed the fingers of his right hand together.

"*La mordida*? You mean a bribe?"

"Yeah, it means 'the bite'. Comes in real handy when you need somebody in the county to do something for you or need to get out of a ticket. That sort of thing."

"Did you, I mean, not that it's any of my business, mind, but did you—"

"—Bribe somebody to get my liquor licence?" Rudy said. "Nah. I just had to transfer the ownership. Still cost a lot, but my cousin Alfonso worked for the county back then, so he took care of the paperwork."

"Quite," I said, "but surely Sky Blue doesn't have a cousin working for the county."

"Maybe he sent Sunflower," Rudy said, grinning. "Bet she could get one of those clerks to act real fast. Alfonso sure as hell would have."

An image of Sunflower *in flagrante* began to form in the grey matter. "But they don't even own the building," I said.

He shrugged. "C'mon, Bennie. You gonna tell me that in England a pretty girl can't get some poor government guy to do what she wants him to do?"

I coughed. "Yes, well, I have the utmost respect for the British Civil Service. Then again, if the old bar had a liquor licence, then would they not simply transfer it as you did?"

Rudy opened his mouth as if to reply, but then closed it. He scratched his head for several moments, before shouting, "Goddamn!"

"What's wrong?" I asked.

"The old bar was abandoned," he said. "Empty for years."

"Yes, and Joe sold it to them even though he does not own the building."

"That little bastard," said Rudy. "I'll tell you what's wrong. First, the old bar probably never had a liquor licence. It wasn't till about ten years ago you had to get them, and it's been closed for longer than that. Second, you can only transfer a liquor licence if a place is in business. That's what I did with the bar. But if a place closes, the licence expires."

"Then I gather Sunflower could not have used her, er, assets to transfer the liquor licence."

"No, because there was no licence to transfer."

"And by 'little bastard' may I surmise you are referring to Joe Garcia?"

Rudy reached for the whisky bottle and poured himself another glass. "You sure?" he asked, offering to refill my glass.

"Why not?" I said, extending my glass towards the bottle. "But what exactly did Joe do?"

Rudy shook his head. "Goddamn Joe sold a building he doesn't own and a liquor licence that doesn't exist."

"So I gather they cannot serve alcoholic beverages, at least, not legally."

Rudy swallowed a large mouthful of whisky and nodded.

"Surely Tiny can, well, do whatever he does in his official capacity as sheriff."

"I can ask him. Tell him what's going on. But it's not gonna change anything."

"Why not? Surely dispensing alcoholic beverages without proper licencing is illegal."

"Yeah, but Tiny's not one for riling up the locals. A few years back, one of the *viejos*—I think it was Armando Trujillo—had a little still on his property. He brewed a few gallons of corn liquor—stuff was so potent it would hold a flame. Armando would sell it to some of the folks in the valley.

"Anyway, one day Tiny found out about it and decided to confront Armando. Off he went, his patrol car's siren blazing. Before Tiny had even stopped the car, Armando had shot out one of the front tires. Tiny tried to put on a brave face. He got out of the car and told Armando he was in big trouble, not only for an illegal still, but for threatening a police officer.

"Armando levelled his rifle at Tiny. Tiny told Armando he was making things worse for himself. Told Armando to surrender peacefully or he would call the state police.

"Well, Armando thought about that for a minute. Then he shot out the patrol car's windshield. He told Tiny to get the hell off his property. Said if Tiny ever set foot on his property, he would end up as coyote food and nobody would ever find him.

"Tiny cursed at Armando, but he backed down. He didn't want a war on his hands, and that's what he would have gotten. A few years later, somebody told me Tiny would sometimes buy a few jars of Armando's hooch. Tiny always denied it, though."

"Surely there is something we can do," I said. "I rather doubt the cafe will withstand the competitive pressures exerted by their restaurant if they serve beer. Unless you suggest we serve alcohol despite our lacking a licence to do so."

Rudy shook his head. "No, I wouldn't do that, Bennie. After all, you and Tiny don't see exactly eye-to-eye, if you know what I mean."

I grunted. On the cafe's opening night, and before I knew Tiny was our local and incompetent constable, I had responded to his rude demands of *sopapillas* for his equally rotund family in an equally rude manner.

"Then what should I do?"

"I dunno," Rudy said, "maybe the food will be real bad. Besides, nobody can cook like *mi querida*."

"Yes, I realize that," I said, "but, you of all people must know the allure of an establishment that will serve beer. I fear Maria's cooking shall be unable to repulse such an attack. Besides, customers who buy their beer at the restaurant shan't be buying it from you, as they do at present."

"Yeah, I know. That's why I'm gonna speak to Joe."

"I suggest a modicum of caution, given Joe's revengeful tendencies. One would not want him to burn down the bar afterwards."

"Thanks, Bennie, but I'm not worried about Joe. You see that?" Rudy pointed to a large shotgun propped up in the corner of his office. "He understands one of those real good."

"Er, yes. Well, I'd best be off to repair the door. Thanks again for the whisky, and the cardboard and tape." I stood up and began to exit his office.

"Hey Bennie," Rudy called.

"Yes?"

"Everything okay with you and Loretta?"

I paused. "Er, well, during the unpleasantness of 1776, I believe your Thomas Paine said something to the effect that 'these are the times that try men's souls.' The Graves soul has been sorely tried; bent it may be, but not broken."

Rudy nodded and grinned. "Glad to hear it, Bennie. Just stay on the straight and narrow, especially with Sunflower around."

"M-hem, yes." I exited Rudy's office and walked down the hallway to the main room. There, sitting at the bar cradling a bottle of beer, was Roger.

"I say, old chap," he said, offering the now usual Cheshire-catish smile, "I've been looking for you."

"Gah," I whimpered. "How did you know I was here?"

I went to your cafe but it was closed," Roger said. "That greasy fat fellow said you have an insect problem. How old-fashioned."

"Yes. I was about to obtain some cardboard boxes to seal the front door. You may have noticed the window is broken."

Roger paused. "I want to film it. That is, as soon as you've covered the window with the cardboard and tape."

"Eh, what?"

"We'll need some graffiti scrawled on the cardboard, too. Can you do that?" He retrieved a notepad and pen from his jacket pocket and scribbled something.

"Graffiti?" I asked.

"Sure." He snapped his fingers. "In fact, we'll scrawl graffiti over the entire front of the cafe. That store owner—what's his name?—he must sell cans of spray paint. But not just black. We'll need several colours. Red will show up well on the brown walls." Roger continued to scribble on his notepad, grunting as he did so. "I'll have one of my assistants at the cafe in an hour. He can take care of it all."

The grey matter reeled. "You wish to deface the front of the cafe? Why?"

Roger eyed me with a distinct air of superiority. "To better illustrate the rebirth, of course."

"Why not simply burn down the cafe and film the ashes?"

Roger paused. "I love your idea, old chap, but burning down the cafe would be tricky. We wouldn't want to set the entire town on fire, now, would we? Usually, we build a separate set and then burn it down. It's much safer that way."

He paused to write something more in the small notebook, which he then replaced into his jacket pocket. "The new cafe literally rising from the ashes," he said to himself dreamily.

"I could show the cafe's slow demise. Empty tables, the graffiti scrawled everywhere, and finally the fire that destroys it. I'm brilliant."

Roger turned to me. "How many fire trucks does your local fire department have? I'll need to look at the building again, but we probably need at least two large pump trucks."

As I listened to Roger's vision of the cafe's destruction, the head began to droop like a wilting geranium.

"Are you mad? There shall be neither graffiti-scrawling nor setting the cafe aflame and reducing it to ash. Before we opened, the cafe endured a fusillade of shotgun blasts, thanks to Coronado's failed efforts to shoot a skunk that had taken up residence beneath the cafe. He almost single-handedly reduced the cafe to rubble."

"That's fantastic!" exclaimed Roger. "I know several animal trainers in Hollywood who deal with skunks. Don't worry, old chap, their scent glands are always removed. The skunks' glands, too." Roger laughed.

I goggled him dully.

"Don't you get the joke, old chap? Animal trainers? Scent glands?"

The Graves cranium was now throbbing in pain. "Er, yes."

"We wouldn't want a skunk stinking up the place, now would we?" Roger stared at the ceiling again. "Perhaps we should write that as comic relief for the audience," he muttered.

I retrieved the roll of tape and began walking towards the front door.

"Wait, old chap," Roger said. "There's one more thing."

"What now? Christians being devoured by lions? Rape of Lucretia in the dining room? Cafe overrun by Visigoths?"

"Ha! Very funny, old chap. But nothing so dramatic. Although I do have a screenplay in preparation about Genghis Khan. Once I have the studio's approval, I intend to out-DeMille DeMille. Anyway, I would like your cafe to cater lunches and dinners for my crew. There's six of them now, although I expect more as we begin filming in earnest. I lose time when I have to send someone to Española for groceries and have them cook meals in the bus. And with a larger crew, I'll have to bring in a catering truck. Very expensive. And, as you know, time is money, eh, old chap?"

"So I have heard."

"How about five dollars per person per meal? Of course, the studio will reimburse you after we finish filming."

I sighed. "I shall enquire with Maria. I'm rather afraid it shall be her decision alone."

Roger smiled and bunged my shoulder. "Thanks, old chap. Would you like me to speak with Maria? I do have a way with the ladies, you know."

I considered the "way" Roger might have with Maria, and shuddered. If anyone was immune to false charm, it was she. "Er, best to let me speak with her."

Roger drained his bottle of beer, placed two dollars on the countertop, and stood up. He extended his hand and shook mine. "Excellent," he said. "Tell Maria I want her to start tomorrow." He turned around and bounded out the door.

"Twit," I muttered. I walked around to the side of the building, retrieved three largish cardboard boxes, and returned to the cafe. As I stepped inside the dining room, I could hear the buzzing of the flies. The broken bottle still lay on the floor. The oozing honey, which had spread further, was now overrun with perhaps a dozen honey-drunk wasps.

I stepped into the kitchen, which appeared abandoned. The food had been put away, the ovens were off, and the lights were out. I flattened the boxes and used a pair of shears to cut away several flaps. Then, returning to the dining room, I quickly covered and taped the gaping hole in the front door.

Having barred any new entry, at least through the door, I turned to the task of ridding the cafe of its current six-legged occupants. We kept a small can of insecticide in the store room to deal with the bolder cockroaches, which I retrieved. I returned to the dining room, approached the wasps stealthily, and opened fire. A small stream drizzled out of the top, rolled down the can and onto my fingers. The wasps appeared unimpressed. I shook the can, aimed, and fired. Again, the contents drizzled out.

"Damn and blast!" I shouted.

Returning to the kitchen, I tossed the can into the rubbish bin. Having been defeated, there now remained only one course of action. Thus I departed the cafe and returned to the ranch, ready to drown the current vicissitudes in several large glasses of whisky.

Chapter 20

U ncle Bill cradled a glass of Dusty Trail from the comfort
of the sitting room sofa. "Let me get this straight," he
said. "Coronado broke the window of the front door
carrying a sign for that new restaurant, and now the cafe's
closed because it's overrun with flies and wasps. Roger wants to
cover the front of the cafe in graffiti to make it look rundown
and then wants to burn the entire thing to the ground. That
new restaurant is gonna serve booze, even though they don't
have a liquor licence. Anything else, pard'ner?"

"As a matter of fact, there was one other item. I also
described Coronado's attempt to reduce the cafe to rubble with
his shotgun whilst attempting to despatch Señor Apestoso.
Roger thought recreating that rather brutish episode would
provide 'comic relief', as he put it."

"So he wants to spray-paint the cafe with graffiti, burn it
down, and blast it to pieces with a shotgun?" Uncle Bill shook
his head in dismay.

"Well, presumably not in that order, but yes, that is Roger's
thinking, if one wishes to refer to such madness as thinking.
Oh, he wants the cafe to feed and water his film crew."

Uncle Bill whistled softly. "Yep, I guess shootin' and burnin'
down a building works up an appetite."

I coughed. "Er, no doubt."

"You ain't gonna allow him to do any of that crap, are you?"

"Good heavens, no. I made it quite clear to Roger I considered his ideas to be barking mad."

Uncle Bill sat silently for a few moments. "Well," he said
finally, "seems to me the real issue is that new restaurant serving

beer. That's gonna draw the locals like moths to a flame. Doesn't matter how good Maria's cooking is."

"I quite agree. Rudy, however, could offer no immediate suggestions. Apparently, our inestimable sheriff has availed himself of alcohol produced from some of the local stills. The expression 'pot calling the kettle black' comes to mind."

"Yeah, Tiny won't be any help. Have you talked to that Sky Blue fella?"

"Er, no. Loretta was rather adamant I not do so, for reasons I need not repeat."

"Dammit, Bennie, when you're in a hole, you got to stop digging yourself deeper."

I stiffened. "I say, Uncle Bill, that's rather unfair. I believe I have behaved honourably, especially in light of Sunflower's, er, unorthodox behaviour."

Uncle Bill shook his head. "Yeah, all right. You know when she and Sky Blue are gonna open that restaurant of theirs?"

"Alas, no, although I gather Pedro has almost completed the refurbishment work. They'll have to secure the necessary comestibles, as we did, of course. One might guess a week or two."

"Well, pard'ner, first thing you gotta do is reopen tomorrow. I got a couple cans of wasp spray in the barn. Look for 'em on a shelf along the back wall. The flies won't live long. You'll just have to sweep 'em up after they're dead. I'll go see Maria in the morning. She's probably pretty riled up. We need to get her back into the kitchen. Then I'll talk to Rudy. Maybe we can figure a way to get beer from the bar closer to the cafe."

"Eh? Are you proposing to relocate the package liquor operations?"

"I dunno, but like I say, I gotta talk to Rudy about it."

"Very well. Things appear to be shipshape, or at least as much as possible, given ill winds and rough seas."

"Oh, there's one more thing."

"Yes?"

"I need you to repair Marjorie's stall before you head into town tomorrow. She kicked a few boards out today. I don't want her to hurt herself."

I considered Marjorie's continual efforts to inflict harm on whatever components of my corpus were within striking range. "Er, yes. Perhaps it would be wise to offer her an especially bracing dose of Farm Calm before I effect repairs?"

Uncle Bill smiled. "Haven't I told you, she's as gentle as a lamb?"

"Indeed. A lamb even the fiercest lion would give way to."

The next morning, having been awakened by a group of especially voluble swallows, eluded Marjorie's repeated attempts to emboss her hoof on the self's hindquarter, and braced myself with several cups of viscous cowboy coffee, I motored into town, armed with two spray cans of what I hoped was accurately named WASP DEATH.

In town, I espied a large crowd gathered around the front entrance of Rudy's Bar. The watch read a cheerful nine o'clock, one hour before Rudy's normal opening hour.

I parked the lorry in front of the cafe and walked towards the milling crowd. The front entrance was gone, replaced by a large gaping hole. Just inside was a lorry, the back of which was covered in dirt and debris.

Amongst the crowd were Sky Blue and Sunflower, the latter dressed in her inaptly named coveralls.

"I say," I shouted, "is anyone hurt?"

Espying my approaching corpus, Sky Blue shook his head. "Bad *chi*, man. Real bad *chi*."

"Er, yes," I replied. I inched my way forwards through the gawking crowd.

"Isn't it awful, Benjamin?" said Sunflower breathlessly. "I think somebody already called the sheriff."

I resisted the urge to guffaw, perceiving that an outburst of laughter might be viewed rather out of context in the situation. "No doubt, Tiny will wish to investigate," I replied.

Sunflower gently took my hand. "We're going to open our restaurant next week. You're invited. Your girlfriend, too. Siddhartha will nourish both your souls."

I glanced down at Sunflower's undulating décolletage. "Yes, they can," I muttered. "I mean, soulful nourishment sounds, er, well, soulful. What shall you be serving?"

"Sky's still working on the final menu, but it's going to be great. Lentil loaf, chickpea curry, tofu *cassoulet*, black bean burgers, and lots more."

I nodded politely, not wishing to enquire as to the precise gastronomic nature of lentil loaf or tofu *cassoulet*. "Er, yes, those certainly sound . . . different. I shall be, er, anxious, to try them, that is."

"We want you both to be our guests on opening night. And don't forget we'll have beer and wine, too. Mister Garcia told Sky the building he sold us came with a liquor licence."

Rudy's theory had been spot-on. "Did he now? Most thoughtful of Joe. Doubtless lentil loaf should be complemented by a *Chateau Margaux* '53."

"We weren't going to serve beer and wine, but Mister Garcia said we would get more customers. And he told us he would sell us beer and wine at special prices."

"Yes, we have always found Joe's prices to be uniquely special."

"That's so cool. And he's such a sweet man, too. Don't you think so?"

"Joe Garcia?" I spluttered. "I mean, 'sweet' might not do him justice, as you will undoubtedly discover."

Presently, Rudy arrived, his lorry screeching to a halt near the gathered crowd. "Get out of my way," he shouted, pushing through the crowd to where I stood.

After a quick review of Sunflower's nearby frame, he turned to me. "Bennie, what the hell happened?" He stared at the debris and grasped his head with his hands. "Jesus Christ," he muttered.

"I gather someone drove their lorry through your front entrance," I said.

"Get away, everyone," shouted Rudy, as he manoeuvred to the front of the gathered mass. Then, eyeing the lorry, he emitted a loud groan. "Goddamn him!"

"What is it?" I asked.

"That pickup. Don't you recognise it?"

"The lorry? Not especially. I mean, it seems to bear a striking resemblance to most of the local lorries, especially the preponderance of dirt."

Presently, I felt a sudden dampness on the trousers. "Gah!" I shouted, and espied Paco retreating into the building. "Nestor?"

"Yeah. C'mon, let's see if he's hurt."

The lorry was covered in debris—rock, adobe mud, splintered pieces of lumber, and glass shards. Peering inside the cab, I espied Nestor slumped on the seat. He was surrounded by numerous empty green and brown beer bottles and snoring like a congested freight engine.

"I gather he was inebriated when he collided with the bar," I said.

Rudy looked at Nestor. Then he looked towards the front of the truck, which had stopped just in front of the large cooler Rudy kept for package sales. The door of the cooler was wide open.

"See that?" said Rudy, as he pointed to the top shelf.

"Yes," I replied. "It appears to be empty."

"Goddamn him."

"I don't understand."

Rudy's face had turned a shade of crimson. "That top shelf. That's where I keep beer—in bottles just like those on the seat. He smashed through the front and helped himself. Jesus!"

Rudy reached through the open driver's side window, seized Nestor's shoulder, and began to shake him violently. "C'mon, wake up, you goddamn drunk! Nestor, wake the hell up!"

Nestor groaned but remained asleep. The crowd now surrounded the lorry, reminding me of the cattle at the ranch who would gather at the fence.

Rudy opened the lorry's door. "Give me a hand," said Rudy. "Let's get him outta here."

"Do you think it's wise to move him? He may be seriously injured."

"The only thing that's seriously injured is Nestor's goddamn liver." Rudy raised the unconscious mass into a sitting position. Nestor's head lolled from side to side and he began mumbling in Spanish.

"What is he saying?" I asked.

"I dunno. Something about the war, I think. Here, when I pull him out, you grab his legs. We can carry him into my office and put him on the couch."

For a smallish individual, Nestor was remarkably heavy. As we carried him into Rudy's office, Paco followed, alternately barking and urinating. We set Nestor down. He resumed snoring. Paco jumped onto the sofa, curled up by Nestor's legs, and began to growl.

"Sod off, you bloody cur," I snarled.

Rudy wiped the sweat from his brow. "I'll let him sleep it off. Pedro can take him home later. I gotta look at the damage to the bar."

We walked back to the front room. The crowd was now slowly dispersing. Presently, Tiny arrived. Lifting himself out of his lorry, he waddled in and began surveying the damage. Glancing in my direction, he grunted disapprovingly, then turned to Rudy.

"What happened?" Tiny asked. "Whose pickup?"

"What do you think happened, Tiny?" Rudy said. "Goddamn Nestor, that's what happened."

Tiny nodded dimly. "Uh, okay, Rudy. You want to file an accident report?"

"What for?" Rudy asked.

Tiny grasped his belt and hoisted his trousers. "Insurance," he replied. "Insurance companies gotta have an accident report before they pay up."

"I don't have any insurance," hissed Rudy. "Nobody around here does."

"Uh, yeah. Sorry, Rudy." Tiny glanced around the wreckage and whistled softly. "Jesus," he muttered. "Where's Nestor?"

"In my office, sleeping it off. Bennie and me carried him inside."

Tiny eyed me dismissively. "Okay. Well, I guess there's nothing for me to do."

"Should you not cite Nestor for driving whilst drunk?" I asked, incredulous at the apparent indifference to the matter of Nestor's wall-crashing lorry.

"What for, *gringo*?" Tiny asked.

"Surely there are laws against driving whilst intoxicated."

Tiny shrugged his ample shoulders and then turned his attention to the cooler. "Hey Rudy, mind if I grab a couple of bottles?"

Without waiting for a reply, he thrust his arms inside it and hoovered up four bottles of beer. "Put it on my tab," he said. Then he snaked his way around the debris on the floor, exited through the gaping hole, heaved himself into his lorry, and departed, leaving a large cloud of dust in his wake.

"Scotland Yard would be proud," I said, shaking the head.

"Huh? You mean Tiny? Yeah, he's pretty useless, but you already knew that."

"What will you do?"

Rudy surveyed the room. "I dunno. Looks like it's just the front wall. Not like the cafe after Coronado got finished with it."

"One can be thankful Nestor's destructive capacity has not reached that of Coronado, at least not yet."

"Anyway, it won't be too hard to rebuild the wall. I'll call the Ortiz brothers. Then Pedro can frame a new door. We should be back in business in a few days. Maybe a week."

"If you need anything, let me know. I must now despatch the wasps and the flies which have taken up residence in the cafe. And, doubtless Maria will be in a foul mood."

"Tell *mi querida* I could sure use some of her *huevos rancheros* this morning."

"I shall inform her of the damage and submit your request. Even Maria might extend you sympathy under the circumstances. Well, cheer-o."

By the time I exited the bar, the onlookers had disappeared. Only Pedro, the town dog, remained. He lay on the *portal* near the entrance and thumped his tail as I approached him. "There's a good dog," I said, bending over to pat his head. Although Pedro was prone to urination on tyres, boots, and any other stationary objects, unlike Paco he was good-tempered.

As I was about to cross the street towards the cafe, Roger's wheeled Moby arrived at the bar. "Fantastic!" he shouted. "Amazing!" He then turned to me. "What do you think, eh, old chap? Is this not a gift from God?"

I gaped at him, unsure how Nestor's motorised excavation was a gift from God, unless He had departed His Heaven and embarked upon a rather less-than-heavenly bender.

"Er, Roger, do you know what happened?" I asked.

"Of course I do, old chap." He barked an order into the bus. Jim, his cameraman, stepped out, Bolex in hand, and disappeared into the gaping hole. "That," he said, pointing to the hole, is our 'before' cafe."

"Rudy's bar?"

"We must leave it like that for, oh, a few weeks or a month, until we finish filming."

"Eh? Nestor's wrecked lorry is inside."

"Even better! The cafe ruined by an unfortunate accident." Roger extracted a pen and the small notebook from his jacket pocket, and began scribbling furiously. "Your uncle's wife, what was her name, the one who died?"

"You mean Celestina?"

"That's it," said Roger. He began muttering to himself whilst scribbling notes. "She has died in a tragic accident. Celestina swerved to avoid hitting an innocent child who was chasing after her puppy into the street. The audience will eat it up."

Roger began to machine-gun orders in the direction of the bus. "Find me a small child in this town. Today. A pretty one, four or five years old. With curly hair and dimples. A Shirley Temple-looking little girl. And a small, cute dog. Not a mangy one like that thing." He pointed at Pedro, who raised his head and wagged his tail, apparently unaware of having been slandered. Pedro was flea-ridden but did not suffer from mange. "A collie would be perfect. You know, like Lassie. Find me one of those!"

Roger continued to scribble notes and mumble. "The child will grow up and reopen the cafe to honour Celestina. Maybe it's her daughter. Yes, that's even better. The mother sacrifices herself to save her daughter. The daughter grows up, moves away to New York. She marries and has children of her own. Her father still lives on his ranch. He's dying and begs her to come back and reopen the cafe that meant so much to her late mother. But her husband doesn't want to leave the city. They argue. The husband flies into a rage and runs off with his secretary. The daughters—Esperanza and Maria, except not ugly—come with her. After triumphing over adversity, they bring the dying father, in his wheelchair, to the cafe on opening night. There is a large picture of Celestina on the wall of the cafe. The father sees the picture, smiles, and dies. Fade to black."

Roger returned the pen and notebook to his jacket pocket. Then he looked upwards to the blue sky and raised both arms. "I am a genius!" he shouted.

I raised an eyebrow.

Roger returned his gaze to earth. "Well, old chap, what do you think?"

Although the vocal cords advocated a high-decibel response of the "raving lunatic" variety, the more diplomatic neurons prevailed. "M-hem," I croaked.

"Excuse me?"

"Er, afraid I must return to the cafe to address our unfortunate insect infestation." I retrieved the two spray cans of WASP DEATH and displayed them to Roger. "Rather less pathos than cute children and smallish dogs, one imagines."

"But I need you to tell Rudy to leave that wreckage alone for now. Make no repairs."

"What?" I replied, wondering whether Rudy's response to such a request would involve discharging the shotgun he kept under the bar. "Yes, well, surely you can explain the artistic significance of, er, wreckage, far better than I."

"My time is far too valuable to deal with such things. After all, old chap—"

"Yes, I know." I glanced at the watch. "I will endeavour to speak with Rudy after despatching the cafe's six-legged invaders. But I should not get one's hopes up."

"The studio will pay for the inconvenience, of course. How about two thousand?"

"Two thousand dollars? I shall inform Rudy of your offer."

"Make sure he accepts it," said Roger. "Oh, and one other thing."

"Yes?"

"I want to conduct a screen test for that pretty young girl who works at your cafe." He winked slyly.

The Graves hackles arose, ready to defend the betrothed maiden's honour. "You mean, Loretta?"

"Yes, that's her."

"A screen test, you say?"

Roger's Cheshire-cat smile emerged. "Oh, it's quite simple, really. I want to determine her screen presence, you know, whether the camera likes her. Does she look natural before it?"

I goggled him warily. "Er, and you shall conduct this, screen test, where exactly? In the cafe?"

Roger laughed. "No, old chap. I always conduct them in the bus."

"Loretta and I are engaged to be married."

Roger's raised an eyebrow briefly. "Engaged? Why, that's wonderful news, old chap." He slapped my shoulder energetically. "Congratulations and all that. Who knows, you may be marrying a new Hollywood star."

Although the hackles remained at quarters, I resisted the temptation to unleash the WASP DEATH on Roger's person.

"Tell her I must see her," he continued nonchalantly. "The sooner the better. You know—"

"Yes, yes," I interrupted, waving my hand, not wishing to hear the vapid expression yet again. "Now, I really must attend to the wasps."

Roger took my hand and shook it vigorously. "Don't forget to tell her, old chap. And don't let that bar owner fix anything." He strutted away, looking like an oiled peacock.

"Gah," I moaned.

The grey matter reeled as I dashed to the cafe. Stepping inside, I ignored the laboured buzzing of the flies, most of which lay on their backs on the floor. The wasps had abandoned the spilt honey, which had solidified into a yellowish mass. I espied them crawling over one of the honey bottles on a table near the back of the room. I approached carefully, raised both cans of insecticide and fired a broadside, and a second. The wasps sank to the table. Lord Nelson could not have relished a victory more.

Entering the kitchen, I encountered Maria and Esperanza. They stared at me venomously.

"Where the fuck you been, *Pendejito*?" snarled Esperanza. "*El Gordo* showed up, tells everybody we're closed. Then he asked Maria to make him some *enchiladas*."

Maria nodded her head, spraying cigarette ash.

"Did you not notice we were overrun with flies and wasps?" I asked.

"So?" Esperanza said. "I got them at home. So does Maria."

"It's rather different. I wasn't going to endanger our customers with wasps."

Esperanza rolled her eyes. "You owe us all money, Loretta, too, 'cause we didn't get no tips."

"That reminds me," I said, "where is Loretta? I must speak with her."

"Uh, she went . . . home," said Esperanza.

I raised an eyebrow, suspecting foul play, or at least something of a conspiratorial nature. "When? Earlier this morning?"

"She went home . . . yesterday. Uh, we ain't seen her since."

Suspicion had by now roused the Holmesian neurons. "You seem rather hesitant regarding Loretta's whereabouts. What's going on?"

"Nothing's going on, *Pendejito*." Esperanza laughed and drew her finger across her throat. "Maybe Loretta don't want to get married no more."

"What?"

"Maybe she figured out she don't like *gringos*, especially ones who sniff around *chichonas* like a dog."

"Stop spouting gibberish, Esperanza," I said. "Do you or do you not know where Loretta is?"

Maria reached out and gripped Esperanza's arm. "*No más, hermana*," said Maria, calmly. Apparently taken aback at the return fire, Esperanza grunted. "Okay. Loretta didn't say nothing about the wedding. She just told us she had to do something this morning. Said she would be here before we opened for lunch."

I glanced at the watch. Loretta had been unusually reticent the past few days, and I began to contemplate whether Esperanza was indeed correct about the wedding, petulance aside.

"Very well," I said. "The wasps have been dealt with and the majority of the flies have expired. I shall prepare the dining room."

"You talk to Rudy?" asked Esperanza. "The bar looks real bad."

"I did, actually. He believes the damage can be repaired in short order. However, Roger wishes to pay Rudy two thousand dollars to leave the bar in its present state of disrepair, including Nestor's wrecked lorry."

"How come?" Esperanza asked, apparently baffled.

"Roger wishes to film the current wreckage of the bar to represent the cafe prior to its resurrection. Oh, and the wreckage is the result of a tragic accident."

"What accident?"

"Ah, Celestina swerved her lorry to avoid hitting her daughter's collie, hence the fatal crash."

Esperanza's cigarette drooped. "Celestina didn't have no daughter," she said. "No dog, neither."

"Er, yes. Roger intends to take what one might call poetic licence with the story."

"I don't care what kinda licence he got, as long as Maria and me get our money."

"Oh, and he would like us to cater lunches and dinners for his crew. Five dollars per person per meal. I informed him the decision was Maria's, and hers alone."

"How many?" asked Maria.

"Six people currently, perhaps a few more at a later date," I replied.

Esperanza began to perform the requisite multiplication on her fingers. "*Hermana*, that's, uh, fifty dollars a day."

"Sixty, actually," I said.

Maria considered the matter for a longish minute. "Okay. What do I got to cook?"

"Merely our standard fare. Should their souls require nourishment, they can ask the Siddhartha restaurant."

"Huh?" both responded in unison.

"The sign, the one Coronado made for them. It said Siddhartha would satisfy hunger and nourish souls."

"What the fuck does that mean?" asked Esperanza.

"I haven't the foggiest. But we shall soon find out. According to Sunflower, Siddhartha will open next week."

Chapter 21

After several hours of work, the dining room was properly spiffed and ready for the luncheon crowd. Owing to hand-and-knee work to remove the spilt honey and the deceased insects, the lower back was rather stiff. As I was in mid-stretch to lubricate the offended muscles, the front door banged open, admitting Sunflower. She rushed at me like an enraged rugby player and flung herself around the self's startled corpus.

"Benjamin," she sobbed, "please help me."

"There, there," I said as I unsuccessfully attempted to dislodge her. "What has happened?"

"The ghost. I heard it." She tightened her grip around my neck like a python.

"You heard a ghost?"

Sunflower's sobs now took on a loud, wailing quality, such as what one might hear from a distraught hyaena. "I know it sounds crazy. I never heard a voice like that. It was horrible."

Although a Graves prided himself on offering a shoulder for the fairer sex to cry upon, ghostly voices had never before been the *raison d'etre*. Attempting to soothe the distraught maiden, I stroked her hair.

The sobbing subsided. "Oh, Benjamin," cooed Sunflower, "you're so kind." She then raised her head and proceeded to kiss me. And not one of those quick, kiss-your-aunt-goodbye-there's-a-good-little-chap pecks on the cheek, either.

"Please, Sunflower. I mean—"

"Shhh, Benjamin," she replied, putting a finger on what was now rather a confused set of Graves lips and then kissing them again. The steel in the Graves spine was now the consistency of warm marmalade.

At that moment, Fate brought its cannons to bear: three of them, in the form of Maria and Esperanza, who stormed into the dining room from the kitchen, and Loretta, who walked through the front entrance.

"Somebody hurt?" shouted Esperanza as she opened the kitchen door, only to espy the untimely entanglement before her. She paused, mouthed something silently, then exploded. "What the fuck, *Pendejito!*"

"Benjamin Graves, you pig!" yelled Loretta.

The Graves ship had been hulled and was now fast taking on water. I pried Sunflower's arms from around my neck. "Gah! I mean, it's not what you think. Sunflower heard a ghost. She was terrified. I was merely providing aid and comfort, that sort of thing."

"A ghost?" shouted Esperanza. "Your *chichona* friend says she heard some ghost. So she runs to you so you can f—"

"Shut up, Esperanza," I roared.

"You pig," Loretta yelled again. She stormed out the front door, wailing.

I pushed Sunflower away and was about to run after Loretta, but was stopped by Maria's iron grip on my left arm. Her stare spoke an Encyclopaedia Britannica's worth of volumes.

"Leave her alone, Bennie," said Maria.

"But Maria, you don't understand." I sighed.

"Please, it's my fault, Maria," said Sunflower. "I didn't know where else to go. A deep voice started speaking to me. It said it was the ghost of Alejandro Mora and that the old bar should never open again. Then it said Sky and I must leave today and go back to California. Then it said Joe Garcia was going to put rattlesnakes inside the restaurant and our bus. And then it called me horrible names and said I had better stay away from Benjamin or else—"

She burst into tears again and covered her face.

Embers of suspicion began to glow brightly in the grey matter. Although the ancestral Graves estate was said to be haunted by several of the more dull-witted relatives past, one had a natural scepticism about the existence of such apparitions. And for someone who had died many years ago, the aural apparition of Alejandro Mora was rather well-informed about recent events, including Joe Garcia's penchant for rattlesnake tossing.

The front door again opened, this time admitting Sky Blue. "Hey, baby," he said, walking towards her, "I've been looking for you." Sunflower fell into his arms.

"Sky, I'm so glad you're here." She kissed him passionately.

"Did you hear this, er, ghost, too?" I asked him.

"Ghost, man?" Sky Blue's eyes widened. "No, I was in the back of the restaurant, working with Pedro, when I heard Sunflower scream. I ran inside, but she was already gone."

"You saw no white-sheeted apparitions floating about, heard no sounds of dragging chains, that sort of thing?"

Sky Blue considered this momentarily, then shook his head. "No, man. But I tell you, there's real bad *chi* in this town."

"I heard it, Sky," moaned Sunflower, resting her head on his chest. "It was horrible."

"Don't you worry, baby. I'll protect you."

"Er, perhaps you should escort Sunflower to your bus," I said. "Chance for her to, well, regain her composure, that sort of thing."

"Yeah, man," he said. "C'mon, baby. Any ghost knows you've got a great aura."

She whimpered softly as he led her out the front door.

The Holmesian instincts were now engaged, and the game was afoot. Joe Garcia was the most natural suspect. Then again, ever eager for lucre, he would hardly benefit from scaring away a new customer. And Esperanza, the other obvious suspect, stood in front of me, stone-faced and silent.

I eyed her suspiciously. "Something is amiss," I said.

Esperanza exhaled a large cloud of smoke at the suspicion-filled oculars. "I got news for you, *Pendejito*, Alejandro's ghost is real. I heard him once. So did Maria."

Maria nodded in agreement.

"No doubt you did. But for someone who died long ago, Alejandro's ghost seems remarkably well-informed."

"Alejandro, uh, always knew what was going on in town," said Esperanza.

"Really? Including the rattlesnake Joe bunged through the window into our kitchen?"

Esperanza remained silent.

"And surely Alejandro's ghost realises Joe profits by selling overpriced supplies, just as he sells to us. And our ghost must also realise avarice is Joe's *sine qua non*."

"What's that mean?" asked Esperanza.

"It means this entire ghost business is tosh and you are the obvious suspect."

"¡*Veta a la chingada*!" she shouted. "I ain't no ghost and Maria and me were in the kitchen when your *chichona* friend came in. Don't you accuse me of nothing, *Pendejito*."

"Then, who?" I asked, both to her and the self.

"Who the fuck cares, *Pendejito*. This town gonna be better when that *chichona* ain't here no more. And when you ain't here, neither. Look what you just done to poor Loretta." Esperanza raised her middle finger in my direction.

"Somehow," I growled, "this is your doing, Esperanza, alibi or no, and I intend to discover how."

"*Hermana*," said Maria, "you do this, like Bennie says? 'Cause if you did, you just hurt our Loretta."

Esperanza looked at Maria and then launched a barrage of Spanish, which included frequent use of the words *chichona* and *Pendejito*.

"What did you say?" I asked.

"I said if Alejandro's ghost gets you and that *chichona* to go, that's real good."

Maria turned to me. "Señor Bennie, I don't think this is Alejandro's ghost. But Esperanza's been here with me. She couldn't do nothing."

"Well, I am relieved you share my suspicions, Maria. But if this is not the work of your sister, then whom?"

Maria shrugged. "I dunno. Maybe that movie *gringo*."

"Roger? He seems quite besotted with Sunflower. Besides, he knows nothing about the rattlesnake incident."

Maria shrugged. The front door opened, admitting two customers. "You gotta wait tables, Bennie," Maria said. "Then you find Loretta and apologise to her real good, *que no?*"

"Yes, Maria."

After the straggling luncheon customers were finally herded out the door, I decamped to Rudy's, as I had yet to discuss Roger's offer for maintaining the bar in its present state of destruction.

I found him behind the bar, clearing the dust that had been raised by Nestor's crash.

"*Hola*, Rudy," I said.

"Hey, Bennie," he replied, wiping his brow. "What a goddamn mess."

"Er, yes. Uh, about the mess, actually, Roger wishes to pay you two thousand dollars to maintain the bar in its present condition."

"Two thousand dollars? Why?"

"I gather he has constructed a narrative—and a rather bizarre one at that—in which the wrecked bar will serve as the cafe after an accident in which Celestina dies, having nobly swerved to avoid her daughter and her daughter's collie."

"What?" he said, eyes widening. "Celestina dying in a car accident? She didn't have a daughter or a dog."

"I believe it is referred to as artistic licence. In any case, what would seem to matter is the financial offer."

"Two thousand, huh?" Rudy considered the figure for a moment. "For how long?"

"He didn't exactly say. A few weeks, a month perhaps. You could still operate the package store, couldn't you?"

"Yeah, I guess. Okay. Do I have to sign something?"

"One would assume."

Rudy shook his head, then retrieved a glass from the shelf and cleaned it. "These *gringos* sure are crazy," he muttered.

"Eh, what?"

Rudy laughed. "Sorry, Bennie, I didn't mean you and El Vaquero."

"No offence taken. Although, speaking of offence, there is rather a mystery brewing."

"Yeah? What's that?"

I proceeded to relay the morning's ghostly events, as well as Loretta's having seen Sunflower delivering an all-too-real kiss upon the Graves lips.

Rudy laughed. "Alejandro's ghost wouldn't scream at Sunflower, he'd be on his knees begging her to stay. As for Sunflower kissing you, tell her she can kiss me. I ain't engaged."

"M-hem, yes. "More importantly, who is pretending to be Alejandro's ghost? Esperanza has an alibi and Joe would never jeopardise his golden egg–laying goose, as it were."

"Maybe Joe wants to sell the building again."

"Perhaps. Then again, who would buy it? After all, the building sat vacant for many years."

Rudy scratched his chin. "Yeah, maybe you're right, Bennie. So who wants them to leave? Didn't you said everybody was at the cafe when Sunflower ran in?"

"Yes. Maria, Esperanza, and I were all present."

"You're forgetting someone," said Rudy.

"Who?" I asked, before the grey matter whirred and offered an answer. "Loretta? How? I mean, she ran into the cafe and found Sunflower and me, that is—gah!"

"Makes the most sense, Bennie. ¿*Que no*?

"Loretta? I mean, she was quite upset, not that I blame her, of course."

"You know the saying, 'Hell hath no fury.'"

"But why would Loretta wish to *cause* such a fury, especially one which caused Sunflower to seek aid and comfort from the self?"

Rudy scratched his head. "I dunno. Maybe Loretta figured Sunflower would leave town. Or maybe that's why I've been divorced four times. Never could make sense of women."

"There are also the practical considerations."

"What do you mean?" asked Rudy.

"Well, presumably, Loretta could not walk up to Sunflower and announce she was actually the ghost of Alejandro. And Loretta's voice could hardly be described as deep."

Rudy pondered for a few moments whilst he cleaned several glasses. "Walkie-talkies."

"Eh?"

"It's an old trick. You hide a walkie-talkie in a room. Then you just talk into another one nearby." Rudy laughed. "When I was in the army, there was this major who lived on the base. Everybody hated him. So one night, we rigged up a walkie-talkie under his bed. Scared the shit out of that little bastard. There's your ghost."

"Most clever. Where would one find walkie-talkies in town?"

Rudy pondered the question. "Joe used to sell them. They come in real handy working on a ranch, or for hunting."

"So Esperanza could have been at the cafe and been the voice of Alejandro's ghost.

"Yeah, I guess so," said Rudy. "Esperanza's voice is kinda husky, too."

"You would make Sherlock Holmes proud, Rudy. What should we do?"

"We?" said Rudy. "I'm not doing a damn thing about this ghost shit. I got enough with that hole in the front wall.

"But surely—"

"Bennie, you want my advice?"

I grimaced. "Er, go down with the ship?"

"Get those other two to leave town. As long as Sunflower's around, Loretta's never gonna trust you. Not that I blame her." Rudy grinned.

"Yes, well, other than delivering ghostly warnings, how am I supposed to accomplish that? Although ultimatums to leave town by sundown appear to be a staple of Uncle Bill's Zane Grey novels, one doubts they would be effective at present."

"I dunno. I'm just a bartender with a wrecked bar."

"I don't suppose you could speak with her. Tell her she has nothing to worry about, a Graves is always faithful, et cetera, et cetera. I'm quite sure you could provide various supportive nostrums."

"You want me to tell Loretta that, with Sunflower around? Are you crazy?"

"My explanations seem to ring rather hollow at present."

Rudy sighed deeply. "Yeah, okay. I'm gonna regret this. Meanwhile, *try* to stay out of trouble."

"Thank you, Rudy. In the meantime, I shall pursue my investigations. I should not be surprised if Esperanza purchased the walkie-talkies."

"Yeah, good luck with that. But even if you do, that won't solve your real problem."

"I suppose not. But at least I shall be able to demonstrate to Loretta the proximate cause of Sunflower's, er, errant behaviour. Thanks, Rudy."

I departed the bar, armed with the knowledge of a ghostly conspiracy, but needing to acquire sufficient evidence before confronting Esperanza with her crimes. Once armed with Esperanza's confession, I intended to speak with Loretta.

My first stop was Joe's store, where I found Coronado standing watch behind the counter.

"*Hola*, Señor Graves. Did you hear? Alejandro's ghost must be real mad."

"There is no ghost, Coronado. The voice that terrified Sunflower was a trick."

"A trick?"

"Yes. The perpetrator used a pair of walkie-talkies to effectuate the deceit."

Coronado goggled me wide-eyed. "Alejandro's ghost has a walkie-talkie?"

"What? No. This is all the work of Esperanza."

Coronado eyes bulged. "*¡Hijole!* Esperanza's a ghost, too?"

I massaged the temples, vainly hoping to relieve the arriving headache. "No, Esperanza used a walkie-talkie and pretended to be a ghost so she could terrify Sunflower."

"How come Esperanza wants to scare Señorita Flower? She's real nice."

"A surprisingly astute question, Coronado," I replied, raising an eyebrow. "I theorise two reasons. First, the new restaurant will compete with our cafe, which will cost Esperanza brass. Second, by scaring Sunflower, Esperanza assumed, correctly as it were, Sunflower would rush into my arms, which would distress Loretta, knacker the engagement, and cause me to exit Vaca Seca permanently. Case closed."

Coronado nodded his head and smiled.

"You haven't the vaguest notion what I mean, do you?"

"Sorry, Señor Graves. Is Esperanza gonna scare me, too?"

"Eh? Why would Esperanza wish to scare you?"

"I dunno. I don't think she likes me much."

"I shouldn't trouble yourself about that, Coronado. For Esperanza, the milk of human kindness soured long ago. Besides, I believe the guns of Esperanza's wrath are aimed squarely at me, not you."

"I like you, Señor Graves."

"I, er, like you, too, Coronado," I said in a tone of sympathy accompanied by several measures of guilt. "Now, about these walkie-talkies. Did you happen to sell a pair recently?"

"Maybe. People sometimes buy them when they go hunting. A couple of years ago, Juan Gabaldón and his brother Freddy got lost when they went elk hunting near Wheeler Peak—"

"No embellishment required, Coronado," I interrupted. "I'm sure walkie-talkies are the hunter's favoured companion, plus bottles of whisky. Has anyone purchased a pair recently?"

Coronado shrugged. He stepped out from behind the counter and waddled down one of the aisles. I followed close behind. He paused before several large cans of hominy, used for *posole*. Next to the cans was a package advertising a pair of walkie-talkies within. Coronado eyed the package and pointed. "I think we had two of those. I guess we sold the other one."

I resisted the urge to enquire why walkie-talkies were located next to the cans of hominy and focused on this potential clue. "To whom did you sell this latest pair?" I asked.

He scratched his head. "I dunno. I can ask Joe if you want."

"Damn and blast," I muttered, as the hoped-for clue gave me the heave-ho.

"Do you want to buy those, Señor Graves," he said, pointing at the box, "in case you and El Vaquero go hunting and get lost? Or maybe you can talk to Alejandro's ghost."

"Er, some other time, perhaps." I wondered now how Sherlock Holmes would proceed. Then, as I walked towards the front of the store, the Baker Street detective's ghost biffed the grey matter. "On second thought, Coronado, I believe I shall purchase those walkie-talkies."

The transaction completed, I returned to the cafe, the package of walkie-talkies underneath the arm.

"*J'accuse* Esperanza!" I shouted, as I burst into the kitchen.

Esperanza, who was grasping a large tomato, raised the cigarette between her lips defiantly. "Huh?"

"I have solved the mystery and know about the walkie-talkies."

Presently, Loretta appeared, walking into the kitchen from the storeroom. She eyed me balefully.

"Ah, hullo, Loretta," I said. "This whole business about Alejandro's ghost scaring Sunflower and which was the proximate cause of this morning's, er, incident—it was your bloody aunt. She used a pair of walkie-talkies, which she purchased from Joe Garcia, to frighten Sunflower. She hid one of them in their building and then spoke into the other one. Voilà, instant ghost."

Loretta's expression remained fixed.

"What the fuck are you talking about, *Pendejito?*" said Esperanza.

"You know precisely what I am talking about, Esperanza. Or should I now call you Alejandro?"

Esperanza fired the tomato and scored a direct hit on the self, amidships. "¡*Vete a la chingada*! I didn't do nothing with no fucking walkie-talkies or no ghost."

"*Hermana*," said Maria softly. "You swear you didn't do nothing?"

"I swear, Maria," replied Esperanza as she crossed herself rapidly.

"Sorry, Esperanza," I said, as I removed the larger bits of tomato from the now reddish-stained shirt, "but given your previous mendacity, I simply do not believe you. Besides, one seeks individuals with means, motive, and opportunity. You possess all three."

"Esperanza swore she didn't do nothing," said Maria. "I know *mi hermana* sometimes don't tell the truth, but she swore and crossed herself. It's gotta be somebody else."

"Very well, Maria," I replied, as my indignation deflated like a worn tyre, "but there simply is no one else."

"There's gotta be."

I turned my attention to Loretta, whose expression had not changed. "Loretta, please, you must forgive me."

"I forgive you," Loretta said, jaw clenched.

"You don't sound especially forgiving," I replied.

Loretta retrieved a nearby carrot and pitched it towards me with cricket-like precision, into the shoulder. She then reloaded, using a conveniently located tomato, and fired, striking the forehead.

"Gah! Why must I be subjected to this vegetable fusillade?" I shouted as bits of tomato streamed down the face like an oozing waterfall.

All three burst into laughter. "Maybe you need some chiles now, *Pendejito*," Esperanza said, "so you can be green chile stew."

"I'm sorry, Bennie," Loretta said, attempting to stifle further mirth. She retrieved a dish towel and walked towards me.

"Are you going to hurl the towel at me, too?" I asked.

Loretta approached, saying nothing. She raised the towel and cocked her right arm back, as if ready to pitch. She moved the arm slowly forward and began cleaning the debris off my face. Then she kissed me on the tip of the nose.

"We're even."

"Er, yes."

Chapter 22

Despite the reprieve from Loretta, I remained resolved to determine the perpetrator of *l'affaire du fantôme* and convinced that Esperanza was the ghostly puppet master. But the Graves pursuit of truth, justice, and honour was now derailed by a lack of evidence. And so, over the next several days, I pursued the daily routine with vigour, if only to calm the nerves.

The gaping hole in Rudy's Bar remained, *sans* Nestor's lorry, which Luis had towed back to Nestor's abode. Although Roger had protested the lorry's removal because it provided "atmosphere" to the demolished bar, Rudy did not wish his customers to have to negotiate through more of the wreckage than necessary.

"Could you not at least cover the hole with plywood?" I asked Rudy on this particular morning. I had espied several mice scurry underneath a nearby wall. Pedro had also taken up residence and was curled up in a corner under one of the tables.

Rudy responded with a stream of invective, no doubt reflecting growing frustration at an inability to effect repairs and return the bar to its rightful place among the locals. There was also the slight matter of Roger's promise of payment.

"Did you enquire of Roger when he would pay you the two thousand dollars?" I asked.

"Hell yes, I did," said Rudy. "Twice. He told me the studio would send me a check after I signed their standard contract and filled out some goddamn form."

"When I was employed by the bank, it was most insistent on forms filled out, generally in triplicate. Have you signed said contract and filled out said form?"

"No. That fucking *gringo* hasn't given 'em to me."

"Why not?"

"He told me he didn't have a 'permission to film' contract or the form. Said that came from the studio directly. Well, I haven't seen it. That's one reason I had Luis tow Nestor's pickup out of here. At least I can get some customers inside now."

"Odd, that. When Roger first enquired of Uncle Bill to film at the ranch, he mentioned a contract. None, as far as I know, has been received."

"Then El Vaquero better get one." Rudy rubbed his grey-stubbled chin wearily. "I know he said a few weeks, but the Ortiz brothers are gonna be real busy. Something about a big job over in Española. I need to get them started soon."

"Have you spoken with Roger? Surely he can ask the studio about the forms?"

"He told me the studio already mailed it to him."

"Er, exactly what address does one give for a bus?"

"It's supposed to go to the post office, so he can pick it up there."

"Ah." Irma Flores, the postmistress, would perform her postal duties when she was so inclined, which was infrequently. "Perhaps you should ask Irma about it."

"I already talked to her this morning. She hasn't seen anything for Roger. Said she'd let me know right away."

I pondered the gravity of the situation. The bank would gleefully pounce on any contractual irregularity to deny payment or impose a penalty on a hapless customer. Presumably, an avaricious film studio would not behave differently.

"We may find ourselves in a similar circumstance," I said.

"How come?"

"Maria agreed to cater luncheons and dinners for Roger's crew for Roger's crew. I've seen no evidence of contractual whereupons and wherefores."

"Well, I know what *I'm* gonna do." Rudy stood up and exited his office. Several minutes later, he returned, cradling the shotgun he kept behind the bar. "This here's gonna be my fucking contract," he said.

I grimaced. "I grant that a loaded shotgun provides a strong inducement to honour contractual obligations, at least in Vaca Seca. But perhaps such a gesture would be, er, misinterpreted by Roger."

Rudy set the gun down on his desk. "I gotta do something, Bennie."

"Allow me speak with him. I owe you a favour, after all, for arguing my case with Loretta.

"Hey, anything for true love. I went over to her mom's house right after you left and spoke to her. She didn't even throw tomatoes at me."

"I should not recommend standing in Loretta's line of fire. Her aim is most precise, rather like your Sandy Koufax."

Rudy laughed. "You a baseball fan now, Bennie, like a real American?"

"Er, not especially. Uncle Bill, however, is. During the season, one can find him glued to the radio most evenings listening to the games."

I glanced at the watch. "Sorry, but I must be off. Morning ablutions at the cafe and all that. I shall locate Roger forthwith and speak with him about the contractual issues."

"Thanks, Bennie. This whole movie thing has turned out to be giant pain in the ass."

"I quite agree," I replied, and bid him good morning.

After returning to the cafe and preparing the dining room, I returned to Garcia's store for needed supplies, whereupon I encountered Sky Blue, who appeared to be doing the same, to the delight of Joe.

"Good morning," I said to both, with false cheer.

Joe nodded silently, engrossed in tallying up the morning's receivables.

Hey, man," Sky Blue said. "We're opening the day after tomorrow. Hoping for some real good *chi*."

"Ah. Sunflower has described some of the menu items. They, er, certainly sound rather unique."

"Yeah, man, it's gonna be a lot different than what your place serves. No offence, man, but *enchiladas* and all that other shit, it kills off your soul."

I considered Maria's cooking, especially her blue-corn chicken *enchiladas* smothered in green chile, to be Heaven-sent. One recoiled at proclaiming such manna to be soul-killing. More importantly, Maria's reaction to hearing such bilge likely would not confine itself to despatching disparaging souls, but also their corporeal containers.

"M-hem. I might suggest you not express your views to Maria directly. She is rather proud of her cooking."

Sky Blue nodded. "That's cool, man. I'm not down on Maria or anything. You gonna come on opening night? We're offering free *lassi* with every meal."

"Good God," I muttered, recalling the emetic reaction to his prior description of that liquid. "I mean, what an excellent idea. Yes, of course we shall be there, welcoming another local business owner, that sort of thing."

"Cool, man."

"Oh, ah, how is Sunflower, by the way? Recovered from her, er, ghostly encounters?"

"She's cool now. I got her *chi* centred."

"Eh?" I replied, not having the vaguest idea of how one's *chi* became centred. "Oh, you may wish to tell her the alleged ghost was a trick, which was performed with walkie-talkies."

"A trick?" said Sky Blue. "Not cool."

"Not in the slightest. Rather in bad taste, really."

"Who would want to trick Sunflower, man? She's got a real gentle soul. That's why she gets real upset by things like mice."

"Er, yes, no doubt the gentlest. As to the identity of the perpetrator, that remains unclear. Afraid the locals have rather a bad habit of, er, practical jokes. But fear not, I intend to severely reprimand the perpetrator, once I identify him."

"That's cool, man. Whoever did it has got some real negative energy."

"Quite."

Sky Blue completed his transaction and departed. I then handed Joe the list of supplies Maria required.

"Liquor licence?" I said, as he began to tally the items. Really?"

"It's a bar, ain't it?" replied Joe. "Had a licence when it was open."

"You do realise you can no more transfer the expired liquor licence of a shuttered bar than you can sell a building which you do not own."

Joe shrugged.

"If they serve beer, it will be ruinous for the cafe's business."

"Why the fuck should I care?"

"A ruined cafe is one which shall not be purchasing supplies from you, that's why."

Joe eyed me silently, apparently tallying receipts from our purchases. "Maybe I'm gonna make up the loss selling to that weirdo," said Joe. He jerked his thumb towards the front door through which Sky Blue had just departed. "He's real stupid, even for a *gringo*."

"How insightful. Perhaps I should inform Maria you believe her to be stupid as well. Doubtless she would be delighted to discuss the subject with you, personally."

Beads of perspiration began to form on Joe's avaricious forehead. "Hey, don't you tell her nothing, *gringo*, I mean, Bennie," he stuttered. "I don't want no trouble from Maria."

"A wise decision. Oh, you have heard about the alleged ghost of Alejandro, have you not?"

Joe grinned. "Yeah, I heard the *chichona* ran straight to you and then Loretta caught you and her, you know . . . " He made the same rude gesture Esperanza favoured.

"Rubbish," I said.

"Hey, I wish she'd come to me. I'd protect her from Alejandro's ghost."

"Yes, yes, you and Rudy both. In any event, I believe the perpetrator purchased the walkie-talkies from the store. To whom did you sell them?"

"It was—uh, I mean, I don't remember." Joe's eyes darted about furtively, like a thief just nicked. He rubbed his chin. "Coronado must have sold 'em. Ask him. Or maybe Alejandro's ghost stole them." Joe began to utter "woo-ooh" sounds and waving his hands in a juvenile manner. He then burst out laughing.

The suspicious neurons were at high alert. "I have already enquired of Coronado. He said you would know."

"I don't know nothing."

"Bollocks. You are hiding something."

Joe shrugged. "Like I said, *gringo*, I don't know nothing."

"Have you considered what shall happen if Sunflower and Sky Blue leave? All that money you are now making? Alas, absent in a flash."

Joe's countenance became pensive. "You said it was a joke."

"Indeed it was, just like the joke which had someone bung a rattlesnake into our kitchen."

"Hey, you can't prove I did nothing."

I raised an accusatory finger. "Admit it, Joe. You are the ghost."

"Me? Hey, I don't want to scare 'em off. Like you said, I'm making lots of money from that Sky Blue *gringo*."

One could not disagree with Joe's fiduciary logic, as he was not wont to bite the hand that enriched the Garcia fisc.

"Then who bought the bloody walkie-talkies?" I asked, as I brought my fist sharply down upon the counter.

"Okay, okay. El Vaquero bought 'em a couple weeks ago."

"What? You sold the walkie-talkies to Uncle Bill?" Uncle Bill, the perpetrator of the ghostly calumny? The grey matter had now run aground.

I stood immobile, mouthing "why" silently, and then walked towards the front door. As I was about to exit, I turned around. "Maria needs those supplies by tomorrow," I said robotically.

"Okay. That's gonna be fifty-five bucks."

"I shall pay you tomorrow after you deliver them."

"But I need some money now. The movie *gringo* bought some stuff last week. Told me the studio would pay me for it."

"Indeed? Well, we shall pay you tomorrow, upon delivery, and not before," I sniffed.

"You think I did what?" said Uncle Bill. He set down the strand of barbed wire he was using to mend a portion of fence, as several steers looked on.

"Joe told me you recently purchased the pair of walkie-talkies."

"Yeah, for when you and me go elk hunting, in case we get separated. You said you wanted to go huntin' with me, remember?"

"I did? Ah, yes, I suppose I did."

"Well, you're a greenhorn who doesn't know his way around these mountains. So I bought the pair of walkie-talkies. That way, if we get separated, I can find you. I got 'em in my closet. Still in the goddamn box, too."

"But Sunflower said the ghost's voice was a man's."

"It sure as hell wasn't mine," shouted Uncle Bill. "Why would I want to scare that poor gal half out of her wits, anyhow? That ain't the cowboy way."

I recalled the means, motive, and opportunity trifecta, and presently found myself without any suspects. "I thought you might, that is, given my, er, troubles, with Sunflower. Perhaps you were attempting to entice her to depart Vaca Seca. Remove temptation, and all that."

Uncle Bill eyed me contemptuously. He retrieved the barbed wire from the ground and a pair of pliers from his trouser pocket. The two steers that had been observing the fence repairs moved closer, the better to eavesdrop.

Uncle Bill wiped his brow with a red handkerchief. "Bennie," he said, "look around. You know how much work this ranch takes, don't you? I can barely keep up, even with your help. I ain't got time for tomfoolery. Now, I've told you

Loretta's a great gal, but if you want to keep her, that's your business, not mine."

One of the steers shook its head in apparent agreement. It lowed loudly, raised its tail and deposited a copious quantity of manure, before sauntering away.

Uncle Bill jerked his thumb at the bovine commentary and laughed. "Not much I can add to that."

"M-hem, yes. My apologies, I should have never even suspected you. As for Loretta, of course I wish to keep her, as you put it, although Fate seems determined to drive a wedge between us."

"Fate ain't the one kissing that Sunflower gal."

"Er, no. By the way, we are all invited for opening night at Siddhartha."

Uncle Bill grimaced. "I dunno. After what you told me is on the menu? Doesn't sound much different than what that steer just left. What the hell is 'lentil loaf' anyway?"

"One prefers not to hazard a guess. But I would appreciate your attendance, in case of any, er—"

"To make sure you behave in front of Loretta? Yeah, okay, Bennie. Now, go get a pair of leather gloves out of the barn and give me a hand with this barbed wire."

After we completed the fence repairs, I returned to the cafe. The investigations regarding the identity of the 'ghost' had come to nought. Absent the guilty party stepping forward, there seemed little one could do but wait for the ghost to emerge again. Besides, with Siddhartha opening soon and promising its patrons liquid solace, an economic typhoon was fast bearing down upon us.

Chapter 23

The next morning, having reached an impasse on the apparitional investigations, I sought out Roger to discuss the lack of payment for Rudy to maintain the bar in its wrecked state, as well as the lack of promised payment for the rights to Celestina's story. As to Roger's lack of payment for goods purchased from Joe Garcia, I had rather less concern, viewing it instead as the hoisting of Joe upon his mercantilist petard.

I stepped tentatively into the bus, which was like a gargantuan and garish version of the campers one would occasionally pass on the expressway in Britain. There was a galley immediately to my left. Towards the centre, I espied a small desk, at which Roger beavered away. In front of him were two stacks of yellow notepaper. Rows of cabinets lined the other side of the bus. And in the very back, a large bed could be seen through a doorway, on top of which lay a bright red, heart-shaped pillow and a large, brownish teddy bear.

"M-hem," I said.

Roger did not look up.

"Hullo," I said. "Do you have a moment?"

Roger glanced up from the desk. He eyed me coolly, apparently disappointed with what stood before him, and mumbled. And, whereas the Graves auditory could not decipher the entirety of his verbiage, it distinctly detected the words "prig" and "jackass."

"Oh, I say, old chap," said Roger with false cheer and falser accent. He goggled me from above his half-glasses, then removed them. "I hear your competition will be opening soon,

Ben. What's the name of the ravishing Sunflower's restaurant again?"

"Er, I believe it is to be called Siddhartha, after the Buddha."

"That's it." Roger put the pen he held down upon the desk. "Do you ever wonder what the Buddha actually ate? Given those statues, he must have chowed down."

"Eh, what? Oh, you mean the Buddha's general rotundity. I gather the menu will include items such as lentil loaf and a tofu casserole. Will you be attending?"

Roger paused. He retrieved the small notebook from his jacket and leafed through several pages. "Why, yes, old chap. I will. It promises to be quite a show."

"Show?" I asked. "Are they planning some form of thespian activities?"

"I meant Sunflower. She told me she will be waitressing, whilst that large boyfriend of hers—what's his name again?—cooks."

"He calls himself Sky Blue, although I gather that is not his Christian name. When did she tell you this?"

"Oh, a few days ago," said Roger, with a gratuitous wink. "She also told me about the ghost. Poor girl must have been scared to death, so to speak. I comforted her as best I could. Sometimes a bit of reassurance is all a girl like that needs, eh, old chap?"

The grey matter contemplated Sunflower's putative comforting and reassuring by Roger with pronounced scepticism. "Er, yes. In any case, I wish to discuss another matter with you."

Returning the half-glasses to his nose, Roger glanced at his watch and pointed at the notepaper. "Sorry, but I'm very busy now. Can it wait?"

I paused, whilst the Graves bursar repulsed the efforts of the Graves courtesy and deference.

"Actually, no, it cannot," I said. "There are some contractual and payment matters to be dealt with, which require your immediate attention."

"Such as?"

"Rudy, for one. He wants to be paid as promised for not repairing the damage so your cameraman can flit about inside and out like a small lizard. I believe the amount you agreed to pay was two thousand dollars. There is also the matter of your promised payment to my uncle for the rights, as you call them, to the story about the cafe. I also gather Joe Garcia would like to be recompensed for the purchases your staff made from his store. And I shall require reimbursement for the cafe catering of luncheons and dinners for you and your staff."

Roger leaned back in his chair. He removed the half-glasses and tossed them onto the desk. "Look, Ben," he said, "I already told that Rudy fellow about the contract he has to sign with the studio and the payment form he has to fill out. It's out of my hands. As for paying your uncle, I've decided to rewrite the entire script, so I don't need to purchase the rights to your uncle's story."

"What? The film no longer will be about the resurrection of the cafe?"

"Well, yes and no, old chap," he said as he reverted to the grating accent and flashed his ivories in a rather mocking way. "I'm still working out all of the details."

I gaped at him, fishlike, but said nothing.

"As for payments for your cafe catering meals and my staff's purchases from that greasy little chap's store, those will be reimbursed through the studio contracts, as I previously explained."

"Yes, but none of us have yet received those contracts."

"They should arrive any day now. That the United States Post Office can even find this godforsaken little town is a miracle."

"I, er—"

"Of course, if Rudy wants to repair his rundown dump of a bar, then he can. As you pointed out, he hasn't signed a contract yet. The same goes for your cafe. Of course, without a signed contract, none of you will be paid a dime."

"I say, do you mean you shan't pay us for what we have already provided?"

Roger eyed me dismissively. "They're called contracts for a reason—old chap."

"Well, yes," I said, "but what about one's word of honour in the interim?"

He burst into laughter. "Word of honour? I'm afraid the only word that matters is 'contract': c-o-n-t-r-a-c-t. Now, I really must finish this new script. Goodbye." He waved his hand, motioning me to exit the bus, and returned to scribbling on the notepaper.

I exited the bus, unsure of what to do next. Roger's reworking of the script would be rather a blow to Uncle Bill, who had already selected—and paid significant brass—for his soon-to-arrive new breeding bull. It seemed Roger had left us little choice: maintain our course and hope for eventual payment, or return to shore with nothing.

"Gah," I whispered

Not wishing to be the bearer of bad news for Uncle Bill, I decided to postpone the inevitable discussion, which would surely require multiple glasses of Dusty Trail and involve dodging fusillades of invective. Instead, I hoofed it to Rudy's and delivered Roger's terms, which at least maintained the possibility of payment.

Rudy slammed down a fortunately empty coffee cup on his desk. "He said what? I'm losing money every day."

"If it is of any consolation, Roger knackered the promised payment to Uncle Bill for the rights to the story. Regrettably, Uncle Bill already spent the promised sum on a new bull. I have not yet relayed the bad news."

"Damn. That ain't good. If Bill needs any money—"

"A most kind offer, Rudy, but unnecessary. I have at least one bull's worth of brass in savings at present."

"Okay, Bennie. Hey, you going to the opening night for the new restaurant? Sunflower stopped by and invited me personally."

"Yes, I received said invitation from Sky Blue. Loretta and I shall both attend, as will Uncle Bill."

"They gonna make sure you behave?"

"Er, yes. In my defence, however, the rumours to the contrary have been rather exaggerated."

"Yeah, I heard Joe talking yesterday."

The eyes attempted a somersault. "Joe previously shared his views with me. One hopes Loretta will not believe him."

"Don't worry," said Rudy. "Most people don't believe anything that Joe says."

"True," I replied. "Then again, Vaca Secans do rather revel in rumours, the more scandalous the better."

"Makes up for our dull lives, I guess."

I sighed. "If only. Well, cheer-o, Rudy. Do let me know if you receive your contract. We await ours for the catering."

"Sure, Bennie."

I departed the bar and returned to the cafe, only to find Roger's cameraman, Jim, filming the dining room.

"I say, why are you filming here?"

Jim placed the camera on a table. "Getting some inside shots," he said. "We'll need those for when we build the set depicting the new cafe."

"I don't understand. I was just speaking with Roger. He informed me the script has changed and the film will no longer be about the cafe's resurrection, as it were."

Jim shrugged. "Hey, I'm just doing what I was told. Roger said to film the dining room, so that's what I'm doing. Oh, and I need to get some shots of the kitchen." He retrieved the camera and continued filming.

"Er, no. As Roger informed me he will no longer be purchasing the rights to Uncle Bill's story, you are hereby banished."

Jim ignored my proclamation and continued filming. I advanced towards him and placed my hand over the lens.

"Don't touch my camera!" he shouted, twisting away. "You know how much it's worth? I'm finished in here anyway."

He walked towards the kitchen door and pushed it open.

"I should not enter the kitchen, if I were you," I said, rather half-heartedly. Jim stepped inside, camera running. Deciding to remain out of firing range, I heard Esperanza curse, then Jim yell, "Give me that," and finally a loudish thud. After a measured silence, one perceived a pronounced whimpering.

Presently, the kitchen door opened and Jim walked back into the dining room, cradling the remains of his camera. "It's ruined," he said.

"Most unfortunate," I replied as I suppressed a smile. "I did warn you not enter the kitchen. Esperanza and Maria are rather territorial."

"Roger's going to have a fit."

"No doubt."

"And he's gonna insist you pay for the camera. A new one costs a thousand bucks."

"You may inform Roger I shall be happy to discuss reimbursement for the damaged camera with him."

"Thanks," Jim said. "I'll tell him."

After Jim departed, I went into the kitchen. Esperanza and Maria were jabbering away like chain-smoking monkeys, whilst Loretta nodded in agreement.

"How many times I got to tell you, *Pendejito*," Esperanza said. "Don't let nobody in our kitchen."

"I did warn the chap. Alas, he paid me no heed."

"Huh?"

"Did you destroy his camera?" I asked Esperanza.

Esperanza glanced at Maria. "That *gringo* comes right up to Maria with that camera thing. I tried to stop him, but Maria, she just grabbed it and threw it against the wall."

"*Sí*," said Maria.

I stifled a laugh. "I suspect we shall have a bit of rough sailing ahead."

"Is Maria in trouble, Bennie?" asked Loretta. "That cameraman practically stuck the camera in her face."

Maria nodded. She pointed the edge of her knife towards her nose.

"Indeed? Did you point that knife at him, Maria?" I asked.

Maria rocked her other hand back and forth. "*Más o menos.*"

"She didn't threaten him, Bennie," said Loretta.

"M-hem. One imagines a stranger might not find a knife-wielding Maria entirely sanguine. Then again, there are extenuating circumstances."

"Does this mean we're not gonna get paid for the lunches and dinners?" asked Esperanza.

"Er, that remains to be seen. There are several outstanding contractual issues to be worked through."

"What the fuck does that mean?" Esperanza growled. "We get paid or not?"

"Once we have a signed contract, yes," I said. "However, we lack such a contract at present. And unless we sign said lacking contract, we will not be paid for the meals already provided."

"How come we got no contract?" Esperanza asked.

"According to Roger, one should be arriving from the studio any day. I have my doubts, however."

"But that *gringo* owes us a lot of money," said Esperanza.

"Er, yes, he does."

Esperanza and Maria chimneyed away and goggled me silently.

"What should we do, Bennie?" asked Loretta.

"It appears we are upon the sharp horns of a financial dilemma," I replied. "Maria, you're the one who does the cooking. I believe the decision is yours."

Esperanza turned to Maria and machine-gunned verbiage in Spanish. Maria shook her head. "So, if we stop now, we don't get no money? But if we keep going, we don't get more money unless we got a contract?"

"That's right. No contract, no money."

"Fucking *gringos*," hissed Esperanza.

"M-hem, yes."

Later, as I was readying the dining room, Roger burst through the front door.

"Who destroyed my camera?" he shouted, nostrils flared like an enraged bull gazing at a matador's red cape.

"That would be Maria," I said cheefully.

"Where is she? I need to speak with her. Now!"

"In the kitchen."

"Pah," Roger said. He began to accelerate towards the kitchen door. I took hold of his arm and set anchor. "Roger, please do not enter. Maria is rather possessive about her kitchen, which is why she rubbished Jim's camera."

"Let go of my arm," said Roger. He wrenched it from my grip. "I don't give a damn about Maria and her kitchen. She destroyed a thousand-dollar camera. I demand you pay for the damage."

"You do understand, do you not, your cameraman was trespassing."

"What do you mean, trespassing? He was filming for my movie. When I get back to Hollywood, we're going to build several sets, one for the kitchen and one for the dining room. That's why Jim was here."

"No doubt, you shall. Alas, the cafe is owned by my Uncle Bill and, if I recall correctly, earlier this morning you stated you were rewriting the script and would no longer be purchasing the story rights from him."

"So? That has nothing to do with destroying private property."

"Yes, but at present there is no contract allowing your cameraman to film inside the cafe. Hence, his presence could well be deemed trespassing."

Roger launched a reptilian stare. "The studio has excellent lawyers, son. You don't want to challenge me on this."

Presently, Esperanza and Loretta emerged from the kitchen. "What's all the shouting, Bennie?" asked Loretta, before espying Roger.

Esperanza moved towards him, raising an accusatory cigarette. "You owe us money, *gringo*. You want food, you gotta pay now."

"And you signed a contract," he boomed, "both you and your sister."

"Yeah, so what?"

"The contract allows me unfettered access to film you and your sister. As your sister wrecked my camera, you violated the contract." Roger eyed me again and smiled. "Afraid your trespassing claim won't hold water, old chap. Now, I insist you pay for a new camera."

"¡*Vete a la chingada*!" shouted Esperanza. She stormed back into the kitchen, followed by Maria.

"What did she say?" Roger asked.

"Er, nothing," I said, attempting to gauge the legal morass. "Perhaps we could—"

I was interrupted by Esperanza's return, shotgun firm in hand and cigarette firm between lips. "Maria and me, we ain't paying you nothing, *gringo*." She levelled the shotgun at Roger.

"No, wait," he screamed as he stepped backwards into one of the dining room chairs. The chair fell over, followed by Roger, who landed on the dining room floor.

"No, please," Roger screamed. "Help! Murder!"

I raised an eyebrow.

"No, *Tia* Esperanza!" shouted Loretta. She gently seized the barrel and took possession of the gun. "I'm sure we can work something out with Mister Victory."

"¡*Pendejo*!" Esperanza muttered, expelling a large cloud of smoke. "You're real lucky Loretta's here. Otherwise, I'd shoot your fucking *cojones* off." Esperanza turned around and stormed back to the kitchen.

I walked over to Roger, who was now sitting on the floor, and extended a hand. "Let me help you up," I said.

"She's crazy," shouted Roger as he remained on the floor. "I want to file charges."

"Er, I rather doubt the local constabulary will be especially sympathetic or cooperative," I replied. "Tiny is not, how should I put it, enamoured of outsiders."

"Then call the Highway Patrol," Roger snarled. "No, call the FBI." He pointed a now shaking hand towards the kitchen door. "She—she belongs in jail."

Loretta glided to Roger and extended her hand towards him. "Let me help you, Mr. Victory," she said soothingly.

Roger took Loretta's hand and stood up. "Thank you, my dear."

"I'm sorry about my aunt," said Loretta. "She, well, she's been so—so excited about the movie since you first arrived. She's really harmless."

The Graves brows rocketed upwards.

Loretta guided Roger to a nearby chair. "Can I get you something to drink? How about a glass of iced tea?"

"Why, yes, my dear. That's very kind of you," he replied, as he continued to hold her hand.

Loretta gently removed his hand from hers. "I'll be right back, Mister Victory," she said. "Bennie, you make sure he's comfortable."

"Er, yes, of course," I said.

"A most charming young lady," said Roger, with a flash of his ivories. "Though I can't say the same for her aunt. Hard to believe they're related."

"Yes, well, 'Esperanza' and 'charming' is rather an oxymoronic combination. As for Loretta's lineage, it is more aunt by convenience." I paused, in hopes Loretta would quickly return with Roger's iced tea. "Ah, about the unfortunate incident, the camera, that is."

Roger appeared lost in thought. "What? Oh, yes, the camera." He waved his hand dismissively. "I'm sure we can work something out."

"Eh, what?" I replied, dismayed by the lamb-like docility which had replaced the roaring lion. "I mean, yes, no doubt we can."

Presently, Loretta returned, bearing iced tea and a basket of steaming *sopapillas*. "Here's your tea, Mister Victory," she said warmly. "I'm sorry to take so long, but I thought you might like some fresh *sopapillas*." She set the tea and the basket upon the table, then reached for the squeeze bottle of honey. "And here's some honey for them."

The soothing aroma of the *sopapillas* wafted about the table. "Oh, those smell wonderful," said Roger. He retrieved a *sopapilla* and took a large bite out of it. "Mmm, oh, that's delicious. Thank you, my dear."

"You're welcome, Mister Victory."

"Please, you may call me Roger," he said.

"Okay, Mister Vict—I mean, Roger. Are you feeling better?" she asked.

"Much better, thanks," replied Roger. I espied his eyes reconnoitring Loretta's curves.

"I've already spoken with my aunts about the camera. I'm sorry they don't have the money right now, but I'm going to ask my mother for some help. And Bennie can help, too."

"I can?" I spluttered. "I mean, yes, er, I have a bit of brass saved for such emergencies."

"Quite all right, my dear."

"I've asked my aunts to write you a formal letter of apology, too."

The eyebrows were too exhausted to rise up yet again. Remorse was not a trait one would ever associate with either Maria or Esperanza.

Roger took Loretta's hand in his and eyed her, Svengali-like. "That's quite all right," he tut-tutted. "I have a spare camera on the bus. As for your aunt, no harm done."

Roger paused, but continued to stare into Loretta's eyes. "You have such beautiful eyes. How would you like a screen test, Loretta? You could be my next discovery."

"A screen test?" said Loretta, who appeared to be entranced. "But I've never been good at memorizing things."

"No need to memorize anything," said Roger. "I just want to film you and see if you're suitable for a role in my movie. How does that sound?"

Loretta emitted a delighted squeal.

"How about I give you the test and we discuss your future over lunch?"

"Lunch?" I said.

"I waitress during lunch," said Loretta.

"Waitress, eh?" said Roger. He stroked his chin with his hand. "Well, let's begin by shooting you going about your work. Your aunts, too. I simply must get some shots of the cafe. I can give you a screen test later in my bus."

"Er, perhaps I should accompany Loretta," said I, not wishing to allow her to enter the fluorescent-toothed lion's den alone. "I, er, have rather more experience with contractual arrangements."

"No need, old chap," purred Roger. "I won't ask this beautiful young woman to sign any legal documents."

Loretta blushed. "Do you really think I could be an actress?" she said.

"Gah," I groaned softly.

"You'd be surprised how many actresses I've discovered, my dear. Ordinary people, just like you, except most were not nearly as beautiful."

Roger stood up. He reached out, took her hand in his, and gently kissed it. "Until we meet again."

"You're such a gentleman," cooed Loretta. "Maybe you can give Bennie some lessons."

Roger glared at me and grunted. Then he returned his gaze to Loretta. "When a woman is as beautiful as Cleopatra, she should be treated like a queen. Now, if you'll excuse me, my dear. I'll have Jim come around at lunch to take some shots of you."

He straightened his sports jacket, put on his sunglasses, and glided regally through the front door.

"Gah," I groaned again, after the door closed behind him.

Loretta stared blankly at the front door, looking very much as Cynthia did when she first told me about Rodrigo.

"Please be careful, Loretta," I said as I attempted to wrap my arms about her. "Roger has rather the Lothario air about him. I know the type."

She escaped from my arms. "I'm sure you do, Benjamin Graves. I'm sure *you* do. It's the same type that goes around kissing *chichonas*."

"Yes, I mean, no. I mean—"

The ability of the fairer sex to knot one's tongue into a bowline strong enough to restrain an ocean liner could make even the most weathered sailor gasp in amazement.

"Never mind," said Loretta. She stormed off towards the kitchen and disappeared through the door.

"Gah," I moaned.

Chapter 24

The lunch crowd proved to be more surly than customary, forcing the self to field numerous complaints regarding erroneous orders, insufficiently temperate *sopapillas* preferred by the Goldilocks dining set, and excessive quantities of ice in the iced tea. One especially annoying customer, an aged and thick-spectacled bat named Josefa Romero, complained the green chile sitting atop the *enchiladas* was insufficiently green and the blue corn *tortillas* were greyish.

Under normal circumstances, one would dismiss such complaints as the ordinary grumblings of the aged; Josefa Romero was not only half-blind, but colour-blind as well. I apologised profusely, ignoring her mutterings about the *gringo* waiter, and announced I would return her *enchiladas* to Maria for the appropriate revisions.

Entering the kitchen, I barely avoided a collision with Loretta, who was exiting whilst laden with a large tray.

"Look out," she shouted.

"Sorry, Loretta," I said meekly, as I wondered how I might return to her good graces. I then directed my attention to Maria. "Ahoy," I shouted, "Mrs. Romero is complaining yet again."

"What's wrong this time?" growled Maria. "Too many beans? Not enough cheese?"

"Surprisingly, not. Apparently, neither the green chile nor the blue corn *tortillas* meet her exacting spectral standards."

"Huh?"

"She says the green chile is not green and the blue corn is grey."

Overhearing this recitation, Esperanza chimed in. "That *vieja* can't see nothing. And she never tips. I'm gonna tell her to get the fuck outta here and never come back."

I sighed. "No you will not, Esperanza, tempting as it may be. Expelling customers, regardless of their disposition, is not something we shall entertain."

"How about I tell fucking Tiny to never come back?" said Esperanza. "You gonna complain about that?"

"Yes, well," I muttered. "Consistency and all that, what?"

Maria expelled a cloud of smoke as a large piece of ash detached itself from her cigarette and vanished into the pot she was stirring.

"I believe you dropped, er, something into that pot," said I, having long since become inured to the ubiquitous presence of cigarette ash in our comestibles.

She glanced downward, lowered the spoon with which she was stirring the mixture, scooped up the intruder, and bunged it into the sink. "*Gracias*," she said.

I extended the offending plate to Maria. "Is there anything you can do?"

Maria inspected the green chile and the blue corn *tortillas*, then wrested the plate from my hand. "*Sí*." She mounded additional green chile on top of the *enchiladas* and hid the exposed blue corn tortilla beneath a spoon of *refritos*. Then she returned the offending plate to the self. "You tell Josefa she better eat it now, or don't never come back here."

"Er, yes, Maria."

As I emerged from the kitchen, the front door opened, admitting Roger, his cameraman, Jim, and another assistant.

"Let's start in here," shouted Roger above the conversational din, "and then we'll shoot the kitchen."

"Attention," he yelled. "Your attention please."

The conversational din ceased, forks and glasses hovering in mid-air.

"Thank you, everyone," continued Roger. "You may all continue with your lunches while we shoot some film of the cafe."

Roger then espied Loretta and glided towards her like a stingray. He collected her hand and kissed it gently. "Hello, my dear. Such a pleasure to see you again."

Loretta giggled and blushed.

"Bloody hell," I muttered.

"Hey, Benny," shouted Luis Chavez. "You better get Loretta to the church real quick."

"Er, yes, thank you, Luis. We are engaged."

"Yeah, but you ain't gonna be for long. That Roger is one smooth *gringo*. Rich, too. *¿Que no?*"

"M-hem."

I walked over to Mrs. Romero and unceremoniously deposited the revised plate before her. "Here. Green chile appropriately greened and blue corn blued."

She picked up her fork and attacked the plate, narrowly missing my right hand. "Thanks, *gringo*," she gargled through a large mouthful.

Roger returned Loretta's hand, and turned towards me. "Hullo, old chap. I do hope you don't mind the intrusion. I simply must experience the cafe in full flower, so to speak." He glanced back at Loretta and winked playfully. "Now, where are Maria and Esperanza? I want to film them in action."

"In the kitchen," I said.

Roger motioned to Jim and pointed to the kitchen door. "Let's go in. Bring one of the lights, too."

"Hold on, boss," Jim said. "They already wrecked one of my cameras."

"Just shoot from the door. I'll set Maria straight."

Jim shrugged and tightened his grip on the camera. "Okay, boss."

"Perhaps you should allow me to warn Maria before you enter. As you well know, she does not like intruders in her kitchen."

"Nonsense, old chap," he replied with a wave of his hand. "Once I tell her how famous she's going to be, she'll be eating out of my hand."

A picture of Maria grazing from Roger's hand emerged in the grey matter, but was quickly extinguished by the more alert neurons. The Graves conscious now wrestled with a dilemma: restrain Roger and prevent needless bloodshed, or allow him to enter the kitchen and suffer the well-deserved slings, arrows, and chef's knives he would surely encounter therein?

I retracted my arm. "You're probably correct. No doubt, Maria will relish her impending fame."

"Of course I am, old chap," said Roger. "Of course I am." He strode confidently to the kitchen door and disappeared behind it. Jim timorously followed, cautiously pushing open the door with his foot, so he could film Maria.

"You shouldn't have let him go in there, Bennie," said Loretta. "You know how Maria is about her kitchen."

I shrugged. "Fools do rush in."

"Why you don't like him, Bennie?" asked Loretta. "He's a perfect gentleman."

Before I could respond, epithets and shouts erupted from the kitchen. Presently, Jim dashed aside and pulled the camera to his chest. Roger burst through the doorway, followed by Maria, apron askew and chef's knife waving, and then Esperanza. With cigarettes dangling, both emitted puffs of smoke, reminding one of a steam train.

"Don't you never come in my kitchen again, *gringo*," she shouted.

"Now, see here, Maria," Roger said as he dashed behind one of the tables. "You signed a contract."

"I don't care about no contract."

"What about the money then? You know you and your sister need it." Beads of perspiration appeared above Roger's brow.

"¡*Vete a la chingada*!" she shouted. Maria vibrated the knife menacingly and stepped towards Roger.

"*Hermana*!" shouted Esperanza. "Think about the money."

Roger grabbed the squeeze bottle of honey from the table he was standing behind. "You don't scare me, Maria," he said, brandishing the makeshift weapon. "You signed a contract. It allows me to film you in the cafe, including in the kitchen. You're the cook, for God's sake."

"Bennie, do something," shouted Loretta.

"Right." I strode to the table and stood between them. "Maria, please lower the knife. No doubt we can negotiate a satisfactory arrangement."

I turned to Roger. "Are you both deaf and stupid? I told you not to go into the kitchen. Yet off you went."

"You of all people should understand what I am trying to accomplish," he screamed. He thrust the honey bottle towards Maria. "Even if she can't."

"I understand real good, *pendejo*," growled Maria.

She brandished the knife again, muttering an extensive list of Spanish obscenities under her breath, and began moving around the table towards him. Roger stepped back and stumbled. Instinctively, he tightened his grip on the squeeze bottle, which erupted, sending a large plume of honey into my right ear.

"Gah!" I shouted, as honey slowly dripped onto my shoulder and the floor.

Roger burst out laughing, as did Esperanza, Loretta, and all of the diners.

Maria supressed a smile. "Don't ever come in my kitchen again," she said. "*¿Comprende?*"

Roger sighed. "Very well. How about we film you here in the dining room, serving a plate of your wonderful food to a hungry customer?"

Maria lowered her knife. "*Sí*, okay," she replied. "Later. I got too much to do now." She turned around and returned to the kitchen.

Roger retrieved a serviette from the table and offered it to me. "Sorry, old chap."

I seized the serviette with my right hand and inserted it into the honey-plugged ear. "Sod off!"

"Now see here, Ben," he said. He stood up and puffed himself like a tanned peacock. "I'm here to make a movie. A movie, I might add, that will put money in people's pockets and this town on the map. And I've got signed contracts. Or had you forgotten about that?"

"Get out!" I shouted. "I don't care about your money, your bloody contracts, or your bloody movie."

"The studio's attorneys won't appreciate that attitude, Ben. And I'm sure some of your customers won't appreciate not being paid their fifty dollars to be extras."

"Avast!"

"Just remember, no movie, no money," said Roger. He motioned to Jim. "Let's go."

After Roger and Jim departed, Joe Romero, who had a large ranch east of town, approached. Well over six feet tall and with a rugby player's build, he towered over me. "That movie *gringo* promised me fifty bucks," he said. He pushed a large, work-roughened finger into my chest, under which the Graves heart beat wildly. "I better get my money."

"Yeah, *Pendejo*," said Esperanza. "A lot of people want their money, especially me and Maria. You got no right to tell him to leave."

Avaricious murmurs of agreement spread through the dining room.

"What? You just screamed at him to get out of the kitchen," I said.

Esperanza shrugged. "Yeah, but Maria and me I don't care if he films in here."

"Er, I'm sure Roger didn't mean it," I said nervously, as Joe's finger continued to press on the chest. "I shall speak with Roger a bit later. Clear up any misunderstandings, eh?"

"You better," Joe grumbled.

"Yes, well, all right. Now, perhaps you would care to sit down and finish your lunch."

"I'm done . . . *gringo*," he replied. Joe walked back to the table where he had been sitting and retrieved his cowboy hat. "Like I said, I want my money." Then he walked out the door.

The heart steadied itself and I turned my attention to Esperanza. "As for you, if you want *your* money, perhaps you should tell your sister to stop threatening Roger."

"She didn't threaten him," Esperanza said, expelling a large cloud of smoke. "Not much. When you go apologise, tell him Maria didn't mean nothing. And ask if we can get some of our money now. Maybe a couple hundred bucks."

Another rivulet of honey began to ooze down the temple. I grabbed several serviettes from the dispenser on the table, and wadded them into the ear as if reloading a cannon.

"I have no intention of asking Roger for your money. Nor shall I apologise. The man is a cad and a fraud."

"You think he's a cat? I think that honey got into your brain, *Pendejito*. Maybe the *moscas* got in there." Esperanza laughed.

"*Cad*, not cat." I shouted. "You know, a blackguard, a scoundrel."

"Just tell him to pay us. I'm gonna talk to Maria."

She took a large pull on her cigarette, exhaled a cloud of smoke into my eyes, and deposited a large clump of ash onto my foot. Then she returned to the kitchen.

"Bloody hell," I muttered.

Around half-three that afternoon, Loretta and I were preparing the dining room for the dinner crowd.

"I think you were rude to Roger," said Loretta, placing cutlery onto a table. "He's just trying to help the town. Besides, everyone could use that money."

"His motives are hardly altruistic."

"Well, I think he's charming. And I'm going to see him now."

"Now? Why?"

"For my screen test, of course."

"What? Loretta, that screen test, as he calls it, is a ruse. The man is a cad."

Loretta responded with one of those glacial stares for which the fairer sex is famous. She dropped the silverware in her hand onto the table. "For your information, Benjamin Graves, I am not a helpless little girl who needs your protection. I can take care of myself. Besides, Roger's been nothing but a gentleman."

"Yes, but—"

"Tell *Tia* Maria I'll be back before five."

Loretta then came about and marched through the front door.

The Graves mental state now entered a precipitous decline. By half-four, the neurons, along with several downed plates and glasses, were in utter disarray.

"What would Lord Nelson do?" I thought. And so, eschewing manoeuvres and with spine stiffened by the admiral's ethereal admonitions, I set course for Roger's bus, which was parked near Rudy's bar.

Upon reaching it, I knocked on the door loudly. "Roger, it's me, Benjamin Graves." I heard laughter from inside the bus. "I say, open the door. I must speak with Loretta."

Presently, the door opened. Roger stood before me, grinning hyaena-like. "Now what?"

"Where's Loretta? I must speak with her."

Loretta appeared at Roger's side. Her hair was dishevelled, as if she had just awoken. Her shirt was torn, revealing a bare left shoulder.

"Loretta! What has happened?" I eyed Roger, who continued to grin. "How dare you!"

"How dare I what—old chap?"

"I shall retrieve Maria's shotgun and blast you myself. Fiend!"

Roger exploded with laughter. "Fiend?"

"Blackguard! Loretta and I are engaged to be married. You have besmirched her honour. I demand satisfaction."

"Satisfaction?" chortled Roger. "You mean, like a duel, old chap? Awfully eighteenth century, don't you think?"

"Nothing happened, Bennie," Loretta said, with what I perceived to be a hint of dejection. She removed a wisp of hair that had fallen in front of her right eye.

I snorted. "Nothing happened? Look at your hair. Look at your shirt."

She attempted to restore the torn piece over her shoulder. "I, um, tore it on a coat hook."

"What about your hair? Did it become entangled in the same coat hook?"

"That was part of Roger's screen test." She ran her hands through her hair, letting it fall naturally. "See?"

"What on earth for?"

Roger eyed me witheringly. "To see how the camera frames her head and hair," he said. He turned to Loretta. "Never settle for mediocrity, my dear. It doesn't become you."

Loretta blushed deeply. "Um, thank you, Roger."

He took her in his arms and kissed her cheek lightly. "Let me know what you decide, my dear."

Loretta stepped out of the bus and sighed. I now feared I had lost her to Roger's venomous Hollywood charm, which seemed far more lethal than the Iberian utterings Rodrigo had used to lure Cynthia from me.

"Decide what?" I demanded.

"Nothing. I'll explain later, Bennie," said Loretta in a rather trance-like voice. She looked at her watch. "We need to get back to the cafe."

"Nothing?" I asked incredulously. "Nothing?"

Roger winked. "She is a pearl of great price, Ben," he said.

"What do you mean?" I growled, straining against Loretta's pull.

"Let's go," Loretta said. She led me away like a puppy that had missed its newspaper, escorting a wounded and much-shrivelled Graves pride towards the cafe.

"It appears Roger has a new career planned for you," I said.

"I don't want to talk about it."

"You told me you would explain. Please do."

She counted on her fingers. "Well, we discussed the broken camera. And the movie. And then he had me do my, um, screen test."

"Well, are you leaving?"

"You sound like you want me to."

"Eh, what?"

"You want me to leave, don't you? Because of her." Loretta burst into tears.

I goggled at her, amazed yet again at the fairer sex's ability to pretzel a situation not in their favour into one in which the male of the species is reduced to apologetic mewling. The world's greatest contortionist would be an arthritic wreck by comparison.

"Who? Sunflower?"

Loretta stopped suddenly, turned to face me, and crossed her arms. "Maybe I *should* go to Hollywood with Roger."

The jaw now undulated silently like a large goldfish.

"Well?" she said. "I'm waiting for an answer."

Not knowing the question, the grey matter readied itself to crash onto the matrimonial reef lying dead ahead. "I, er—"

"Fine. Don't answer, then. That's an answer in itself."

"No, that is, I mean—"

Before I could finish, I heard a loud squealing of brakes and espied a lorry bearing down upon us. I tackled Loretta and dove with her out of the way. The lorry screeched to a halt perhaps ten feet past where we had been just standing. A cloud of dust enveloped it.

"Loretta, are you injured?"

She rubbed her arm. "I'm okay, I think."

I stood up, then helped her to her feet. As the dust cleared, before us stood Coronado, eyes bloodshot and blinking in the sunlight.

"Shorry, Señor Graves, shorry Loretta," he slurred. "I didn't think anybody would be standing in the road."

Coronado's face had the same greenish pallor I had seen the day I arrived in Vaca Seca and which had preceded his vomiting upon my trousers. I pulled Loretta backwards beyond what I hoped was emetic range.

"You're drunk!" I shouted.

Coronado stared blankly, but said nothing. Then he began to sway to-and-fro slowly like a pendulum.

"Stand clear," I shouted as I pulled Loretta towards the edge of the macadam. Coronado leaned against his lorry and unleashed an emetic torrent that pooled around the front tyre.

Then he straightened himself and began slowly walking towards us like an inebriated Frankenstein's monster.

"That's quite far enough, Coronado," I said. Still holding Loretta, I stepped backwards with her onto the steps of the cafe. "Do you intend to vomit again?"

Coronado smiled. "I don't think so, Señor Graves," he said. "But I'm kinda hungry. Could Maria make me some *tacos*?"

"No. You can have dinner later this evening."

"Okay." He began walking towards Rudy's bar.

"I say, Coronado."

"Huh?"

"Should you not move your lorry?"

"Where?"

"Perhaps you should park it in front of Rudy's."

"How did you know I was going there?"

Another headache had begun to build within the cranium. "A lucky guess, one imagines. Good day."

"Señor Graves?"

"Yes?"

"How come you and Loretta were standing in the middle of the road?"

"What? That is, we were, uh, engrossed in a discussion."

"Were you talking about Señorita Flower?"

The jaw dropped. "How could you possibly know that?"

"I dunno," said Coronado. He wiped his lips on the arm of his grease-stained shirt. "I guess 'cause her cafe is gonna open real soon. Señorita Flower invited me. Did she invite you and Loretta? I can chaperone if you want me to."

"Er, uh, well, Sky Blue invited us."

Coronado beamed. "Señorita Flower told me I get to have dinner for free. She said my soul is gonna be real happy afterwards."

Only the most desperate of souls would be contented by lentil loaf and *lassi*, I thought. "No doubt, it will," I said.

"Is your soul happy, Señor Graves? It should be, 'cause you get to marry Loretta."

I glanced at Loretta, who met my gaze briefly before dropping her eyes towards the ground. "Er, I suppose it is, especially having avoided your lorry. You do realise we could have been killed."

"Sorry, Señor Graves." Coronado's eyes widened. "But if I had, you and Loretta would be ghosts, and you could ask Alejandro how come he scared Señorita Flower."

"Yes, well, one prefers a more corporeal existence at present. And that is one reason you ought not to drive whilst intoxicated."

He shrugged. "I'm only a little drunk."

"Yes, of course," I said. Loretta's face was rather pale. "Excuse us, Coronado. I'm afraid the encounter has left Loretta feeling rather poorly."

"Okay. I hope you feel better real soon, Loretta."

She nodded silently.

"Do you still want me to wash dishes tonight?" Coronado asked.

I eyed his vomit-stained shirt and trousers, the malodour of which was attacking the olfactory. "Er, perhaps we can manage without you this evening."

"Okay, Señor Graves." He shrugged his shoulders, returned to his lorry, and drove off slowly.

I helped Loretta up the steps and into the dining room. She sat down heavily in one of the chairs and lowered her head onto the table.

"We could have been killed," she moaned.

"Best not to think about it," I said.

Loretta's moans increased in volume. I called out to Esperanza and Maria, who came into the dining room. Esperanza put her arm around Loretta's shoulders. "What'd you do to her, *Pendejito*?"

"Shut up. Coronado almost despatched the both of us with his lorry. As you can see, Loretta is quite shaken."

"You okay, Loretta?" asked Esperanza.

"*Sí, Tía* Esperanza," she said, "Bennie saved my life." She began to cry.

Esperanza and Maria eyed me, but said nothing. "I shall return momentarily with the lorry and escort her home. She needs to rest."

"Okay, Señor Bennie," Maria said, patting my arm. "*Gracias.*"

"*Sí, Pende*—Bennie," Esperanza added. "*Gracias.*"

"Er, *de nada*," I replied, the Graves pride restored to its rightful place. "I shall return."

After I'd seen Loretta home, the remainder of the evening proved uneventful; an unusually well-behaved group of customers at the cafe and a large glass, well, two, of Dusty Trail before retiring for the night steadied the Graves ship, although not before gobsmacking Uncle Bill with a recitation of Coronado's near-knackering of Loretta and the self.

The next morning, Loretta arrived at the cafe, apparently recovered. Esperanza and Maria displayed never-before-seen maternal instincts, hovering over her like chain-smoking mother birds. More remarkable still, Esperanza employed an almost civil tone in her dealings with the self, going so far as to utter the word "please" in a request to assist with needed scullery work.

One almost wished for more frequent opportunities to save distressed damsels from out-of-control lorries. Even the execrable dinner presence of Tiny Roybal and his brood of overfed and underbrained spawn failed to cause upset. A song was in the Graves heart of the "Whistle a Happy Tune" variety.

Then again, the events of the previous day left unresolved Loretta's meeting with the oily and untrustworthy Roger, as well as the alleged coat hook-caused blouse tearing and Hollywood-star offering thereof.

The Graves ship, whilst steadied, was still navigating through rough and uncharted seas. And when a more sober and less fouled Coronado burst into the cafe to tell us Siddhartha's opening day was tomorrow, I presumed the seas were to become much rougher still.

Chapter 25

We thought it best to shutter the cafe for the evening, reasoning that all our customers would be lured by a free meal and beer with which to wash it down. "Will you be attending tonight, Maria?" I enquired. "You could evaluate the competition's offerings."

She glared at me balefully. "What kind of food you say they got?"

"Vegetarian fare, I gather."

"They got *enchiladas*?" she asked.

"Doubtful."

"*Tamales*?"

"Most unlikely."

"*Posole*? *Carne adovada*? *Burritos*? *Sopapillas*?"

"Perish the thought."

Maria grunted. "Nobody's gonna want to eat there."

"Perhaps, but what they serve tonight will be free. And it shall be served with beer, which the locals will most certainly want."

She shook her head. "I'm gonna stay home."

"What about you, Esperanza?" I asked. "Loretta and I are attending."

"Uh, I got something else to do," said Esperanza. She looked at Loretta. "You go with Bennie."

A large crowd was already gathered in front of the Siddhartha restaurant, art gallery, and spiritual centre when Loretta, Uncle Bill, and I arrived. Coronado had prepared another sign for the evening's opening, promising a free meal and free *lassi* for all.

Presently, Sunflower unlocked the front entrance. She was dressed in dark jeans and a tight-fitting, orange-ish pullover shirt. Her hair flowed loosely, framing her eyes, which glowed radiantly.

"Welcome to Siddhartha," she announced, "where we will satisfy your hunger and nourish your soul. Please come in and sit anywhere you like." She turned around and walked inside as the crowd's male eyes tracked the gracious swinging of her jean-fitted derrière. Several of the female guests swung large purses like halyards into their male companions' heads, as they commanded "Stop looking at that *chichona*," followed by cries of "Ow, I didn't do nothing."

"Jesus," Uncle Bill whispered to me. "That gal's got curves and then some."

"Er, yes," I replied, as Loretta eyed me suspiciously.

I took Loretta's hand conspicuously as we walked inside. The walls were covered with pictures of the Buddha, jungle temples, and pious worshippers from the subcontinent. Along the back wall were three golden Buddha statuettes, each surrounded by burning candles and incense sticks, the latter conveying an almost sickly sweet aroma to the room. The auditory discerned wounded-cat sounds from a sitar, a discordant reminder of Subba Krishnamurundi, an Indian chap I knew at Oxford who owned and played said instrument, at least until his was found dismembered in a local rubbish bin.

"What's that smell?" Loretta whispered.

I directed her attention to the fingers of smoke arising from burning incense sticks. "I believe those are the source. A chap I knew at Oxford would burn them to mask his roommate's— well, the roommate lacked a certain familiarity with the benefits of proper bathing."

"Eww."

"Yes, quite."

We seated ourselves at a small table near a corner, on which a small candle was burning.

"This place looks like a goddamn cathouse," Uncle Bill said. "Smells kinda like one, too."

Coronado and his sister arrived and sat down at the table next to us.

"*Hola*, Señor Graves. *Hola* Loretta," Coronado said as he glanced about. "*Hijole*. I hope the food's good. I'm real hungry."

Sunflower shimmied from table to table, welcoming her customers and pouring out small glasses of *lassi*. As she drew nearer to our table, Uncle Bill gaped and Loretta stiffened.

"Hello, Benjamin," she cooed, "I'm so glad you came tonight." Then she bent across the table to extend a hand to Uncle Bill. "Hi, I'm Sunflower," she said, shaking Uncle Bill's hand.

"Why hello, young lady," replied Uncle Bill. He raised his hat with his left hand and forced his eyes to focus on Sunflower's face. "I'm Bill Graves, Bennie's uncle. But a lot of folks 'round here just call me El Vaquero."

"El Vaquero?"

"Yep. Means 'the cowboy'. Always wanted to be one, and that's what I am."

Sunflower giggled. "That's so cool. I didn't know Benjamin had an uncle living here. But you don't sound English."

"Nope. Came out west a long time ago. Figured if I was gonna be a western cowboy, I ought to talk like one."

"It's very nice to meet you, Mister Graves, I mean, El Vaquero. I never met a real cowboy before."

"Well, young lady, I hope I haven't disappointed you too much."

Sunflower giggled again. "Let me pour some *lassi* for you to try and tell you about tonight's menu. Because it's our opening night, Sky's cooking a few special things. We have lentil loaf, chickpea casserole, and vegetable quiche."

"I'll try the quiche," said Loretta.

"Do you want me to drop it in your lap, like you did to me?" Sunflower said icily.

I raised an eyebrow, but remained assiduously silent. Loretta's face turned a crimson shade as she silently mouthed the word *chichona*.

"How about you, El Vaquero?" Sunflower said softly as she leaned down towards him.

"Well, little lady, I, uh, why don't you choose for me. How's that sound?"

"I would love to, El Vaquero."

Sunflower then turned towards me. "And Benjamin, what would you like to nibble on?"

God would I, I thought, the neurons short-circuiting. "Eh, what?"

"What would like to order, silly?"

"Oh, yes. Ah, well, I, that is, perhaps you could make the choice for me, the same as Uncle Bill." I felt a sharp jab in the right shin. "Bloody hell," I muttered. I eyed Loretta, who responded with a tight-lipped smile.

"Did you say something?"

The shin throbbed. "Er, no. I believe I shall try your *lassi*." I reached for the small glass before me and downed it in one swallow. The taste reminded me of curdled milk.

"Isn't it delicious?" said Sunflower, beaming. "And it's really good for you."

One could have said the same to the wasps I had sprayed with insecticide.

"Did you hear that?" said Loretta suddenly.

The auditory strained but detected only the din of multiple conversations. "What?" I asked.

Sunflower's eyes widened. "What?"

"I thought I heard someone groan," said Loretta. "It's probably nothing."

"Groaning?" said Sunflower in a quavering voice.

"It almost sounded like it came from below the floor," Loretta said. "It's probably just the floorboards creaking."

Sunflower looked at the floor beneath her. Then she went down on her knees and pressed her ear to the floor. "I don't hear anything."

There was a loud thud against the wall that faced the alley behind the building.

"What was that?" Sunflower said, jumping back up. Her face was distinctly pale.

"Now, don't you get upset, little lady," Uncle Bill said. "Probably one of those old elm trees banging against the wall in the wind."

"Do—do you really think so?" asked Sunflower.

"Yep. We got one at the ranch. When the wind blows, its branches scrape the side of the house."

"Yes," I added. "The sound disturbed me initially, but I do not even notice it now."

"I'm sorry," she said. "I guess it's this old bar." She rushed into the kitchen.

"Are you trying to frighten her, Loretta?" I asked.

"You want to protect your little *chichona*?" she replied. "I said it was probably the floorboards."

"C'mon, you two," Uncle Bill said. "That gal's just trying to do her job."

A cold silence descended upon the table as we waited for our meals.

"I could sure use a beer," Uncle Bill said.

"Yes, quite," I said. "Er, what about you, Loretta?"

Loretta's right elbow was on the table and her head was listing to starboard, supported by her right hand. "Sure, why not," she said.

Several minutes later, Roger entered the premises in his full Hollywood regalia—navy blazer, pink sports shirt, sunglasses, and ivories polished to a high lustre. The din of conversation stopped, and all eyes turned to him.

"Please, everyone, don't let me interrupt your dinner," he declaimed. "You have such a wonderful town."

Several of the locals began to clap. Roger bowed slightly, then raised his hands. "Thank you, all. You're very kind. The movie is going quite well, by the way. We've been doing some location filming and it all looks quite promising, thanks to all of you."

"When do we get our money?" shouted one of the diners.

"Soon, everyone, very soon," he replied.

Sunflower returned from the kitchen. Espying him, she shouted, "Roger!" Then she dashed over and pressed against him, as all eyes in the restaurant followed her. "I'm so glad you're here. Please stay for dinner."

He released her embrace, reluctantly. "I would love to, my dear, but I must attend to some other business. And don't forget, you still need a screen test."

"That's so exciting," said Sunflower. "How about tomorrow?"

"Tomorrow would be fine, my dear."

Sunflower returned to the kitchen and Roger walked over to our table.

"Hello, young lady," said Roger, as he placed a well-manicured hand on Loretta's shoulder. She looked up at him and smiled, rather rapturously, I thought. Then he turned to Uncle Bill. "Nice to see you again, Mr. Graves." Finally, he looked at me and grunted. "Well, I hope you all enjoy yourselves this evening. Such a lovely restaurant."

"Don't want to stay for some of this here soul food?" Uncle Bill asked.

Roger swallowed. "Uh, as much as I would like to, I have a previous commitment. Perhaps some other time." He glanced at his watch. "Look at the time. Well, cheerio, as Ben would say."

He turned around and glided out the front door.

"Tosser," I muttered.

"I don't feel well," Loretta said. "I think I'm going to go home and lie down. I guess I'm still a bit shaken up from yesterday."

"Would you like me to drive you home?" I said.

"No! I mean, that's okay, Bennie. I think I'll walk home. The fresh air might help."

Loretta excused herself from the table and quickly walked out the door. I looked at Uncle Bill, who shrugged his shoulders.

Presently, Sunflower arrived with our dinners. "Where's your girlfriend, Benjamin?" she asked as she placed our dinners in front of us.

"Uh, she wasn't feeling well."

"Too bad," replied Sunflower.

I glanced down at the steaming, greyish-green mass. "Er, what does one call this, precisely?"

"Chickpea and broccoli casserole. It's one of Sky's specialties."

Uncle Bill eyed his plate warily. "Uh, thanks, little lady. I don't suppose I could get a beer, could I?"

"Of course. I'll bring one out. I never knew Sky's cooking went so well with beer. Everybody's asking for them. Would you like one, Benjamin?"

"Please God yes, I mean, I shouldn't wish Uncle Bill to drink alone."

Sunflower vanished back into the kitchen. I glanced down at the plate and then at Uncle Bill. I searched for salt and pepper dispensers, but found none.

I dipped my fork tentatively in the mass and extracted a small quantity of casserole. "Er, *bon appétit*," I said, before placing the laden fork into the hesitant mouth.

"Well?" Uncle Bill asked.

I swallowed. "The flavour is, er—different."

Uncle Bill sampled a tentative forkful. His mouth twisted. "Damn, I could sure use that beer."

"I quite agree. Well, one hopes Sunflower will return with our libation shortly."

We picked at our plates to maintain a fiction of gustatory enjoyment. Suddenly, a deep voice rumbled through the dining room. "Sunflower, I am the ghost of Alejandro. You have made me very angry. Leave this place at once."

All conversation ceased. "Did you hear that, Uncle Bill?" I whispered.

"Yep."

Startled by a sudden tap on my shoulder, I turned around and found myself goggling a wide-eyed Coronado. "Señor Graves, did you hear that? It's Alejandro's ghost."

"Yes, the voice did say that, Coronado."

"You think he's mad at me?"

"Why would Alejandro's ghost be mad at you?"

"I dunno. I guess 'cause ghosts are supposed to be mad."

"Yes, well, this particular ghost is a fraud who is speaking through a walkie-talkie. You remember our conversation about that?"

"*Sí*. Alejandro's ghost bought a pair of walkie-talkies from Joe."

I sighed.

The disembodied voice spoke again, louder. "Do you hear me, Sunflower? Run away. Run away before I strike you down. You are an evil harlot, a slut. You will leave Vaca Seca or I will punish you."

"One would expect a ghost to have more creative discourse," I said.

"You recognize the voice, Coronado?" asked Uncle Bill.

"*Sí*, El Vaquero," said Coronado. "It's Alejandro. I know it."

The eyes rolled. "Coronado, how old were you when Alejandro died?"

"I dunno. I was a kid. Maybe five or six."

"Did you and the other five-year-olds often visit Alejandro's bar, stop for a quick pint after kindergarten, and all that?"

"No, Señor Graves. I had to come home right after school and do chores. Sometimes, my mother told me to walk down to Velasquez's bar and get my father. He never liked this bar."

"Then how can you possibly know that is his voice speaking through a walkie-talkie?"

Whilst Coronado pondered, the ghost spoke yet again, this time adding some rather poor "woo-wooing" and chain-dragging sound effects.

"Sunflower," the voice moaned. "Sunflower." The voice then cackled like one of those cartoon witches of the Hansel and Gretel variety. "Sunflower, I will haunt you until you leave. Slut! Harridan! She-devil!"

I was about to comment to Uncle Bill regarding the appalling theatrics of the "ghost" when I espied Sunflower, who was peeking through the kitchen door. Her eyes were saucer-like and one could see the tears flowing down her cheeks.

"Mice!" she screamed suddenly. She began to claw violently at her shirt and ran towards the front door, crashing into one of the tables. The collision launched the occupants and their dinners onto the floor. Sunflower screamed again. She tore off the shirt and threw it violently. Then she disappeared out the front door and into the night.

The orange shirt now dangled over the head of one of the nearby male customers. He appeared startled, but not displeased, despite his spouse's bludgeoning him like the biblical Jael, albeit with purse rather than peg.

"Baby, wait!" an aproned and spoon-carrying Sky Blue shouted, as he laboured after her. "Baby! Sunflower! Come back!" Then he, too, disappeared through the front door.

The numerous jaws that had been dangling slowly restored themselves to their rightful places. Several customers finished their beers, stood up and left. Others, who apparently lacked functioning taste buds, continued to eat. The ghostly voice had become silent.

"Ghosts and mice," said I. "Rather puts our opening night to shame."

"That gal sure don't like mice," said Uncle Bill, as he shook his head. "And she's sure got some fine-looking equipment under her hood."

"Really, Uncle Bill," I said, unable to stifle the image of Sunflower streaking through the dining room.

"Hey, like I told you, pard'ner, I may be old, but I ain't dead. Not yet, at least."

"Do you think we should attempt to find her? Damsel in distress and all that."

Uncle Bill rubbed the stubble on his chin. "I don't think that's a real good idea," he said, "especially not for you."

"Er, no, I suppose not."

"Look, Bennie, I'll mosey around, maybe ask Rudy to look for her, too. Meantime, you can herd all these folks out." He paused. "I never got my beer."

"Perhaps a glass of Dusty Trail at the ranch will provide you solace."

"Damn right it will. I'll see you later." He returned his cowboy hat to his head and walked out the front door.

"I say, everyone," I shouted. "As our hosts have abandoned ship, as it were, perhaps we should do the same."

"Maybe we should form a posse," said the orange-shirted chap, as his spouse whipped the shirt from his head and threw it onto the floor.

"You gonna have a show like this at the Dos Abuelas, Bennie?" said another chap, only to be biffed violently by his spouse with her purse.

"Do you think I should look for Señorita Flower, Señor Graves?" Coronado asked. "I'm pretty good at finding people."

"Thank you, Coronado, but probably best for Sky Blue to locate her."

"How come?"

The image of Sunflower's unbridled departure bubbled up in the grey matter. "Uh, we wouldn't want to cause her further embarrassment, given her state of undress, as it were."

"You mean 'cause she don't got her shirt no more?" Coronado grinned.

I goggled at him. "M-hem."

With both Sunflower and Sky Blue gone, dinner came to a rather abrupt end. After the last of the customers had left, I checked the kitchen to ensure the stove and oven were off, extinguished the lights, and exited, followed closely by Coronado.

"Do you think Alejandro's ghost put mice in Señorita Flower's shirt?" he asked.

"For the last time, Coronado, there is no ghost. Someone, someone very much alive, was speaking into a walkie-talkie. As for the mice, they could be pure coincidence, given Sunflower's previous encounter with them. Then again, coincidence and events in Vaca Seca have always seemed rather incompatible. The game is afoot, as Holmes would say."

"Did you hurt your foot playing a game, Señor Graves? Once, when I was a kid, I stepped on a nail playing baseball. It hurt a lot."

"What? No, I meant—never mind, it's not important."

"Okay. I guess I'm gonna go to Rudy's and get a six-pack. *Buenas noches*, Señor Graves."

"Good night, Coronado." I watched as he waddled towards Rudy's and then disappeared through the gaping hole, which had been covered in plastic sheeting. The game was indeed afoot, although Fate had yet to divulge the rules.

Chapter 26

As I approached the lorry, I espied the great white bus, parked and shimmering in the moonlight like a wheeled Flying Dutchman. A soft glow emanated from behind drawn curtains. Detouring towards it, I pounded on the door.

"Hullo? I say, Roger, are you in there?"

There was no response. Then, I discerned the muffled sounds of feet, a soft giggle, and a distinct "Shhh!" Presently, the door opened, revealing an unusually dishevelled Roger—shirt untucked and half-buttoned, barefoot, and trousers askew. I raised the left eyebrow discreetly.

"Jesus Christ. What do you want?" he said.

"Sorry, but there was rather an incident in the restaurant earlier involving Sunflower."

"An incident? Did she squirt honey into your ear?"

"No," I replied slowly. "Alejandro's ghost returned, that is, someone speaking through a walkie-talkie pretending to be Alejandro's ghost. He threatened Sunflower, as well as called her various names. Most uncivil. She was then attacked by several mice, which led to, well, she ran out into the night, screaming. Perhaps you saw her?"

"Can't say I have, old chap," he said with a wolfish smile. "Ghost, you say? Did you recognize the voice?"

"No. It was rather deep and sonorous. One was reminded of Ezio Pinza."

"That good?" Roger said with an oddly proud intonation.

"Well, the voice may have been ghostly, but what the ghost said was quite pedestrian. Rather what one would expect in an old Boris Karloff film, complete with the cartoonish, cackling laugh."

Roger's countenance took on an oddly wounded look. "Afraid I can't help you. However, if I see Sunflower, I will let her know you're looking for her."

The auditory detected another muffled giggle. "What was that?"

"I didn't hear anything," he said curtly. "Now, I'm quite busy. Goodnight." He slammed the door shut before I could respond.

The grey matter whirred. A wave of jealousy swept over the Graves ship. Was Loretta the source of the giggling? Had she been seduced by his false charm? I pounded on the door. "Loretta!" I shouted. "Loretta, are you in there?"

The door opened again, revealing a now fully tucked and buttoned Roger. "Will you please leave? She's not here."

"Liar! I heard her giggling. Fiend!"

"Not that *fiend* nonsense again. Look, I saw Loretta earlier this evening, but I don't know where she is now."

"You saw her? What did she say?"

Roger's eyes darted about. "She, uh, she said she was not feeling well and was going home."

"She stopped and told you that?"

"Why, yes. She did."

The neurons were now at full battle stations. "Liar! She's with you now." I began ascending the steps into the bus. Roger blocked the doorway and extended his right arm to block my entrance.

"Stay out!" he roared.

I pushed his arm away and forced my way into the bus. It was dark inside, except for a small light near the back, which illuminated the bed. Sitting upon it, wrapped perfunctorily in a blanket and noticeably *sans accoutrement*, was Sunflower.

"Sunflower?"

"Hi, Benjamin," she said, with a schoolgirl giggle. "Please don't tell Sky. I don't think he'd understand."

I gaped at her grouper-like, unable to speak.

"Idiot!" shouted Roger. He shoved me towards the door. "Get out, now."

"Gah," I moaned, before beating a quick retreat out the door and into the cool evening.

I staggered towards the lorry, hands pushing against the now-throbbing cranium. Whilst I attempted to retrieve the key from my trouser pocket, Coronado appeared, carrying a six-pack.

"*Hola*, Señor Graves," he said cheerily. "You okay? You're walking kinda funny, like you're drunk."

"Go away. I must get back to the ranch."

"Maybe I better drive you."

"No," I said, recalling the first, and only, time I had motored with Coronado, on the day of my arrival in Vaca Seca. "That is, thank you for the offer, but I am not inebriated. A bit shell-shocked is all."

"Did you see Alejandro's ghost?"

"Please, no," I moaned.

"Alejandro was moaning? *Híjole*, I'd be real scared, too."

I wrenched open the lorry's door, climbed inside, and groaned.

"You sure you can drive, Señor Graves?"

I glanced sidelong at Coronado. Then I opened the lorry door and slid out. "Is Rudy at the bar?" I mumbled.

"*Sí*, but maybe you shouldn't drink nothing more."

"I'm not drunk, but I hope to be soon." I walked unsteadily towards the bar, the legs feeling as if they were weighed down with iron. Coronado waddled behind.

"Rudy!" I called out, as I stepped through the plastic sheet and threaded my way towards his office.

"You want me to wait for you, Señor Graves? I don't mind driving you home."

"No, thank you, Coronado. I must speak with Rudy privately."

"Okay. *Buenas noches*, Senor Graves."

I nodded and waved dully, then walked down the hall towards Rudy's office.

"Rudy?" I said, knocking on the door.

"C'mon in, Bennie."

He was sitting behind his desk, scribbling figures in his accounts book, a glass of whisky on the port side. He glanced at me as I sat down heavily. "Jesus. What happened to you?" He retrieved a bottle of whiskey from the bottom right drawer of the desk along with a glass, dispensed a large dose, and handed it to me.

I vanquished the contents summarily and leaned back in the chair.

"I heard about what happened tonight. Poor girl." He took a sip from his glass and laughed softly. "Did she really tear her shirt off and throw it on Paul Martinez?"

"I don't know the chap's name, but yes, that is what happened."

"Did Sky Blue find her?"

"I'm quite sure he has not." I extended the now empty glass towards him. "Would you mind? This is rather difficult."

"Sure." Rudy refilled the glass and returned it to my waiting hand.

"I found Sunflower."

"You did? Is she okay?"

"Yes. She was with Roger. In his bus. In his bed. Unclothed and apparently fully recovered from her ordeal."

Rudy's eyes widened. "*Híjole*," he muttered.

"Anyway, after the, er, incident, I got everyone out of the restaurant. I planned to check on Loretta; she left earlier complaining she was still feeling poorly—you know that Coronado almost knackered the both of us with his lorry."

Rudy nodded.

"Anyway, I espied Roger's bus and decided to enquire if he had seen Sunflower. Then I heard giggling. I knocked on the door. Roger presented himself in a state of, well, he appeared to have clothed himself rapidly. Of course, I assumed he was with Loretta, but he denied anyone was there and dismissed me summarily. Then I heard giggling again. So, convinced it was Loretta, I banged on the door and demanded to see her. Roger tried to prevent me from entering, but I pushed him aside and found—Sunflower."

"*Chichona*," he muttered. "So she and Roger were—"

"Quite."

"Hey, at least it wasn't Loretta."

By now, the whisky had steadied the neurons. "Not tonight," I said. "But what about yesterday, when he gave her that bloody screen test, as he called it? Her shirt was torn open at the shoulder."

"Look, Bennie, let me give you some advice. Unless you caught Loretta, uh, you know, with Roger, take her word. Otherwise, you'll drive yourself crazy. Trust me, I know." He held up four fingers. "Four marriages, remember?"

I nodded reluctantly.

"Why don't you head back to the ranch and get some sleep? You look like you could use it."

At the mention of the word *sleep*, I yawned. "Thanks, Rudy."

"Did you recognize the ghost's voice?"

"No. It was rather deep, which eliminates Esperanza as the source, much as I would like to accuse her. Anybody in town have such a voice?"

"Nobody I know." Rudy pondered silently for a few moments, drumming his fingers upon the desk. "Nestor!"

"Eh? Nestor's voice is rather scratchy. Besides, why would he wish to frighten Sunflower?"

"I don't think Nestor's your ghost, Bennie. But I bet he knows who is.

"How?"

"Because Nestor's always been kind of a pack rat. Maybe he has a pair of walkie-talkies from the war. Maybe he let somebody borrow them."

The eyes widened. "I say, Rudy, a capital deduction, worthy of the Baker Street detective himself. Care to participate in the interrogation?"

Rudy glanced at me through half-shuttered eyes. "Sorry, I'm beat. Besides, Nestor's probably drunk. I'd try him in the morning."

"Tomorrow morning, it is, then. Thanks, Rudy."

I departed the bar with a spring in the step, hopeful the mystery soon would be resolved. As I walked back to the lorry, I noted Roger's bus had vanished.

The next morning's first task, after enduring the slings and arrows of Daisy and Marjorie, was to enquire about Loretta's health. Motoring to her mother's house, I rang the doorbell, instinctively recoiling upon hearing Chata's heavy footfalls and guttural barking. Loretta opened the door, which precipitated a drooling attack.

"Avast, bloody cur," I said, grasping the dog's front paws, which had been on my shoulders, and placing them onto the floor. Chata began to push against my legs like a canine battering ram.

"Chata, leave Bennie alone," said Loretta. She swatted the dog's backside, causing it to retreat. She laughed. "I heard about last night. Alejandro's ghost and mice."

"I assumed you would have. The efficiency of the local gossip telegraph never ceases to astound. I came by to see if you were feeling better this morning."

"Huh? Oh, yes. I feel fine, thanks. Is it true her shirt ended up on Paul Martinez's head?"

"Er, yes. Mrs. Martinez appeared to disapprove of the final resting place; she was beating a grinning Mr. Martinez most energetically with her purse."

"Where did she go?"

"Mrs. Martinez?"

"No, the *chichona*."

"The bus."

"You followed her?" said Loretta angrily.

"What? No, I mean, I assume she sought out the sanctuary of the dilapidated school bus. Sky Blue chased after her."

Loretta appeared lost in thought.

"I say, Loretta, if you are feeling better, would you like to accompany me? I intend to speak with Nestor, who is more likely to be sober at this hour of the morning."

"Nestor? What for?"

"Rudy believes he could well be the source of the ghostly walkie-talkies—World War II surplus and such."

"No! You can't."

"What? Why not?"

"Uh, because Maria needs us at the cafe." Loretta glanced at her watch. "Yeah, she needs us there right now. I'll get my coat and we can go."

"You spoke with Maria? When?"

"Uh, last night." Loretta glanced at her watch again. "Damn," she muttered. Presently, she wrapped her arms around my waist. "Bennie," she cooed, "would you mind waiting outside for just a minute. I, um, need to take care of something. I'll just be a minute."

The right eyebrow twitched. "Is everything all right? You seem rather disconcerted."

"I'm fine!" she shouted, prompting Chata to emit a thunderous "woof."

"Perhaps a strategic retreat is in order."

I stepped outside and waited. Through an open window into the sitting room the auditory detected a muffled but frantic-sounding conversation, which caused the left eyebrow to twitch.

Presently, Loretta stepped outside. "Ready?" she chirped.

As we motored to the cafe, Loretta drummed her fingers nervously on her knees. Before I had even switched off the motor, she dashed out of the lorry, ran up the steps, and disappeared through the front door.

I stepped out of the lorry and shut the door, only to espy Coronado waddling rapidly towards me.

"Señor Graves," he said. "Did you see Señorita Flower?"

I wondered if Coronado knew about Sunflower and Roger. "No, that is, not since last night's incident. Why?"

"She came into the store this morning with Señor Blue."

"Oh. Then he found her. Is she all right?"

"I don't think so. She was real mad at Señor Blue."

"Why?"

Coronado paused. "I dunno. He was buying some stuff and then she just started yelling. Then she threw a bag of flour at him and ran out of the store. I tried to sweep it up, but it's real hard."

If anything, after the events of the previous night, one might have expected Sky Blue to yell at Sunflower. Then again, aspersions cast at the fairer sex did have a tendency to ricochet.

"Yes, well, never mind the difficult-to-sweep flour. Do you know what, exactly, Sunflower said to him?"

"She said she didn't want to be suffo—suffo something. She sure was mad."

"Do you mean suffocated?"

"I think so. What's that mean?"

"It means to have one's breathing stopped, forcefully."

"You mean, like choked?" said Coronado.

"Uh, yes."

"You think Señor Blue tried to choke Señorita Flower in the store? I didn't see nothing."

"Er, no, Coronado. She probably meant it metaphorically. That means, well, he wasn't choking her physically, just mentally."

Coronado shrugged, but said nothing.

"Well, it's not especially important. Was Sky Blue angry?"

"I think so. He kept shouting at Señorita Flower to remember her cheese. I guess she forgot, 'cause she didn't buy none. Maybe Señor Blue wants cheese so he can make some *enchiladas*." Coronado's countenance took on a faraway look, as it often did when he focused on comestibles.

"I believe Sky Blue was telling Sunflower to remember her *chi*, not her cheese."

"Señor Graves, can I get some enchiladas for lunch from Maria? I'm kinda hungry."

I glanced at the watch. "It's not even nine o'clock yet. Perhaps there is something in the store you can consume. Try aisle three. Now, if you'll excuse me, I must be going."

"Okay, Señor Graves. What's on aisle three?"

"How should I know? But surely there is something you can eat."

"Okay." Coronado turned around and began to waddle towards the store. I bounded up the steps and into the cafe. Hearing voices from the kitchen, I went inside. Loretta and Esperanza were conversing heatedly, but stopped immediately upon observing the self's presence.

"Right then, where's Maria?" I said.

"Uh, she ain't here, yet," said Esperanza, looking like the proverbial canary-consuming feline.

"Well, what does she need?"

"Uh, she didn't say exactly," said Loretta.

"Rather odd behaviour on Maria's part, what?"

Esperanza shrugged and exhaled a large cloud of cigarette smoke. "Don't be so fucking impatient."

Before I could reply, Maria entered through the outside kitchen door. All eyes turned towards her. She paused, eyeing us suspiciously. "How come everybody's staring at me?" she asked, inspecting her person. "Did I spill coffee or something?"

"No, you're okay," said Esperanza. "Uh, we're here, like you wanted."

"Okay," Maria said.

Loretta and Esperanza remained motionless, as a tense silence engulfed the kitchen.

Feeling rather confused, I eyed the assembly. "Maria, I gather you wished to discuss a matter of some urgency with all of us," I said. "Pray, what is it?"

Maria remained silent as she furrowed her brow.

"*Hermana,* the menu," said Esperanza, head bobbling up and down. "You remember, we were talking about changing the menu?"

Maria glanced about nervously. "Uh, *sí.*"

Holmesian doubt was now seeping into the grey matter. "You wish to change the menu?" I asked. "How, exactly?"

Maria goggled Esperanza, but remained silent.

"Well, I suggest we remove *enchiladas* and *carne adovada* from the menu. No doubt, our customers will prefer lentil loaf in future. After all, that is the competition, what?"

Maria's countenance darkened. "Are you crazy?" she growled.

"Merely suggesting some changes to our menu, Maria," I said. "We could abandon the *refritos,* the green chile stew, and the stuffed *sopapillas,* and serve a chickpea and broccoli casserole in its stead. The version Uncle Bill and I were served last night was quite, er, different."

"I think that El Vaquero's horse musta kicked you in the head or something," replied Maria. "Everybody like what I cook."

"*Carajo,*" Esperanza said softly, as she stared out the window.

"I quite agree, Maria. What you cook is perfect, as is the cafe's menu." I turned and directed my attention at Esperanza. "Well? Do you intend to reveal what perfidy underlies this allegedly important meeting?"

"*Pendejito,*" Esperanza muttered.

I sighed and directed my attention to Loretta. "Can you please tell me what this meeting is really about?"

Loretta lowered her eyes to the floor. "*Chichona,*" she muttered.

"Sunflower? I don't understand."

"Leave her alone, *Pendejito,*" shouted Esperanza.

The fog that had enveloped the grey matter suddenly lifted. "Nestor!" I raised an accusatory digit and pointed it at Esperanza. "It was you! The walkie-talkies. You took them from Nestor. My God, Esperanza, if the ghost's voice were not a man's, I would suspect you for that, too."

"¡*Vete a la chingada, Pendejito!*" Esperanza yelled as her face began to turn crimson. "You can talk to that fucking *borracho* about his fucking walkie-talkies. Loretta and me didn't do nothing and Nestor ain't gonna know what you're talking about."

I turned to Loretta. "Well?"

"Well what?" she replied, crossing her arms across her chest defiantly.

"Is that why you did not want to accompany me this morning to speak with Nestor?"

"No," said Loretta, lip quivering slightly.

"Loretta, please," I sighed.

"I had to do something," she said.

"About Sunflower? The poor girl was scared half out of her wits."

Esperanza laughed. "I hear she got scared outta her shirt, too."

"Yes, about the mice," I replied. "How did you manage that?"

Esperanza raised her middle finger in silent response.

Presently, Loretta ran out the kitchen door and disappeared down the alley.

"Loretta, please," I shouted, as I followed her outside and watched her disappear around the corner.

For several minutes, I remained in the alley, disconsolate. When I returned to the kitchen, I found Maria aproned and attacking several onions. Esperanza had vanished.

"Maria, did you know about the walkie-talkies and the ghost?"

Maria shook her head and wiped her brow. "*No se nada.*"

"Do you think your sister is behind this?"

"Maybe," Maria said in a defeated sort of tone. She placed her chef's knife on the cutting board and paused. "Yeah. But who is the ghost? You said it was a man's voice."

"I intend to discover the culprit. Although the only one male who is on good terms with Esperanza, if one wishes to call it that, is Hector. Is he staying with her at present?"

"Hector? I don't think so. Esperanza said he got a construction job in Albuquerque and was gonna be there a couple weeks."

"Could she have asked Nestor to voice the ghost?"

"I dunno. Did your ghost sound real drunk?"

"Er, no. The voice was quite clear and strong."

"Most nights, Nestor can barely talk, he's so drunk. You seen him eat here."

"Yes, quite." The list of usual suspects was rapidly diminishing. "Joe Garcia? I know they despise each other, but both are equally avaricious. Perhaps they reached a *modus vivendi* of sorts."

Maria burst out laughing. "Joe? I don't know what this modo vivo is, but Joe never did nothing for Esperanza and he's never gonna."

"He does have rather a squeaky voice, too," I added.

"How come you want to know, Bennie?"

I considered Maria's question. "Because, well—I don't know, really. Your sister has gone to great lengths to terrify Sunflower, likely on Loretta's behalf because of an, er, mistaken belief I am besotted with her. Sunflower, that is. But Sunflower is smitten with Sky Blue and—" I paused, recalling Coronado's description of the couple's earlier argument and Sunflower's subsequent lobbing of bagged flour artillery at Sky Blue. "Er, yes."

The wheels of intrigue now dug deeper into the local mud.

Chapter 27

Despite Esperanza's denial, I was certain of her having solicited the walkie-talkies from Nestor. The remaining mystery was the chap whose voice had so terrified Sunflower. As Nestor was the presumed source of the ghostly apparatus, he might well know the identity of the ghost himself.

Telling Maria I would return forthwith, I dashed out of the cafe, only to nearly collide with Roger, who was dressed in full Hollywood regalia.

"I say, old chap," he said with false cheer. "I need to speak with you."

"I am rather busy at present."

"Yes, of course you are, old chap. Uh, won't take a moment."

"Well?" I asked.

Roger removed his sunglasses and approached. "About last night," he whispered, glancing about in search of anyone within earshot.

"Ah."

"I was simply offering the poor girl a bit of aid and comfort. She was pounding on the bus door, shrieking for help. When I opened it, she jumped inside. I mean, the poor girl was half naked. She ran back to the bed and hid under the sheets. Was I supposed to throw her back outside? For all I knew, she had just escaped an attack by a vicious animal."

"She did. A mouse."

Roger laughed softly. "Yes, I know. Well, naturally, I wanted to help. I asked her what had happened. She sat up and told me. Then she buried her head in my chest and began to cry. After that, well, she, that is—"

"I believe I know the rest of the story."

"A fun-loving girl," he added.

Having experienced Sunflower's fondness for the tactile, one could not disagree with Roger, even if he was a cad.

"Er, yes," said I.

He slapped me on the shoulder. "I knew you'd understand, Ben."

I sighed. The Graves code meant one kept a respectful silence about another chap's indiscretions.

"By the way, I've been rethinking the storyline. This Alejandro's ghost of yours. Excellent dramatic effect, don't you think? The tragedy of the cafe. An evil ghost who haunts the premises, terrifying the beautiful and brave girl trying to restore it. Rather dramatic, don't you think?"

"But there is no ghost," I said. "It was all Esperanza's doing. She borrowed, if not stole, several walkie-talkies from Nestor. She placed one in the restaurant—where, I know not. Speak into the other one and, voilà, ghost."

"Nestor?"

"Do you recall the chap who Florence Nightingaled your ankle?"

"The old drunk?"

"The same."

"Interesting theory, old chap, but Sunflower told me your ghost had a man's voice, a DEEP GHOSTLY voice."

The eyebrows rocketed upwards. "You?" *You're* the ghost?" The grey matter cried out for a tankard of Dusty Trail. "But last night—Sunflower—you, you cad."

"Hold on, Ben. Esperanza asked me to do this. I'm an actor, so I jumped at the chance. Besides, I wanted to see whether changing the premise of my movie was believable. Sunflower convinced me."

Roger winked slyly.

"This beggars belief. And what about the mouse in Sunflower's, er—was that your idea, as well?"

"Until Sunflower told me, I had no idea. Then again, I suppose I should thank that particular mouse." He winked again.

"What about Loretta?" The Graves pugilistic instincts were now at the ready. "That bloody screen test of yours? Her torn blouse?"

"A sweet girl," he said reassuringly. "But she really did tear her blouse on a coat hook. As for the screen test, I'm afraid she would be a terrible actress. I didn't have the heart to tell her." Roger paused. "By the way, Loretta thinks the world of you, for whatever reason. Esperanza, however—"

I raised a hand. "I know all about Esperanza. We shall have words. What about Sunflower? Are you going to tell her the truth?"

"I already have," said Roger.

"What?" I spluttered. "She must be furious."

"On the contrary, old chap," she thanked me. "Besides, she is going to be my next discovery."

"Eh, what?"

"I'm taking her back to Hollywood."

"But what about Sky Blue? What about their restaurant, spiritual centre, and art gallery?"

Roger shrugged. "What about them? This is Hollywood, old chap." He glanced at his watch. "Well, off I go. I have a few things to do before I leave."

"You're leaving? What about the movie?"

"I just told you."

"You mean, the ghost story?"

"That's right," replied Roger, as he flashed his ivories.

"What about the locals? Rudy's bar? You were going to pay Uncle Bill for the rights to the story."

Roger removed his sunglasses. "You really don't understand, do you?"

I goggled him silently. Presently, Roger's bus drove up and parked beside us. The door opened and I espied Sunflower. She stood up and bounced down the steps.

"Hi, Benjamin," she cooed as she enveloped me in an embrace. "Isn't it exciting! Roger's going to make me a star."

"But what about Sky Blue?" I said. "How can you abandon him and, er, Siddhartha?"

Sunflower rubbed my cheek playfully. "You're so naïve, Benjamin. It's cute."

"Eh?"

Roger snaked his arm around Sunflower's waist. "Well, time is money, old chap," he said. "I have a new star to create."

Releasing his grip on Sunflower, Roger walked onto the bus. "Good-bye, Benjamin," she said. "Wish me luck." Then she bounded up the stairs of the bus. The door closed and the bus roared away, leaving me engulfed in a cloud of exhaust.

"Good luck," I muttered.

With Sunflower destined for Hollywood stardom under Roger's tutelage, the tide of normalcy, or at least its second cousin, thrice removed, quickly returned to Vaca Seca. The cafe hummed, disrupted only by Esperanza's serial complaints about overwork and the peculiarities of the clientele. The jealous, savage beast within Loretta had been soothed and our engagement was now back on course.

There had been much grumbling about the money Roger had promised everyone, but it had receded into glum acceptance of lost riches. The Ortiz brothers were rebuilding the front wall of Rudy's bar. Uncle Bill had cancelled his purchase of the new bull. Siddhartha was shuttered.

A few days later, I was sweeping the luncheon debris off the floor of the cafe when the front door opened, admitting Sky Blue, who had not been seen since Sunflower's abrupt departure. I glanced up and was immediately shocked at what stood before me. Where there had been blue coveralls, there was now a smartly tailored grey suit, crisp white shirt, dark blue tie, and black shoes. He was clean-shaven and the olfactory detected a hint of scent.

"Sky?" I said, placing the broom against the wall. "Are you quite well?"

"Yeah, I know, man," he replied, offering a rather dispirited grin as he widened his arms to display the new raiment. "Not what you were expecting, is it?"

"Er, well, no. Not that I disapprove, of course. Merely rather perplexed. One doesn't imagine you as the banking sort."

"Stockbroker, actually."

"A stockbroker?" The left eyebrow raised itself warily.

"Yeah, man, I know it's hard to believe, but I figured it was time to get back to reality." He looked around the room wistfully. "I guess things didn't work out like I thought."

"Well, in my experience, things rarely do, less so in Vaca Seca." I retrieved the broom. "As for reality—"

"At least Sunflower's happy," he interrupted.

"Er, yes. Sorry." An apparition of Sunflower *au naturel* scurried through the grey matter, chased by a second apparition of Loretta, which stopped, espied the self, and mentally biffed the cranium with an imaginary saucer. "Gah!" I cried instinctively. "I mean, fate has been rather more cruel than normal."

He stared out the front window, shaking his head softly. "I wonder if he knows what he's got."

"Who?"

"You know, man, the movie man. He's got a tiger by the tail."

"Ah," I replied. A most voluptuous tiger, I thought, but a tiger nevertheless. "Shall you be returning to California?"

"No. I've had enough of that scene. I'm going to New York City. Gonna get a job at a brokerage there."

I thought of my own previous escape from London. "Yes, I quite understand the sentiment. Will you be motoring there in the intrepid bus?"

"You mean Siddhartha. No. I traded that piece of crap to Joe Romero for a pickup."

I wondered if Joe Romero even owned the lorry he had sold to Sky Blue, but chose not to raise the subject, deciding it would be unnecessary salt in Sky Blue's wounded pride.

"Well, man," Sky said, extending his hand. "Guess I'll be going. Good luck, here. I dunno how you do it. This place sure has bad *chi*."

"Er, yes. It is something one often contemplates."

I shook Sky Blue's hand and wished him Godspeed. He turned around and walked slowly towards the door. Then, as he opened it, he stopped and turned around slowly. "You know, Sunflower's got this power—"

I cut him off abruptly, not wishing any further reminders of Fate's having tasked the Graves soul with temptation. "As Lord Nelson said, 'Never mind manoeuvres, go straight at 'em.' No sense contemplating the past, eh?"

"Yeah, I guess you're right," he replied, with a defeated shrug of the shoulders. "Well, later, man." He waved halfheartedly, then walked through the door and down the steps. I watched as he climbed into a rather rusty, greenish lorry, started its motor, and drove away, leaving behind a large cloud of dust as the final fleeting evidence of Siddhartha in all of its brief glory.

Perhaps a year later, long after Sunflower, Siddhartha, and Roger had faded from Vaca Seca's collective consciousness, Loretta and I found ourselves in Santa Fe, enjoying a short respite from our daily obligations.

As we walked downtown, we passed the El Farol, the local movie theatre. We glanced at the marquee, shrugged, and were about to continue our perambulation when our jaws weighed anchor simultaneously.

Inside a glass-enclosed case announcing coming attractions, a colourful poster announced the impending arrival of *The Resurrection*, starring Roger Victory. The description read "A woman wages a fight against the supernatural to restore her family's honour." Below his name, the poster announced, "introducing Veronica Lee," with an illustration of a voluptuous and half-naked actress.

"He really did make her a star," I muttered.
Loretta's purse scored a direct hit on the cranium.
"Gah," I whimpered as she dragged me towards our hotel.

THE END